SUITCASE NUMBER SEVEN

Irish Examiner

SUITCASE NUMBER SEVEN

A rugby story with a difference

WITHDRAWN FROM STOCK

Ursula Kane Cafferty

A CIP catalogue record for this book is available from the British Library.

ISBN
0-9551258-0-4 (paperback)
0-9551258-1-2 (hardback)

Published by
Ursula Kane Cafferty
ucafferty@ireland.com

in association with
Personal History Publishing
45 Herberton Road, Dublin 12, Ireland

Designed & produced by Personal History Publishing
Front cover photograph by Kenny Studios, Dublin
Back cover photograph by Irish Examiner
Printed by Colourbooks Ltd, Dublin

About the Author

Ursula Kane Cafferty is a nurse and midwife by profession and has worked in the Irish health service since 1974, apart from two years working in a Central African mission hospital in the early 1980s. She also holds qualifications in Microbiology, Communication Studies, Project Management and Critical Incident Stress Debriefing. She is a graduate of "The Maeve Binchy's Writers' Course" programme held at the National College of Ireland in 2003–2004. Ursula has always had a keen interest in writing verse. This is her first book.

Contents

POST MORTEM

PART ONE

Ursula

Passing

"SORRY for your troubles ..."

"Thanks."

"Sorry for your troubles ..."

"Thanks for coming..." *What exactly does that mean, sorry for your troubles?*

"Your uncle was a gentleman ..."

"Thanks, I appreciate that ..." *OUCH. What a bone-cracking handshake. A rugby player for sure! Thank God I took off my rings.*

A silent sympathiser came next, a gentle touch, a tender gesture.

"That's the girl who broke Tom's heart," someone whispers beside me. I hardly get a chance to look at her as wave after wave of sympathisers alternatively squeeze, pump and shake my hand. I hope I meet her later. Isn't it odd that people travel all this distance and then we don't have time to talk to them?

"He was my hero ..."

"Thank you ..." *Hero?*

"Many's the drink I had with him ..."

"Thanks for coming, Johnny ..." *I know, I know!*

"What a character ...." *...Could bore the backside off us at times but he was a character alright.*

"He was indeed ...."

And on and on they go, filing past us, as we sit in the front row of St. Paul's Church, Mullingar. It should have been the Cathedral, but that was closed for restoration. Tom liked space. He deserved the space of the Cathedral, the church where he so often prayed. He was at least entitled to that long walk of mourning down the Cathedral aisle, I thought.

"FRIENDSHIP ...." A man, whose face I know vaguely, saluted, tears in his eyes. "He'll be sorely missed."

And on and on they go, sympathising and paying their respects.

When everybody has filed past us, we follow his coffin up the short aisle of St. Paul's into the autumn sunshine and lay him to rest in Ballyglass cemetery outside the town.

It is October 1997.

* * *

Ireland is a great place for mourners. You have to be invited to a wedding but anybody can go to a funeral! As it turns out, about 100 people assemble for a meal in a local hotel following Tom's burial. Friends, family, and lots of people from his past. Stories are told, matches replayed, various occasions are recalled and there is lots of chat, backslapping and laughter.

The morning after Tom's burial, an in-law of an in-law[1] of his, who has stayed at my house, is sitting at the breakfast table, no doubt a little worse for wear after the previous night's indulgences. Despite how he feels, this large, solid man tucks into a huge feed of a fried Irish breakfast.

"Great night," says he.

I can see his wife getting edgy at the other side of the table.

"You were at a funeral," she reminds him.

"Still a great night," he spits, biting into a sausage. "But, who the hell was he anyway?" he goes on. "I mean, I heard so many stories about the bastard yesterday that I can't make them all out. Was he a fucking saint or what?"

"Hardly a saint," I muttered.

"Please, don't start," his wife pleads.

"Start what?" he thunders, "I was only asking a question. I didn't really know the man and I am simply asking a fucking question here, IF YOU DON'T MIND."

Silence.

"Well...?" He looks around at us all. "All those well known rugby players, but it turns out most of them haven't seen him since God's own time – what's the story?"

"It's a long story," someone says.

"You haven't enough time to hear the full story unless you decide to stay another night," someone else jokes.

"If you ask me, nobody knew him," he says and he starts scraping the clotted egg off the plate.

As it happens, I am beginning to think the same thing myself.

Over the following few weeks, as we read the letters of sympathy, some from people we don't even know, a picture of the younger Tom begins to form in my mind. Then copies of the obituaries from various magazines and newspapers arrive and we read them too:

> There were few better scrum-halves on the Ireland scene in the fifties and early sixties than Tom Cleary, the former Bohemians and Munster[2] scrum-half, who died in October.

---

1 Some details have been changed. This memoir is partly fictional.

2 The province of Munster is comprised of 6 counties in the southern part of Ireland, namely Clare, Cork, Kerry, Limerick, Tipperary and Waterford.

> A native of Carrick-on-Suir[3], he first revealed his considerable talents in the colours of Castleknock College. Tom was cruelly unlucky that the ultimate honour eluded him in a distinguished career during which he toured South Africa with the Ireland squad in 1961. He played in several final Irish trials and was a reserve for Ireland on 17 occasions without gaining the distinction of a cap.
>
> His career coincided with the days when replacements were not allowed in rugby and he was certainly among the best players of his generation not to be capped.[4]

Poor Tom, I think to myself, *how or why did he let it all go?*

* * *

3 Carrick-on-Suir, Co. Tipperary. Also referred to more simply as 'Carrick' throughout the book.
4 'Obituaries' – *Rugby Ireland International*, vol. 1, no. 3, December 1997, p. 81.

Limerick
20/2/98

Dear Helen,[5]

Even though you already know of our heartfelt sorrow at the passing of your dear brother, Tom, I would like to place on record, at this late stage, the deep sympathy of my wife and entire family.

Those of us who knew Tom so well in the context of sport, be it rugby, tennis or golf, were, one and all, enriched for having known him. The good Lord endowed him with many gifts, not priced out in money terms, but which he shared with us all. I refer to the gifts of good fellowship, good friendship, a sense of fun and laughter, and compassion towards lesser-endowed people, in a spirit of true generosity.

Our journey to Tom's funeral, in its essence a sad occasion, was ironically, a happy, enlightening and rewarding one because it rekindled recollections of old times and happy memories amongst his friends from Limerick. (As I mentioned to you at the funeral, he was best man at our marriage.) It gave us all the opportunity to share in his funeral Mass which was most edifying, dignified and uplifting.

It would be remiss of me if I did not thank you sincerely for your so generous gesture of inviting so many of us to a beautiful lunch which we will always recall amongst our treasured memories of Tom.

With kindest regards and very best wishes.
Sincerely,

A true friend.[6]

Some time after his funeral the time came to go through Tom's "things". He didn't have much. His clothes were fit for nothing but the bin. His trophies were already on display in his sister Helen's house. A few little mementos were in his room, small tokens for nieces and nephews. One of his suitcases was heavy though. His brother, Gerry[7], lifted it down from the top of the little wardrobe

5 Tom's sister. See list of Tom's relations in Post Mortem section of the book.
6 Some details have been changed in this letter.
7 There are three family members called Gerard/Gerry mentioned in this story. See list of Tom's relations in Post Mortem section of the book.

and brought it to the sitting room, and there we sat on the high, hard, old-fashioned couch, Gerry and his wife Ann, Helen and I, as we read the musty story and saw the long-forgotten pictures of Tom's life, the joys, sorrows, triumphs and disappointments. When we reached the bottom of the case, it was lined with a green plastic property bag from the hospital where I worked and where Tom had first been treated a year earlier. The hair stood up on the back of my neck and a shiver ran down my spine as I realised Tom had known he was dying during the past year of his illness and had sorted out what he wanted us to have and see. His story.

It was then I knew I had to write this book.

* * *

One of the first things we lifted off the top of your carefully packed suitcase, Tom, was a diary extract[8] which came from the daughter of a man who emigrated from Tipperary to America in the late 19th century. It was dated 1928, when she visited Carrick-on-Suir while on holiday in Ireland from the States and she describes her visit to the Feehans in West Gate (your maternal grandparents). It gave me a good picture of what life in Carrick was like around that time, not long before you were born:

> I trembled a bit when I entered the town through the old gate. It is a little town of about five thousand people located prettily on the river Suir. We walked slowly through the town and asked a young policeman how we could best see the town and he laughed and said "Look at it, it's here befinxt[9] you". We found the castle that was built in the thirteenth century and the monastery ruins probably dating to the fifth century and the old bridge where my father sat and dreamed of far-off America. We went into the narrow streets and saw poverty and squalor and idleness that was appalling. How could it be otherwise? These people have nothing to do, no place to go. No incentive. The only interest in their lives is the Church and that is not sufficient for the youth. It is all very distressing and hopeless. Is it any wonder that America is a fixation with them? The picture changed however as we continued walking and came to the better part of town.
>
> I easily located my uncle's friend, Mr. Feehan. He was the owner of a fine store well stocked with groceries and canned food and liquors. He greeted us cordially and with much surprise when I made myself known and was overjoyed at seeing anyone who belonged to his dear old friend, Andy. He introduced us to his wife

8 Extract from the diary of the daughter of Richard Ryan who emigrated from Carrick-on-Suir to America in the late 19th century (reproduced here by kind permission of Ms. Connie Miller, U.S.A. Great-niece of the visitor).

9 In front of.

Main Street in Carrick-on-Suir, Co. Tipperary in the early part of the 20th century.
(The West Gate's Town Clock can be seen at the end of the street.)
Photo published by R. Cleary & Sons.

Feehans' shop front, West Gate, Carrick-on-Suir, in the early 1900s.
These are the premises and house mentioned in the diary extract.
(The name over the door refers to Mary Anne Sheehan, Tom's Great-Grandaunt.)
[10]Male shop assistant, female customer in background, John Feehan (1862-1945, Tom's grandfather), Kitty Feehan (1900-1977, Tom's mother as a child.)

---

10 Unless otherwise stated, all group and team photos are named from left to right.

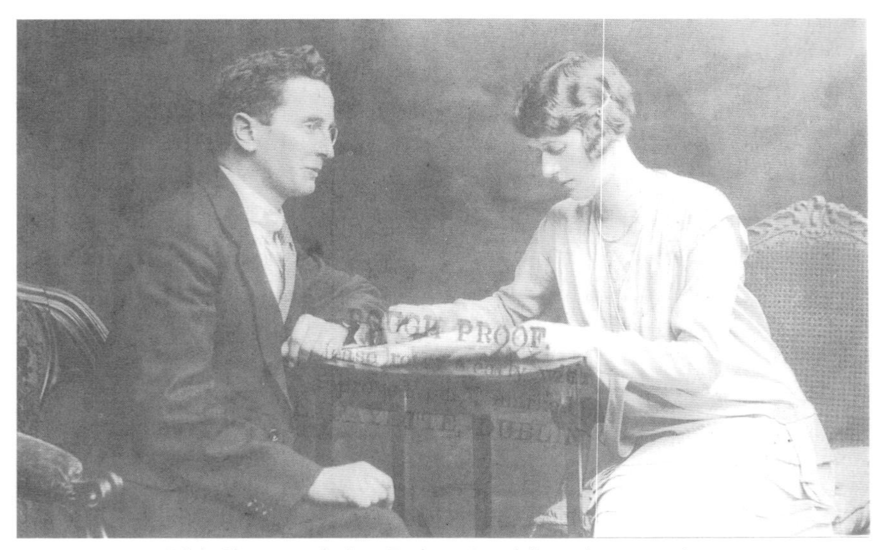

Dick Cleary and Kitty Feehan. Wedding photograph, 1927

and we had a long talk about old family changes that had taken place in the town. One of the things I spoke of was the sordid condition in the poor part of the town and he said, "That was always and I fear always will be".

We then went into his fine house and found a bathroom as modern as our own. There was a large conservatory which housed all sorts of growing plants and little indoor pools. We then went into the dining room to tea and it was a delightful affair. Mrs Feehan sat at the head of the table and served tea from a handsome silver service and a little maid did her bidding. We had tea and jams and hot breads and little fishes and scones and we observed that the teapot and hot water kettle were both covered with tea cosies.

We were then introduced to a young Franciscan Friar whom Mr. Feehan said laughingly was eating him out of house and home and he was a very delightful young man. He talked with a rich Dublin accent and spoke of affairs of the world in general and of the Irish "dilemma" and enlightened us on much of the situation. He was tall and fair and wore a brown habit and sandals. He certainly was a picturesque figure sitting at the table.

So this is what life in Carrick was like in those days! Of course you wouldn't remember it, because you weren't born until two years later.

PART TWO

Tom

GROUNDING

I HAVE left a neatly tied bundle of the trading accounts from my father's business, for my family to find when I'm gone. Some of these documents date back to before I was even born. Carrick was a not a prosperous town in 1930. Tales of hardship in the lanes and hovels full of under-nourished children are plentiful to this day. But looking through the balances, it is obvious that I was born into a life of relative advantage. Underneath the numerous profit and loss accounts, my birth certificate is tucked into a little plastic folder. I was born in the family home in Castle Street.

It has always been said that my father, Dick, also referred to as "The Boss", was a delighted man when his darling Kitty gave birth to me. I was their first born son, a brother for little Helen who was not yet two. Our parents weren't young. Dick was 41, Kitty almost 30. My Uncle Paddy once told me that my father felt as if his heart would burst with joy that day. As a child I never tired of hearing how he called in to the house in Bridge Street to tell his plump, elderly mother the good news and then, strolled up to the West Gate, into the house under the shadow of the town clock opposite, to tell the Feehans, his in-laws. I was christened Thomas after my paternal grandfather.

And they all thought I'd be the fourth generation to run the family business. Little did they know! Just as well that my father didn't have the gift of foretelling the future. Even though he'd lived most of his life in the shelter of the mountain called Sliabh na mBan[11], where Fionn MacCumhaill[12] was supposed to have received his knowledge, he could never have guessed what life had in store for me.

As children, we were all surrounded by love and attention as we grew up. Doted on, in fact. Our parents had plenty of time to devote to Helen and me, in those early years, and we wanted for nothing. It was a charmed life by the standards of the day, in a time when others in the town lived in slum conditions where they didn't even have running water. Maids looked after mundane household matters and my mother was free to enjoy life, as the wife of a prosperous businessman. We were reared with a strong sense of security and belonging, and a firm knowledge of "who we were".

When I was two, after my Granny Cleary died, the family moved to her huge house in Bridge Street and that was the day I truly entered a privileged, but small, world. The entire lives of our families were contained in that neat rectangle

---

11 Mountain overlooking Carrick-on- Suir. The English spelling is *Slievenamon*. Pronounced *sleeve-na-mon*.

12 Legendary Irish warrior.

between Bridge Street, the Quay, the Rookery and the West Gate. In later years, when I spoke of my childhood, I often pretended that the bottom had fallen out of my world the day my baby brother, John, was born (though in truth I adored him). All the same, I realised that anyone could tolerate an older sister (even knowing she was Daddy's little dote) but a brother would mean competition. Horror of horrors, I was going to have to share my mother with this interloper. But even at this young age, as I watched the impostor progress from the carrycot to the playpen inside the back door of the kitchen, I was determined that this was a competition I would win!

Kitty and her first four children. Circa 1937
Helen, Tom, Kitty, Michael (on Kitty's knee) and John (kneeling).
Gerry was not yet born when this photograph was taken.

By the time I was three, things were happening in Carrick. My mother[13] opted for the new electric light, which had come to the town. Our home was lit up as never before when the old gas lamps were taken out, and then, not long before my fourth birthday, further upheaval as another baby boy, Michael, arrived. It was a time of great change for me.

Number 14 Bridge Street was a busy, split-level, house with lots of comings and goings. The family had two live-in maids, a charwoman who washed the clothes and a full-time gardener. At four storeys high, it was a wonderful house for any child to live in, but even better for a child like me, because I was always a bit of a loner. There were lots of nooks and crannies, pantries and larders for me

13 Kitty Feehan-Cleary (1900-1977).

to hide in, places where I learned to smoke and conceal the butts. When I was six I was allowed to join the adults in the main dining room at the front of the house and got to use my own, numbered, silver serviette ring.

The homework schoolroom was up over the kitchen. The hot press in this room was a brilliant hiding place for me. It was an enormous, walk-in, press and it was cosy too. I used sit in there for hours on end, hiding amongst the sheets and hairy blankets, waiting for the chance to eavesdrop on Helen and her friends. It was a fertile source of ammunition for teasing. I loved that spot.

We had a big water pump in the yard and we all loved the chore of priming the pump. I'd usually take charge and make the rest of them (especially Helen) beg for a chance to swing the arm. The general aim was to be the first to be draw clear water. I'd let them take turns at pumping, and many buckets of dirty water would have to be thrown out before the clearer water would start to flow. I always made sure to be the one to draw the first, full, clear bucket. Even at this simple task, I'd have my strategy worked out in advance. Never going first. People often called to our house for water if the town's supply ran low, which often happened, but it was fun for us, rather than work. If I thought it was work I wouldn't have done it!

Our childhood games of conkers and marbles, hoops and rounders were played in the Rookery at the back of the house. Sometimes, along with my pals, I'd sneak past Dad's parked car and all the ploughs and ironmongery in the yard to steal a look at the grown-ups' tennis games and "tea drinking" in the pavilion. Our private grass tennis court and surrounding gardens were out-of-bounds to us children on summer tennis-party occasions – we were usually sent out walking with the maid. But it wasn't long before I became the centre of adult attention when they realised I had a talent for tennis. I was allowed to join the parties at quite a young age – even before Helen. Occasionally, I used to hear anxious whispered snippets of conversation among the men about world affairs, but was too young to worry about things like that. By the time my last baby brother, Gerry, was born, I was eight years old and a bit of a loner. People told me I was showing great promise and had a natural talent. By then I was already playing many sports, including tennis, hurling and golf. Whatever I wanted, I got. And I failed at nothing.

Tom's brother Gerry as a child at the pantry door of the Bridge Street house. Note the water pump in the background.

When the time came for the Cleary work ethic to be instilled in us, my parents saw it as an important development in our lives, but I simply could not understand its purpose. We were all given our allocated posts in the shop. I watched from my father's office as the others worked on diligently, John at the ironmongery counter, Helen serving stationery while Michael was usually out delivering messages on the bike. I had to find a way out of this drudgery.

I decided to coax my mother into playing a daily round of golf. I somehow convinced her (don't ask me how) that I would be doing more for the family business by being seen to actively support the club. And there was nothing Dad could do but give in when the two of us pleaded with him. After all, I'd argue, he and my mother were two of the founder members of the club. And how would I manage to reduce my handicap if I couldn't practise? My general aim at this stage was to match my mother's handicap of 12. I knew she was secretly delighted that I was taking after her father who had been an outstanding sportsman in his youth and I continually played on that. My father gave in easily!

* * *

To this day I don't know how I didn't spot the hardware manager, Willie Power, watching me one morning from his post at the dusty counter towards the back of the shop. I suppose I was bent in concentration over near the window. It was early, and Kitty Hurley, another member of staff, wasn't due in to work at the stationery counter for at least a quarter of an hour.

In later years we used to laugh when Willie would tell the tale of how he saw me putting a copybook into my schoolbag, and he immediately felt sorry for doubting me. Then another copybook, and another, and another. He almost shouted at me when he saw a box of pencils disappearing into my packed school bag.

"Well the brass neck of you...you're nabbed," he caught me by the scruff of the neck. I had been swiping stuff and selling it below cost to my classmates in the Christian Brothers school for some time before I was caught. I had to fund my developing smoking habit. My father was furious. Kitty Hurley felt betrayed. At first, my mother didn't believe the tale. Later, when we were alone, she told me she was proud of me for such a display of entrepreneurial skill.

On the Sundays when there were no plans for tennis parties, we used to go out for dreary driving trips or visit relations. After morning Mass in the Friary in Carrick-Beg and a visit to the family grave, we'd all enjoy a late breakfast, before climbing up the step and piling into the old Ford car. Taking a "pique-nique" which had been prepared by the maid, we'd all get away for the day. I hated those trips. Squabbles in the back, Helen pinching me, a snotty-nosed Gerry whinging and us all singing silly songs on the way home to keep us "occupied".

When I was very young, our annual holidays were usually spent by the sea in Tramore, but as that resort became more commercialised, the family began to

The Cleary children. Circa 1940
Gerry (2), Michael (6), John (9), Tom (10), Helen (11).

spend more time in Ardmore, which was quieter and more refined. Eventually my mother used to rent a house from the Nugents in the Cliff House Hotel for the month of August every year. It was hard for me to get any peace and quiet in Ardmore. I'm not boasting when I say nearly everyone in the resort wanted me to play tennis with them. I even hid under the bed once to avoid partnering a girl. But as soon as I got on the court I was in a different world. I had a good repertoire of shots, I played instinctively and I loved every minute of it.

For most of my happy childhood existence I had been oblivious to anything outside that small world of mine but when the War (or the 'Emergency' as it was called in Ireland) began to bite, my father had no choice but to let some of the staff go. Much to my distress, my mother had to work daily in the shop. This had a big impact on my routine, because she was not as easily accessible as she had been up until now, and on top of that she was tired all the time.

One lasting memory from around this time is the obnoxious smell coming from the tannery. At certain times of the day the pong was overwhelming. I had the misfortune to complain. My father, usually a mild-mannered man, got very annoyed with me that day. He told me, in no uncertain terms, that that smell would bring money to the town and a new Carrick was in the making. It was a lecture I never forgot, for the simple reason that he gave so few. I learned to live with that awful, clinging stench quite close to the family tennis court, but the last straw was when that court was dug up to sow potatoes because of the 'Emergency'.

"This isn't the way things are meant to be," I said to myself. No way was I joining them all up at the shop. Let them at it, I decided. And what's more I got away with it.

PART THREE

Ursula

Fielding

The night we first open your suitcase, my Uncle Gerry's reminiscences are mostly sporting. He hops around from competition to competition, venue to venue and sport to sport, smiling fondly but sadly. Mostly he recalls your tennis. He tells me you were nicknamed 'Spalding' on the tennis court. All the trophies on Helen's sideboard begin to take on a different meaning for me as he speaks. Up to this they have been just so many more items to buff-up, on the occasions when I drew the short straw down the years and got the chore of polishing the silver. The thought occurs to me that I have never absorbed the inscriptions, never thought about the effort involved in putting them there, or the talent required for such achievements. They were there. That was all.

That night I hear about your precious first trophy when you won the American Tennis Tournament in Tramore at the age of 14; how, as a teenager, winning the South Tipperary Junior Tennis Championship Cup three times in-a-row meant you won the trophy outright. I finally understand your achievement when you had taken part in the Irish Under 18 Junior Open Tennis competition in Fitzwilliam. As I listen, I know I have been aware of all these achievements down the years, but subconsciously. It was something which was taken for granted, and given very little thought ... by me at least.

* * *

As the others leaf through papers, opening flittered envelopes which are bent in dirty creases from many handlings down the years, I come across a large bundle of photographs. Professionally taken, many of them show you in the prime of your youth, beaming smiles, with the inevitable trophy, medal or plaque either clutched closely with pride, or nonchalantly displayed at your feet.

"These must be from Castleknock," I venture.

Each one has a short story to tell, as I peel them away from each other and, gradually, I have a longing to know the entire tale. No names adorn the backs, but I have no difficulty picking you out. They record your progress, from lanky childish-looking boy to handsome young man, over the space of the three years you spent in boarding school.

I glance over at Uncle Gerry. He has a series of newspaper cuttings in his hand. Helen meanwhile has a collection of what appears to be social welfare documents in hers. And Ann is looking at a photograph of a plumper, 30-something-year-old Tom, briefcase in hand, ready for work. They all look drawn and tired.

"It's getting late," I say. "Plenty of time to look through all this."

We close the lid on the case.

But for me, Pandora's box has been opened and, from that day on I have made it my purpose to try and understand.

* * *

At the start of my mission, Helen and I travel to your alma mater, Castleknock, to have a look at some of the file copies of the *College Chronicles*[14] from the time you spent there. It is a school steeped in tradition and history, dating back to 1835, when, soon after the passing of Catholic Emancipation in Ireland, four young Vincentian priests leased, and eventually purchased, four fields of an estate in Castleknock, one of which contained the ruins of an old castle, and another the grave mound of Coohal.[15] In time, an old house built by John Warren, standing in the shadow of the historic Cnucha Castle ruin, became the nucleus of Castleknock College. Demolished in 1890, the house was on the site of what was later to become the school's concert hall. To this day, on the south side, Cnucha is often described as "over-hanging the Liffey."[16]

I can't quite describe the experience of actually being there. It's not that I was never there before! After all, my own brother, Gerard, had the distinction of being the first member of the fourth generation of the family to become a pupil there in the late 1960s, so I had visited him and attended numerous Union Day celebrations then. But somehow, this is different ... eerie almost. The first five people we meet clearly demonstrate the cosmopolitan mix of nationalities studying there today, but the building itself seems to be stuck in a time-warp. Structurally and decoratively, little has changed (that I can see) from Gerard's time there and I'm sure not a lot had changed between your time and his. Modern equipment such as photocopiers and computers are evident in the reception area and co-exist easily with the hallowed halls and aged high ceilings. Energetic boys dressed in the modern 'uniform' of sweatshirts, combats and trainers, bounce past on tiles worn hollow by generations of feet, heads popping in and out of doors here and there, but I still feel as if I'm in a venerable institu-

14 The *Castleknock College Chronicle* was (and still is) the title of the college annual, published in Castleknock College Dublin 15.

15 Coohal is the anglicised version of Cumhall (father of the legendary Irish warrior Fionn Mac Cumhaill). He was the leader of the Fianna of Leinster, killed in battle by Goll Mac Morna, leader of the men of Connacht and his burial mound is said to be located in Castleknock.

16 *Castleknock Tradition and Castleknock 1660 to the present,* http://www.iol.ie/~svc/history5.html accessed on 19th April 2005.

tion, not a modern place of learning. To all intents and purposes it is still a world of tigers' heads and leopards' skin.

The priests and staff are more than accommodating and we're escorted down the corridor towards a lobby of beautifully panelled Austrian Oak. As we walk, I note portraits and busts of saints and scholars, one of whom is St. Vincent de Paul himself. Soon we're settled in the staff library, at a large round mahogany table, rooting through the volume of chronicles relating to the time you spent in the college. Frankly, I am amazed. Once I spot your first ignominious mention in the junior football notes of 1945-46 ("A difficult kick was missed by Tom Cleary."!) either your photograph or name hops up at me from almost every page I turn. I make myself busy sticking yellow 'post-it' notes on the pages I want to photocopy and record some extracted details on my little dictaphone for future reference. Helen, meanwhile, is enthralled as she traces the progress of her ancestors and all her four brothers through the college.

St. Vincent's College Castleknock, circa 1940

PART FOUR

Tom

TRYING

I'll never forget my first day at boarding school. My parents had been talking about sending me there for some time, but I never thought they were being remotely serious. Even though I knew that the tradition of the Cleary boys from Carrick-on-Suir going away to St. Vincent's College, Castleknock had started when my grandfather became a pupil there in the 1860s, I never thought my mother would let me go. Innocent, eh? My father's generation had followed suit around the turn of the century. And so it was, bearing the mantle of the third generation to attend this fee-paying boarding school, that I first saw those ivy-clad walls and slid into the house between the hills, in September 1945.

It was a very different world for me as a 15-year-old "new boy". I felt as if it was a million miles away from Carrick. I knew I was continuing tradition, but my parents also told me that this move was necessary to help in the formation and moulding of my character. Imagine telling a teenager that nowadays! So I entered that world of huge arches, banisters and busts, slate and chalk, black clad priests, tinkling bells, "scuts" and codes of conduct. I can still remember (vividly) how our footsteps echoed on the combination of highly-polished wood-block and tiled floors, and bounced off distant ceilings as I went down the corridors of the building that first day. I trembled, as I stood there, flanked by my parents, as the three of us waited patiently to be greeted by the assembled priests. It was a terrifying experience.

My first view of the dormitory is still imprinted on my mind – in bright colour. Multiple, narrow beds with iron frames were lined up in two neat, opposing rows.

"Am I supposed to sleep here?" I wondered.

I could feel myself almost panicking at the very thought. Bed-screen curtains in a bright, multi-coloured, cotton material were pulled back neatly at each bed head and a small white towel was draped over each bed end. I was horrified to think that there would only be a thin piece of cotton separating me and the next boy as we slept. I looked upwards. Holy pictures of various sizes adorned the walls, some of them hanging precariously on picture rails located just below the high ceiling. Wouldn't fancy one of them dropping on my head, I thought. Three mean-looking light bulbs dangled over a double-sided, extended version of an old-fashioned washstand. This contraption stretched down the centre of the sleeping area, and seemed to hold a white, delph washing bowl for each boy's morning wash. I decided that the four mirror sections of the washing area might

save me the horror of looking straight across at the boy opposite me each morning as we washed. The only visible storage space was a row of low-level cupboards underneath the washstands.

I eyed-up the last cubicle on the left, near the window, hiding nicely behind a rather large pillar but I knew, as a greenhorn (though not a "scut"), I was more than likely designated a sunken bunk halfway down the row. The corner would have suited me better. I'd have been less obvious and able to observe others. I could have lain on my side, facing into the clear glass of the large window rather than the face and breath of another boy. But it was not to be. The corner bed went to a huge fellow from Carlow. I never really warmed to him after that.

That first night as the other pupils obediently prayed for blessings on the boys, the community and all activities associated with the college, I fervently pleaded with the Lord to grant me strength and consolation. I implored my recently deceased grandparents to guide and protect me in those strange surroundings. Somehow I felt the loss of the West Gate's John and Ellen, who had both died within days of each other just four months previously, more intensely then. At lights out, in the unfamiliar lumpy bed, close to tears, I wondered how I would ever survive the separation from my parents, sister and brothers, who were all at home safe in Bridge Street.

But I didn't cry.

Ladies in hats and stoles (probably fox-fur) chat on Union Day,
Castleknock College
Tom's mother, Kitty, second from left

The next day, I was enrolled in Class Four B and was registered to take nine subjects, including Latin and Science, in preparation for my Inter Certificate exam. But I had more than lessons on my mind. I was very interested in getting involved in schools' tennis at a competitive level and had also thought about trying my hand at basketball and table tennis. I discovered that my golf would have to wait until I got home for the holidays – no course in 'Knock! As it turned out, I was soon identified as a promising and outstanding junior at tennis, and I once overheard a priest say that, in his opinion, I was able to give a more remarkable performance every time I picked up a racquet.

As time moved on, I spent many dreary days studying Latin verbs and declensions in the classroom. To this day I recall, word for word, the Dean's familiar mantra that Latin would help us boys to develop "logical thinking, clarity of expression, and enjoyment of literature". To be honest, I would much rather be anywhere else, preferably on a tennis court or golf green.

* * *

I had heard the game of rugby described by my father and Uncle Paddy (a Clongowes boy) but had never shown much interest in seeing it played before now. Hurling was my preferred sport and I had even been tipped locally as a possibility for Tipperary teams of the future, before my father rudely interrupted those fantasies of mine by despatching me off to boarding school on the outskirts of the capital city. However, I decided I might as well make the most of where I was, and if this game involved a ball, I'd surely like it. One afternoon, not long afterwards, I voiced my interest to Fr. Maurice Carbery, the man who had the almost heartless task of blending the available material into a junior rugby team. I'd heard on the grapevine that the padre was worried about 'Knock's poor prospects on the rugby front in 1945–46. He studied me from top to toe, said I was a gangly youngster, and announced that he'd give me a chance to tog out. Yippee!

Many years later he told me that he immediately recognised my raw but naturally-gifted talent, but never one to miss an opportunity, he went on to remind me that he was the one to hone the talent into the skill that made me a welcome member of many well-trained, efficient and disciplined teams for the next 18 years of my life. He liked the fact that I was mainly right-footed, but had the ability to kick with my left foot when necessary. From day one, 'Muscles' (as we used to call him) constantly instilled in me that the object of the game was, "in a sporting spirit", to score as many points as possible by carrying, passing, kicking and grounding the oval shaped ball.

"Don't bother starting to play if you are not prepared to get fit and stay fit," he said sternly.

I resolved to cut the smokes back from my current five a day.

"When you attempt a tackle, go for the ball," he went on. "No point in pounding the other lad into the ground. It's the ball that counts. REMEMBER THAT! And when you have that ball, never, EVER waste your possession. There is no place in my team for anyone who is too shy or foolish to use the ball to 'Knock's advantage."

I further resolved to cut the smokes back to two a day. One each morning and evening.

It wasn't all plain sailing. Most of my playing mates had the advantage of being trained from under 13 level at the school so, in order to catch up, I was out on the pitch every chance I got, perfecting my technique, passing and kicking to imaginary team-mates and targets. I quickly learned to pass the ball laterally or behind, never forward, while remembering to stay behind the ball or the group of players trying to win the ball. I soaked up all the information that the coach had to offer, as I heard about rucks and mauls, tackles and techniques. It was from 'Muscles' that I learned that competitive rugby was first played in Ireland at schools' level. He also taught me that originally a rugby ball was made from pig's bladder, inserted into a leather casing and then blown up by mouth. Hence the oval shape. At the time I thought that was disgusting.

The trainer soon had to decide what position I should play in. 'Muscles' told me I didn't have the physique to be suited to the pack, but he could see me handling the ball well, making long passes, cutting through an opponent's defensive line, maybe even kicking for position and possibly scoring for 'Knock. Others told me he spoke openly to them about my competitive nature, which it seems was evident to him, even in practice. After a few tentative trials at various back positions, including full-back and fly-half, 'Muscles' eventually tried me at scrum-half. I took to the position very quickly and before long I felt the place was my very own.

At night, in those early days of rugby playing, I had dreams of scrummages where forwards packed together with their arms across one another's shoulders. Then with an enormous grunt, and eyeballing their opposing forwards, they locked together with them, trying to wheel and push against them, all the time attempting to use their feet to hook the ball back to where I patiently waited. As scrum-half, I sometimes ran with the ball, sometimes passed it to my team-mates or alternatively kicked it downfield. Very rarely in these dreams was I downed in a crushing tackle. Invariably, my moves resulted in a try. I was the hero!

Back in the real world my tackling around the fringe of the scrum was soon rewarded with a place on the junior team, and I wore 'Knock's number nine shirt for the first friendly of the season against Clongowes Wood College. It was a great feeling. I knew that lots of eyes would be on me, so I was determined to give a good account of myself. As part of the preparation before the match, one of the boys from the senior team instilled us all with passion and commitment, by speaking about what it means to play for 'Knock. We hardly needed to be told.

Rugby soon became my world. From my earliest days, I always thought that it was better to play an adventurous, open game and risk losing it, than to play a dull, tight type of kicking game and win. I lived it and loved it and even at the very end of my life these games retained their importance. And I hope that by hearing my story, you will grow to love that world too, or at least begin to understand it.

* * *

The day was fine as we travelled to Clongowes for the match. Castleknock kicked off and hammered at the home line for the first five minutes and eventually we were rewarded with a try at the corner flag. Suddenly, the spotlight was mine for the conversion but I was presented with a very difficult kick which I unfortunately missed. After all that practice and 'Muscles' faith in me, I was devastated and angry with myself. Boiling inwardly to be precise. But I had to put those feelings aside and I did my best to defend well from that to half time. We stuck at it and managed to prevent the other team from scoring before the break. A second chance at a conversion came soon into the second half of the match and this time I brought the 'Knock team to eight points with a well-taken, precise kick. The supporters' reaction was overwhelming and for me to see the sky and navy banners waving in excitement made my teenage heart soar. I was hooked for life.

Despite not being able to play in some of the subsequent matches due to injury, I was instrumental in many of the scores in the lead-up to the Junior Schools Cup competition of 1945–46. Sometimes against physically superior teams, I was able to put into practice 'Muscles' advice on how the backs could outwit the brawn of the bigger boys. In this way, we trounced Belvedere 19-0 and went on to meet a much-improved Clongowes team once more in the final friendly of the season. 'Knock kicked off and went straight into the attack and after a few minutes play, I got sweet revenge for those first-time nerves of six matches previously, by cutting through and passing the ball for a try and a three point lead. Phew! Despite the match ending in a draw, I left that pitch renewed and hopeful of being selected in the coming junior competition proper, which was due to start on 28th February 1946. I was not disappointed and went on to do my best for myself and for my team-mates, but especially for the man who had put his faith in me, a raw newcomer and beginner, my mentor, 'Muscles' Carbery.

The 'Knock team was successful in the first rounds of the competition with superior hooking from the set scrums, availing of ball on the blind side and sometimes almost effortlessly slipping over for tries. Good defensive kicking saved the team on some occasions and we gained a place in our school's first Junior Cup Final for nine years. The atmosphere in the college in the days leading up to the game was fantastic. I'll never forget that feeling. I got such a thrill out of the experience and I knew I wanted more.

In the final match against Blackrock on 3rd April, we never let ourselves become disheartened, despite being pinned in our own 25 from the start. Eventually, the opposition put in some amazing finishing attacks which were both consistent and ferocious and, when the final whistle blew, they came out victorious. I remember the *Chronicles* later reported that on our return home even the walls appeared to weep sympathy for us tired and emotional boys, both players and supporters, who had narrowly failed to bring home the trophy. Everyone was bitterly disappointed. As for me, used to winning at tennis and golf in Carrick, defeat was a new experience, one I didn't particularly relish and one that didn't sit well on my young shoulders. And to make matters worse, all I had to look forward to was Fr. Sullivan pleading with everybody to knuckle down for the forthcoming exams!

This was my first taste of real failure. So public too – it rankled. But, being young, I soon recovered from the bitter disappointment of losing the rugby final and it wasn't too long until, from a scratch handicap, I progressed through the ranks of more experienced players in the table tennis tournament. Having travelled a rough enough path to the final I eventually lost there too, in the best of seven games. Runner-up again. Uh-oh! I have to admit, I didn't like that feeling.

Meanwhile in lawn tennis (as it was called then) I was also being considered as an outstanding junior; some people recognised my promise in the sport and I was regarded as favourite to win the school final. Soon, priests and students alike were tipping me for success. I proved invincible in the inter-schools competition, representing the college at both junior and senior levels, and was seeded in the College Championships. At senior level, I put up a good third round performance in taking a St. Columba's player to 10-8 in the first set.

In the tennis junior cup, I was a member of the team of six boys and, we all gave an astounding display in going through the competition without losing a match. In fact, as a group, we only lost three sets out of 24 matches. We romped home against established teams and when we went into the dining hall the evening of the final, the cheer which greeted us was deafening.

By the end of my first year in Castleknock, the priests were full of praise for me, saying that I was blessed with quite an intellect. (High praise indeed.) My mates told me I was a gifted athlete. (Big of them, I thought!) I myself was aware that almost everything seemed to come easy to me. Although I didn't relish the limelight off the pitch, I was beginning to recognise that I had the gift of drawing people close and that I could be the life and soul of any gathering ... if I chose to be.

The terms passed quickly in a welter of sport and study. Before the end of that academic year, I had grown to love rugby, a sport new to me, but I was runner-up in the final of the junior tournament at table tennis. I had also represented the school on both the winning junior and promising senior inter-schools competitions at tennis.

In June 1946 I sat for the Inter Cert exam in nine subjects, getting honours in

all, except Irish. Indeed, in the dreaded Latin, I achieved 317 marks out of a possible total of 400 so, just turned 16 years of age, I was fairly pleased with myself on my return to 'Knock, the following September, for a second year of sport and study. In that order!

Castleknock College, Junior Tennis Team 1946
Tom (head above the rest!), Jerry O'Donoghue, Derek Reddin, Brian O'Hegarty, Billy Casey and Walter O'Donoghue

Photo by Evening Mail

Castleknock College, Junior Basketball Team 1946-47
Standing: M. Quirke, R. Shipsey, J. Grene, M. Harvey, J. F. Fitzgerald.
Sitting: T. J. Cleary, R. O'Meara, J. Nestor.
Ground: A. Connolly, J. O'Donoghue.
Photo by C. & L. Walsh, Lower Mount Street, Dublin.

Tackling

On my arrival back to school in September 1947, Fr. Kevin O'Kane was taking over as Dean of Discipline and my good friend Frank Maher was made second captain of the house. Over the noisy chat about the summer holidays, we were all reminded of the book of rules. I took some good-natured slagging about the newly-announced restrictions on the use of snuff, as most of my mates were familiar with my likeness for a quiet smoke any time the opportunity presented itself. A far cry from the "new boy" experience the previous year, I was quite casual and relaxed on my return for fifth year.

I had progressed nearer to the corner in the dorm by now, though it didn't worry me as much this year. A wee bit taller, I was just past my 16th birthday and fresh from the summer tennis tournaments at home. I was radiating confidence and secure in the knowledge that the other boys naturally liked me. Having proven myself the previous year, I had won many friends, both in class and in the sports arena. Not so many thoughts of Helen, my parents and the boys this year! The previous term's loneliness forgotten, I bounced back into all the activities from the preceding year and entered into school life with great enthusiasm.

Miss Tighe (Aunt Aggie), our kindly and devoted matron, continued to face the challenges of rationing after the War, as she tried to make greyish-looking bread seem edible. The joke amongst the lads was that she had split the atom to find hidden caches of butter for us. As for the rare event of jams or marmalades, nobody knew how she was able to come up with these treats in such difficult times. Nonetheless, parcels of goodies from home were always eagerly awaited and duly devoured on their arrival.

The barbers regularly braved the weather to come and scalp us. Evening treats included picture shows, compliments of the college projector, and films such as *Shine on Harvest Moon* and *Conspirators* offered the possibility of escape from reality, even if just for a couple of hours. A song I loved dearly at that time came from the musical film starring Alice Faye. My eyes used to get all misty and the lads used to joke that I was like an old sentimental drunk hearing the song he courted to. To this day, I don't know why that song appealed so much to me.

High Masses, numerous Feast Day observances and early rising resumed for us all. Free days in honour of Saints were commonplace and new members received into the Children of Mary were rewarded with time off study in the evening. Competition was encouraged in all areas from the sports field, to the games hall, to the classroom, even down to amateur class concerts in singing. I thrived on the rivalry.

The chosen opera for the year was *The Gondoliers* and I was one of many to take part in the chorus. We had great fun on the day of costume fittings and dress rehearsals. Our first audience consisted of our schoolmates, who couldn't (or wouldn't) sing and this was followed by the performances proper, in front of many dignitaries, together with parents and other guests. It was quite a success. So much so, that the President of the Union requested a free day for the school in honour of our achievement. But, in the middle of exams, most of the students used the spare time to cram, so the treat was wasted on many.

After Christmas, the dreaded 'flu spread through the school and the weather took a major turn for the worse. We experienced ice cold days and there were snow storms almost every day. The freezing water in the washstands had to be cracked open in the mornings and the heating pipes were frozen more often than not. "Winter Sports" became the order of the day for "Vins" and students alike. Some took to skating in the quarry and sleighs were made out of just about anything as the hill became crowded with shrieking boys hurtling down at great speed. I was a member of the team who pounded the speedsters with snowballs as they tumbled to the bottom. We had great fun most of the time, but meanwhile, poor Miss Tighe wondered how she was supposed to feed us all – our appetites were colossal after the fun and games and, despite her best efforts, her scant offerings made little impact on our starving stomachs.

Anyway, life in 'Knock went on as usual, mostly in its age-old routine, but I was very disappointed when some of the friendly rugby matches had to be postponed due to the bad weather. The pitches were constantly covered with blankets of snow and, although a band of willing workers tried to clear it aside for the team to practice, shovelling it away was a huge task, destined for failure. Yet some of the juniors continued to try and break winter's grip on their patch and all they asked in return was the senior cup. Cheeky little devils they were too!

We had frequent problems with the electricity supply in the classrooms and study halls. Occasionally, the lights failed altogether and we had great fun with our adolescent jokes and romantic notions about candlelit suppers with the girls of our dreams. At least it provided us with some light relief. After all, at this stage, we were wearing our coats or using rugs to keep warm in the study hall and, amazingly for a Catholic boarding school in those days, regardless of Lent, we were getting an extra hour in bed in the mornings to help preserve heat.

As well as my usual table tennis exploits, I decided to take an interest in basketball for the duration of the bad weather, which often confined me indoors. I took quickly to this new sport and enjoyed it immensely from day one. I ended up representing the school at junior level that year in basketball and was also on the table tennis team, which secured first place in the Leinster Schools' League.

Although I enjoyed life as a "basketeer", it was just a diversion. Rugby had become my true love and my mates and I watched the weather with more then a passing interest as that awful winter slowly progressed. When the year moved into spring, the long period of cold and snow was followed by flooding, so it was towards the end of March before I got back on the rugby field ... at last! I was hoping to join the senior team, as the talk from the very beginning of the season was that 'Knock would be going "all out" to bring the senior cup back to the ref, just as the boys of the 1943–44 team had done. The weather delays had only strengthened that resolve. We were a determined bunch as we set out on our campaign.

In the autumn term, for the friendly matches, I had been (thankfully) selected for the senior team but strangely enough, to begin with, I actually felt a bit intimidated in the presence of some of the older players. Many of them were sixth year students and much older and stronger than I was. I started out by being a bit slow, and got the blame for handicapping the back division but Fr. Michael Walsh, as trainer of the senior team, had belief in me. I suppose, in his wisdom, he knew that once I got over the shyness I might shine. His faith was rewarded when I was selected to wear the blue jersey as a Leinster inter-provincial and was capped against Ulster in a team captained by another 'Knock boy, Peter McCabe. I've left a tiny snapshot, which was taken on that occasion, in the bottom of my suitcase! My good friend, Frank, is there with me and the Leinster crest is clearly visible on our jerseys.

By the third friendly of the season against Clongowes, I was working very smoothly with my out-half, Frank Maher. Our combined timing was viewed as outstanding and we developed a rapport where my passing, together with his deceptive running, became a sight to see for the juniors. I was delighted with that. By the time 'Knock played Belvedere in the semi-final of the cup later in the season, most people had forgotten my shyness and initial lack of speed, and all were beginning to tell me that I was a brilliant scrum-half. I could hardly believe it. I was on cloud nine and I loved every minute of it.

Castleknock inter provincials 1946-1947[17]
Standing: Paul Cullen, William O'Neill*
Sitting: Frank Maher, Peter McCabe, Tom Cleary
Photo – snapshot from Tom's suitcase.

17 Later capped for Ireland. See Endnotes in Post Mortem section for details of the international careers of the many players of Tom's era who are mentioned in the book, marked throughout with an asterisk (*).

Castleknock College, Rugby Action Shot
Tom on extreme right
Photo courtesy of Independent Newspapers Ltd

Castleknock College, Rugby Action Shot – Schools' Final, Lansdowne Road 1947.
(Tom, though mainly right footed, kicks the ball with his left in this shot.)
"Tom about to kick the ball, Frank Maher in the background with, possibly, Cecil Kilgallon in the centre. The photo is taken from the angle of the 'posh' West Stand end and shows the old East Stand in the background. The Lansdowne Road end terrace (standing room only) can be seen behind Frank."
(Description kindly given to me by Paddy O'Byrne, a classmate of Tom's, now living in Mullingar).

Photo courtesy of Independent Newspapers Ltd

Scoring

On the day of the Senior Cup Final against Blackrock, the anxiety was palpable in the school despite the ongoing chanting and singing of our supporters. I was worried about the continual drizzly weather and its potential to go against good back play, and the nerves became almost overwhelming at times. I did my best to contain the emotion in an effort to channel it into good rugby. As the school bus pulled up at Lansdowne, aware of the history of the place, I soaked up the tumult and the uproar, the hubbub of the supporters, the commotion at the bus, the orders of the stewards. It was such a thrill.

Fr. Walsh had drummed it into us that Lansdowne Road was a place of great history. He fired us up on the legend that Lansdowne was laid down in 1872 by a man called Dunlop, the founder of Lansdowne Football Club. Seemingly, at that time, it ran at right angles to the present international pitch at the Havelock Square or northern end of the ground. It was so low lying that Mr. Dunlop liked to recall that he "paddled a canoe between the goalposts in eighteen inches of water one winter, while a few sheep stood on a little island in the middle".[18]

As it turned out, on my first day to play in Lansdowne, the bad weather was not a problem for our team. Almost as soon as the match started, the 'Knock backs showed their superiority, often kicking the heavy ball well up the field and following it relentlessly. The Blackrock defence had many worrying moments as Frank and I were working very smoothly together all through the first half. The excitement was obvious throughout Lansdowne, as the sky blue and navy scarves and flags waved and the supporters shouted themselves hoarse in efforts at urging their team on. Meanwhile the backs never let up as, about three minutes from half-time in a close shave, a 'Rock movement brought one of their centres inches from the line, but a combined clean tackle by myself and our full back saved the day. This maintained a slender lead for 'Knock and, at half time, we were ahead by 3 points to nil, compliments of Frank's impressive drop goal taken with ten minutes to go. My heart was thumping with adrenaline at this stage of the match.

In the second half, despite the rain becoming heavier, 'Knock attacked from the kick-off and got most of the balls from the tight and the loose, even though

---

18 'Some Irish Rugby Firsts' Michael J. O'Connor, *Irish Rugby Union Programme Ireland v England*, 14th February 1959. p. 5.

the ball was getting very difficult to handle. By now I felt I could do no wrong. Ten minutes into this half I went around the blind side from a scrum near the corner flag, and drawing a wing forward sent Frank over for the try. I felt brilliant! This was special. I sensed the match was ours already. The team defended well for the remainder of the match and at its end, victory and the cup were Castleknock's to enjoy, six points to nil.

When the final whistle blew, I really let go and enjoyed the occasion, the associated drama of the presentation, the ecstasy of being a member of the winning team in a competition of great renown. While I was aware of the barely disguised emotions of heartache and agony on the faces of the 'Rock lads, I didn't really give them too much thought, except to think I was glad I wasn't wearing their devastated boots. We laughed and sang the whole way back to the school with our trophy, we paraded it up and down when we got back, every one of us wanted to touch and hold it and, at the end of the day, when we headed for the dormitory, we reluctantly handed it over to Fr. Walsh for safe keeping.

As I went to bed that night I joked with Frank Maher about my position in the team photographs. As scum-half I was always seated on the ground.

"It seems to me" I said "that the only way I'll ever get a seat on a chair for the photo is to be named as captain next year!"

Frank looked at me, bemused.

"I've worked hard enough," I reminded him.

He still didn't answer. Maybe he thought the captaincy would be his.

Due to the fast approaching Easter holidays, the main cup celebrations weren't held until a month later when we had all returned to school for the summer term. As it turned out, the party was well worth waiting for and each team member had a course on the specially compiled French menu dedicated to their achievement. I was listed as the self-confident salmon salad and was quietly chuffed at such an accolade. There it was printed on the menu in black and white for all to see – *Saumon Froid – Cléri Sang-froid.* Frank was *Sauce Mayonnaise – Marqueue Súr.*

Such a meal had not been seen in the school for many moons and we all washed it down with deliciously sparkling Taylor Keith red lemonade, jokingly referred to by us boys as bubbly Vintage 1947. All the deprivations and difficulties caused by the previous term's awful weather conditions were consigned to history as we thoroughly enjoyed the food and fun. Following the meal and speeches, Fr. Willie Sullivan distributed a commemorative silver pencil to each team member, kindly donated by the parents of *Scrummage de Fruits à la grand Capitain Pierre!* And to top it all, later that evening, we were treated to a movie called *Seven Sweethearts.*

To my eternal regret I lost that silver pencil somewhere along the line. The last time I remember using it was in a pub in Baggot Street, Dublin, many years later after an international match. A rugby pub: I was there, with the gang, for a few scoops, on my way back to the Shelbourne Hotel from Lansdowne that day. I was raging the following morning, when I missed it, because it was always particularly precious to me. I retraced my steps, even though my head was thumping with a hangover. I recalled writing down the telephone number of a girl I met in the pub. I had written it on the inside flap of my cigarette packet.

The barman was very helpful.

"Have a hair of the dog and I'll have a look around," he suggested.

No luck. Had I dropped it? Had it been stolen? I hadn't a clue what I had done with it. I rang the girl in question to see if she could enlighten me. No joy there either. I may have offended her by being more interested in the pencil than I was in her! She was never available any time I phoned her after that. I never found my pencil.

* * *

However, back to my schooldays in Castleknock. Tennis beckoned as the evenings began to stretch. Having won the College Championship for the Murphy Cup at both junior and senior levels the previous year, I was picked for the senior team of 1947. Unfortunately the team was out of practice due to the continual rain and 'Knock lost a match which should have been won easily, in the opening fixture against Belvedere. However, as I progressed through the competition, I felt my flair returning and the team went on to win the senior cup against Terenure College in the final. The Suir-side summer months beckoned once more and I was looking forward to sunny holidays, spending time on the beach and

Ready for tennis
Tom at 17 years of age

Castleknock College, Senior Rugby Team 1946–47
Winners of the Leinster Schools' Senior Cup
Standing: Tom Cleary, Leo Lynch, Maurice Shipsey, Brendan Guerin*,
Richard (Dick) Kinneen, Tim Ryan.
Sitting: John Nestor, Denis Connolly, Frank Maher, Peter McCabe (captain),
William (Boldy) O'Neill, Paul Cullen, Roger Shipsey.
Ground: Richard (Dick) O'Neill, Paddy Donegan.
Photo by C. & L. Walsh, Lower Mount Street, Dublin

doing the rounds of tennis tournaments in Clonmel, Tramore and the resorts of the south. I was well able to beat my brothers John and Michael at tennis at this stage, but young Gerry was beginning to show that he might be a talented competitor of the future. I might have to watch my back there!

In my third and final year in Castleknock there was no trace of reluctance in my step as I bounded towards the college door on my return after a wonderful summer. I remember feeling very grown up, wearing a smart new sports coat, open necked shirt and turned-up trousers. By this stage I was losing my boyishness and people often commented that I was developing into a handsome, toned and fit young man. Soon I enrolled in Leaving Certificate Second Year A, renewed my membership of Sacred Heart Confraternity and was appointed Secretary to the Children of Mary. At the request of Fr. Desmond ("Dart") MacMorrow, I also joined the chorus of Dukes, Marquises, Earls, Viscounts and Barons for the proposed Gilbert and Sullivan opera *Iolanthe*, which was due to be performed the following December. I quietly thanked God that I was too mature to become a member of the faerie chorus, and most of that group were recruited from junior classes!

All through the month of September, we wondered who the prefects for the coming year would be. On the last day of the month, which was a lot later than usual, it was eventually announced at assembly that I, Tom Cleary, had been made captain of the house (therefore the rugby team) and prefect. What an honour. I was all smiles. (And the title carried the added bonus of being allowed to smoke openly in the prefects' room!) My vice captain was John Nestor and Hon. Secretary Dick O'Neill. Lots of backslapping and congratulations followed as all three of us received the good wishes of the boys, teachers and priests alike. Life was good.

With seven of the previous year's cup-winners available to form the mainstay of the 1947–48 senior cup team for 'Knock, the prospects of retaining the trophy were looking good. Five of those players were in the pack where their quick-breaking excellence and ability to pack tightly in the scrums was recognised. Third captain Dick O'Neill was looked on as sound in both attack and defence. My back-line was not so lucky, though. Only myself and my vice captain stayed put. Nonetheless, Nestor's strength combined with my tireless work rate were being seen as a good omen for the team. Later, on looking through the available boys coming along behind, and others returning from injury, I realised that the trainer had plenty of material on hand to fill in the gaps, and that many of the players were capable of filling any vacancy in the back-line. It looked promising enough.

However, in the first friendly of the season, my first as captain, I was both proud and anxious as I led an injury-weakened team, with four major players missing, onto the pitch. Even in the face of that shortfall, the team tried to play open rugby but on the day we were not allowed to do so by the "spoiling" tactics of our opponents, who came out the winners of the match.

'Knock only scored once when I broke away from the scrum at the half way line and ran with the ball, heading for the corner flag. In what was later described as a deft move, I opted to pass it back to the wing forward rather than the backs, and the action resulted in a try. Unfortunately it wasn't converted, so the people who were hoping this match might give an idea of the team's merit walked away dissatisfied.

I was very disappointed that, in my first real test as a leader, I had not come out on top. No matter how the others tried to explain it away, I still felt slightly dejected. But it was only a friendly, so I soon knuckled down to train with the lads for our following matches. But, to be honest, when I attempted to get rid of the taste of defeat, I only managed to bury it slightly below the surface.

Some time later, the fourth friendly was against the visiting Clongownians and the home flags waved triumphantly at full-time, as we smugly recorded a winning score of 8-0. I had to go off in that match just before half time, with an injured ankle, when after a neat dummy near the Clongowes 25 I went on to touch down, a bit awkwardly, for a try. I watched the rest of that game from the sideline. This injury resulted in me missing some of the next few games but by December I was prominent in the inter-provincial trials at Donnybrook and even succeeded in scoring. I was selected, once more, to represent Leinster and was confident that, by the time the competitive matches came about, I'd be fully recovered from injury and back in harness, leading my team.

* * *

The following term, in the first cup game of the 1947–48 season, on 16th February, my team was given a rare fright by Masonic, who more than held their own up to 15 minutes from the end. A fast paced game to begin with, the opposing forwards proceeded to gain possession from the set scrums, and outplayed 'Knock in the loose. However, my team stayed in the game and, finishing the stronger, came out the winners with a score of 15-9. The next challengers were St. Andrew's and we were confident going into the match as we had beaten them easily earlier in the season. Although we took a while to settle down, I was equally pleased with my own try, the overall performance and the final score of 35-0.

In the semi-final, against Belvedere, 'Knock expected a difficult match, but Lady Luck was with us when Belvedere knocked-on straight from the kick-off. The scrum quickly heeled and, in a series of brilliant moves, Liam Burke, evading three opponents in the process, flashed across for the try. With a magic start like that a lot of the fight went out of the challengers and the final score was 8-0 for 'Knock.

The anticipation leading up to the final was mind blowing. The team carried the hopes of everybody, from schoolboys to past-pupils, from professors to parents. On a personal level, I was already the proud owner of a senior medal and now I had the opportunity to captain a winning team on an historic occasion for the college. For me, the hum of excitement was even greater than the previous year. As captain, I was feeling extra pressure What if we failed? But knowing I had already battled successfully at Lansdowne the previous year in the cup final, was a bonus. That steadied the nerves a little bit.

Our old rivals, Blackrock, were the adversaries in the cup final on St. Patrick's Day 1948 but very few doubted that 'Knock would return the precious silverware to the refectory. Fervent prayers were offered to the Lord and St. Patrick for fair weather, especially following the defeat of the junior cup team by an exceptionally heavy and fast Blackrock team just two days before. And now the seniors of the same two schools were to face each other. As our team relied on its speedy and skilled rear division to do its utmost, we hoped for a dry ball and firm footing.

When the dorm woke up to horrendous conditions outside, with wind and rain lashing at the sash windows, rattling them in their cradles, any hope of a good game seemed to be blown away. With our hearts sinking, we began the day with High Mass, in honour of St Patrick, with a sermon in Irish. Lovely! Just lovely! Great preparation, I'm sure, but one which very few members of the congregation were in a position to relish. As the boys sang a hymn in honour of the saint, where was my heart? It was in my boots. But, surely 'Knock had faced similar weather conditions before and came out victorious? Hadn't they?

When we arrived at Lansdowne, the wind coming up the river, from Ringsend, would cut the skin off you. Our supporters had been there for three or four hours before we arrived. It was quite a long wait before they saw any action. There was no such thing as "curtain raisers" because the pitch couldn't be disturbed. But when the match started they forgot all about the cold and discomfort and cheered us on wildly.

It was a bad game for 'Knock. Many of the backs never got going and although the forwards played well in the loose, they couldn't round off with a score. At half-time Blackrock was in the lead by six points to nil and when the second half commenced it was obvious that they were prepared to sit on that. They employed tactics which the 'Knock team could do little against. I led my gallant army, and worked tirelessly in both attack and defence, but between injuries and some having an "off-day" 'Knock was destined, as the final whistle sounded, to end the season defeated at the very doorstep of glory and history. (It was to be eleven more years before the cup was brought back to 'Knock again.) I had to watch as the opposing captain's mother presented him with the cup. I avoided looking over at my mother, Kitty, there in the stand, all dressed up in her fur stole, ready for the moment that never happened. I was devastated.

It was such a disappointing end to a rugby season where I had led by example, putting my heart and soul into it, because of the faith that others had placed in me; a season where I had once more represented Leinster as an inter-provincial by being "capped" in a match against Ulster. Five days after this latest defeat, as the school broke up for Easter, I still felt downhearted, but few would have known. Already, I was a master at suppressing my emotions, and wore a smile, though I felt anguish in my heart. Oh, I got out of bed as usual in the mornings though, if I had been given a choice, I might have remained under the blankets. It was my youth, you see. I was still able to absorb the blows.

On my return to school after a fortnight's break, I concentrated on tennis. The standard was very high, as 'Knock had won the senior cup for the previous two years, only dropping five matches out of a total of 48 played. So, by the time the first post-war Union Day dawned, after a lapse of eight years, on the 13th June 1948, the final of the Murphy Cup was one of the main attractions. Following the annual lunch in the boys' refectory and junior play hall, the celebrations began with a performance of physical drill and gymnastics in front of all the guests.

As I posed for the photos that day I was impeccably dressed in long whites and plimsolls, and ready for action. My outfit was topped off with an intricately patterned, white sweater, hand knitted by my mother, especially for the warm up. I knew that it would be absolutely essential to get my first service in against Jerry O'Donoghue, the previous year's winner, and was determined to play a convincing game right from the start. I was well aware that the slower pace of my second service could offer too many options to this talented opponent. The early morning's dew just a distant memory, I faced the defending champion across the net, watching as the spin of the wooden racquet decided who would have choice of side or service. It was all immaterial really, as conditions were perfect for tennis on that lovely summer's day. I remember it as if it were yesterday.

An epic struggle followed which more than pleased the onlookers. Most of my shots were sharp and speedy and my ability to stay low to the ball on the groundstrokes was about equal with his. I took the lead early in the game, employing my strong forehand drive well and placing the ball excellently, often within a hair's breadth of the tramline. Leading 5-3, I thought an easy first set was mine but as I eased my foot off the pedal slightly, Jerry fought back bravely and won the next two games. There was a huge gasp of frustration from the spectators, as the umpire called one of my cross-court volleys out. I was letting this set slip away.

But I rallied and I pulled out classic low volleys, holding the racquet far out in front and bending my knees to stay low as I hit the returning ball. I went on to play a risky, but winning, drive volley on a crucial point until, eventually, I pocketed the first set 10-8. This removed the initiative from the reigning champion and an element of cautious play entered his game. Some floating mistimed serves followed and soon, after a subdued second set (6-3), I won the Castleknock College Murphy Cup 1947–48 for the second time in three years.[19]

And so, on one of my final schooldays in Castleknock, I added another trophy to an accumulating list of sports' honours which I had achieved in my three years at the college, with winning encounters in the four main sporting spheres of interest to me: champion in tennis, table tennis, basketball and rugby. I left Castleknock on a high. I was a true champion. Everybody told me so.

---

19 Tom also won the "Castleknock College Kevin Smyth Cup, Best All-Round Athlete 1947–48" that year.

Castleknock College, Prefects 1947–1948
Standing: P. Cooney, C. Kilgallon, B. O'Flynn, A. Austin, C. Hunter, E. McCabe, J. Glynn, J. O'Donoghue.
Sitting: T. Ryan, P. O'Byrne (now living in Mullingar), T. J. Cleary (Captain of the House), B. Guerin, J. Bolger, J. Morris, Jn. Nestor (Vice-captain), R. O'Neill (Hon. Secretary), A. Connolly.
Photo by C. & L. Walsh, Lower Mount Street, Dublin

Castleknock College, Table Tennis Team 1947-48
Winners of the Leinster Schools' Shield
Standing: B. McAuliffe, M. Harvey, M. Quirke,.
Sitting: W. O'Donoghue, J. O'Donoghue, T. J. Cleary.
Photo by C. & L. Walsh, Lower Mount Street, Dublin

Castleknock Senior Tennis Team 1947-1948
Winners of the Leinster Senior Schools' Cup
Standing: John Cleary (Tom's brother), Walter O'Donoghue, John Nestor.
Sitting: Jerry O'Donoghue, Tom Cleary, John Bolger.
Photo by C. & L. Walsh, Lower Mount Street, Dublin

Castleknock College, Senior Rugby Team 1947-1948
Runners-up in the Leinster Schools' Senior Cup

Standing: T. Ryan, A. Austin, L. Burke, D. McMahon, M. Ward, R. Shipsey
Sitting: B Guerin, R. Kerr, J. Nestor, T. J. Cleary (Captain), R. O'Neill, J. Morris, L. Lynch.
Ground: A. Connolly, M. Lynch.
Photo by C. & L. Walsh, Lower Mount Street, Dublin

ÉIRE 1s

12 JUL 1947
CLONMEL
DIVISION OF TIPPERARY

Síniú an tSealbhóra
Signature of Holder: Thomas J. Cleary

Sloinne
Surname: CLEARY

Ainmneacha
Christian Names: THOMAS JOSEPH

Sloinne a hAthar
Maiden Name:

Seoladh
Address: Bridge St. Carrick-on-Suir, Co. Tipp. (Castle St., Carrick-on-Suir Co. TIPPERARY)

Gairm
Profession: Student

Dáta Breithe
Date of Birth: 10.8.30

Dáta Eisiúna
Date of Issue: 12.7.47

Bailí go dtí
Valid up to: 11.7.52

Leanaí—Children

Ainm Name	Dáta Breithe Date of Birth	Gnéas Sex	Gaol leis an Sealbhóir Relationship to Holder

VISA
UNITED KINGDOM PERMIT OFFICE, DUBLIN.
Visa No. .... Date 21 JUL 1947
Valid for any number of journeys to and from the United Kingdom within a period of Twelve Months from date hereof, subject to review as necessary, and to the continued validity of the Passport or Travel Permit Card.
Signature of Permit Officer: E. J. Keating

IMMIGRATION OFFICER (20) 13 DEC 1947 LIVERPOOL

IMMIGRATION OFFICER (15) EMBARKED 20 DEC 1947 HOLYHEAD

Tom's Travel Identity Card – Issued 12-7-1947
This travel card was required for a holiday taken by Tom and his sister Helen in Sheffield in 1947.

Tom takes part in All Ireland Boys Senior Tennis competition, Fitzwilliam 1948
Photo courtesy of Independent Newspapers Ltd

PAGE 14
THE STANDARD, NOVEMBER 17, 1950
WE MAY HEAR A LOT ABOUT THE YOUNG LAD
FROM CARRICK-ON-SUIR

The Open Air
By "Fanfare"
****

OVER IN GALWAY RECENTLY I WAS SHOWN A PHOTOGRAPH OF PILGRIMS TAKEN OUTSIDE ST. PETER'S, ROME. IT REPRESENTED A SECTION OF ONE OF THE FRANCISCAN HOLY YEAR PILGRIMAGES AND I WAS ASKED IF I COULD PICK OUT THAT MEMBER OF THE HOUSEHOLD WHO WAS THERE "SOMEWHERE". I COULD NOT.

BUT, STRANGE TO RELATE, MY GLANCE FELL STRAIGHTAWAY UPON THE FIGURE OF A VERY GOOD FRIEND OF MINE FROM CARRICK-ON-SUIR, A MR. RICHARD CLERY (sic). THERE HE WAS, STANDING SLIGHTLY APART AT THE END OF A ROW IN SPORTS JACKET AND FLANNELS.

When I reach Carrick, Mr. Cleary assured me that he himself had not seen the photograph. However, I mention the photograph because but for it I might not have called upon the Cleary household at all. Inevitably, the conversation swung around to young Tom Cleary, an up-and-coming lad, of whom Rugby followers may hear a lot in the near future.

Tom Cleary was a stylish hurler, who, in the opinion of local judges, would have eventually found his place on the Tipperary team had he continued with the game. However, he was sent to Castleknock College as a boy, and took to Rugby almost at once. Having tried his hand at many positions in the three-quarter line, he settled down finally at scrum-half.

He was on the senior cup winning team of 1947, and the following year played on the team eventually defeated in the cup final.

Lawn tennis attracted young Cleary in the summer months, and so he proceeded to make his mark in this sphere also. He won the senior cup presented by the college, and in 1948 he captained the team of six, which captured for Castleknock the Leinster Senior Tennis Cup.

Back home in Carrick-on-Suir while on holidays, Tom took a hand at this game of golf on the local course. It is a rugged and very interesting nine-hole course, if a little short.

Last summer Tom was playing to a handicap of six! He has a natural flair for games and the big occasion never ruffles him. This, to my mind, along with his aptitude for games, is the secret of his really fine record as an all-round sportsman.

RECORD

He was eighteen when leaving college in 1948, and for a time he busied himself around his father's shop in Carrick. Early this year he began his apprenticeship with a firm of accountants in Limerick; joined a Rugby Club, of course – Bohemians, actually – a local Tennis Club, and, if I remember correctly, Castletroy Golf Club.

He was selected to play by Munster as scrum-half for their first inter-provincial encounter of the season versus Connaught, and acquitted himself more than well. Munster won this game, eight points to six, and Tom Cleary contributed three points by means of a delightfully taken dropped goal.

In a way, I suppose it was natural to expect that Burges*, the International scrum-half of last season, should have found his place on the Munster team versus Ulster, at Cork, last Saturday; but by all accounts Cleary would have suited the job better. Be that as it may, it seems more than likely that we shall see more of this young lad from Carrick-on-Suir, before the Rugby season ends.

NEW BLOOD NEEDED

There is no denying the fact that we are badly in need of scrum-halves again this year, and it is to be hoped that all available talent will be brought to light as early as possible. The display of Burges last Saturday was nothing to write home about they tell me; while Cox and Dillon seem to have sizzled out recently, despite a spate of publicity.

Tom Cullen of U.C.D. has had many chances, and his general form is known, so that to my mind the issue would seem to rest between Cleary and Reggie O'Reilly of Wanderers, who has certainly staked his claim with a flourish already. Might not an Irish Trial with these two ambitious youngsters in opposite camps be an interesting experiment, to say the least?

Lining Out

In the early 1950s things in general began to improve for the people of Carrick. Miloko, a new chocolate crumb factory, was opened on the outskirts of the town. This gave much needed employment to many of the townspeople. After a short time in U.C.D. when I lived in Hatch Street, I returned home to work in the shop. University life was not for me. It didn't take long for my father to see that my commitment to the family business left a lot to be desired also. Despite my progress in Castleknock, remnants of the spoiled boy were still obvious to my astute, but caring father. My mother continued to lavish attention on me for my sporting achievements. She made excuses for many of my lapses and I realise now that I was probably the subject of many frank and animated conversations in the Cleary household at night.

My father was having difficulty understanding me, his eldest son. At school I had shown that I was quite intelligent. I had proven leadership abilities and could be hard-working on occasions; I was popular, talented, had a natural flair for games and seemed difficult to ruffle. But, since I came home, it appeared to my Dad that my interests lay more in keeping my golf handicap at six than progressing in the business ethic of Richard Cleary & Sons. It was high time, my father decided, that I should take up commercial studies of some kind that might instil a bit of business sense into that head of mine. He came to a decision that was to have a life-long impact on me and those who loved me.

* * *

At this stage of my life I was twenty years old and an unsettled young man. To be honest, I was missing the hustle and bustle of the life I imagined all my school friends were having in different parts of the country. I often thought of how my sister and her pals used to throw a dandelion, picked from the quayside, over one side of the old bridge and then run across to see it come out at the other side. They thought that if they made a wish while the yellow plant was falling into the stream and it floated out on the other side, then that wish would be granted. If only I could have made a wish, like Helen used to as a kid, mine would have been to get out of Carrick.

One evening, not long after he made his decision, I watched my father, as he walked slowly down towards our home in Bridge Street with that day's letter tucked neatly inside his sports-coat pocket. Pat Barron, of O'Neill-Barron in

Limerick, had offered an accountancy apprenticeship to me – where my father hoped I would avail of the general experience of working in an accountant's office and eventually bring the know-how to bear on the family enterprise. On his way to break the news to my reluctant mother, he steeled himself for an evening of high emotion.

That evening, instead of a single boiled or scrambled egg per person, a glorious fry complete with tripe and onions was being served at teatime. One of the friars from Carrick-Beg joined the family, as we continued the tradition started by my grandmother Feehan at the West Gate house years before. Plates of back rashers, pork sausages, black and white pudding, with drisheen, all swimming in a thick pond of off-white cow's belly, diced and cooked in an onion and white sauce mix, were the order of the day. These delights were accompanied by a slice of fried bread, crispy from the dripping, and all was about to be eaten with relish by each person – when my father announced that I was to go to Limerick.

I could see that my mother was finding it difficult to take in the news, but she was holding things together fairly well in front of the priest. I realised she was thrilled to have me back home, what with Helen now working miles away up in the midlands and John and Michael back at school in Castleknock. She'd been enjoying the extra activity of having me in the house and loving our rounds of golf together. Young Gerry adored me and had been trying very hard to be like me in all things sporting. My father really wanted things to work out business-wise, but for some reason he decided that I was having difficulty applying myself in the shop. Let's face it ... I was bored silly. In her wildest dreams, however, my mother had never thought I'd receive such a prompt and attractive offer. She was stunned into silence and realised there was nothing to be discussed. I could see on her face that she felt she'd lost me. This was it!

But how did I feel? Maybe at first I was not altogether sure how I felt. I wondered if this was just another choice my father was making for me, when maybe I should be making decisions for myself. But I knew it would be a way of getting away from the drudgery of my present life. And to the Mecca of Munster[20] rugby at that. I could feel the beginnings of a little excitement bubbling deep in my belly, but no one would ever know it to look at me. I did not agree to the move that evening... not before talking it over with my much-loved Uncle Paddy first. But there was no doubt in my mind – I already knew that my answer would be a resounding YES!

So my mother was devastated and my father was worried, while I, in my own head, was already in Limerick making sporting contacts. Baby brother Gerry

---

20 'Munster was the first Irish province to arrange a cross-channel tour, when it sent a team in 1897 to play the Welsh clubs Newport, Swansea and Neath. The Munstermen defeated Neath and were narrowly defeated in the other two games'. 'Some Irish Rugby Firsts' Michael J. O'Connor, *Irish Rugby Union Programme Ireland v England* 14th February 1959. p. 7.

was trying to work out what could be in this for him. Maybe he'd get my bed. At least he'd have the undivided attention of his mother again.

* * *

When the day came for me to leave home, snowy peaks were still visible on Sliabh na mBan. The morning was spent with my mother and the maid bustling between the upper floors of the house, to the short corridor hot-press and down to the kitchen, fetching and gathering all the requirements for a boy's extended stay away from home. Their list was long. Suits for work, casual clothes, flannels, shirts, collars, ties, a spare pair of braces, socks, tennis whites, laundry bag, new vests and other underwear from Morrissey's, new shoes from Meaney's, toiletries from Coghlan's, all would have to be accommodated in the luggage. I accepted the new or laundered, neatly folded clothes offered by the two women and stored them carefully in my suitcase.

Later, in the slight warmth of the early afternoon, my father walked around to the yard to collect the car. When the time came to kiss my mother goodbye inside the door of Bridge Street, I felt strangely emotional. My baby brother, Gerry, stood beside her, looking up at me expectantly. I tweaked his ear and told him to be good. I hoisted my, by now, heavy but spanking new suitcase with my wash bag and all the belongings and clothing it could contain into the trunk of the car. I next loaded a separate sports tackle holdall containing my boots, plimsolls, and racquet with wooden press.

Once again my father guided me, his first born son, onto the next step on life's journey as he personally drove me to my destination. My mother had been able to organise suitable accommodation with the O'Neill family friends, in their home on the North Circular Road, and was happy that I'd be comfortable, warm and well fed there. My father and I travelled in comfortable silence, through the long basin which extends from Carrick to the plains of Limerick. Founded by the Norse and sitting at the entrance to the mouth of the Shannon River, I knew that Limerick boasted a noble history and tradition, but it was its sporting folklore that mainly beckoned as I listened to my father pleading with me to apply myself to this new business position.

I remember hoping that my father was proud of me. After all I had achieved things in my young life to date that he could only dream about. Duty meant that he'd had to leave school and knuckle down prematurely to supporting his siblings after his father's death and so he didn't have the opportunities that were being afforded his offspring. And now, here he was urging the next generation forward in his own quiet way. I felt an unfamiliar stab of loneliness as I sneaked a look at the bespectacled old man beside me in the car. I promised myself that I would not let him down.

What I did not realise at the time is that it was no coincidence that my father had chosen to write to these people in search of an apprenticeship. He'd had some little chats with my Uncle Paddy! While the main reason was dictated by the business sense of his head, deep down in his heart he wanted Munster rugby to recognise my raw talent, and, although I had played in the Leinster jersey at inter-provincial level, my father wanted to see me in the red of my native province. It was, after all, where he felt I belonged.

On our arrival in Limerick city we passed the Treaty Stone off Thomond Bridge. I remembered from my history lessons that a war between England, France, Holland and Ireland had brought the town of Limerick under siege way back in the 1600s and, ultimately, a treaty had been signed in 1691 on that very stone.[21] I noted that there was great movement to this city, something that my home town lacked, and all the people seemed to walk with a purpose. Historically a very class-conscious society, where professional and business people thrived side-by-side with those living in dismal poverty, it was the more affluent side of Limerick I was to see in my first days in the city.

I actually never talked that much about my time in Limerick, yet it was the one place in my life where I truly felt alive. When I first went there I had plenty of money in my bank account, following a recent bequest from my Grand-Aunt Bid.[22] For most of my time there, I lived well, dressed well, socialised a lot and was very sporting ... in every sense of the word. With Aunt Bid's dosh in my pocket, I was doing OK.

I was to be employed at 93 O'Connell Street, where a well-polished brass plaque announced that this was the premises of O'Neill, Barron & Co., Accountants and Auditors. The strange smell of polish combined with ink hit me forcefully that first day but I soon grew used to it. Thus began my initiation into a world of balance sheets, trading accounts, profit and loss accounts, capital accounts, gross profits, nett rents, liquid assets, current liabilities, dividends received, stock-taking, percentage rates, statements, debits and credits. Wow, what a lot to learn. Firstly, however, I learned that my main role was to prepare accounts to final stage for checking by the partners before their ultimate submission to the Inspector of Taxes. Soon I was recording the details of businesses with massive turnovers of £15,000 or more per annum. I settled in and enjoyed the work, the camaraderie of my colleagues, the peripheral presence of pretty girls and it was not too long before I become an established member of staff.

On the nights when small groups of us were asked to work late at stocktaking, everyone automatically headed for the pub afterwards. At this early stage, although quite a heavy smoker, I was still a mineral drinker, but it wasn't long before, with a little coaxing from colleagues such as Joe Benson, Brian Gubbins, Pat McGuigan and Frank Butler, I was persuaded to "try" a glass of the black stuff, Guinness. I liked it. It wasn't long before I progressed to pints. I loved them.

---

21 *Streets of Limerick* by Darina Raleigh. http://www.limerick.com/alimk/auld1.html, accessed on 19th April 2005.

22 Bridget Mary Hurley (neé Feehan) (1867-1946), the childless sister of Tom's maternal grandfather. She married Frank Hurley. For details of her will see Post Mortem section of the book.

Scrum-ptious

A forward needs enormous calves,
  A back needs mounds of muscle,
Three-quarters, not to mention halves,
  Need sinew for the tussle.
And Rugger men whose thinnish thews
  Have hardly any kick in 'em,
Know Guinness is the stuff to choose
  To build 'em up and thicken 'em.

GUINNESS

FOR STRENGTH

G.E.3085

A Guinness advertisement from the 1950s
Designed to appeal to "Rugger Men"
This advertisement is reproduced here courtesy of Guinness Archive, Diageo Ireland

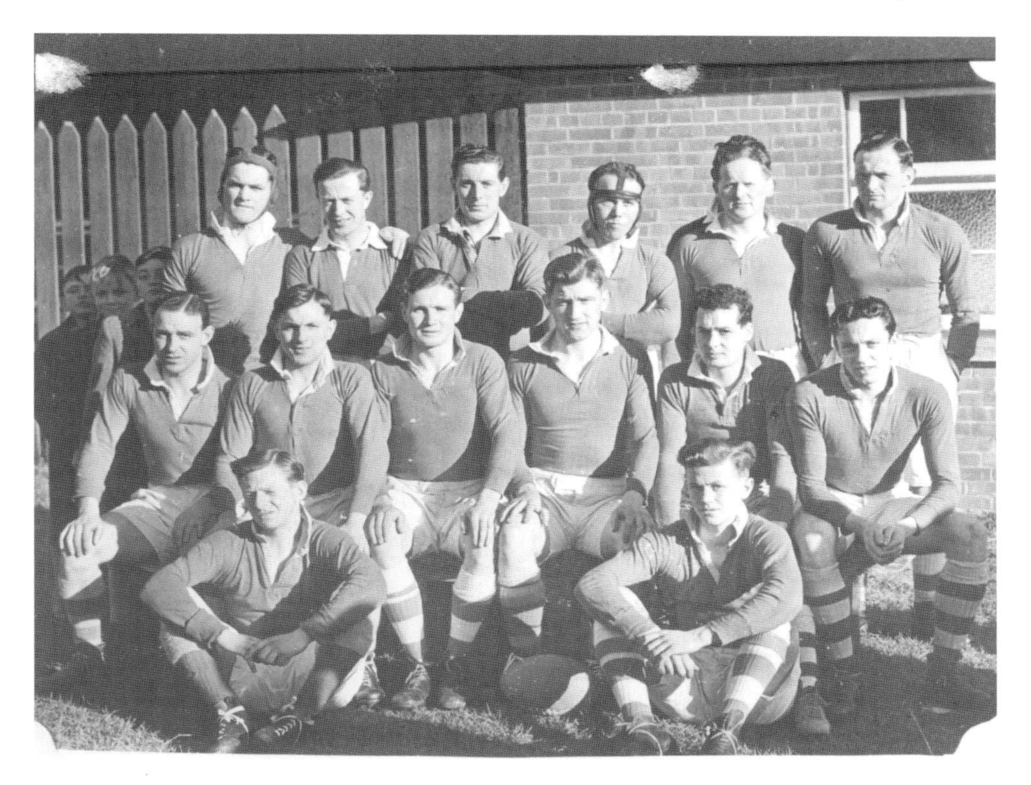

Bohemians team – early 1950s
Standing: Joe Gilligan, Paddy Ryan, Alfie Mulcahy, Ger O'Sullivan, Tom McCarthy,[23] Robin Bolster
Sitting: Brian Keogh, Joe Murphy, Vernon Lane, Dom Dineen, John Lane, Tom Fitzgerald
Ground: Mick Walsh, Tom Cleary

23 Ger South was playing Gaelic football in Dublin at this time, and the code of rules dictated that he should not have been playing rugby. So he hid behind Tom McCarthy for this photo!

BALLHOPPING

Soon after my arrival in Limerick, I discovered the expression 'ballhopping'. It was a Limerick term for swapping stories and gossip. Anyone who remembers me will recall my own favourite phrase "Just hoppin' the ball", one frequently used by me, especially on those nights when the family were trying to get me to shut up and go to bed, when I had a few pints on board. They knew what I meant, without it ever being explained. To me that phrase meant stirring things up a bit when I was having a banter, but always in a light-hearted friendly way. But they never fully realised that it wasn't just a phrase of mine. It belonged to the people of Limerick, where rugby is like a religion.

Not long after my move to Limerick, I was invited to join Bohemians Rugby Club (fondly known as Bohs). I also joined a local tennis club, and a golf club. Bohs origins dated back to the mid 1920s and I was aware that they were no strangers to long spells in the wilderness, most notably in the few years since the recent war. One of the first men I met was Dom Dineen, a great rugby man, who had given wonderful service to the club since the mid 1940s, with no trophies to show for it. I also met my soon-to-become regular out-half partner – who became my good friend – the now legendary Mick English.

People often wondered why I chose to join that particular rugby club – a club that had lived for years in the Limerick shadows. They all felt I could have had my pick. What they didn't realise was that I had been "head-hunted". Dom had been told by Fr. J. G. Guinane S. J. [24] that I was coming to Limerick and the padre had recommended approaching me to join Bohs. I often said that Bohs was the first truly ecumenical rugby club in Ireland. The club's initial Munster cup triumph was in 1927, just a few years after its foundation. Since then it hadn't achieved much of note especially in the decade before my arrival. In those barren years the popular club anthem, sung to the tune of Bye, Bye, Blackbird and starting with the line 'we are the boys in red and white', had seldom been heard.

As early as the following autumn, I made my Munster Senior Cup debut on Bohemians' First XV. The match was played on Saturday 4th March, 1950 against University College Cork at the Mardyke. Dom often recalled over the years that not long after this debut, in one of my early matches for the club (possibly against Instonians) the opposition hooked the ball and I, in a move which went against the general theme of training in those days, decided to go across

---

24 Fr. Guinane was President of Munster RFU when Tom was Captain.

the back line and make a tackle just on the line to prevent them scoring a try. I earned a lot of respect by making such an innovative move that day. I appreciated the admiration. It was not too long before I was chosen to captain Bohs First XV. Things were going well for me.

* * *

However, it was the 1957–58 season before I was selected by Munster to play as scrum-half for their first inter-provincial encounter of the season, versus Connacht. I still cherish the moment I first put on that red jersey and wore the emblem of three crowns on my chest. I had a good match. In fact, the press reports said that I made everyone at Thomond Park, including the Irish hooker, Karl Mullen[*], sit up and take notice as I demonstrated my skill in attack. I got great length into my passes and, although to the observer, I never appeared to be hurried, I still managed to get the ball away quickly. Every fling sent the ball out of the reach of the opposing wing forwards, but unfortunately for Munster and for me, my out-half often failed to hold on to the passes and so nothing spectacular came from the scrum-half play. The forwards were disappointing, and it was generally felt afterwards that when the ball should have been distributed among the backs, it was more often than not trapped in the second and third rows. Munster was fortunate to scrape home in this game, 8-6, and, as the papers were later to report, I contributed three points by means of a "delightfully taken dropped goal".

My hopes, therefore, of being selected for the next game against Ulster in Cork on 11th November 1957 were extremely high, as were the expectations of most of Limerick. Rumour had it that Munster people, outside of Limerick, were asking questions as to who this new chap was and where he had come from. Reports that I had been Bohs scrum-half for years, and was an ex-Castleknock student, who had played at inter provincial level for Leinster, only added to the interest. I knew that, in Limerick, rugby (especially Munster rugby) was a deeply held religion that filtered into every aspect of daily life in the city. I was treated like a champion after one game.

Success tasted sweet. I was offered morning coffee with a pink iced bun "compliments of the house" in the Stella Restaurant. Celebratory pints were the order of the day in Bohs and anywhere else I went in Limerick. I wanted more of this.

Munster Shock Was Dropping Cleary

By
Des Hanrahan

THE first inter-provincial Rugby game of the season, that in which Munster were exceedingly lucky to scrape home against Connacht, and the subsequent developments—nominating a team to play Ulster in Cork, on November 11, etc.—have kept tongues wagging lustily.

The new selection surprised most people but the dropping of Tom Cleary simply astounded them.

In last Saturday's game the Bohemian and ex-Castleknock scrum-half made every one at Thomond Park, including Irish hooker Karl Mullen, sit up and take notice. He got great length into his passes and never appeared to be unduly hurried.

That, however, does not mean that he did not get the ball away quickly. Every fling sent the ball way out of the reach of the opposing wing-forwards, but unfortunately the Munster out-half did not often fulfil the important function of holding on to his passes and in consequence nothing spectacular came from the scrum half play.

I have never regarded Dan Daly as anything but a good club stand-off with a flair for dropping goals, but I did have hopes of Tom Cleary and it is hard to believe that the selectors have turned a blind eye to this youth, who, as a student, played for Leinster.

If the action in alloting his position to J. Burges was taken out of consideration for the Irish Five, then we can well afford to await later developments.

This criticism does not imply t[h]e least intention to detract from t[h]e ability of the Roslyn Park scru[m] worker, but is simply to emphasi[se] that a worthy challenger has arisen [in] Cleary, whose class and skill in atta[ck] in last Saturday's game were suprem[e]. A match against Leinster would te[st] his defensive strength, and if a ne[w] partner has to be found for him, wh[y] not Joe Keane of U.C.C., who, practi[c]ally off his own bat last year, be[at] Garryowen in the Munster Cup fina[l]. He has represented his province as [a] junior and has clearly shown the rig[ht] temperament for the big occasion.

The presence of Tom Clifford* and Jim McCarthy* should bring a pleasing atmosphere into the work of the Munster pack against Ulster, but personally I rather doubt if the Irish selectors' eyes will be cast in the direction of any other Southern forward. Height and weight these days tend to invest Rugby forwards with qualities they never really possessed, and at least two Munster men included in the team to play Ulster are disappointing in this respect.

Final Irish trialist of last yea[r] Paddy Lawlor quite obviously has n[ot] made the required improvement [to] earn him a "cap," but he certainl[y] had a better game against Connac[ht] than the Constitution second row fo[r]ward and would have once more bee[n] my choice.

In all, the Munster forwards wer[e] the most disappointing section of th[e] team, and no one player can b[e] singled out for special mentio[n]. When the ball should have bee[n] circulating among the backs it wa[s] more often than not stuck in th[e] second and third rows.

The outlook for the game against Ulster is more optimistic. Mick Lane* should give strength to the attack and Berkery,* at full back, has only to reproduce last week's form to be a tremendous success.

He started nervously, but later o[n] was supremely confident when fieldin[g] difficult punts and, in his favour, h[e] invariably found touch.

One thing clear in the minds of a[ll] after the Munster-Connacht game wa[s] that the code has come on a "ton" i[n] Connacht. The Irish Five cannot pos[s]ibly ignore the claims of Verno[n] Lane. His straight bursts down th[e] centre take stopping, and a couple o[f] runs towards the end in his best styl[e] almost pulled the game out of the fi[re] for the visitors.

Aengus McMorrow,* now devotin[g] some of his time to soccer, is still [a] very consistent full back, and it wa[s] due largely to his good defensive wor[k] that the score sheet, penalty kick apart, was kept blank for so long las[t] week.

* See end notes (pp.304–307) for details of these players mentioned. No newspaper title or date on press cutting found in suitcase.

With bated breath, all of Limerick waited for the team announcement. All this time I was trying, with great difficulty, to concentrate on balance sheets and such like at work. Tongues in Munster and further afield started wagging furiously once the team was announced and people realised that the selectors had turned a blind eye to their newly-found, up and coming, talent. Arguments were made that the decision to give the position to Burges, the international scrum-half of the previous season, made sense, but most people thought that I'd have suited the job better. Poor consolation for me. I was very disappointed. I vowed to do my utmost at club level to display my defensive strength and prove myself a worthy challenger as a scrum worker. I hoped that people would see more than my flair, because I knew I had substance behind the style. I was quietly confident.

It's small comfort to me that Burges's display on the day in Cork was only average and all the talk was that Ireland was, once again, badly in need of scrum-halves. All I could do was make myself available and hope that my talent would be noticed as early as possible. I was all too aware that my other predecessors, Cox, Cullen and Dillon, seemed to have fizzled out recently, despite plenty of exposure. It seemed to many observers that the issue lay between me and O'Reilly of Wanderers, who had undoubtedly shown his budding talent. Hopes were high of an Irish Trial with the two of us on opposite sides.

I enjoyed the novelty of being in the centre of all this speculation. It felt great to have my name mentioned in the same sentence as the Munster and Irish teams. I was determined to keep my feet on the ground and not to get too bigheaded. Difficult though. Through it all I remained patient. I was prepared to continue waiting.

As it turned out I waited for years and years. Some said that I was disadvantaged by the fact that Munster rugby had two centres of strength, Cork and Limerick, and the rivalry between them was intense. For the years of my prime, Munster's international selector was Cork based. Provincial rivalry may have played a part in what was to become my long and frustrating career as a permanent substitute, but who am I to say?

In contrast to my exasperating experience, my out-half partner at Bohs, Mick English*,(a Limerick man by birth, and a Rockwell graduate, three years my junior) went on to play 16 times for Ireland between 1959 and 1963, after succeeding the famous Jack Kyle.* His international career was quite sporadic, with the appearance of six other out-halves in those four years. And through all his ups and downs I kept hope alive in my heart that one day the two of us would line out in the Irish jersey together. I wanted it with all my heart. But it seemed I was destined to remain on the sideline as his career seemed to go from strength to strength. In 1959 I could only look on as Mick was chosen to travel with the Lions to Australia and New Zealand.[25]

25 Due to a bad leg injury, Mick didn't play in a test and so was not capped on the Lions tour.

And all that time I continued to partner Mick at club and provincial levels but never got to the peak like he did. At club level, we were so in tune with each other that I was able to pass the ball, and he was able to accept it, intuitively. I realise his memory of me has faded in the intervening years, but I also know that he still refers to me variously as a very talented sportsman ... a most talented footballer ... a fine scrum-half with a great pass. Mick would be the first to admit that while he and most others had to struggle to improve their skills, I was a natural and it all came easily to me. Maybe too easy! As Mick once wrote about me in a letter:

> As his out-half partner I was really spoiled by his great passing – I remember a match where I missed a drop goal because I used my left foot (I was mainly right-footed). I blamed Tom for not passing to my right foot side. His answer was to hand the ball to me and tell me to play scrum-half and out-half at the same time.

Despite my father's high hopes, as the 1950s progressed, work was not a high priority for me. I failed my Institute of Chartered Accountants Exams and by 1955 moved from O'Neill-Barron (by now W. H. O'Donnell) to work at stores control in Limerick Cement Ltd. My fondness for rugby, tennis, golf and socialising was beginning to take its toll even at this relatively early stage in my life. I returned to Carrick to work in the family business for a year in 1958. I was very unsettled around this time. My mother's brother, Uncle Paddy, seemed to be the only person who had any understanding of how tormented I felt. I was always able to be totally frank and honest with him. Drunk or sober, I could communicate with Paddy. He always listened, in a totally non-judgemental way, to my hopes, fears and concerns. Sometimes, when I felt the world was pressing in on me, Paddy gave me the ability to breathe.

While living in Carrick, I developed a new social routine, in that several evenings a week I would arrange to meet up with Paddy in one of the many pubs of the town. People observing the two of us used to think our behaviour was a bit odd. We'd go into the pub separately, sit down together, and drink silently. Not one word would be exchanged between us until enough porter had been consumed to lubricate the thought processes. When the conversation started it was likely go on for about two hours non-stop and from there we'd move on to the men-only Kitty Club off Castle Street. But we didn't go there to play snooker like most of the members. We merely wanted to finish the night's quiet tête-à-tête together and often stayed there until about two or three in the morning. As my mother used to say, "talking about God only knows what!" By now I had discovered that alcohol made it easier for me to talk freely. Paddy understood that. And he was patient with me.

In the meantime, Helen's share of Aunt Bid's legacy had gone almost half way towards the purchase of a new home and business in Mullingar and I was best

man at her wedding to Brendan Kane in 1953. John had entered the priesthood at this stage and Michael was making plans to marry Maureen O'Callaghan from Cork, and take up his position in the business at home. Soon, a new bungalow was built for my parents, Dick and Kitty, on the site of the family tennis court, while the Bridge Street house became home to a new generation of Clearys, when Michael and Maureen took over there. And most of this time I spent in Limerick, following my dream, having fun with the boys and romancing a select few of the ladies. The girls were all mad about me, but I was a choosey enough escort and was not that interested in longer-term relationships or "lines" (as they were called then).

* * *

I was a big hit with the ladies, even if I say so myself. I never had any difficulty finding a partner for club or Munster functions. Most of those girls were very dear to my heart. In a way I loved every one of them and they left me with very fond memories of those times; Rita Guinan, Greta Fulham, Jo Lane, Joan Corbett, Irene Brady and others. Many of them went on to marry friends of mine in later years, but in the beginning we were all just one big gang, who socialised together and looked out for one another.

I remember, one Saturday, a large group of us travelled to Enniscorthy in Co. Wexford, for a dinner dance. We were a carefree bunch of lads, such as Dom Dineen, Tom Kavanagh, Gerry Saunders, Paddy Ryan (the postmaster), myself and others, as we travelled along in convoy with our selected partners and girlfriends. We were to pass through Carrick en route, so I had arranged that we would call in to Bridge Street for a bite to eat. I was a proud man that day as I introduced my Limerick friends to my parents. A lot of the talk was of rugby and Bohemians' and Munster's prospects for the season, but my mother managed to put a few subtle (but searching) questions to the ladies. I could see what she was at. She wondered which of the beauties was my partner, but she was none the wiser when we left!

My true love was in the group that day. Anyone with eyes in their head could probably see that I was mad about her. She had everything going for her, as far as I could see. I was totally smitten. I can still visualise her in the kitchen in Bridge Street, standing with her back to the big Esse cooker at the far end of the room, both hands behind her. When she laughed, it was so infectious that everyone automatically joined in. The light coming in through the window caught the natural highlights in her fair, wavy hair. She wore a set of pearls around her neck.

I can recall every single detail, from the colour of her two-piece, tweed costume which picked up the blue in her bright round eyes, to the fact that she wore very little make-up. I was glad of that. I didn't like the latest trend of overdoing it on cosmetics. It was a joy for me to see her so relaxed and at ease in the presence

"Women adored him"

Formal Photographs by Franks Photographers, 49 O'Connell Street, Limerick

of my parents. I can still recall her scent. Don't ask me the name of it, but sometimes even to this day, I can be caught unawares and transported back to that kitchen, by someone wearing the same perfume. I could be anywhere when the memories assault me and the grief overwhelms me; in the pub, in a queue, at Mass or just walking up the street.

* * *

I kept many of the menus from celebratory functions held in the southwest city, and elsewhere. The 'bill of fare' will be fun for people to look at from the view of their discerning palates nowadays. Invariably garden peas were served. Haute cuisine of the 1950s! There are a few cartes-du-jour from the days I captained Munster against Leinster, Connacht and Ulster in the autumn of 1959. I would have replied to the toasts on those occasions, but I usually spoke off the cuff and entertained everybody with a fairly easy style so, unfortunately I didn't leave copies of any speeches in the suitcase. Maybe it's just as well.

Weary Beery Cleary is probably the only nickname I ever mentioned in latter years, but I was also known as Pipey, a favourite term of mine when I thought I was getting a bit 'tight' or 'jarred'. Believe it or not, I was known for being very polite and the most profane word to come out of my mouth (in those days) was the mild mannered "jeepers". As you all know, I accumulated a few stronger versions in my repertoire for the night-time ramblings of my life after Limerick, but more of that later. "Fair enough – 50 percent" was my calling card when discussing tactics and strategy at the start of many games. This meant that if the forwards were able to supply me with that amount of ball, I would undertake to do the rest.

In my Limerick days, Dom Dineen had access to some self-drive cars, which were often used by the club as transport for away matches. Usually terrible crocks, they were referred to as "Dom's submarines". Once, when I was driving back from Belfast the wipers packed up. There happened to be a lady's umbrella in the car and I wrapped some newspaper around it. Every now and then I would open my side-window, put my arm out, while still driving and wipe my side of the windscreen. Somewhere outside Drogheda the lads in the back persuaded me to stop for two young ladies who were hitchhiking (not considered so dangerous in those days of innocence). We set off again and eventually I had to use my wiping device. The reaction from the ladies – "Janey Mister, your windscreen wiper is very psychedelic!" in the broadest Drogheda accent. We had it for a 'cant' for years afterwards[26].

Great times were launched for Bohs in 1958 soon after Dom's playing days ended when he became club coach. He immediately masterminded the second

26 Anecdote compliments of Dermot Geary, former Bohemians and Munster team-mate.

Munster Cup triumph in Bohemians' history. I was on that team. In the semi-final against Old Crescent, there was a thrill-packed opening 20 minutes when Bohs chalked up 14 points without reply. And five minutes from time I touched down at the posts after a loose maul and Mick added the points. The club's first Munster Cup Final in 19 years beckoned in a fortnight's time.

The weather was poor enough during the final match against Highfield, with an early blinding shower of rain, followed by a sweeping gale force wind, which played queer tricks with the ball. But we won. I served Mick English well that day, allowing him lots of scope to give Bohs an advantage in defence. Bohs were back with a vengeance and the team was able to put the dark, desolate days of the previous decades well behind them. How I enjoyed that feeling of being victorious. We made such a great team – men like left-winger and captain Paddy (Mo) Moran, hooker Dermot (Gooser) Geary, and Mick English's brother Christy in the three-quarter line.

Afterwards, the press reports credited Mick English's gifted right boot with spear-heading Bohs' irresistible surge to this, their first of three Munster Cups in five years. They also said that Mick and I were considered the best club partnership in the country. It was generally agreed that, on many occasions, my good service allowed Mick the scope he needed to gain long touches with his clearances and the resulting territorial advantage for the Bohs team.

Bohemians Winners Munster Senior Cup, 1957–58
Photograph taken at the back of the stand at Thomond Park, Limerick
Inserts: Jim Walsh, Eamonn Purcell, Maurice Mortell
Back row: Jim (Tish) Auchmuty, Billy Hurley, Johnny Ryan, Caleb Powell, Dom Dineen (Coach), John Mulcahy, Johnny Nagle, Ted Watson, Donal Holland
Front row: Kevin Doyle, Paddy Downes, Dermot Geary, Paddy Moran (Captain), Christy English, Basil Fitzgibbon, Billy Slattery
Ground: Mick English, Tom Cleary

Bohemians R.F.C. Committee (Early 1950s)
Back row: D. Dineen, T. Carey, W. W. Stokes, T. J. Cleary, J. W. Stokes
Middle row: G. A. Saunders, P. Downes, P. Quaid, D. Holland
Front row: J. W. Auchmuty (President), M. Murphy

Bohemian First XV - 1958-'59

—★—

Played 25 matches. Won 18, drew 3 and lost 4, with 240 points scored for and 129 against.

MUNSTER SENIOR CUP

March 17th. Second Round—Beat Sunday's Well in Cork by 1 penalty goal, 3 dropped goals (12 points) to 1 penalty goal (3 points).

April 4th. Semi-Final—Beat Constitution in Limercik by 1 try (3 points) to nil.

Bohemian XV in both matches—P. N. Downes; P. T. Moran, C. M. English, J. B. Fitzgibbon, W. J. Walshe; M. A. English, T. J. Cleary; P. L. O'Callaghan, D. J. Geary (Captain), W. G. Hurley, J. J. Meany, B. G. O'Dowd, W. J. Slattery, C. C. Powell, J. G. Ryan.

April 25th. Final—Drew with Shannon in Limerick, 1 dropped goal, 1 try (6 points) to 1 penalty goal, 1 dropped goal (6 points).

May 2nd. Final Re-play—Beat Shannon in Limerick, 1 dropped goal, 3 tries (12 points) to 1 try (3 points).

Bohemian XV in both matches—P. N. Downes; P. T. Moran, C. M. English, J. B. Fitzgibbon, M. J. Walshe; J. M. McGovern, T. J. Cleary; P. L. O'Callaghan, D. J. Geary (Captain), W. G. Hurley, J. J. Meaney, B. G. O'Dowd, W. J. Slattery, C. C. Powell, J. G. Ryan.

MUNSTER SENIOR LEAGUE

Played 9 matches, won 8, drew 1. Points for, 80; against, 34.

LIMERICK CHARITY CUP

Beat Old Crescent in the Semi-Final, 16 to 5, after two drawn games, 6 all and 3 all.

Beat Garryowen in the Final, 8 points to nil.

URBS ANTIQUA FUIT STUDIISQUE ASPERRIMA BELLI

BOHEMIAN R.F.C.

—★—

DINNER

In honour of the

FIRST XV, 1958-'59

Winners of

THE MUNSTER SENIOR CUP
THE MUNSTER SENIOR LEAGUE
THE LIMERICK CHARITY CUP

CRUISE'S ROYAL HOTEL

Saturday, 6th June, 1959

—★—

Chairman - J. W. Stokes, Esq.

W. H. O'DONNELL & CO.
INCORPORATING
O'NEILL, BARRON & CO.
CHARTERED ACCOUNTANTS

88, O'CONNELL STREET,
LIMERICK

W. H. O'DONNELL, B. Comm., F.C.A.,
PUBLIC AUDITOR

Telephone No. 646

Friday 7th March.

Dear Mammy
Many thanks for your letter, which now as I look at it again is undated. You have however the new address which reads well. Glad to hear that Daddy is delighted with the life as of course Michael and Maureen must be. Tell Michael that I have two stand tickets for him – in what stand I don't know, as I have not yet collected them. I will send them on early next week.

My leg is grand at the moment. I had two matches and no ill effects. I was hoping to get down this weekend but as things stand regarding the scrum-half position I intend training to-morrow and on Sunday here with Mickey[27] English. It's great news about Mickey and of course he is delighted. He certainly deserves the honour. I really don't know about my own chances. Had I been playing the whole season and especially in the Australian game here they would be stronger. If Johnny O'Meara[*] plays well tomorrow and escapes injury then we feel here that he is on. If his injury re-occurs then anyone could be on. I probably will be in the running.

I met Gerard[28] on Sunday last after the Bective match. He was playing in Belfield. I also met the O'Callaghans[29] going into the stand on Saturday. I am sending on some clothes tomorrow. If any clean ones are ready they'll be welcomed.

Kindest regards to all
Love, Tom

---

27 Michael Anthony Francis English, also known as (and referred to in press reports as) Mick, Mike and/or Mickey.

28 Tom's brother Gerry (Ref. 1). See list of family relations in Post Mortem section of book for reference and further details.

29 Michael's (Ref. 2) in-laws, Maureen's (Ref. 1) parents. See list of family relations in Post Mortem section of book for reference and further details.

I suppose the letter, which I wrote to my mother around this time, is poignant when read with hindsight. My parents had just moved into the bungalow around the time Mick English got his first cap. My hopes were high, and I was prepared to sacrifice a trip home for the weekend in order to put in some extra training and so make the Irish team. And my mother was still organising my washing! I never asked how herself and Mrs. O' continually managed to get it over and back from Carrick to Limerick. It just seemed to arrive at my digs. Clean clothes were almost always there when I needed them.

On the 6th February, 1958 Ireland was defeated 6-0 at Twickenham. Although they had got their first caps the previous month against Australia at Lansdowne Road, this was the Five Nations International debut for four guys who were to become good friends of mine in my playing days: Ronnie Dawson*, Noel Murphy*, Dave Hewitt* and Bill (Wigs) Mulcahy*. How I wished I could add my name to that list. Most people felt that I should have been called for an Irish trial before now. Just over a month later, on the 15th March, Ireland played Wales at Lansdowne Road. Mick English got his first cap that day. There was great excitement in Bohs, in Limerick, in Munster and further afield when the news broke. We were all thrilled for him.

Mick acquitted himself well on the day. Scrum-half, John O'Meara, scored a fine try (in what was to be his last international appearance) but he sustained an injury and was taken off during the second half. Ireland was down to 14 men in the closing stages of the match and was not able to hold out against the Welsh who won 9-6 with three late tries. Would O'Meara's injury mean the selectors would start looking at alternative scrum-halves, I wondered?

I was destined, however, to remain on the fringes. It was around this time we had to learn some major revisions in the laws of rugby, set by the International Rugby Board. Most of them made perfect sense, but they all took a bit of getting used to. I can't remember if I paid much heed to the rule regarding the prohibition of shoulder pads "unless for the protection after injury and not of hard material[30]". If I'd known what I was to suffer with my shoulder towards the end of my life, I may have taken more care of it. That's youth for you. I never imagined then that one day I would get old.

I recall one particularly busy weekend in September 1958 when I played for the Wolfhounds XV[31] against Oxford and Cambridge in Dublin on the Saturday and the following day played on Tom Clifford's XV versus the Wolfhounds touring side in Limerick.

In the first match that weekend, at Lansdowne Road, we were beaten by a

30 'Revision of the Laws of the Game – January 1958. International Rugby Football Board (To come into operation next Season)' *Irish Rugby Union Programme, Ireland v Wales,* 15th March, 1958 pp. 22-23.

31 The Wolfhounds (now defunct) were founded with the idea of bringing exhibition style rugby to the provinces. The concept was based on the Barbarians principle (see footnote 65 on page 115). A Wolfhounds XV consists of a conglomerate of international and provincial players. (Note that Tom played on a Wolfhounds XV on a Saturday and the next day, Sunday, he played versus a Wolfhounds XV.)

goal and three tries to a goal and two tries. The new rules were in force so it was thought that play should have been faster and more open. Afterwards observers felt that the visitors had made the most of the rule changes. It was generally agreed that the amendments held great promise for a more dazzling type of rugby in the future. I was happy enough with my own game that day. It was well recognised that Mick and myself were every bit as good in all respects as our more well known opposites.[32]

> English was admirably safe-handed and notably unselfish at out-half and received very adequate support from Cleary, who, even so early in the season, emerges as a serious rival to Mulligan, the man in possession on the Irish team.[33]

The next day (Sunday) I was on Tom Clifford's XV versus the touring Wolfhounds (consisting of many of the Oxford and Cambridge men of the previous day and a few internationals). There were six changes to the visiting team which played in Dublin and they were considered to be stronger as a result. Sadly, my team was beaten once more. The final score was 28-6. It was an entertaining game for the crowd as the visitors put on a bit of an exhibition. They were never at a loss as to what to do. On the other hand we were slow on our feet and did not attack much. In contrast to the previous day, Mick and I were outplayed. It was heavy going – playing, travelling and socialising – so maybe we were to be forgiven for tiring a little towards the end of the second day's activity.

* * *

At club level, I played out of my skin when Bohs repeated their win of the Munster Cup Final in 1959. Along the way I was credited in the press reports as being one of the reasons for Bohs superiority in the final replay against Shannon. I felt that should augur well for me at international level. I kept a copy of a subsequent article written in 1985 (26 years later) in the *Sunday Independent*, about the final match. It was a very interesting article to read, from my perspective.

32 'Visitors Used New Laws To Advantage', *The Cork Examiner*, 15th September, 1958, p 7.

33 'Rugby Is better This Way', *Sunday Independent*, 14th September, 1958, p 18.

SPORT 2
3rd NOVEMBER 1985
BMW
SUNDAY INDEPENDENT
THEIR FINEST HOUR
Pool of water saved day for Bohemians
By Philip Quinn

The 1959 Munster Senior Cup Final between Bohemians and Shannon will long be remembered as "the burning and dousing final", a controversial affair which was a topic of many impassioned conversations in the Limerick area for years to come.

The venue was Thomond Park. The weather was foul and torrential rain had churned the surface of the pitch into a quagmire. Despite the inclement conditions, interest in the final was immense.

Shannon had never won the cup before, while Bohs were attempting to repeat their success of 1958. Prior to that their previous success had been in 1927.

The score was 6-3 for Shannon with time running out when Bohs full back Paddy Downes lofted the ball for the Shannon touchline. The ball appeared set to run out of play when it rolled into a pool of water and stuck there. This gave Bohs winger Maurice Walsh the chance to outspeed his cover and pounce on the ball for a try that levelled the scores.

FAIR AND SQUARE
Discussing that incident recently with Bohs' players involved that day, one got an impression of the "tongue-in-cheek" attitude as they protested that the try was fair and square.

However, Dom Dineen, the coach of the side was quick to point out that Bohs should never have found themselves three points behind at all.

"Earlier in the match, Shannon dropped a goal that should have been disallowed as Caleb Powell got a hand to it and "burnt it" but the referee failed to see this and awarded three points to Shannon" said Dineen.

While the discussion continued apace as to the rights and wrongs of both incident, everyone in Limerick, it seems was making it their business to be in Thomond Park for the replay the following Sunday.

The day was bright and sunny with a firm pitch and another

colossal crowd. This time there were no contentious decisions. Instead, Bohs ripped Shannon's challenge apart, though Shannon were without the injured Eamonn Clancy and Brian O'Brien.

Two superb tries from centre Maurice Walsh, another by winger Basil Fitzgibbon and a drop goal by Jimmy McGovern, deputising for Lion's absentee Mick English, countered an early Shannon try by Frank O'Flynn.

GOLDEN PERIOD

The victory put the seal on Bohs' "golden period". Already that season they had won the Munster Senior League and the Limerick Charity Cup to complement their Cup win in 1958.

That first Cup win marked the end of a period in the wilderness. The Cup was last brought back to Thomond Park in 1927 while the previous League success was in 1931.

That Bohs kept going during the lean times was due in no small measure to the efforts of the Stokes, the Treacys, Pat Power, Seán Carey, Ted Russell and the great Dom Dineen.

Dineen was a loyal servant for many years and good enough to play in the second row for Munster against the Springboks in 1951 when Munster went down with all guns blazing 11-6.

He retired in 1957 with an eye injury and went on to become one of the game's finest administrators – he was President of the IRFU in 1971-72.

Dineen was appointed coach to Bohs at the start of the 1957-58 season and by placing emphasis on iron discipline and fitness, he moulded together a terrific side, capable of beating the best in the country.

TOUGH AS TEAK

Dineen was fortunate to have the services of the inimitable Mick English at out-half. English was the catalyst behind Bohs' success. When he was in full flight the team were virtually unstoppable.

Tom Cleary at scrum-half was another stalwart – "he was a most natural footballer and always stayed on his feet to pass" (Dineeen); and there was Gooser Geary, the captain and hooker; Billy Slattery, Billy Hurley, Johnny Nagle, Christy English, Paddy Moran and tough-as-teak Johnny Ryan.

In 1957-58 when Bohs regained the Cup by beating Highfield easily in the final, the famous old trophy disappeared in the midst of the celebrations on the night of the final.

It caused the "Limerick Leader" to frown ... "the practical joker responsible for this "coup" would be well advised to return the trophy without delay. Bohemians officials have a shrewd suspicion as to the whereabouts of the Cup and its return is regarded as certain within a day or two".

The Cup was "discovered" in Mick English's front garden the following Thursday morning.

In season 1958-59 Bohemians played, in all, 27 matches. They won 21, drew three and lost three – to Instonians, Garryowen and Clontarf.

UNBEATEN IN LEAGUE

They were unbeaten in the League and beat Sunday's Well and Cork Constitution on their way to the final clash with Shannon.

A memorable highlight was provided when Wanderers, laden with internationals Ronnie Dawson, Gerry Culliton*, Wally Bornemann*, Kevin Flynn* and the Kavanaghs, came to Limerick and were trounced 13-6.

It was ironic in the light of that result that Bohs' own international representations had been thin on the ground. True, Mick English earned 16 caps but Cleary was on the bench 14 times without earning a cap, while Geary and Paddy O'Callaghan were Irish trialists.

In order to understand the significance of Dom Dineen's comment (that I always stayed on my feet to pass) in that 1985 article, I should clarify that most scrum-halves used a falling pass in those days. The object of the exercise was that the scrum-half would retrieve the ball out of the scrum and pass it to the out-half. So the quicker the ball was retrieved and passed, and the further the out-half was away from the scrum, the better the advantage he had, because he was also further away from the opposing wing forward.

Very few scrum-halves passed the ball standing in those days, for the simple reason that the old ball couldn't be moved in the same way as those of today. Nowadays, people see the way Peter Stringer* and other modern scrum-halves fling the ball, torpedo-like, and it flies aerodynamically – the new ball has a more oval shape and a modern rugby ball can actually be held with one hand. In the old days a player would have needed a big hand to grasp the laced, leather ball. It was totally different and, although my hands were fairly big, if there was any bit of moisture it was like trying to catch a bar of wet soap.

I had developed the ability to spin the ball and therefore I was able to generate the power to move it out the same distance as any player who was using a falling pass, at that time. My theory was that once the scrum-half fell with the ball he was out of the game for a few moments and by the time he'd get up again the game would have moved on by 30 yards or more. By catching it and standing to pass, I remained on my feet, the ball was already gone, but I was still in the game. Perhaps the fact that I was 15 years of age by the time I first played the game meant that I was physically more mature and better able to develop my standing pass than the other boys of my age, who had started their training, two years before me, when they were only 13 years old. In later years, some people compared my skill to that of the great scrum-half and lynch-pin of the Welsh Grand Slam international team of the 1970s, Gareth Edwards*. Many observers reckoned that he was the first player to come on stream after my day, whose (seemingly unorthodox) technique resembled mine.

* * *

My summers in Limerick were spent mostly playing golf and tennis and generally enjoying life. I was a naturally gifted player in both of these sports also, but they never really meant as much to me as rugby. I have kept one large group photo (taken in Belfast not long after our big rugby win and just a few weeks before my brother John's ordination) which was taken at an inter-provincial tennis tournament. You will see me there, are at the edge in the back row, all dressed up in my whites and looking quite mature. I was a winner of a South of Ireland tennis

PATRON:
RET. J. CALLANAN, C.C.

President : Mr. Rd. Cleary
Vice-President : Mr. T. Morrissey
Hon. Sec.: Miss M. Kelly
Hon. Treas. : Mr. Tom Walsh
Captain - Mr. J. O'Keeffe.

COMMITTEE : Misses C. Dickenson, Vera McGrath, Messrs. N. Treacy, Ml. Cleary T. Glascott, J. O'Keeffe, N. Elattery.

Castleview Lawn Tennis Club,
Carrick-on-Suir

☆ ☆ ☆

MEMBERSHIP CARD

Leahy & Co. Carrick-on-Suir

Membership Card from Castleview Tennis Club.
Tom's Dad Richard (Dick) was President of the Club
and his brother Michael was a committee member.

championship in the late 50s. Partly as a result of my interest in the sport, but also because my brothers, especially the youngest, Gerry, were showing great promise on the tennis court, the Cleary Perpetual Challenge Cup was presented to Castleview Tennis Club in Carrick by my father, Dick, in 1958. It went on to be a hotly contested tournament for many years.

Inter-provincial Tennis Championships (Ulster, Munster, Leinster and Connacht)
Held in Belfast 1957
Tom Cleary Standing on extreme left, middle row[34]

34 Some of the other people (E&OE!) in this photo include:
C. Pedlow, R. O'Connor, D. Dempsey, M. Fleming, H. Barniville, T. Rafter, G. Jackson, V. Gotto, A. Haughton, D.Sweetman, J. Fitzgibbon, T. Crooks, P. Jackson, J. Hatchett, E. Heddermann, G. Burke, A. Blake, M. Foley, G. Burke, Mrs. Fann, Mrs. Morton, H. Robinson, M. O'Sullivan, E. Kirkpatrick, C. McGuinness, T. Duncan, D. Kilgannon, A. Walsh, B. Lombard, A. Cormann, F. Quinn.

Group photo taken at Castleview Tennis Club, Carrick-on-Suir
Tom centre at the back, v-necked jumper (arrowed)

Team photo taken at Castleview Tennis Club in Carrick-on-Suir.
Standing: Fred Nagle, Gerry, Michael and Tom Cleary
Kneeling: Joan Nagle, Maureen Cleary, Margaret Galvin and Eleanor Murphy

Tom beaten by Harry Crowe in the Final of a tennis match.

Brothers in sport:
Gerry and Tom before one of their many finals as opponents in the late 1950s[35]

35 Much to Tom's disappointment (his Uncle Paddy reported afterwards) Gerry won this match – The Gent's Singles Championship of Munster – played at Waterford in the late 1950s. The match was refereed by Vincent Tunney. At this stage, Tom was starting a decline in his fitness levels while Gerry's star was in the ascendant.
Gerry had been Number One under-age tennis player in Ireland from Under 15 all the way through to senior level. He won the Leinster Under 18 title at Fitzwilliam and went on to represent Ireland at the Wimbledon Junior Invitation Championship in 1956. At the time of this match against Tom, Gerry was playing inter-varsity tennis for University College Dublin, competing in the Dublin League, while also playing for Fitzwilliam Club.

Jerry Moran and Tom at Castleview Tennis Club, Carrick-on-Suir in 1948
(Jerry's widow, Bernadette, married Tom's widowed brother, Michael, in 1980).

Castleview Lawn Tennis Team
Standing: Dr. P. O'Brien, M. Cleary, G. Cleary, T. J. Cleary
Sitting: Miss K. Phelan, Mrs. B. Dowley, Miss E. Murphy, Mrs. M. Cleary

As for golf, I was winning trophies galore. My name is engraved as a former winner on the Cleary Cup at Carrick Golf Club. I played off a handicap of 4. I laugh when I recall the day a Limerick based friend of mine (who fancied himself as bit of a golfer) invited me out to play a few holes, with the express intention of beating me.

I took up position on the first tee in the clothes and shoes I had arrived in!

"Where are your golf shoes?" asked my friend (who shall remain nameless to save his blushes).

"I don't need any," was my reply.

"Of course you do," he said.

"All you need to play good golf is balance," I informed him and began to demonstrate, finding my balance, by moving from one foot to the other. I then loosened my collar, brought my tie down a bit and started playing. On the second hole, a par five, I had an eagle, and my mate soon realised he may have bitten off more than he could chew. I was on form, so there followed a demonstration of some of the finest golf I had played for many a day. Afterwards, over a few gins in the clubhouse, and for many years to come, my mate regaled all who would listen to his story of the man who played his round of golf, in a shirt and tie, without spikes...and won!

I remember also in my latter years, my brother, John, brought me out to caddy for him, while I was staying with him in Cork for a couple of days. He encouraged me to play a few holes. I hadn't touched a club for well over 25 years; yet he was to say later that my grip, posture, swing and subsequent shots were a joy to watch. I'd be lying if I said I can recall the number of shots it took me to play the few holes, but I had at least one par. He told me I made the difficult shots look easy and the easy shots were like putty in my hands and he couldn't understand why I hadn't kept it up. How could I tell him it was partly out of fear of not being able to hold my own, financially, at the 19th?

PART FIVE

Ursula

Subbing

Many of your obituaries mention that you had been a substitute on the Irish team on 17 occasions, but the suitcase had no obvious trace of this. I knew that, as those were the days when there were no replacements on the field of play, you had never got an Irish cap. Your Limerick buddies, Paddy Moran, Bill Mulcahy and Dermot Geary, tried to fill me in on some of the details, but somehow they never seemed to add up. Then I re-read the 1985 article on "Bohemians' Finest Hour"[36] and it mentioned that "Cleary was on the bench 14 times without earning a cap", so needless to mention I was a bit confused. I wrote to the I.R.F.U.

Imagine my disappointment when I received a phone call from their Hon. Archivist, Willow Murray, who told me, as far as he could glean from the information he had available, it was "unlikely" that you had subbed at all, never mind 17 times. He asked me where I got the information and I had to admit that it was mostly anecdotal. (Shit, I thought! What am I at here? Sure it's all a myth!) Willow went on to mention Moffett*, Mulligan* and O'Meara*, who were the main playing scrum-halves at that time, and he gave me the dates of some of the international matches they had played. He outlined your record as a player and captain for Munster, but sure I already had most of that. I was shocked and disappointed with the news.

But not for long! As I was looking at some press reports of the day, didn't I see where you got a mention as one of four subs travelling with the Irish to Twickenham in February 1960. Bingo! If there was one, there could be 17. Always the optimist, it would be a bit of a hill for me to climb as an amateur sleuth to find sixteen more, but it was a start. Then I found details of where you had played on a Wolfhounds XV versus Oxford and Cambridge in 1956 and again in 1958. You captained a Rest of Ireland team at the Mardyke in Cork against Combined Universities in January 1961. Surely they meant something, though they wouldn't have been capped matches.

A few months later, Willow rang again. Following our previous conversation, he had carried out further research and, sure enough, he identified three dates when you were on an Irish trial and the many times when you were listed as sub to attend. Suffice to say that for the seasons 1959, 1960 and 1961, he found twelve internationals and one combined services match. Add to that (possibly) the

---

36 See pp. 79–81.

Springboks v Ireland game in December 1960, the Shamrocks' South African matches where you were a sub three times (although two of these were against provincial sides and not full internationals) and played once (against South Western Districts). I was beginning to see where the claim of 17 times as a sub came from.

Then, apart from Munster matches and Irish trials, there were at least five other occasions when you actually played in very high profile sides – Tom Clifford's XV, (v. a touring Wolfhounds side, December 1956 and September, 1958) an Irish Wolfhounds XV, (v. Oxford and Cambridge, September, 1958) the Waterpark Selected XV, (v. a touring Wolfhounds side, September, 1959) and the Rest of Ireland (v. Combined Universities, January, 1961). Always the best man, never the groom.

There were other occasions when you were selected on teams but I am not sure whether you actually played or not.[37] You were named on a Wolfhounds XV versus Skerries Selected on 13th September 1959 and a Young Munster Selection versus a Wolfhounds XV on 18th September 1960.

As part of my research, I also wrote to sports psychologist, Dr. Donal O'Shaughnessy, Hon. Medical Officer, IRFU, who had written an article in one of the rugby magazines which had featured your obituary. I asked him if he had any advice, theories or otherwise for me which might help my understanding of what happened in your life, as I was at a loss to know why you were unable to transfer all that leadership and competitive ability to your personal life in the years after Limerick. Unfortunately, he was unable to comment specifically as he had never known you personally but what he did say was:

> In the present day the players have many aids to help them get capped – diet, training, supplements and scientific back-up with medical care second to none. The amount of games played also ensures all the "subs" will get a run at some stage during the season.

I have to admit that it truly annoys me these days when I see subs trotting on to the pitch for the last minute or so of an international, knowing that it will mean a cap for them. Because every single time I see it, I think of you and the caps that never were.

Another man, who responded to my letter, when I started researching for this book, was Karl Johnston (since deceased) who actually worked with you in W. H. O'Donnell & Co. all those years ago. He remembered many conversations during that time that didn't necessarily relate to debits or credits or a balance sheet. Simpler days, no doubt, but spirited ones also by the sounds of things.

Of all the men I spoke with, every one of them recalled you as a "gentleman", some going so far as to elaborate on how lovable you were. (Not an easy thing for

37 Details of the selected teams can be seen in Post Mortem section of the book.

men to admit that they found another man lovable.) Without fail they mentioned your competitive spirit. And thirdly, they talked of your extreme bad luck! Bill (Wigs) Mulcahy recalled how on one occasion you had to cry off a trial due to injury, and that the cap went to the fourth or fifth choice scrum-half of the time, due to various circumstances of the other players. That was hard luck alright, Tom. Very hard luck. He mentioned another time you had to go off in an important cup match against Thomond in Limerick due to an injury to your shoulder on very hard ground. That was the injury that came back to haunt you later in life, as your final illness progressed.

Bill also related an anecdote from Cardiff in 1963 when the flight was delayed after an Ireland versus Wales match. (Could that be another time where you were sub that I haven't counted? Or were you just a tourist? It sounded as if you were with the team and I later found the match programme in your suitcase.) He remembers that you were all invited for drinks to a summer house belonging to some prosperous Welsh connections. You decided to introduce a bit of "pomp" to the ceremony and started off with the "cúpla focal"[38] for "mein hosts"! After lots of waffle you announced that you would make a presentation, in thanks for their hospitality. The Irish lads were looking at each other, wondering what surprise you had in store, when gathering all the flourish required to present a beautiful piece of Waterford crystal, you produced a battered Bohs' membership card. It was the first time the crowd had been quiet all day and then, simultaneously, they all erupted into laughter at your cheek. I believe the party went on for quite a while!

Anyone who knows anything about rugby must have heard the story of the day Mick English was left 'holding the hyphen', but for those readers who don't it refers to the hyphen in the name of J. P. Horrocks-Taylor*, who played for England nine times between 1958 and 1964. Fable has it down the years that, once, in a match, Horrocks went one way, Taylor the other and Mick English was left with the hyphen! I remember the laughter in Bloomfield after your burial as tales like this were recalled and recounted.

Many stories have been told about the 'holding the hyphen' story down through the years and some say it couldn't have happened because Horrocks-Taylor never actually played against Ireland. So, according to Sean Diffley, whose articles I also found in your case, "many people thought that the famous occasion where Mick English was left holding the hyphen must have happened in some rugby clubhouse!"

Others pointed out that English and Horrocks-Taylor were members of the same team on the 1959 Lions tour of Australia & New Zealand, the latter joining as a replacement. Sean Diffley suggests, "Perhaps it was in some club house in Wagga Wagga that English was left clutching the hyphen?"[39]

---

38 Irish for "a couple of words".

39 'Rugby Chat – Laying Ghost Of Horrocks-Taylor' Sean Diffley (no newspaper name or dates on cutting in suitcase).

The solution might also have been in your suitcase, Tom. On 29th December 1956 at Thomond Park, Mick English in partnership with your good self, played for Tom Clifford's XV against the Wolfhounds, for whom Horrocks-Taylor and Andy Mulligan* were the half-backs. Your team won 19-16 and the Irish Independent report proclaimed, "Horrocks-Taylor, the Cambridge out-half was neat enough but never devastating".

Sean Diffley writes:

> From that we can assume that on that particular occasion at Thomond Park that Mick English managed to take both Horrocks and Taylor as well as the hyphen. But it was different two years later. On September 13, 1958 Mick English, again partnered by Tom Cleary, played for the Wolfhounds against the combined Oxford-Cambridge team at Lansdowne Road. And the Oxbridge halfbacks were Horrocks-Taylor and Andy Mulligan.
>
> But this time English was on the losing side. Oxford-Cambridge won 14-11 and the *Irish Independent* report had a significant passage. It read "Early in the second half Horrocks-Taylor waltzed through the Wolfhounds defence with a series of jinks and passed inside for Davies to score between the posts".
>
> Was that the time English was left grasping the hyphen?[40]

Sean Diffley told me he saw you playing on many occasions and his first ever Munster Cup Final (your last as a medal winner) was the 1962 Bohs win at Thomond Park. It was also his first ever visit to "that holy ground". He recalls that in the lead up to the match the opposition said they "would 'concentrate' on Cleary because they would not be able to 'get' English". He also mentions that in your day, teams were picked by the "Big Five"[41], two each from Leinster and Ulster and one from Munster. I often wonder if the fact that there was only one Munster selector put you at a disadvantage.

Apart from your three big wins with Bohemians, you have many other rugby successes in the 1950s and early 1960s. Again, not much in the suitcase except for the menus from the after-match functions, but it was not too difficult for me to track the detail down. From your first selection for Munster, in the 1957–58 season versus Connacht, you went on to play for, and eventually captain, the province on numerous occasions. I also found a programme for a Bohs v Taunton[42] RFC dated Saturday 24th September 1960. Bohs, fielding a strong

40 'Rugby Chat – The Solution To The Great Hyphen Query' Sean Diffley (no newspaper name or dates on cutting in suitcase).

41 In 1961/62 the "Big Five" selectors were Karl Mullen and Gerry O'Reilly from Leinster, Jack Siggins and Harry McKibben from Ulster and Charlie St George from Munster and Limerick.

42 The Taunton-Somerset team included 8 county players.

side, were 'on tour' and were the first Irish team to play the First XV at Priory Park since before the war. You also saved a programme from a Cornwall v Surrey[43] friendly held a few days later in Camborne.

Another story told at your funeral was about the biggest margin ever recorded by Leinster over Munster. It was in 1958, November to be precise. Seemingly the *Independent* headline read afterwards "Leinster run up a cricket score". They won by 32 points to nil!

Ronnie Dawson captained Leinster while Noel Murphy captained Munster and you, Dermot Geary and Mick English were three Bohemians players on the southern team. Munster were the reigning inter-provincial champions so the result was considered a reverse beyond belief. The report of the match said that:

> Seldom does such a one-sided affair sustain interest but the brilliance of the Leinster backs kept the 5,000 crowd in their places until the final whistle when the referee's blast brought merciful relief to the southerners who had taken a real drubbing in the second half.[44]

As for Munster, the verdict was:

> When they had their tails up in the early stages the Munster pack looked real fire-eaters, Nesdale*, Spillane*, Wood* and Murphy* being especially good but alas, Wood was the only one to maintain the standard and the Garryowen front row forward was perhaps the one member of the losing side to enhance his reputation.[46]

Leinster went on to beat Ulster in the final at Ravenhill by 16-12 and became inter-provincial champions in 1958 .... for the first time since 1948.

However, back to the suitcase where I discover that 15 spirited southerners, despite a greasy ball and less than perfect conditions, got sweet revenge in November 1959. With you as their captain at Thomond Park, the Munster team defeated Leinster by 18 points to 14, after a hard fought game and become inter-provincial champions for the second time in three years. The newspaper photograph of the team shows you, proudly holding the ball, surrounded by your team, your torso leaning forward slightly as you sit, almost as if the adrenaline is still, to this day, coursing through your veins.

43 Surrey team included internationals J. R. C. Young (Harlequins), J. J. McPartlin (Harlequins), and T J. Baxter (Blackheath), and trialists P. J. O'Donovan (London Welsh), H. G. Greatwood (Harlequins) and D. Thompson (Harlequins).

44 'The Day Noel Murphy Would Like To Forget' Question Box (no newspaper name or dates on cutting in suitcase).

45 Mick Spillane. Old Crescent.

46 'The Day Noel Murphy Would Like To Forget' Question Box (no newspaper name or dates on cutting in suitcase).

Munster v Connacht
Galway Sports Ground, October 1959
Tom Cleary, the Munster scrum-half, clears to touch[47]
Final Score: Munster 6, Connacht 0

Photo courtesy of Irish Examiner

47 Some of the other players in this photograph include Mick English (extreme left), Tom Coffey, (second from left), Tim McGrath, Paddy O'Callaghan and Tony O'Sullivan (centre of photo) and Brendan Guerin (third from right).

Munster are Inter-provincial Champions, 1959

The Munster team which defeated Leinster after a hard fought game by 18 points to 14 at Thomond Park, Limerick, on Saturday 28th November, 1959.
Back row: M. Holland (referee), G. Wood, M. Spillane, N. Murphy, T. Nesdale, F. Buckley, P .O'Callaghan, D. Geary, T. McGrath
Front row: M. English, R. Hennessy, L. Coughlan, T. J. Cleary (captain), T. Kiernan, G. Walsh, D. Kenefick

Photo courtesy of Irish Examiner

With a group of Bohemians on tour to Cornwall in September 1960[48]
Tom (front row, second from left)

48 Some of the other people included in this photograph are Eddie Murphy, Peter Quaid, Peter Irwin, John Nagle, Ted Watson, Donal Holland, Ronnie Lawlor, Owen Ryan, Nickie Dalton, Paddy Moran, Jim Crotty, Tony O'Sullivan, Mick English, Billy Hurley, Brendan O'Dowd, John Holland and Paddy Dowley.

PART SIX

Tom

Handling

By early 1959 I had competed in two Irish trials, so imagine the thrill when I was listed as 'sub to attend' for the match between Ireland and England in Lansdowne Road on the 14th February 1959. I could not hide my excitement. My hopes were extremely high, especially as O'Meara was doubtful, but Andy Mulligan was named as partner to Mick English that day. This was Andy's tenth cap, Mick's third. Never mind! I was closer to the ultimate honour than I had ever been before, so I settled down to watch the match with interest.

We all loved it when the English came to town. More than any other side at the time, we used to eagerly await their arrival every alternate year. Only once since 1947 had they beaten us in Dublin. We were confident. Lansdowne Road had an atmosphere all of its own on days like these but, despite my resolve to enjoy every aspect of the game, when the selected 30 men lined up to face each other, I couldn't help wishing I was one of them, out there standing on the finest playing field in rugby. The magic of Jack Kyle would still be greatly missed by the Irish and was talked about over and over (even though he had played his last international match almost a year before, against Scotland). However, Mulligan and English were given plenty of respect in the pre-match discussion, and it was hoped that the pack would be heavy enough to contain a powerful England eight.

The result was a lucky win for England by one penalty goal to nil. For much of the first half England defended by the skin of their teeth. Our pack gave an outstanding display all through that hard and uncompromising game and there were a few moves where we could have scored tries, but our tactical skills and lack of pace let us down. A penalty goal, by Bev Risman* (their fly-half playing in his second international) taken from near our 25, was the only score of the match. Ominously though, for the fourth game in a row, Ireland had failed to score against England. Not a record we cherished; it had not happened since the 1890s.

Afterwards, writing about the back play in this encounter, O. L. Owen remarked:

> English, the Limerick Bohemian, playing in his third international, proved a strongly built but rather clumsy player with a powerful kick. A. A. Mulligan played only moderately well while Ireland were having the better of things in Dublin, but roused himself to some

> gallant efforts in the closing stages when the English pack began to get a little of their own back.[49]

I felt hurt for Mick. I dared to hope for myself.

* * *

On the 14th March 1959, as we travelled to Cardiff, we were hoping for a victory against Wales. It had been 27 years since we had triumphed at that venue, so it was a tall order. The situation between the sides, at this stage, was very interesting, as every team had a chance of winning the Championship, while the Triple Crown could not be won by any side:

> England have three points and could end with five; Scotland have two and could end with four; Ireland and Wales have two apiece and both countries could end with six, while France has the best chance of winning the championship outright, since victories over Wales and Ireland would give her seven points and the overwhelming joy of achieving a long-awaited ambition.[50]

Irish hopes were dashed in the match against Wales. The final score was Wales 8, Ireland 6. In Murrayfield we won against the Scots that year. The score was 8-3. When the French came to Lansdowne they beat us 9-5.[51] They got one dropped goal, one penalty goal and one try, to our one converted try. I was a sub for all of those matches. All I could do was watch, hope and pray. It was frustrating and at times I felt quite agitated. I was bursting to get into the action. The tension was unbearable. Would I ever make it onto the pitch in an Irish jersey?

* * *

In September 1959 I had some small consolation when I played for a Waterpark Selected XV against a Wolfhound XV which included French and Welsh internationals such as Danos*, Davies*, Main*, Celaya*, and our own O'Sullivan* and Dooley*. My partner that day was Gerry Hardy* and we worked well together but it was generally felt that he could have fed his outside men a bit better. Waterpark played with great spirit and led for most of the game. In the end however the luminaries were lucky enough to beat us by one point. The final score was 17-16.

---

49 'Ireland's Murrayfield Record' O. L. Owen, *Scottish Rugby Union Programme, Scotland v Ireland,* 28th February, 1959, p. 21.

50 'Two Prize – Championship and the Tour!' J. B. G. Thomas, *Welsh Rugby Union Programme, Wales v Ireland,* 14th March, 1959, p. 3.

51 France achieved their long-awaited ambition by winning the Championship outright for the first time in 1959 (they had previously shared it with Wales in 1955).

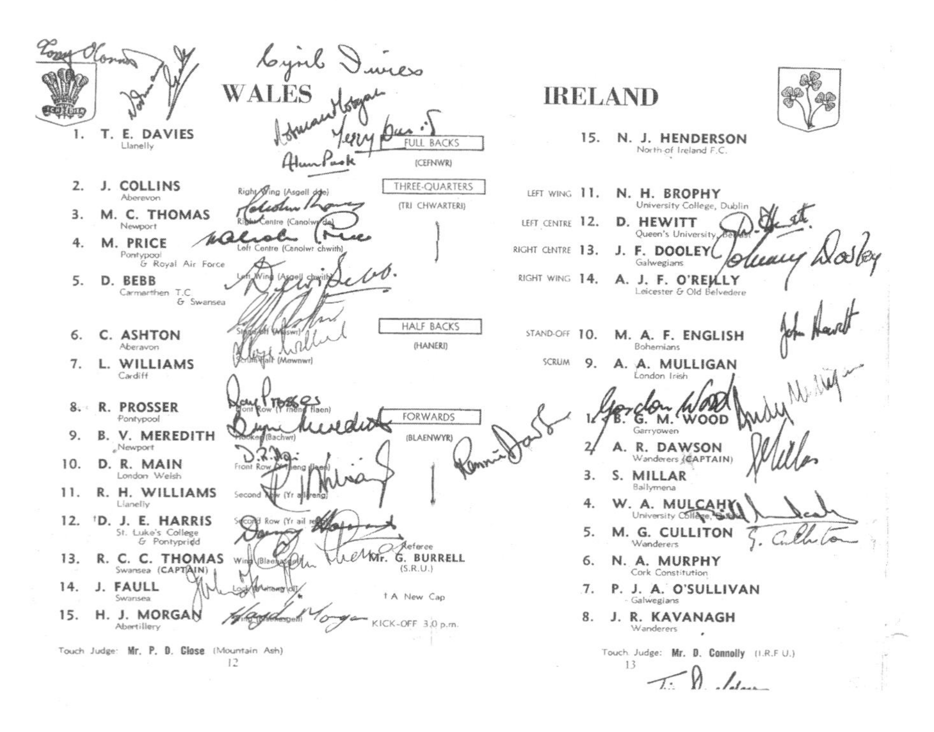

WALES **IRELAND**

WALES

1. **T. E. DAVIES** Llanelly

FULL BACKS (CEFNWR)

2. **J. COLLINS** Aberavon — Right Wing (Asgell dde)
3. **M. C. THOMAS** Newport — Right Centre (Canolwr dde)
4. **M. PRICE** Pontypool & Royal Air Force — Left Centre (Canolwr chwith)
5. **D. BEBB** Carmarthen T.C. & Swansea — Left Wing (Asgell chwith)

THREE-QUARTERS (TRI CHWARTERI)

6. **C. ASHTON** Aberavon — Stand-off (Maswr)
7. **L. WILLIAMS** Cardiff — Scrum Half (Mewnwr)

HALF BACKS (HANERI)

8. **R. PROSSER** Pontypool — Front Row (Y rheng flaen)
9. **B. V. MEREDITH** Newport — Hooker (Bachwr)
10. **D. R. MAIN** London Welsh — Front Row (Y rheng flaen)
11. **R. H. WILLIAMS** Llanelly — Second Row (Yr ail reng)
12. †**D. J. E. HARRIS** St. Luke's College & Pontypridd — Second Row (Yr ail reng)
13. **R. C. C. THOMAS** Swansea (CAPTAIN) — Wing (Blaenasgell)
14. **J. FAULL** Swansea — Lock (Wythwr)
15. **H. J. MORGAN** Abertillery — Wing (Blaenasgell)

FORWARDS (BLAENWYR)

Referee Mr. G. BURRELL (S.R.U.)

† A New Cap

KICK-OFF 3.0 p.m.

Touch Judge: **Mr. P. D. Close** (Mountain Ash)

12

IRELAND

15. **N. J. HENDERSON** North of Ireland F.C.

LEFT WING 11. **N. H. BROPHY** University College, Dublin

LEFT CENTRE 12. **D. HEWITT** Queen's University, Belfast

RIGHT CENTRE 13. **J. F. DOOLEY** Galwegians

RIGHT WING 14. **A. J. F. O'REILLY** Leicester & Old Belvedere

STAND-OFF 10. **M. A. F. ENGLISH** Bohemians

SCRUM 9. **A. A. MULLIGAN** London Irish

1. **B. G. M. WOOD** Garryowen
2. **A. R. DAWSON** Wanderers (CAPTAIN)
3. **S. MILLAR** Ballymena
4. **W. A. MULCAHY** University College, Dublin
5. **M. G. CULLITON** Wanderers
6. **N. A. MURPHY** Cork Constitution
7. **P. J. A. O'SULLIVAN** Galwegians
8. **J. R. KAVANAGH** Wanderers

Touch Judge: **Mr. D. Connolly** (I.R.F.U.)

13

Autographed programme from Tom's suitcase.
Wales v Ireland, Cardiff Arms Park, 14th March 1959.

The following February (1960) I travelled to London with the players and officials, one of four subs.[52] Before departure we had our photograph taken at the steps of our Irish Airlines plane, which was called FRIENDSHIP.[53] I was on the periphery of that photo (just as I was on the periphery of the team) dressed in my overcoat and cap, still full of hope. Tom Kiernan* and Wally Bornemann* were both due to get their first caps that day. There was great talk about the fact that the entire match would be televised.[54] Different times surely! This match was being viewed generally as a Triple Crown decider, but the Irish were very aware that they hadn't won at Twickenham since 1948, a full 12 years earlier. It was hoped that the Irish half-backs would be highly instrumental in winning the match for Ireland.

My heart took a leap the following morning when I heard that right-centre Kevin Flynn (Wanderers) had to cry off due to a thigh injury, which he had sustained in practice. I dared to hope I might be named as a replacement. Silly really, because I knew Dion Glass* would be the obvious choice, but although he was considered to be a utility back, the three-quarter line would have to be shuffled to accommodate him. My hopes were dashed. I was not named on the team. We were beaten.

Two weeks later, I was still a sub. Andy Mulligan was captain when the Scots came to Dublin. We were expected to do well. It was a dour and close game, but the Scottish men broke their losing sequence with a try from Ronnie Thomson* and a dropped goal from (the aptly named) Ken Scotland*. Gordon Wood scored a try for us and it was converted by David Hewitt, but the final score was Scotland 6; Ireland 5. Worse was to come. When the Welsh came to Dublin, I watched from the sideline as we were beaten by another narrow margin of 10-9.

---

52 'Flynn off Irish Team – Pulled Muscle In Practice' B. S. Nolan, *Irish Independent*, 13th February 1960, p. 14. (note: The four subs were: D. Glass (Collegians, four caps in his career), J. Thomas (Blackrock College, no caps), L. Butler (Blackrock College, who went on to gain one cap) and T. J. Cleary (Bohemians, no caps).

53 'Friendship' was to become Tom's catch-phrase, immediately identifiable with him. It was a term that peppered all his conversations and one he used constantly throughout his life.

54 'Irish Half-Backs May Lay Twickenham Bogy' B. S. Nolan, *Irish Independent*, February 12th 1960, p.16.

SCOTLAND			IRELAND
1. K. J. F. SCOTLAND Cambridge University	FULL-BACKS		15. N. J. HENDERSON North of Ireland F.C.
	THREE-QUARTERS		
2. A. R. SMITH Gosforth and Ebbw Vale	RIGHT WING	LEFT WING	11. N. H. BROPHY University College, Dublin
3. T. McCLUNG Edinburgh Academicals	RIGHT CENTRE	LEFT CENTRE	12. D. HEWITT Queen's University, Belfast
4. G. D. STEVENSON Hawick	LEFT CENTRE	RIGHT CENTRE	13. J. F. DOOLEY Galwegians
5. T. G. WEATHERSTONE Stewart's College F.P.	LEFT WING	RIGHT WING	14. A. J. F. O'REILLY Old Belvedere
	HALF-BACKS		
6. G. H. WADDELL Cambridge University	STAND-OFF		10. M. A. F. ENGLISH Bohemians
7. S. COUGHTRIE Edinburgh Academicals	SCRUM		9. A. A. MULLIGAN London Irish
8. H. F. McLEOD Hawick	FORWARDS		1. B. G. M. WOOD Garryowen
9. N. S. BRUCE Blackheath			2. A. R. DAWSON Wanderers (CAPTAIN)
10. I. R. HASTIE Kelso			3. S. MILLAR Ballymena
11. M. W. SWAN London Scottish			4. W. A. MULCAHY University College, Dublin
12. J. W. Y. KEMP Glasgow High School F.P.	Referee: Mr L. M. BOUNDY (England)		5. M. G. CULLITON Wanderers
13. G. K. SMITH Kelso			6. N. A. MURPHY Cork Constitution
14. J. T. GREENWOOD Perthshire Academicals (CAPTAIN)			7. P. J. A. O'SULLIVAN Galwegians
15. A. ROBSON Hawick	KICK-OFF 3 p.m.		8. J. R. KAVANAGH Wanderers
Touch Judge: Mr J. I. MORRISON (Stewart's College F.P.)			Touch Judge: Mr P. J. LAVERY (I.R.F.U.)

Autographed programme from Tom's suitcase.
Scotland v Ireland, Murrayfield, 28th March 1959.

In the spring of 1960, once more, I travelled with the team; this time to Paris. The match was to be played on 9th April. What a beautiful city. Full of cherry blossoms and glorious sunshine. Warm enough to go around in shirt sleeves, and despite our position on the table, we relished the prospect of the last match of the season for Ireland. Ronnie Dawson, just returned from injury, was promoted to captain that day. Andy had been the leader for the three losses against England, Scotland and Wales, so he was glad of the reprieve.

The ground was several miles out from central Paris and the traffic jams were so bad that some of us almost missed the kick-off. The lads told me afterwards that the tour bus had been escorted by police outriders, who went so fast that they were all nervous wrecks by the time they got to the dressing room. Maybe there was an ulterior motive there!

Unlike the Lansdowne Road ground, there was a low-level running-track surrounding the pitch where all sorts of officials seemed to be gathered: ambulance men, police officers, men in white coats, press reporters and photographers and others whose function I could not determine. Numerous missiles were aimed at the touch judge on my side and they seemed to come from the direction of the dangerous looking terraces. The resounding noise of the cheering crowd produced an echo that hurt my sensitive ears.

France was leading 12-3 at half-time and at the end we were trounced 23-6. Under their captain, Francois Moncla[*], this was France's biggest ever victory over us. Pierre Albaladejo[*] became the first player to kick three drop goals in an Ireland v France game. I watched as men like Michel Vannier[*], Guy Boniface[*] and Jean Dupuy[*] went through us like a hot knife through butter. But it was the pack who proved to be truly amazing. Flanker Michel Crauste[*], and props Roques[*] and Domenech[*], would surely become famous.

The meal that night was the best I had ever tasted. Despite my disappointment at the result, I was able to enjoy the pomp and ceremony. The French had style, that's for sure. The pace was leisurely and a pleasant mood spread through the function room at the Hotel Lutetia. As usual, toasts were made by the Presidents of the two unions and responded to by the captains. I was very happy to be there and felt I would never tire of this. I was loving every single minute of the evening. Ronnie Dawson did us proud with his response to the toast. As I nibbled at the delicious cheese board and sipped my glass of Champagne, Agne Taittinger Brut 1952, I was thinking that only one thing could make my life better than this! Shouldn't be much longer now. I continued to live in hope.

* * *

A few weeks after my trip to France, I was on a team which made history in Carrick. Captained by Paddy Dowley, we defeated the holders, Cashel, in the

final of the Garryowen Cup in Clanwilliam Park, Tipperary, in April 1960. It was quite a feat, as it was only Carrick's second season to play since the club was reformed after the war. It was a beautiful sunny Sunday afternoon and quite a crowd had gathered. I had the most awful hangover but I couldn't let the side (or the supporters) down, so I put on my bravest face and joined my team-mates. I was to play at out-half, with my brother, Gerry, at scrum-half. Gerry's friend, Leslie Dowley, partnered another brother of mine, Michael, in the centre. In my mind, ever after, I always thought of it as the game of two halves.

For the entire first half I felt as if my head would explode. Thump, thump, thump. My temple was throbbing in time to my pulse. My moves were sluggish as a result. I knocked on my first two passes from Gerry, and despite the mugginess of my brain I could see Michael gesturing frantically in my direction. This wasn't what the crowd had expected to see from me, the player with the highest profile on the pitch. After my two errors, Michael shunted me into the centre and took over at out-half.

"What are you playing at?" he thundered in my right ear.

"I'll be alright in a while," I said meekly.

"Let me know when your eyes start to focus. I can't believe you went on the tear LAST NIGHT OF ALL NIGHTS!"

What could I say?

Initially, Cashel's performance was excellent (partly thanks to me) but, mercifully, Carrick managed to keep them scoreless for the first half. They were unlucky. (I admit that now!) By the time the second half started I was 'coming to' and I began to rise to the challenge. I moved back to out-half and went on to give quite a good display. So much so that the *Munster Tribune* singled me out in the match report afterwards:

> Out-half, Tom Cleary was Carrick's star performer. His magnificent handling and fielding, together with his vast experience, proved too much for Cashel. When it came to touch finding, or dodging through, he was always a menace to the holders. Gerry Cleary, a brother, performed very well at the base of the scrum, and got his passes away cleanly all the time. Centres Leslie Dowley and Michael Cleary (another brother) were also safe, the former being very prominent. He took his scoring chances in fine style. Galvin and Morrissey on the wings ran well and were always dangerous in possession, while full-back, O'Keeffe gave an impeccable display throughout, his handling being particularly good. Carrick's forwards, ably assisted by final trialist Robert Dowley, were a lively bunch.[55]

---

55 *Munster Tribune* (no date on cutting in suitcase).

In the second half, Leslie made the opening score with a superb try and I added the points with an accurate kick. We were on our way. We increased our lead with another try by John Connolly and once again I put the additional points on the board with my kick. The final score was 10-0 and we were declared worthy winners. It was a great achievement; one of the triumphs in my life that meant most to me in the years afterwards. It was lovely to be on a winning team with my younger brothers. I realised my days in the game were numbered, so it was a particularly pleasant experience. A warm memory which helped sustain me in lonelier times.

* * *

The following autumn, 1960, I watched once more with interest and hope in my heart, as preparation and planning began for the arrival of the South African Springboks on tour. By now I had been named as 'sub to attend' eight times in all. The ninth time I was named as sub was in November of that year. An Irish XV team was to play the British Combined Services at Ravenhill. Andy Mulligan of Ulster and London Irish was, once again, first choice scrum-half, as he had been on so many occasions before. This match was looked on as a full-scale test, which would stretch the players to their limits. There was a lot at stake. The selectors needed to be impressed, as they eyed up individual players for possible potential for the coming match against the mighty touring Springboks. Once more, I was desperately disappointed when I didn't get a chance to show them what I could do.

Even though the team consisted of tried and proven international players, doubts had been expressed in certain quarters following some of the performances in the recent inter-provincial series. I knew that the half-back combination of Mulligan and Dooley had yet to be proven, so their play would be under the microscope. The main question was "Would they display enough skill, toughness, stamina and pace for a full 80 minutes of international rugby, in order to gain a place on the team for the big match?" Outwardly, I joked with my mates that John Dooley and I would be a better half-back combination and we should perform well together because he shared a birthday with me (although he was four years my junior) but inwardly I wasn't so confident.

Maybe there was a glimmer of hope for me. I wasn't sure whether to wish for a decisive win for the Irish XV in this match or hope for a poor performance so that the selectors might have to take a serious look at the substitutes. Secretly, I hoped that Andy might be on the sideline on 17th December. After all, I was only human.

However, my hope was dashed again. The selected Irish team, which played on 17th December, did not include me. It was devastating. Small consolation that it didn't include Mick English either. I can't remember if Mick was out through injury or not, but I can recall vividly that he had already gained something like seven caps by now, to my none.

The chairman of the South African Rugby Board, Dr. Daniel Craven* (who was considered to be one of the shrewdest judges of players and teams in the world at that time) had said before the tour that, in his opinion, the 1951-52 Springboks had been the greatest all-round side. I had seen them play when they toured all those years before and had been very impressed. The most commonly asked question now was "Would this present team live up to that high standard?" It was a tall order. In the four previous tours, the Springboks lost only seven and drew three matches out of 108. Their sole international defeat had been against Scotland, on their first tour, in 1906.

As they arrived in Ireland, it was generally felt that they were competent rather than brilliant. However, they had succeeded in beating Wales in Cardiff, on a day when they had to battle against very poor weather conditions and an atmosphere which was electric with the singing of the "men from the valleys". No mean feat. Their props, Piet du Toit* and Franie Kuhn* pushed hard to allow Ronnie Hilll* outhook the famous Bryn Meredith*. And the second row of Claassen* and Malan* were a force to be reckoned with.

The Irish had observed, with great interest, how the flankers and the number 8 adjusted their game and curbed some of their natural instincts, to suit the pouring rain and swampy pitch. They gathered the ball from the heel and burst straight past the fringes of the scrum. Hopwood* in particular looked dangerous when in possession and was identified as a potential problem for the Irish. He had, however, taken tremendous pressure in front of the pack and made enormous exertions rummaging in the Cardiff mud. Afterwards, the word was he had hurt his back and had been brought to hospital in Swansea.

Due to the awful weather it was difficult to assess the back division, but we would not be taking anything for granted. All in all, it was agreed that the task facing the Irish was formidable, but we had the incentive of boosting our reputation prior to the upcoming tour to South Africa the following May.

* * *

On the day of the match the Irishmen gave a good display against the tourists at Lansdowne Road, but were beaten (8-3) in the end. South Africa got a pushover try which was converted by Lockyear* and then, later in the game, Gainsford* got another try, while Ireland only managed a penalty goal from the boot of Tom Kiernan.

At the after-match function, I mingled with the great and good of international rugby from two continents. Some time after the meal I wandered into the foyer of the hotel where there were many small groups holding post mortems on the day's play. "Has anyone seen Doug Hopwood?" I asked for the umpteenth time.

I bumped into Andy Mulligan on the corridor, but he hadn't seen him. "Might have gone back to his room," he ventured. "Might be nursing those injuries of his."

I had all the Irish and almost all the Springboks' autographs on my match programme. Just Hopwood's and Baard's* to get. Hopwood hadn't actually played that day and I was just about fed up looking for him. I decided to retire to the bar. If they were around they'd surely arrive in there at some stage before the end of the evening. As I approached the door I met Charlie Nimb* and Adriaan Pieter Baard on the corridor. "Would you mind doing me the honour?" I asked Adriaan, handing him the programme opened at page 15. I pointed to his pen picture and he wrote his name diagonally across it.

Only one more signature to go and my souvenir would be complete. As it turned out, I got distracted and I didn't manage to get the autograph of Douglas John Hopwood, Springboks' loose-forward. Had a good night though!

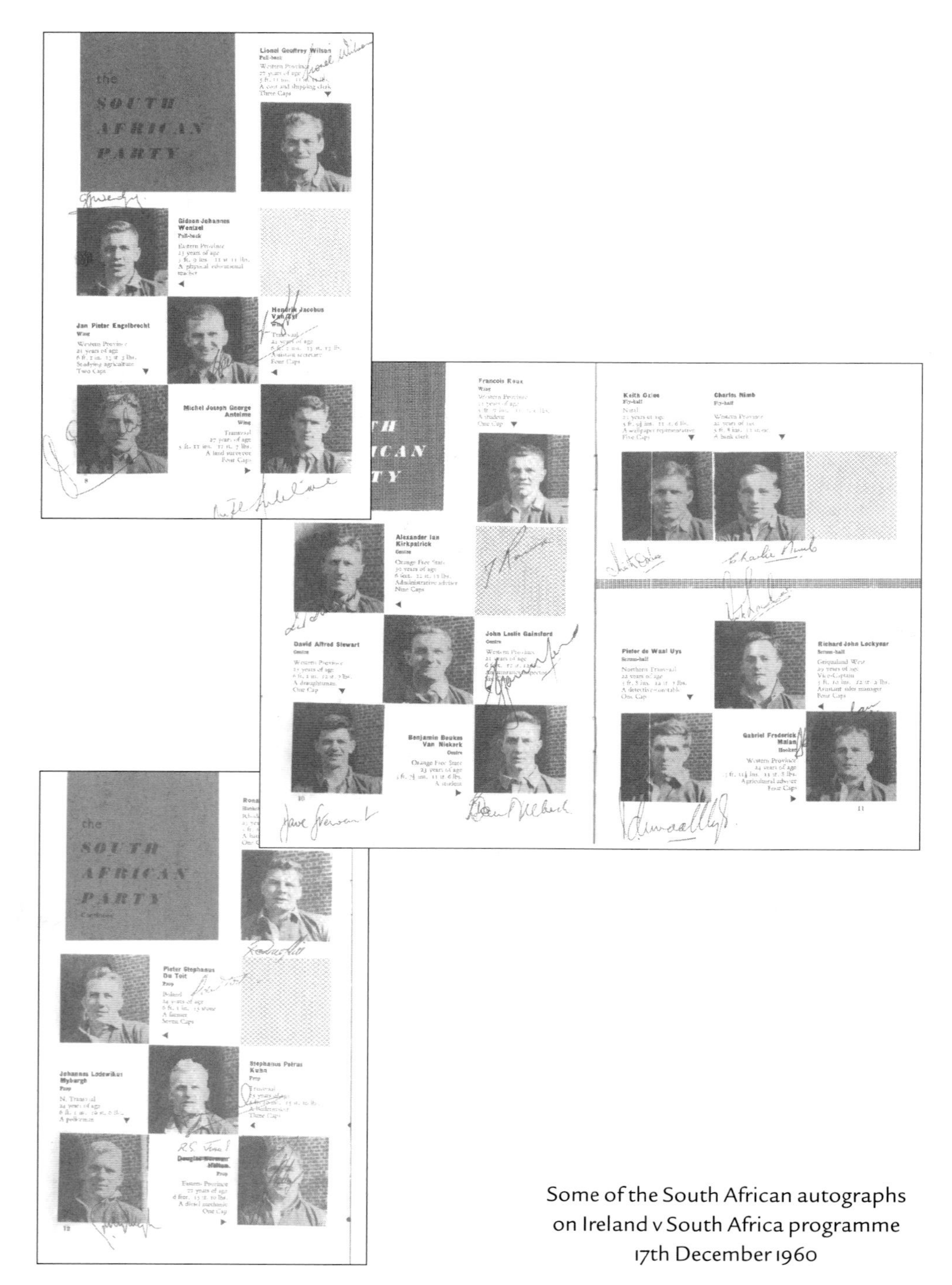
the SOUTH AFRICAN PARTY

Lionel Geoffrey Wilson
Full-back
Western Province
A coat and shipping clerk
Three Caps

Gideon Johannes Wentzel
Full-back
Eastern Province
23 years of age
A physical educational teacher

Jan Pieter Engelbrecht
Wing
Western Province
21 years of age
Studying agriculture
Two Caps

Hendrik Jacobus Van Zyl
Wing
Transvaal
Assistant secretary
Four Caps

Michel Joseph George Antelme
Wing
Transvaal
27 years of age
A land surveyor
Four Caps

8

Francois Roux
Wing
Western Province
A student
One Cap

Alexander Ian Kirkpatrick
Centre
Orange Free State
30 years of age
Administrative adviser
Nine Caps

David Alfred Stewart
Centre
Western Province
A draughtsman
One Cap

John Leslie Gainsford
Centre
Western Province
21 years of age

Benjamin Beukes Van Niekerk
Centre
Orange Free State
23 years of age
A student

10

Keith Oxlee
Fly-half
Natal
A wallpaper representative
Five Caps

Charles Nimb
Fly-half
Western Province
A bank clerk

Pieter de Waal Uys
Scrum-half
Northern Transvaal
22 years of age
A detective-constable
One Cap

Richard John Lockyear
Scrum-half
Griqualand West
Vice-Captain
Assistant sales manager
Four Caps

Gabriel Frederick Malan
Hooker
Western Province
24 years of age
Agricultural adviser
Four Caps

11

the SOUTH AFRICAN PARTY

Pieter Stephanus Du Toit
Prop
Boland
A farmer
Seven Caps

Johannes Lodewikus Myburgh
Prop
N. Transvaal
A policeman

Stephanus Petrus Kuhn
Prop
Transvaal
Three Caps

Douglas Norman Holton
Prop
Eastern Province
A diesel mechanic
One Cap

12

Some of the South African autographs on Ireland v South Africa programme 17th December 1960

Some of the South African autographs on
Ireland v South Africa programme
17th December 1960

Ireland	KICK OFF 2.30 p.m.	South Africa
15 T. J. KIERNAN Full Back, UNIVERSITY COLLEGE, CORK	FULL-BACKS	15 L. G. WILSON Full Back, W. PROVINCE
14 W. W. BORNEMANN Right Wing, WANDERERS	THREE-QUARTERS	13 A. N. OTHER Left Wing
13 J. C. WALSH Right Centre, UNIVERSITY COLLEGE, CORK		12 A. I. KIRKPATRICK Left Centre, ORANGE FREE STATE
12 A. C. PEDLOW Left Centre, C.I.Y.M.S.		11 J. L. GAINSFORD Right Centre, W. PROVINCE
11 N. H. BROPHY Left Wing, BLACKROCK		14 J. P. ENGELBRECHT Right Wing, W. PROVINCE
10 *W. K. ARMSTRONG Stand Off, NORTH OF IRELAND	HALVES	10 K. OXLEE Stand Off, NATAL
9 A. A. MULLIGAN Scrum, LONDON IRISH		9 R. J. LOCKYEAR Scrum, GRIQUALAND WEST
1 S. MILLAR Front Row Outside, BALLYMENA	FORWARDS	1 S. P. KUHN Loose Head Prop, TRANSVAAL
2 A. R. DAWSON Front Row Hooker, WANDERERS, CAPTAIN		2 R. A. HILL Hooker, RHODESIA
3 B. G. M. WOOD Front Row Outside, LANSDOWNE		3 P. S. du TOIT Tight Head Prop, BOLAND
4 W. A. MULCAHY Second Row, UNIVERSITY COLLEGE, DUBLIN		4 A. S. MALAN Lock, TRANSVAAL, CAPTAIN
5 *M. G. CULLITON Second Row, WANDERERS	* Denotes new cap.	5 J. T. CLAASSEN Lock, W. TRANSVAAL
6 J. R. KAVANAGH Back Row Wing, WANDERERS		6 G. H. van ZYL Flank, W. PROVINCE
8 P. J. A. O'SULLIVAN Back Row Lock, GALWEGIANS		7 H. J. M. PELSER No. 8, TRANSVAAL
7 N. A. A. MURPHY Back Row Wing, GARRYOWEN		8 *A. P. BAARD Flank, W. PROVINCE
Touch Judge: COMDT. T. FURLONG (IRFU)	Referee: G. J. TREHARNE (Welsh R.U.)	Touch Judge: D. A. STEWARD (S.A.R.T.T.)

The Irish autographs on
Ireland v South Africa programme
17th December 1960

The following Wednesday, the disappointment of not being named in the international was well behind me, when I was once again named as captain of the Munster side, to play at Musgrave Park against this touring Springboks' side. I was on a high. And we gave them a good run for their money. . . until injury time. It was a tight match until the very end. In fact Munster threatened to win it until the 41st minute of the second half and we certainly did not deserve to be beaten by six points in the end:

> Munster upheld their proud name as great battlers against touring rugby teams when they fought bravely, but unsuccessfully, against the South Africans who were victorious by two tries and a penalty goal (9 pts) to a try (3 pts). The ground was packed, the attendance being around the 12,000 mark, and even before the teams took the field one could sense an atmosphere of expectancy that it would be a battle royal.
>
> So it turned out as the fiery Munstermen proceeded to rock the Springboks with all-out foot rushes, full-blooded tackling and an eagerness, which the visitors can have experienced in few of their previous matches. Indeed, at one stage it seemed that the South Africans were shaken to the roots, but as always, they had that all-essential bit of extra stamina and steadiness to enable them to apply the pressure necessary to give them the winning points when Munster's tremendous effort lost some of its momentum.
>
> However, as in last Saturday's international at Lansdowne Road, the tourists did not get their heads in front, until the match had run its full course and "broken time" had been started.[56]

And I was the captain that day! It was awesome to hear the roar of 12,000 people in my ears as we took to the pitch. We used to joke that rugby teams competing against Munster would come to understand what it must have been like for the Christians in the Colosseum.

I can honestly say, I felt like an emperor!

* * *

The actor Richard Harris, a passionate Limerick man and a hell-raiser by reputation, often spoke glowingly of Limerick city and Munster rugby. In his youth he played in two Munster schools' finals and represented Munster schools and Munster under-20 before being struck down by tuberculosis. He took great

56 'Munster's Gallant But Vain Bid – Springboks Again Win In "Injury" Time', B. S. Nolan, *Irish Independent,* 22nd December 1960, p. 12.

Tom Cleary, the Munster scrum-half and captain, tackles a South African forward with Mick Spillane and Mick O'Callaghan, Munster forwards, backing up. Snapshot from Tom's suitcase.

pride in that red shirt, which he still had in his possession many years later, and he used to say that he intended to be buried in it. He also said:

> I would give up all the accolades – people have occasionally written and said nice things – of my showbiz career to play just once for the senior Munster team.[57]

And there was I, Tom Cleary, and I *captained* Munster – not once – but many times[58]. What an honour and a privilege... and what an achievement. I realise that I should never have buried it down so far. Maybe I should have given people a chance to look before now.

* * *

---

57 'Limerick Rugby Full Of Heroes', Richard Harris, *The Telegraph*, 24th May 2002.

58 Tom made 14 senior appearances for Munster between 1957 and 1961. He captained Munster to inter-provincial championship honours in 1959–1960. He also led the side in the four matches played by Munster during the 1960–1961 season. See footnote 127 on page 250 for full details.

The Springbok touring side, which had almost been rocked by my Munster side, went on to beat England at Twickenham a couple of weeks later, a goal to nil, in a game that was described as "a dreary 80 minutes – there was happily no over-time".[59] Puts things in perspective for me, all these years later. The provincial team I captained performed as well as the chosen Irish side, and so much better, and in a more exciting manner, than the English international team did, against the same opposition.

A few weeks later, in January 1961, I was named on a 'Rest of Ireland' team to play against Combined Universities. The match was played in the mud at Donnybrook and Universities won the match by six points to nil. The surface of the pitch was very bad and the mud was sticky, the ball was difficult to hold and any sort of quick manoeuvre was liable to send the players' feet slithering help-lessly.

The following day's newspaper reported that, while the Universities were happy with the result:

> ...the spectators, the Irish selectors and those engaged who might be considered to be on or near the fringes of international honours must have been far less content. [60]

The article went on to report:

> Gerry Tormey[61] emerged with almost as much credit as his better-known opposite number, Mick English, who drew a lot of moans and groans from the onlookers by his persistent kicking. Some of the criticism was justified especially in the second half, but the Varsity wing forwards and the trajectory of Tom Cleary's passes often left English with no other alternative.[62]

I didn't fare much better in Monday's *Cork Examiner*. Maurice Mullins, the Universities scrum-half was declared a star while I got some more bad press, declaring that I had "an unhappy day at the base of the Rest scrum, giving English an erratic and rather slow service."[63]

Even the weather was against me. To add to my woes my Bohs team-mates lost 6-0 to Constitution. They had missed the services of Mick and myself while we were away on Rest of Ireland duties. When the teams for the Irish Trial to be

---

59 'England Pack Steamrolled, Springboks sit on unstoppable try' Mitchel Cogley, *Sunday Independent*, 8th January 1961, p. 11.

60 'Tony's Form Hidden In Donnybrook Mud' Noel Dunne, *Sunday Independent*, 8th January 1961, p 11.

61 Gerry Tormey (University College Dublin). Playing on the Combined Universities team. (Referred to as 'Jerry' in some of the press reports.)

62 Tony's Form Hidden In Donnybrook Mud' Noel Dunne, *Sunday Independent*, January 8th 1961, p 11.

63 Donnybrook Game Little Help to Irish Selectors, *The Cork Examiner*, January 9th 1961, p. 9.

played later in the month were announced I was devastated to see that I was not considered. But by now, to everyone except myself perhaps, I was old news. The biggest surprise to most onlookers was the selection of Jonathan Moffett to play scrum-half for the Blues XV. Everyone thought that Mullins would get the nod after his display for the universities. I hardly got a mention in all their chat.

Nothing was going right. Did this mean my chance was gone? My heart was in the dumps again. But gradually, I was learning to live with my sense of disappointment and frustration at being consistently on the fringes of international honours, though at times the emotions were extremely overwhelming and seemed magnified out of all proportion.

* * *

A month later, on 4th February, I read with interest that the Barbarians[64] recorded an historic win when the tourists lost their only match of the tour, at Cardiff, after 15 weeks and 29 matches. The Barbarian forwards forced the Springboks to play more often to their backs than they might otherwise have done and so succeeded in isolating the Springbok backs from their usual forward support.

The final score read Barbarians 6, South Africa nil. Hardly believable! The "invincibles" crashed to two tries by Haydn Morgan*, the Welshman and William Morgan*, the England back-row man. Irish internationals such as Wood, Dawson, Millar*, O'Reilly and Culliton played on the Baa Baas team. What a pleasure to see the pictures of Ronnie Dawson accepting the coveted trophy (a Springbok head) as the first side to defeat the visitors. We were all looking forward to our tour in May. Even if I wasn't selected I was determined to travel. I'd find the money somehow.

---

64 Barbarians – the Club with no Ground. Also known as Baa-Baas (sometimes spelt Ba-Bas) and often referred to as the United Nations of Rugby. Founded in Bradford in 1890. A team consisting of a conglomerate of (mainly international) invited players from a variety of countries playing in an exhibition style match.
Baa-Baas Team on this historic occasion: J. C. R. Young, H. M. Roberts, S. Millar, B. Price, H. J. Mainwaring, R. A. W. Sharp, W. G. D. Morgan, M. G. Culliton, B. G. M. Wood, W. R. Evans, A. R. Dawson (captain), A. J. F. O'Reilly, H. J. Morgan, B. J. Jones, W. R. Watkins.
Officials: H. L. Glyn-Hughes (President), H. Waddell (Vice-President), M. R. Steele-Bodger (Hon. Secretary), V. G. Roberts (Touch Judge), M. F. Turner (Referee)

Touring

I was thrilled to be selected for the short Irish tour of South Africa in May 1961. By then, I was getting on a bit in years. Soon to be 31 (although many press reports put me at 29), this was definitely the last chance saloon if I were ever to attain that elusive green cap. Most people agreed that I deserved it, though there were some murmurs about my selection above Jonathan Moffett, who had been declared a hero in the match against England and played quite well in our defeat by the Scots at Murrayfield.

Indeed, in general terms, disappointment reigned in the Irish camp, which had started out on that season's campaign with high hopes. Initially there was talk of Triple Crown and possibly even Championship glory but in the end we were defeated 16-8 in Murrayfield and were well beaten in a 9-0 debacle at Cardiff when Richards* scored a try and two penalty goals.

The May 1961 edition of *Rugby World* magazine declared that Ireland's selectors had slipped up. They were described as a harassed committee who showed little faith in potential and it was felt that much of their trouble was of their own making. It mentioned the "whims of the provincial selectors, of whom they themselves were part and parcel". I could certainly identify with those whims and I know there were many times over the years when supporters and players alike thought that some of their decisions were erratic and capricious.

There were five of us included in the touring team who had not yet represented our country. The article made particular mention of James Thomas and myself:

> Cleary and Thomas are both 29 and have had long and frustrating careers. Cleary, incredible to relate, was on the Munster inter-provincial team before John O'Meara, who appeared 22 times as Ireland's scrum-half and retired from the game three years ago.
>
> Thomas is also a hardened campaigner, and both he and Cleary must have been resigned to careers as permanent substitutes. The latter had filled that role 10 successive times for Ireland.[65]

65 'Ireland's Selectors Slip Up' *Rugby World*, May 1961, pp. 12-13.

The article went on to ponder individual selections describing mine as "strangest of all". Regarding Jonathan Moffett and myself, it posed two questions:

> What did he[66] do to lose favour, or how did Cleary suddenly regain it?[67]

Some people saw it as a consolation selection for all the times I had been a sub but not capped.

* * *

March already. It was the day after Paddy's Day and I had seriously drowned the shamrock the previous night. I had to shake my skull in an effort to clear the muggy feeling across my forehead. I slowly made my way out to Shannon Airport for my vaccination against yellow fever in preparation for the trip of any man's lifetime. The letter gave me directions to attend the Clare County Medical Officer's office and informed me of the appointment time. I folded the page in two, and put it in my pocket.

There was no one in the waiting room, so I knocked on the door to the inner sanctum.

"Come in." The doctor, peering over his glasses, looked up from the desk. "Mr. Cleary, I presume", he joked, making a pun on the famous encounter of Dr. Livingston at Victoria Falls, one of the very places I was to visit shortly, "Come in Sir, sit down," he urged.

"This won't take long, vaccination isn't it?" He was one of the many people, in Munster and further afield, who were delighted to see that my distinguished career was finally about to receive the ultimate honour of the tour in an Irish shirt. "Cruelly unlucky you have been, Tom, ...cruelly unlucky." He emphasised the words by shaking his head.

I took the praise on board. I was used to it. I put the niggling doubt that Andy Mulligan was still first choice to the back of my mind. I was determined to enjoy this experience from start to finish, even the dreaded injections.

"Vaccination contre la Fièvre Jaune," I jokingly put on my best French accent as I read aloud from the little orange coloured booklet. I could see that it was issued by the World Health Organisation under the rules governing International Sanitary Regulations. To the side of the booklet I noted an Aer Lingus shamrock symbol and title, and, in case anyone was mistaken as to what it meant, the words Irish Airlines were written below that.

"Not bad for a Tipperary man!" the doctor remarked on my accent.

---

66 Jonathan Moffett.
67 'Ireland's Selectors Slip Up', *Rugby World*, May 1961, pp. 12-13.

"A Tipperary man, an adopted Limerick man and a MUNSTERMAN!" I reminded him.

"Better still, so!"

I watched then as he expertly prepared for the procedure. I felt a little apprehensive as he opened the steriliser and took out a prepared hypodermic, attached a needle and placed them in a little stainless steel kidney dish, beside a small ball of cotton wool.

"Wellcome batch No. 2935" he declared aloud, as he read the maker's label on a vial of liquid from the cabinet on the opposite wall.

"Easy for you to welcome it," I laughed nervously, "it's not going into your arm!"

"Good joke, Tom, good joke!" He looked up towards the window as he carefully withdrew the plunger and the appointed dosage was sucked into the syringe. I continued to observe him as he flicked the side of the cylinder and a few air bubbles fought to get to the needle, only to be squirted into the atmosphere in a tiny spray. I was so intent on the other man's course of action that I remained sitting, pen poised in hand.

"Did you fill that out yet?"

I quickly rallied those wandering thoughts of mine and proceeded to sign the page in two places. I then filled in my date of birth in Roman numerals and put a capital "M" to indicate my gender. I wondered aloud if I should have filled the top line in capital letters.

"It'll do grand," I was assured. "Up with the sleeve now."

Taking off my jacket, I undid my gold cufflink, placed it on the desk beside me, and rolled up the sleeve of my crisp, white shirt. A liquid with the overwhelming smell, which I usually associated with hospitals, was produced and dabbed onto the wool ball. A vigorous rub on the injection site and it was all over in a jiffy.

"Never felt a thing," I remarked seriously.

Pulling the book over to him, the doctor then recorded the relevant details from his perspective. Lastly, he took up the official stamp, pressed it into the green ink-pad on the desk, carefully made the impression on the orange page, then signed and dated in the allotted spot.

"Your smallpox booster will have to wait until nearer the travel date. You needn't come all the way out here. I'll contact Dr. Corboy and he'll oblige you in the city, say 4th of May . . . how would that suit you?" the doctor asked, looking at the calendar on the wall. I could see that he had circled Monday 8th May, the date the tour was due to fly out from Ireland. It's true, I mused (although I have never doubted it), rugby is a religion here.

"Marvellous, I agreed, "Thanks Doc!"

"Don't let us down out there now!" the parting shot.

A cold March wind was whipping up as I left the surgery. I pulled up the collar of my jacket against the elements and considered going for a hair of the dog.

* * *

Seven days to go. I was in fairly high spirits as I entered the O'Connell Street branch of the Munster & Leinster Bank in Limerick to collect my foreign exchange for travelling expenses on the trip. I filled in the forms, watched admiringly by the young female bank clerks and I knew that in no time at all I'd be back outside again with the 20 pounds sterling tucked away safely in my breast pocket. But silly me. I forgot to bring my passport along to be stamped by the bank. However, knowing me and knowing the important business I would shortly be conducting abroad on behalf of Irish sport in general and Limerick sport in particular, the teller let me away with that and gave me a small stamped receipt docket, impressing on me the importance of fixing it to the last page of that little green book as soon as I got home. But I never got around to it. I left it loose.

Before I left on my South African trip, I wrote to Uncle Paddy on a sheet of the good quality headed notepaper, which had been issued to me some time prior to our departure. I knew he'd get a kick out of that letter and would have fun showing it off down in the Kitty Club.

It was headed "Irish Rugby Union Touring Team, South Africa & Rhodesia[69], 1961" in green writing accompanied by the shamrock symbol. My tour number was 7 and I was issued with a suitcase with that number on its side. 'Lucky for some' was the usual comment when I imparted that piece of information to my pals and family.

Tom's Passport Photograph
Issued in 1958, his passport cost him 29 shillings and six pence.
(Quite a lot of money for the times.)
It includes the 1961 stamps recording his entry to South Africa on 9th May
and his re-entry to Ireland on 21st May.

68 Southern Rhodesia is now Zimbabwe. Northern Rhodesia is now Zambia.

Photographs from the Western Transvaal v Ireland programme, Potchefstroom, 20th May 1961.

> The short tour was really inaugurated in 1960 by Scotland to South Africa and Ireland followed that same trail in 1961. At that early stage the wide range of problems had not been studied with sufficient care, for our first fixture, 48 hours after a long, tiring journey, was the international ...... almost before the visitors realised they had arrived.[69]

It was some scene as we arrived at Jan Smuts Airport in Johannesburg in the afternoon of 9th May 1961, having left Dublin the previous day at nine in the morning and flown via London. I had never seen anything like it on my travels to date. Avril Malan, skipper of the 1960-61 Springboks in Britain and Ireland was on the reception committee and the first bit of 'good' news we overheard, from the Irish perspective, was that he'd be out of the test on Saturday due to a heavy tackle on the right thigh in a club game, which hadn't recovered enough for him to declare himself fit. Everyone, including the thousands of spectators, who had seen Malan lead his team the previous winter, unbeaten until that dramatic Barbarians game, would know just how much his captaincy meant to the Springboks.

We were thrilled, despite the heat and exhaustion after an arduous journey this far, to see a crowd of about 1,000 people at the airport, to welcome the team, along with officials of the Transvaal Rugby Union. A photographer was heard asking a group of visitors to pose in front of an Irish tricolour but was surprised to hear that they were from the North. It was all cheerfully laughed off.

There was a three-hour stop at the airport before we took off again for our flight to D. F. Malan Airport in Capetown. When we eventually landed in Capetown, it was to brilliant sunshine with the temperatures in the 70s. We were shattered after a tiring journey of nearly 26 hours, but everyone was fit and well. This was to be our headquarters for the first week of the tour.

I could hardly wait to get to bed. The weariness in my bones was overwhelming. It was obvious though that the tiredness, and the after effects of a few scoops here and there throughout the long journey, was beginning to tell on more than me. Once the welcoming ceremonies were over, we were taken by bus to the hotel at Sea Point, but the booking-in procedure and the room allocations took ages so, it was late by the time the team members hit the sack. Between the excitement, the unaccustomed heat, the long journey and what would, in later years, become known as 'jet lag', I and many others hardly slept a wink.

The next day, Hennie Muller*, the Springbok team manager, was not in a cheerful mood about practice arrangements for his test team. The Springboks were due to arrive in Capetown from midday onwards, but, due to it being the

69 '... An Idyllic Existence. Australia 1967' Paul McWeeney, *Irish Rugby Union Programme Ireland v Australia,* January 17th 1976, p. 4.

religious and public holiday, Ascension Thursday, any special practice for them was ruled out. On Friday morning, the day before the test, the Springboks gathered for a team picture, and then for another one in the company of the Irish team. In the afternoon, entertainment was lined up for the two teams in the form of a cocktail party organised by the South African Board. It looked like Hennie was going to have a tough time squeezing in a practice for his boys.

Another point worrying the South Africans was the announcement that Johan Claassen would be taking over from Malan as skipper and many considered that this was likely to be Ireland's greatest asset. Claassen was the Springbok captain three years previously when the French shattered South African rugby pride by winning one and drawing the other game. Claassen's captaincy on the field was still the subject of detailed criticism.

The morning after our arrival, exhausted, the Irish management held a squad talk and announced their team, prior to our first training spin on South African soil, before an interested crowd on the Hamilton ground at Green Point. Andy Mulligan was to play at scrum-half. I had expected that I wouldn't be named, but I was nonetheless a little disappointed to hear Andy's name called out. I decided to put my efforts into bolstering those colleagues who would be playing in the test. But deep down I wondered why they could not give me the nod just this once.

The training session lasted two hours, the greater part of which was devoted to loosening up and exercising under the direction of the captain, Ronnie Dawson. In the last 45 minutes the team got down to serious practise, the forwards splitting up under the supervision of Dawson and the backs under Andy Mulligan. The South Africans noted that Dawson had Saturday's test pack scrummaging against the rest who were augmented by Peter McMullan, the *Belfast Telegraph* correspondent. They thought that it was significant that the Irish captain drilled them thoroughly and called for a concentrated powerful shove. Different times, surely.

Afterwards, Noel Murphy Senior*, the Irish manager declared that the boys were fit – he announced that they had just had a season of rugby and, shortly before leaving home, the team had two practice sessions in Dublin. He announced that we were only limbering up today and would probably have another light training session before the game. He felt secure in the knowledge that all the Irish, except the 19-year-old centre Ken Houston*, a science student from Queen's University, Belfast, were experienced internationals. Some observers were surprised by Houston's selection (as he was scarcely known south of the border and had not even played for Ulster) but he got his chance, firstly because injury and studies kept three of Ireland's top backs at home and, secondly, because of his startling and consistent club form in the latter part of the previous season. I looked on wryly. If only...? I wondered, quietly, if I might have gained a cap easier if I'd been born in a different province. One other selection and one omission caused a few raised eyebrows in Capetown. Dion Glass was selected as standoff half, after winning his three caps at either wing or centre, and Gerry Culliton, Wanderers wing forward and 13 times capped, was omitted.

But the Irish themselves had one or two pointed views on the strength of the opposition. We planned to capitalise on the selection of Dave Stewart* at centre, and vowed to make the most of his poor defensive qualities, especially in view of Houston's love of the dashing break. We looked on Avril Malan's injury, which deprived the Springboks of their finest leader for years, as by far the strongest factor in any chance of a shock win. What with the missing captain and John Gainsford's absence due to a thigh injury, I recall that there was a lot of speculation in some circles on the possibility of an Irish win.

Seemingly there had been a lively debate up north, in Transvaal, when the South African team was announced. Their team had visited Capetown and beaten the Western Province not long before and it was being said that with eight Western Province men in the Springbok side, an Irish win would be welcomed almost as much in the Transvaal as in Ireland. Everyone hoped that the controversy would at least ensure a good crowd.

Meanwhile, we heard that the Springboks planned to have at least three team talks. The first to get them together as a team – thinking rugby. Then, before the second practice, the manager would outline the essentials for rehearsal at practice. On the eve of the test, he hoped to have them set as a team and the fundamentals of their tactics well drilled into them, and he said he would drive home his message of:

> the importance of the match itself, the honour of their being the select of South African rugby. What it means to play for the Springboks, more especially in a test match. I know I will get the best out of those boys. I hope they play well and they win: but should we lose which can easily happen, we will be the first to congratulate our Irish visitors. You know how things go in rugby, you can never be too sure of winning! We will play attacking rugby, on orthodox lines – on a solid foundation .... Of course there will be tricks and variations but you cannot publish them.[70]

It seemed that Hennie Muller was adamant about wanting the Springboks to have their run on Newlands before the game. He knew the team would benefit from having a training spin there on the day before the test and felt the team needed to get the feel of the turf and the Newlands atmosphere. He also knew that South Africa was going into the test without a recognised goal-kicker since

70 'No Blackboard Of Test – Says Hennie Muller' Maxwell Price, Sport 1, p. 24. (no other details on newspaper cutting in suitcase).

they'd chosen Piet Van Zyl*, rather than Frik Du Preez* who had kicked so well not long before in Britain and especially in Ireland.

He also knew that they were up against a very experienced Irish front row in Gordon Wood, Ronnie Dawson and Syd Millar, who had played together for Ireland in 14 internationals. They had also been the Lions front row in three of the four tests in New Zealand in 1959 and were said to have given the Irish scrum a very professional appearance.

Elsewhere, Noel Murphy (Senior), the Irish Rugby Union President and senior tour manager, was being interviewed by Donald Mosey, staff reporter with the *Daily Mail* and others who were travelling with the team, and he voiced the hope that the tourists would play attractive rugby, saying that Newlands was a beautiful surface and had a wonderful rugby atmosphere. The scene was set.

However, many observers had been saying that there were numerous question marks over the Irish team, not least the ones relating to our obvious fatigue after that recent energy-sapping, long-distance journey from Ireland, just three nights previously. Pundits wondered if we would be able to take the strain for 80 minutes, against the formidable South African front row of Du Toit, Hill and Kuhn. Others asked how Glass, in his first international at out-half, would fare against the Springbok breakaways. There was ongoing discussion on the omission of the two proven campaigners, Culliton and Murphy, and several wondered if it was a wise selection in a match of that importance. However, the good news was that Friday's newspapers were tipping the Irish to beat the Springboks.

From Donald Mosey
Daily Mail Staff Reporter who is travelling with the Irish Team

First Test forecasts are puzzling the Tourists
IRISH BACK THEIR PACK
And tipsters say they'll beat this Springbok side
Capetown, Friday

The last official photograph has been taken, the last official party has finished, and the stage is set for Ireland's first ever Rugby test match in South Africa.

They came out here not even giving themselves a chance, apart from the natural fighting response of the Irish to a challenge. Today they find themselves being widely tipped to beat the Springboks.

It is forecasting they cannot understand, because it is based on a negative approach to tomorrow's game.

The tipsters are not looking at the potentialities of the tourists at all, but at the many faults they find with the South African selectors and with a handful of the men they have picked.

THEIR PLAN

The advice most freely given to the Irish is "give the ball to your backs and let them run, and the Springbok pack will never get into the game."

But the fact is that the tourists are not too happy about the strength of their backs and are working understandably on the idea that their main force is in the forwards.

If David Hewitt, Niall Brophy*, and Mike English had been here their approach might have been different, but the strength of the backs as a combined force, with so many enforced changes and positional switches, is problematical.

The poker-faced Tom Kiernan is safe enough at fullback and the rampaging Springbok forwards will not ruffle him.

Tony O'Reilly* is just as likely to fade out of the picture in an overseas test, as he is to justify his tremendous popularity.

Versatile John Hewitt* is just about incapable of playing a bad game in any position and Andy Mulligan and Jerry Walsh* have plenty of experience to add to their ability.

ORDEAL

For Ken Houston the game will be something of an ordeal. To take a man who has not played provincial rugby in Ireland and put him against the Springboks at Newlands for his first big game is rather like taking a Fourth Division footballer in England and dropping him into the F. A. Cup Final at Wembley.

Dion Glass has not played for Ireland at standoff half but has three caps in the three-quarter line and it is generally accepted that his best work is done in the halfbacks.

As for the forwards, the front row came off far better against the Springboks on their tour of Britain than any three have done for a long time, and that includes the All-Blacks, while Ronnie Dawson is a far greater captain than Claassen.

In the second row the two doctors, Bill Mulcahy and Ian Dick*, look capable of diagnosing any trouble from the opposition and treating it in the approved manner.

TIRELESS

The back three prove something of a contrast from Ronnie

Kavanagh,* the most capped Irishman, through the roving and tireless Tim McGrath* to Dennis Scott,* who played nearly all of his first international against France a few months ago as an emergency full back when the team were crippled by injuries.

The South African critics who feel the Irish have more than an even money chance say the Springboks are weary after their own six months season – a visit from the All Blacks, an exhausting tour of Britain and now their own new season starting with last week's trials in Port Elizabeth.

They have had no time for team training for this game.

The Springboks met yesterday, five days after being selected and had no chance to work-out because Ascension Day is observed very strictly here, with banks, shops, pubs, and cinemas closed, and no sport taking place at all.

So they were left to make all their preparations on the day of the test.

PEP TALKS

They will have a loosener at Newlands and three pep talks from Manager Hennie Muller, who scorns theoretical rugby and the use of a blackboard.

Whatever the result, the game promises to be a classic example of a fight between the Irish, averaging 14st. 7 lb. and the Springboks, 15st. 6 lb.

If Ronnie Dawson's men can hold these heavyweights, South Africa might regret going into the game without a recognised goal-kicker, but I doubt whether it will become merely a matter of penalties.

The Irish can expect a good deal of support. Apart from the traditional backing of the coloured fans, they will be urged on by many rugby followers here who would be delighted to see the lordly Springboks humbled at their own headquarters.

If I doubt whether this can be done, it is in no way a criticism of the Irish but born of a wholesome respect for the supreme efficiency of South African rugby.

As it happened, a crowd of 35,000 delighted people turned out to throng Newlands for the test the following day, and they were not to be disappointed. Contests didn't come much better than this and it was reported that the multitude would willingly have returned to see it all again if that were possible. It offered sparkling attacking play, which resulted in an attractive type of handling game.

I kept the green and white programme for the day's test match. It was written in two languages, English and Afrikaans, and included both the Shamrock and Springbok emblems. The message of introduction was by the man referred to as "Mr. Rugby"[71] at that time – test captain, prophet and administrator, Dr. Daniel Craven, who had been President of the Board since 1956 and was one of the dignitaries to meet the Irish party when we arrived. A legend already in his own lifetime, he was head of the Department of Physical Education at the University of Stellenbosch, but seemingly that didn't prevent him from flying away to meetings of the International Rugby Board, and writing with a seemingly inexhaustible pen about the game in which he was so very involved. I was aware that the 'Doc', as he was called, was South Africa's first noted contributor to the worldwide administration of the game:

> For the first time in our history we shall have the privilege of meeting our friends from Ireland, and it gives me great pleasure to extend to them the warmest of welcomes. We trust that they will never forget this short visit to our country, that they will make friends with the many people they will meet and as such make the ties between our two rugby playing countries firmer.
>
> We hope that their matches will be so enjoyable and outstanding that these games will always live in their memories. We know that the approach to all their matches and the spirit in which they will be played, will be what it should be, namely in the best interest and traditions of this wonderful game of ours. We are not unduly interested in winning or losing; we want the game to profit, as also relationships.
>
> We are glad that the Irish Rugby Football Union found it possible to accept our invitation, and we hope that this will be a prelude to many more visits to our country.
>
> D. H. Craven, Pres. S. A. Rugby Football Board.

---

71 'They Call Him . . . 'Mr. Rugby'.' Reg Sweet ("Natal Daily News") *Rugby World*, August 1961. Charles Buchan's Publications Ltd., pp. 17-19.

Irish Rugby Union Touring Team, South Africa & Rhodesia

1 9 6 1

Hon. Manager

Hon. Assistant Manager

Secretary

Full Back:

Threequarters:

Half-Backs: Stand Off:

Half-Backs: Scrum:

Forwards:

(CAPTAIN)

An autograph sheet signed by all 26 members of the I.R.F.U. Touring Team, South Africa and Rhodesia, May 1961.

RUCKING

There I am, at the back, in the top left hand corner of the touring team photograph, wearing the Irish jersey. Hands by my side, proud chest puffed out, but maybe putting on a bit of condition when I compare it to other photos. But I knew I was fit and wished in my heart that I'd have the chance to display my ability on a world stage. However it was not to be, so I settled into my seat to enjoy the atmosphere of the display which was about to unfold on the pitch. Subs didn't tog out in those days. I viewed it from the sideline.

Irish Rugby Football Union Touring Team 1961
Back Row: T. J. Cleary, W. G. Tormey, J. S. Dick, J. Thomas, T. J. Kiernan, K. Houston, D. C. Glass, J. C. Walsh, W. J. Hewitt.
Middle Row: N. A. A. Murphy, J. F. Dooley, N. Brophy, W.A. Mulcahy, C. J. Dick, T. McGrath, D. Scott, M. G. Culliton.
Front Row: A. J. F. O'Reilly, S. Millar, B. G. M. Wood, N. Murphy (Senior) (Hon. Manager), A. R. Dawson (Captain), T. A. O'Reilly (Hon. Assistant Manager), A. A. Mulligan, R. W. Jeffares (Secretary), J. R. Kavanagh.
Photo courtesy of Mr. Willow Murray, I.R.F.U.

I watched with intensity as South Africa playing in white, Ireland in green, battled in a classic competition[72]. And even though at the end, Ireland was beaten 24-8, when my shattered mates went, wearily, back to the dressing room, I joined them as they sang "When Irish eyes are smiling" with great pride to a magnificent Springbok team who would have beaten any 15 in the world that day with their wonderful display of rugby at its greatest. It has often been said of the Irish that 'all their wars are merry and all their songs are sad.'[73] That night we showed the mighty Springboks that our songs can also be uplifting. That episode in the dressing room is quite an emotional memory for me. My heart was very full.

Despite all the questions beforehand, the lads completed the match only two scrums down against the head, though our pack was constantly under considerable strain. The game developed along the lines of repeated thrust and counter, and the Springboks made the most of their chances with good handling and incisive running. But we showed our spirit of adventure when we pulled out some brilliant attacks against the Springbok's defence in the second half.

Though some may have looked on at it as a humiliating loss for Ireland's first team to play in South Africa, it was suggested afterwards that we had come out of a game in which we were outclassed, with our dignity intact, because of our attractive type of handling game. In defeat the Irish made more friends than any victory could have done. All our points came in the last four minutes, when we were still throwing the ball about as if this were the start of an exhibition game. One of the Western Province Board said afterwards:

> As long as Rugby is played like this the crowd will still roll in. We shall remember Ireland not as a team who were heavily beaten here, but as the boys who helped to make this into a Rugby classic.[74]

Before the match it had been said the South Africans were stale after 15 months' continuous playing – so they went out to play this game as if it was their first for six months and the most important of their lives. It had also been said they were asking for trouble going into an international without a recognised goal-kicker, but stand-off half Charlie Nimb in his first test, and despite having a recently-lanced bad boil on his cheek, kicked four beauties from acute angles and fantastic ranges.

Nimb's dummy scissors with Dave Stewart set up the Springboks' first try, scored by Ben-Piet van Zyl. He scored three conversions and also kicked a colossal 56-yard penalty kick. We were very impressed with this youngster, playing in his first (and what turned out to be his only) international.

---

72 All descriptions of play in this chapter are taken from the press reports in Tom's suitcase.

73 G. K. Chesterton. "The Ballad of the White Horse", BOOK II, line 796. G. K. Chesterton web site: accessed 13th June 2005. http://www.cse.dmu.ac.uk/~mward/gkc/

74 'Defeat Won Friends'. Donald Mosey, *Daily Mail,* 15th May, 1961, p. 16.

Even by their own elevated standards, these Springboks were declared to be truly great. I overheard our own magnificent full-back, Tom Kiernan, say that Doug Hopwood's performance was "incredible". Despite taking a bad knock after 17 minutes, where he looked to be in trouble, the South African played a game which rivalled anything he had ever done to date in his distinguished career.

Some described it as a masterpiece match and it was said that Avril Malan, the injured Springbok skipper, who had to miss the game, might have been right to worry about his place. Piet Van Zyl, the man who replaced Malan, had a tremendous game. He, with Johan Claassen, was responsible for wrecking the Irishmen's carefully-planned and exhaustively-rehearsed campaign in the lineout.

Our mighty Irish front row was forced literally to bow to the incredible strength of the South Africans who had a 3-1 advantage against the loose head, less from any technical skill of Ronnie Hill than from the fierce push of the men with him. Ireland's was a defeat by a vastly superior team rather than the result of any individual deficiencies, but one or two names were singled out to give a true picture.

Kiernan, apart from scoring the eight points, refused to be jolted out of his usual unruffled calm and that in itself was regarded as an achievement. He hit a post with a 35 yard angled penalty kick and put an astonishing 50 yard effort from near touch a couple of feet under the bar – both when the score was only 5–0. Ken Houston, who could not have landed in a more testing game for his first big match appearance, ran well and afterwards was very definitely viewed as a prospect for the future. However, as Don Mosey noted in the *Daily Mail*, Tony O'Reilly, the man all South Africa wanted to see in full cry, found it difficult to get into the game. It was 15 minutes before he got a touch of the ball at all, and 55 minutes before he got a running chance, which proved to be his only one.

For the South Africans, Colin Greenwood[*], the new Springbok, got off to a wonderful start in international rugby by scoring in the twelfth minute when he took an inside pass from Ben Piet Van Zyl[*]. Charlie Nimb made the running for the score and converted with a glorious kick from the touchline. Greenwood and Nimb opened up the cover for Hopwood, backing up as always, to dive over in the corner, and Nimb landed another fine goal. He missed his conversion of Greenwood's second try after 31 minutes, so the Springboks turned around with a 13-0 lead and the game in their pockets.

In the second half, Martin Pelser[*] ran into the ruck, but shrugging off the horde of green shirts surrounding him, leapt into the air to throw out a huge one-handed pass to Ben Piet Van Zyl, who went 40 yards to score in the corner, and again Nimb converted. Lionel Wilson[*], whose uncanny positional sense stopped every Irish threat, had to go off for nine minutes with a damaged shoulder. However, he was back in time to see Nimb put that fantastic 56 yard penalty kick high over the bar.

It almost looked like a consolation prize when Kiernan kicked a straight penalty goal four minutes from time but the Irishmen were still opening up every time they got the ball and a minute later Walsh and Houston moved out to the left. Walsh put in a cross kick which Hennie Van Zyl* fumbled with a "leisurely contempt" to let Kiernan pick up and score by the posts to give himself an easy conversion. Just to show they were still running the game their way, the Springboks finished off with another try by Ben Piet Van Zyl, carved out by Piet Uys*. Afterwards we all agreed that if the Springboks had played like this on the tour, they would have been cheered off every ground in the four Home Countries.

Most onlookers in the months and years afterwards, and still to this day, say that the one marked shortcoming of Ireland's short tour of South Africa in 1961 was the actual timing of the test match. It was generally felt that we would have provided much better opposition if we had been given ten days to find our feet in a couple of games against provincial sides. As it was, we went down highly praised in defeat, winning all round acclamation for our determination to carry out the 'open rugby' policy advocated by Noel Murphy Senior. Without exception the players would have preferred to have played the international as their final fixture, despite the obvious risk of prior injuries, but we were informed that the decision to opt for the test first was made in an effort to avoid further weakening a team that had already been deprived of its usual centre and winger, due to the players' exam commitments in Ireland.

Once the test match was over, the team was to be known as the Shamrocks for the remaining three matches against provincial sides. Despite all those who advised us not to be discouraged by that Saturday's result, there was still a lot of talk about the wisdom of opening this short tour with a test match. However, there was more work to be done, further matches awaited and, looking forward to gathering some happy memories, there was a buzz of excitement in the camp as we set out on the next part of our trip.

* * *

The first of the Shamrocks' matches was to be in Cape Province near the middle of South Africa's southern coastline. On the Wednesday following that defeat by the Springboks, a 75-minute, early morning flight from Capetown, in two Dakota airplanes, brought us to a lovely little town called Oudtshoorn. It was a good road journey inland from Mossel Bay[75], where the second game of the tour, against South-Western Districts was to be played.

From the airport our entire party was whisked away to visit the famous Cango Caves, reportedly in a valley more beautiful than anything even the hills of Kerry have to offer. The tour guide rattled on a bit about the local agriculture in

75 All descriptions of Mossel Bay are from V. M. Fitzroy, Mossel Bay Official Guide (W. J. Flesch & Partners, Cape Town.)

Cape Province, the western part of which is seemingly famed for its wine industry. Fruit growing is a flourishing industry throughout the country and forms a valuable part of their exports with large quantities of fresh grapes exported annually.

We heard about the Karoo, which formed the greater part of the Cape Province, and vast stretches of South West Africa which had a very small rainfall. It's a far cry from my usual, mundane, day-to-day work in a Certified Accountants office in Limerick. What a different world from the one I lived in. Except for the sheep, of course. They looked slightly familiar! She went on to mention the wealth of wild animal life in South Africa, one of its foremost tourist attractions. Some of the lads said they hoped to tour at least one of the game parks, but I was just bursting for a pint.

No such luck! Before the 56 mile drive over the mountains to Mossel Bay, the group visited one of the biggest ostrich farming centres in the world. We were all fascinated by the animals but the heat and the smell was a bit overcoming. Noel Murphy Junior took a seat on the back of one of the more docile birds and I saw the hefty figure of Syd Millar standing on an ostrich egg without breaking it[76]. Later I examined an empty shell and was surprised to see how robust it was. The local native curio carvers had engraved pictures onto the surface of some of the shells and were trying to sell them. I watched while Tom Kiernan and Gordon Wood tried to out-bargain one of these men but all to no avail.

The trip from Oudtshoorn, through George and a pleasant river valley reminded me a bit of home. As we travelled towards Mossel Bay, we got our first opportunity to take in some of the unforgettably beautiful African scenery. Pints forgotten for a while, I could see, even on this short journey, that this part of the world deserved its reputation.

The tour guide was describing it as a commanding country, immense, majestic, exciting.... a place of ageless significance. A bit over the top you might think but I could see what she meant. As I gazed out the window of the coach, she told us a bit about its chequered history, but emphasised that throughout all that time man had not succeeded in dimming its beauty. We heard that since the nearby Cape of Good Hope was discovered originally in 1486, there had been many struggles, from the first Dutch settlers who landed at the Cape in 1652, to the 1688 French Huguenot refugees. She touched on the tribulations of the 1820 British settlers, the history of the Voortrekkers who began their epic 'trek' from the Cape in 1836 and the discovery of diamonds in 1866. There followed the discovery of gold in 1886, the struggle for independence by the Transvaal and Orange Free State Republics at the turn of the century and the formation of the Union in 1910. It was a fascinating history but one which seemed to ignore the

76 'Champagne Shamrocks' Peter McMullan, *Rugby World*, August 1961. Charles Buchan's Publications Ltd., p. 27.

native African story. Although the team had not been exposed too much to the apartheid system, I was very aware of it since my first sight of the "Whites Only" signs at Johannesburg airport.

We were knackered by the time we approached Mossel Bay. Between the heat, the tiredness, the lingering disappointment of losing the test match and the, by now, interminable drone of the tour guide, I thought I'd never reach my destination to freshen up and have a drink. I'd have settled for a long cool drink of water at this stage.

We all brightened up a bit, on the last lap of our journey, when the smell of the ocean greeted us. The air felt cooler: there was a pleasant breeze in Mossel Bay. My initial impression of the town was that it was bright and welcoming. Most of the buildings had a yellow hue and they all backed on to a deeply-contrasting, blue sea. The place had a hilly aspect with a neat little harbour filled with small, interesting boats. In some ways it reminded me of Carrick, but in others it couldn't have been more different. There was a wide sweeping coastline, of which the guide (finally!) pointed out Knysna Heads, the furthermost point, out on the horizon to the east.

Thankfully, the booking-in procedure was dealt with very quickly at our hotel and, after some quick refreshment a gang of us headed off into town to explore. Armed with our little guide books, we found the ornamental gateway to the local park looking up at the rare type of Australian Flame trees, unfortunately not in bloom at the time of our visit. Marsh Street is full of shops and businesses. It's very colourful in its display of window boxes and shrub containers, all painted uniformly in a bright yellow.

We discovered that the local stone was used for most public and private buildings and they were roofed with corrugated iron, painted red or green, the likes of which were not too familiar to the men from the four provinces of Ireland. Pleasant sunshine and cool sea breezes enticed us towards the ocean. The locals were friendly, smiling at us and wishing us luck for the following day. We were amazed at the 'natives' touching their hats and bobbing their heads in greeting. We headed out the Point Road towards the lighthouse of St. Blaize, passing the war memorial on the rocky headland that guarded the bay at its southwestern extremity. Finding a spot where the rocks made a glorious playground, and hid a spot where two of the largest reefs were set wide apart to form a lovely pond, we decided to go for a dip.

Seemingly this inlet was known as the Poort, one of the finest natural bathing pools in the world. A sheltered, safe spot for anyone who could swim, a few of us ventured into the water. With its lovely depth and walls of living rock, one small bit of built-up wall formed a bridge from one side to the other. The water flowed freely, however, so that the sea surged in from one end of the pool and out at the other. Nowadays people are all so well travelled they may take such sights for granted, but to me, a young Irish man of that time, it seemed like heaven on earth. I could feel the disappointment of my non-selection for the international slipping into the back of my mind as I slid into the water.

I went on to splash around in the mild water of the Indian Ocean, sometimes tipping the lovely sandy bottom of the pool with my toes. This was one of the highlights of my entire trip (off the field). The breakers were thundering and pounding a stone's throw away from me, sending up spray showers, but I was well protected from that rough commotion by the surrounding walls of rock. Would that life in general had been so kind to me.

One of the non-swimmers came back to tell us that he had been exploring. He said that he had gone down to the lighthouse, to see the edge of the cavern known locally as Bats' Cave, silhouetted against the sky, and (supposedly) looking a bit like Gladstone's profile. However, he didn't venture as far as the floor of the cave still deep in mussel shells, or dare to enter the area where, it was said, bats still hung in festoons from the cave's rocky roof and walls.

After our swim, we sampled the hospitality of the Poort Restaurant under the lighthouse. It had a shipboard atmosphere, and was under the personal supervision of two wonderful ladies called Miss Fish and Miss Brown. They indulged our taste for some light refreshments and advised us to follow that up with a spot of souvenir shopping in places where we had choices as varied as ostrich and springbok leather goods, down to feather dusters.

"Not much Connemara marble here," I heard a comment, to laughter from my other companions. I eyed out a leather foot-pouffe for my mother but was so undecided as to whether or not to buy it that the lads went on ahead of me.

They were at Bland Street, past the harbour, beyond the Railway Station and approaching the Yachting Club by the time I caught up with them, breathless. After a short rest, we went on towards the colourful and sunlit Santos Beach. It was absolutely beautiful. A curve of dull gold sand was set off beautifully by the turquoise sea. A little paradise where people could swim, surf and laze around in the summer months. It was a bit cold for the locals and other holidaymakers the day of our visit, but we thought the weather was gorgeous, just like a good summer's day at home. Going up Grave Street, we came across a little stream. A local man, who was sitting nearby, told us that this stream had given fresh water to those thirsty sailors of long ago, and had never yet run dry in all the time since. It had been recently enclosed in a stone catchment to protect it from 'progress', and it was feared that this might result in its eventual loss beneath paving stones and tarmac. Our new friend (Anthony he said his name was) then pointed out the white, square-set Police Station in the distance, and told us it was due to be torn down in the near future. It had been built for utility in 1861, of sound, simple proportions and at the time of our visit it still stood in a commanding position on the high side of Marsh Street, looking out to sea, its sturdy walls adding character to the town.

As Anthony fell into step beside us, we moved beyond the stream towards a stretch of lawn. He was directing us towards one of the oldest living things in Africa, known locally as the Post Office Tree. It was an old milkwood tree which had been there for over 500 years and he filled us in on its history. Already a sizable tree when Diaz[77] sailed into the bay, it was said that a few years later, Jaoa da Nova[78] left letters there in a sea-boot dangling from its branches. It was a little thicker around the trunk when the port's name was changed from the Portuguese Aguada de Sao Bras to the Dutch Mossel Baai in 1602. Many notable people in history availed of the shade it offered, and some less notable such as the ordinary wagoners of 18th century, who brought their wheat from inland farms for shipping to Batavia. Fishermen, whalers and oystermen all knew this tree. It had seen the rise of the ostrich feather and aloe industries, the opening of the railway, the arrival of buses, the oil refinery, the power station, speed boats and now a group of Irish rugby players were standing at its gnarled feet, its foliage still green and vigorous after all that time.

Before we parted company, Anthony told us that Mossel Bay was Southern Africa's first port of call, visited by the Portuguese in 1487, and early visitors from Europe, approaching by the sea, found shelter on that lovely beach under a hillside on which aloes and milkwood trees made a frieze against the skyline. Finally, he said that the first trade between white man and black man took place at Mossel Bay, when Vasco da Gama[79] bartered a bull from a Hottentot tribe, in exchange for a red sailor cap. I looked over my shoulder, for one last glance towards the sea, and when I turned back Anthony was gone.

---

77 Captain Bartholomew Diaz, the Portuguese explorer, who named the most southerly tip of Africa as the Cape of Good Hope.

78 Admiral Jaoa de Nova, the Portuguese explorer who is said to have discovered Mossel Bay. He also discovered the Ascension Islands and St. Helena Island.

79 Vasco da Gama, the Portuguese explorer who was attempting a voyage around Africa to find a route by sea to India. His ships rounded the Cape of Good Hope in November 1497.

Scrummaging

The team for the following day's match against Western Districts was due to be announced later that evening, and I hoped my name would be included. Although I knew I'd missed another opportunity to gain an Irish cap, by not being named in the test match, my disappointment gave way to excitement as I headed for the team talk in beautiful Mossel Bay. After all, I had captained Munster against Avril Malan's Springboks not long before.

It was generally felt that this fixture would give the Shamrocks a chance to find their feet, for South-Western Districts were reputedly the weakest provincial side in the country at that time. But, as this judgement was by the current South African standards, the team knew it would be far from a walkover. It was not looked on it as an easy game because the Districts put up a good show against the All Blacks not too long before. While the Irish were aware that the Districts finished bottom in the last Currie Cup Tournament, they also knew that many touring teams in the past found that it was wrong to underestimate the weaker South African provincial teams.

Eventually it was announced:

> All the players who were not included in the Irish team beaten by South Africa in the International at Capetown on Saturday will be in action tomorrow, plus Niall Brophy, wing three-quarter of the 1959 Lions who joined the Shamrocks party on Sunday.[80]

My heart took a jump. My chest puffed out just a little bit. My battered self-esteem got a well-deserved boost when I got the nod on South African soil.

And so the talk and planning began. Most agreed that the Districts had two fast wings in Horne and Sefrontein, but it would be too much to expect them to outpace Tony O'Reilly and Niall Brophy, one on either side to round off the open game, while John Dooley and Jerry Walsh should give us the advantage at centre. It was well known that the opposition had a mobile pack; although light by South African standards, the average weight was just over 14 st. 4 lb. So the Shamrocks expected to have a weight advantage in the scrum, but we knew that Jimmy Dick*, in his first game of the tour, would be up against a fine hooker in Ben Piet Van Zyl.

---

80 'Hewitt forced to cry off' *Irish Press Special* (no date on press cutting in suitcase).

The personality of the opposing side was known as Bruce Lynn, a No. 8, who made the Junior Springbok trials for the Aussies tour two years previously. For the next day's game, I noted that the Districts' side's scrum-half would be Geldenhuys, who had never played in senior rugby of any kind. Also playing was Koos Dotoit, the former Boland centre.

Gerry Tormey[81], brought into the Irish party when Mick English was forced to withdraw with an injured calf muscle, was named at out-half. Tormey was out-half partner to my own brother Gerry at scrum-half on the Dental Hospital team at this time so I was familiar with his style of play. I was in no doubt that we would 'click' as a partnership. More importantly, the management team felt confident that, with me at scrum-half, Gerry would have good service. One disappointment was that John Hewitt, who was to have captained the Irish team, was forced to withdraw after testing his injured knee. Hewitt received the injury in the previous Saturday's test match against South Africa and had been having treatment for fluid on the knee. Tom Kiernan, who excelled in the international, was named to play at fullback instead, and front row forward, Syd Millar, received the honour of captaining the Irish side. The Shamrocks plan was to play another fast open game, an exhibition style match, where we would throw the ball about as much as possible, letting our forwards get on top early in the game, with a weight advantage of about 7 lbs. a man. With Gerry Culliton, Syd Millar and Niall Brophy in the pack, we expected to beat the Districts forwards and give the backs all the chances. As we left the team talk to prepare for an early night, and by now feeling more rested, we all knew in our hearts that we had it in us to register the first victory of this South African tour in the beautiful Mossel Bay, Cape Province.

That night while sleeping in my hotel room, having had a bath in warm, soft, amber-coloured water, I dreamt of an Irish victory, and a trophy in the shape of an enormous tree, delivered by a beautiful woman on a surfboard, who spoke directly to me in breathy tones... and as she said "welcome to Seth Efricah, Thom" I turned over in my cosy bed and descended into a peaceful slumber.

* * *

After shaping like comfortable winners in the first half, following a good dribbling rush putting us early on the attack, we had to play for all we were worth to beat a spirited South-Western Districts side before a crowd of about 5,000. The

81 Interestingly, Gerry Tormey had been Leinster out-half to Tom's brother, Gerry (Ref. 1), who played at scrum-half in the schools inter-provincial matches in 1957. They were also the half-back partnership on the Dental Hospital rugby team for three years around the time Tom went to South Africa. Although compared to a young Jack Kyle in the September 1961 issue of Rugby World, and tipped as a key individual in Ireland's future international planning, Tormey, like Tom, did not gain the ultimate distinction of a cap for Ireland.

final score was 11-6. It was the first international rugby visit to Mossel Bay for 51 years so the build-up and level of excitement was huge. The crowd was at fever pitch during the second half due to the close nature of the game and there was a real buzz about the place. On the whole, we demonstrated greater activity and speed behind the scrum than our opponents. We led eight points to nil at half-time, and overall scored a goal, a penalty goal and a dropped goal to two penalty goals. Kiernan contributed eight of those points in an outstanding game at full-back, with an easy penalty, a touchline conversion of hooker Jimmy Dick's try and, just before time, a drop goal from a five-yard scrum. The opposition's penalties were goaled by the No. 8, Bruce Lynn, with a sensational start to the second half when he made a kick from just inside the half-way, and with 17 minutes to go, following an incident in the lineout, Koos Hanekom scored a goal from the 25, near touch.

Jimmy Dick scored the only try of the game when myself and flank forward Noel Murphy (Junior), combined in a clever move from a set scrum, and out-hooked Philip van Zyl. It was magic! I was chuffed with that move and the resulting score. And at the lineouts Ian Dick and Gerry Culliton gave Ireland the advantage, though Strydom worked hard in this department also. Jim Thomas, that tough mauling forward, displayed his useful knack of dispossessing at the lineout, and kept himself busy as a prop who now and then also showed a fair turn of speed.

There was much local excitement when Hanekom kicked his penalty to make the score 8-6 in the 24th minute of the second half and the result was in doubt almost up to the final whistle. The great pace of the game and the fact that the Irish were prepared to attack from their own half added to the general excitement. Afterwards, my move in picking up well from the wheeled scrum and passing to Murphy was acknowledged as the making of Dick's splendid try. And Tom Kiernan's steal of a drop goal, from my pass out of a scrum at the posts, three minutes from time, was another brilliant move that allowed the entire team to breathe easier in the closing moments.

I'd be the first to admit that it was far from being an exceptional game because of numerous handling mistakes but the Shamrocks were much the more enterprising side and fully deserved to win. The excellent defensive work of the South Western Districts men, with their tenacious tackling and covering, was all that kept them in the game with a chance. In this respect, the performances of Nortje at centre and Lynn at No. 8 stood out. The South Western backs, who saw far less of the ball, hardly had a single line movement, but the value of fly-half Barnard's strong kicking with both feet in driving the tourists back, was a considerable factor in the home team's respectable performance.

Afterwards, some observers felt that Gerry Tormey proved a better fly-half than Dion Glass had done in Saturday's test. However, personally, I felt that the line still lacked a bit of punch, though once it was only a great cover-tackle by

Lynn that stopped Walsh on the corner flag. I was very pleased with my own game as I left the Mossel Bay sports field off Van Riebeck Street. I knew I had substituted ably for Mulligan. But deep in my heart I realised that, at the end of the day, it wouldn't make much difference to the scrum-half position, in the grand scheme of Irish rugby.

Although the reports in the next day's newspapers were favourable, the forecasts were not good. Many were of the opinion that, judging by the form in the Mossel Bay match and despite our win, there was reason to doubt whether the tourists had the capacity to beat Western Transvaal or Rhodesia.

The next day, Thursday, we found ourselves travelling once more. Firstly, by coach for 30 minutes, then we boarded two Port Elizabeth-bound aircraft at George, for a nine hour journey, with a whole series of stops from there, to Johannesburg. The Shamrocks were due to stay in the 'golden' metropolis, at the Carlton Hotel in Eloff Street (nowadays referred to as the Old Carlton, it was a great rendezvous point in those days) until Friday night so that we could fit in some shopping. My school friend Paddy O'Byrne was living in South Africa at that time and we met at the hotel for a few jars and a bit of craic. While other members of the team were off promoting various business opportunities or recommending Ireland as a tourist destination,[82] I was more interested in socialising and renewing old acquaintances. It wasn't long before Paddy had me singing my old favourite Alice Faye song, despite the fact that we hadn't met for 13 years. A certain tune about a little yellow bird had an outing that night too. It was late when I eventually hit the sack.

The following day I dropped in to visit my father's brother, Michael,[83] who was resident in the city's very comfortable Rand Club. A bachelor, he had been a Chief Superintendent in the Indian Police and was the holder of a King's Police medal. He retired to South Africa some years previously, when someone told him the climate there would ease the crippling pain of his arthritis. The reality that he was more likely to have servants in South Africa than in the Carrick of the 1950s helped focus his mind, I'm sure.

It was a very colonial looking club. Men only. I introduced myself to the broadly smiling concierge, who politely directed me to a seat while he padded off at a leisurely pace to call my uncle. I felt I was stepping back in time as I waited in the lounge for his arrival and I noted all the stuffed heads of wild beasts that adorned the walls. And then I saw him. Although he was the youngest member of that generation, he looked like an older version of my father in many ways. As he shuffled along slowly, I moved towards him, hand outstretched. He had been expecting my visit and seemed pleased to see me.

"Nice to see you, my boy," he said, taking my hand in both of his and holding

---

82 Andy Mulligan and Tony O'Reilly had recently founded an import-export market research business together. Ref. 'Handy Andy', Denzil Batchelor, *Rugby World*, May 1961, pp. 9-11.

83 Michael (Ref. 1)

it warmly for a few moments. "Welcome to the most comfortable place one can live in," he said as he waved his arms around expansively.

When we were settled with two, ice-cold, gin and tonics on the table between us he asked about home. I filled him in, as best I could, on the up-to-date details of all the family. He spoke fondly about his sister, Kitty Cheasty, who had died after a long illness a number of years before. We then chatted about the Irish rugby tour. He was very well informed about the team members and had been following the press reports avidly. Then he told me a bit about his own life. Generally he led a very quiet existence, filling up his time playing bridge, reading, listening to the radio and going to the cinema. He sometimes dabbled in stocks and shares, though he failed to make his fortune. He was planning a trip to Natal and the more temperate climate of Maritzburg and said he would be spending the months of June and July there. It sounded like a lonely enough set-up to me, though he assured me he had lots of friends there and wanted for nothing. When the time came for me to leave, he handed me a folded newspaper cutting which he had saved for me. It was taken from the *Cape Argus*, dated Wednesday, the 19th April (3 weeks before my visit) giving a profile of all those on Irish Rugby Union tour of South Africa & Rhodesia, 1961. He wished me well and, telling me never to lose hope, he shook my hand and said farewell.

As I walked away, I was feeling very subdued. The visit had been mere duty really. I could not go home and say I hadn't had a chance to call and see him. I'd never be forgiven. But somehow he had touched me in a way that few people in my life to date had managed. Pity he never married, I thought. I sneaked a look at my pen picture which had been written in Africa a few weeks before we travelled. It took a year off my age but apart from that it was fairly accurate. It read:

> First played for Munster in 1950, captained Bohemians in 1952–53 and Munster inter-provincial team in 1959–60, 1960–61. Played against South Africa for Munster last December. Was in the final trials in 1958/59 but has not yet been capped for Ireland.[84]

Not much to show (on paper at least) for all that effort and supposed glory, is it? It was difficult at times to keep my spirits up. However, I was chuffed that this uncle that I hardly knew still had faith in me after all my time on the fringes and I promised myself I'd keep in touch with him when I got home. (But I never did.)

Making my way back to the hotel, I looked up at the modern skyscrapers, making myself dizzy in the process. Those gins had been served with a heavy hand. The highways of Johannesburg, the likes of which I had never seen before,

84 'Pen-Pictures Of Irish Rugby Team To Tour S.A. Next Month', *The Cape Argus,* April 19th 1961, (no page number on newspaper cutting in suitcase).

made quite an impression on me, despite my travelling experience. I heard afterwards that the new Railway Station had cost something in the region of (at that time, a staggering) £10 million. On my stroll back to the hotel, I saw few traces of the traditional tribal origins of the many people who made up the bulk of the workforce, although I can recall noticing the occasional mineworker wrapped up in his blanket ambling down the street.

Home to a million people, Jo-burg with its mine-dumps (often referred to as 'ant heaps in gold') and great modern buildings was the dynamo of South African industry and commerce. Like a vast complex machine, it was in a perpetual state of high pressure, throbbing, opulent and energetic. A total contrast to the lovely Mossel Bay area. The biggest city in the world not built near a river, lake or sea, it had risen out of the veld in the space of a mere human lifespan. It was only 70 years before my visit that the world's richest reef of gold had been discovered, lying beneath the bleak Witwatersrand (or White Water's Ridge as it was called in English). Prior to that, only lonely jackals had scavenged the area for scraps of food as the occasional lion preyed nearby. It was difficult for us tourists to comprehend that quite suddenly, there was a huge, spread-eagled mining camp of fortune hunters from all over the world who had trekked to the new goldfields of President Paul Kruger's Transvaal Republic. And so soon, to me at least, it seemed to contain touches of the sophistication of other, more established cities – maybe a bit of London's West End, a little of the essence of Bond Street, or Paris and the Rue de la Paix. It seemed to boast as much as, if not more than, those other, more familiar, cities with its own Art Gallery, numerous museums, law courts, memorials, centres of excellence in health and education, and the longest runway in Africa (at 10,500 feet, located at its £6 million Jan Smuts airport, the air gateway to the city). It was some sight to behold for a lad from Carrick.

Our next match was to be on Saturday in Potchefstroom,[85] where we were due to meet a Western Transvaal side. However, some of the snags of a short tour involving four games were beginning to show and the team was getting little opportunity to rest. The Shamrocks had very little time to treat casualties. At this stage of the tour, Ron Kavanagh had a bruised heel, Tim McGrath a badly blistered foot and it looked ominously like John Hewitt's game at Newlands was to be his first and last of the tour, as he was receiving ongoing treatment for his damaged knee, on which the fluid was proving difficult to move.

Despite all of this, we continued to prepare for the next match, and the journey to Potchefstroom, which could prove to be the team's greatest challenge yet. At an altitude of 4,600 feet, it was feared that a burst of 25 yards might result in

85 South Africa's Transvaal (South African Tourist Corporation) describes this venue as the oldest town in the Transvaal. Founded by the voortrekker leader Potgieter in 1838.

laboured breathing in the fittest. Add to that a forecast temperature of 75 degrees in blazing sunshine and we knew this could prove to be some contest. Andy Mulligan was called up once more for this match, much to my disappointment, but I rallied behind the team and supported it in every way I could.

On the day of the match I was pleased to see that further effort had been put into preparing a souvenir programme. Another item for my suitcase. I was gathering quite a little bundle of souvenirs at this stage. It was a fairly substantial booklet, the cover of which was in the green, white and orange colours of the two teams. The crest consisted of a sheaf of yellow corn on the cob, while the inevitable shamrock was given a nice twist as it rose from a wide road surrounded by buildings and clouds. A symbol of the team's journey thus far, I presumed. There was a welcome message from the President of the Western Transvaal Rugby Union, Mr. Bosman, written in both languages.

It was strange for me to see my own profile in Afrikaans, on page seven, where I was listed as the Skrumskakel. I noticed that they were still taking a year off my age. Maybe that was no harm, I decided. My photo on page 14 was half profile with the collar up. I took some slagging from the lads over that pose. Verrrry fashionable, they agreed!

Paddy O'Byrne and a crowd of the lads decided to travel from Johannesburg to our next match. They chartered a bus and, just as well because I'll tell you what, if any of them had to drive home that day there would have been 20 or 30 corpses on the side of the road. After quite a few bevies at the Impala Hotel before the match, they arrived at the ground – Olen Park – a lovely place, with blue gum trees all around. They immediately headed for the opposition dressing room where, the renowned captain at that time of Western Transvaal and of South Africa, Johann Claassen, was leading his team members in prayer. Paddy was the spokesman for the group of Irish supporters and he went up to tell the captain that he wanted a nice open game, and advised the team to get the ball out to the wings. They were looked at with mingled resentment and contempt before being ushered away back to their places in the stand by a burly bunch of stern-faced security men.

The outcome of this third match was a morale and prestige-boosting win, a triumph for the tactical brilliance of Ronnie Dawson and the result of a tremendous all-round improvement in the work of the lads, regardless of the clinging, clammy heat at that elevation. Despite my personal disappointment at being consigned to watch once more from the sideline, I was happy with the result. We beat one of the mightiest packs in South Africa, led by test skipper Johann Claassen in his greatest form. Our leader, Ronnie Dawson, managed to play for three quarters of the game despite being in intense pain from badly torn ligaments in his right wrist. Noel Murphy Junior was taken off for treatment for five minutes in the first half, but he limped gamely through the remainder of the match with a nasty twist of his right ankle. Despite these setbacks the team brought off a notable, clear-cut win against a side which had beaten both the Lions and the Barbarians on their last visits.

The Irish lineout was excellent. My good pal Bill Mulcahy and team-mate Ian Dick were up against Claassen at six feet four inches and almost 17 stone, and 'Tiny' Pretorious, the biggest forward in South Africa at six feet six inches and nearly 18 stone. Yet, through the supremely efficient working of a system we had practised diligently and which involved the vital co-operation of Ron Kavanagh and Gerry Culliton, Shamrocks got the ball back 24 times to the Transvaal side's 23.

Mulcahy's marking of Claassen was terrific. So was much of Dick's individual effort. And Kavanagh was still going better than any man on the field at the end of those exhausting, energy-sapping 80 minutes. The backs too deserved a share of the credit. Most observers said that this was by far the best game Tony O'Reilly had played on tour. His try, three minutes from the end, was a model of how to capitalise on the standoff half kick to the wing. Gerry Tormey who also had a good game, placed his punt perfectly. Andy Mulligan varied his game cleverly and worked a dropped goal for Tom Kiernan with a brilliant feint.

The magnificent Kiernan (whom everyone in South Africa, by now, hoped they would see the following year with the Lions) had a personal haul of ten points, making a total of 26 out of the 35 the tourists had scored in the three games so far. Again Shamrocks experienced a little referee trouble. A South African official completely missed a mark by Mulcahy which cost the Irish the one try they conceded, and he further mystified us by disallowing what looked like a perfectly good dropped goal by Ken Houston. Fortunately, it didn't matter this time.

Afterwards, the South African critics blamed the Western Transvaal backs for the defeat. Apparently, they had not stopped to consider how much their performance was governed by the way Dawson skilfully dictated the course of the game, and how magnificently his plans were carried out by his men. This was not always an attractive game to watch, but a win for the Irish was important both for our own spirit and the success of the final game yet to come at Salisbury[86] in Rhodesia. Dawson who, allegedly had no time for pious phrases like "the game is the thing and the result unimportant", was determined to win and had laid his plans accordingly. He got immense credit for doing so, and for his personal example in playing while plainly suffering agony from his damaged wrist.

The day after the match against Western Transvaal, still in high spirits following that decisive win, we were treated to a trip to the East Rand Proprietary Mines[87] for a demonstration of their tribal dance routine, courtesy of the mine

86 Now Harare.

87 All descriptions of mine dances taken from East Rand Proprietary Mines Ltd. Tribal Dances, Brochure. The display was presented by African employees of E. R. P. M. Ltd.

management. At the start of proceedings when we were all seated, an official outlined the rules of admission as listed in the pink programme.

Admission to the dance was free, but refreshments were on sale to raise funds for charity. He stated that the dance was organised primarily in the interest of the native workers, and European visitors were present only by courtesy of the management, which reserved the right of admission. Some of the lads laughed out loud when he requested that ladies be suitably dressed, but a stern look from Noel Murphy Senior silenced them quickly enough.

The official continued with his introduction.

"Abbreviated shorts are not considered suitable for women on these occasions," he droned on to suppressed giggles from the back row.

"Visitors are not permitted on the dance floor and although photographers are welcome, they are requested not to interfere with the dancers or obstruct the view of other members of the audience." He continued, "In no circumstances should coins be thrown to the dancers."

What did they take us for?

He next announced that in no case should any of the dances be termed "war dances"; few of the dances retained any special meaning, but, he said, all were still enjoyed as a recreation, and on festive occasions by the workers.

"Visitors are not allowed into any other part of the compound unless accompanied by a European official." the official ended triumphantly.

The mine we attended consisted of four compounds, with approximately 50 dance teams representing 18 different tribes. The teams were organised and encouraged by the Mines' Welfare department and the company supplied all the equipment and costumes. We were told that an inter-tribal dance display was held every month, each time in a different compound. Consequently, over a period of time all of the teams got the opportunity to perform. However, today's display was a special Sunday 'Invitation' Dance, where up to 15 teams would be actively engaged in the dancing and not all were from this mine.

Every team in the compound was allocated a Sunday on which to hold a dance and they then invited up to five teams of their own tribe from various other mines to dance competitively with them. In their turn they were invited back to other compounds, with the transport being provided free by the mines. Can you even begin to imagine what this experience was like for a bunch of 'youngish' Irish lads? At first we were amazed, ...then surprised, ... some seemed fascinated, ... but by the time it was over, I must admit I felt a bit bored. Less would have done me.

First up were the Pondo Tribe. The programme informed the us that they were from Cape Province and found mostly near the coast north of Umtata. The visitors were treated to a type of line dance, performed to their own peculiar music rhythms and, at the end, all the dancers completed the routine by turning and crouching at the same time. This display was followed in speedy succession by other tribes whose names I could hardly pronounce such as, the Yanganyika, the Pondomise, the Ramakhobotle and the 'Ndau from Portuguese East Africa; and finally the Zulu Tribe from Natal came on before the break.

The Zulu Tribal music comprised a combination of singers, hand clapping and drums, seemingly copied from the British forces during the Zulu wars. They were dressed in coloured skirts, bead necklaces and calf-hide aprons, called betshu. Sticks and legs were decorated with angora goatskin. The dance they performed originated in Durban about 50 years previously and was based on a similar one performed in the country by both men and girls. After the shouting of the clan cries, the team leader first performed alone, then called the others to join him by stamping his foot. They went on to complete two routines, called Iqulu, which they concluded by falling to the ground.

At the tea interval we were reminded that proceeds from the sale of refreshments would be donated to charitable institutions. I bought a few minerals and a sticky bun. As mine management circulated among the men who had triumphed over the mighty Western Transvaal the previous day, their talk turned to rugby and bravery on the field. Very little discussion took place on the exhibition we had just witnessed.

The Bachopi Tribe took to the floor at the start of the second half. The orchestra of xylophones (timbila) performed in five pitches, from treble to double bass, accompanied by rattles and occasional drumbeats. The dancers appeared in their traditional dress of lemon yellow loincloths and jackal skin capes, carrying shields, sticks and wooden spears. They performed a dance called the mchopi ngodo, the most complex of all Southern African dances, performing it in about nine movements. The climax of the performance occurred when the dancers advanced towards the orchestra and sang in a haunting natural harmony, which they must have learned in their faraway homelands.

These were followed by tribes such as the Shangaan Makwaya, the Xhosa from Cape Province, the Baca from Umzimkulu in the Cape and Natal Provinces, and finally the Zingili Tribe performed. By now, the dancers were all beginning to look the same to me. I was getting restless in my seat. To me, these latest dances and traditional dress looked the same as the Zulu dancers who had performed earlier. The accompanying music consisted of drums, cymbals, clappers and one flute, but there were no singers this time. The dance leader directed the drummers with actions, and the dancers by whistling. At this stage, all of the boys were shifting around in their seats.

And then it was over. I was looking forward to a few pints after all that. Idly, I wondered if the referee would have missed the mark, had the tribes been playing in the match the previous day!

* * *

Our fourth and final match was to be played four days later in Salisbury, the capital of the Federation of Rhodesia and Nyasaland in Central Africa, another city which was barely 70 years in existence. It was quite a bit closer to the Equator than South Africa and felt fairly warm to us boys. On Tuesday, 23rd May, His Worship, the Mayor of Salisbury, Councillor Dennis Divaris, hosted a civic luncheon in honour of the visiting team at the Grand Hotel. The delights on offer included Fillet of Kingklip, Mornay and Baba Marignan. I tasted everything on the menu. It was a grand affair, in a beautiful setting, all served to us by a bevy of native waiters. Their attention to detail was unbelievable.

The next day I bought an enormous, colourful map of the area.[88] It detailed how the Federation was one of the largest British States in Africa and consisted of Southern Rhodesia,[89] Northern Rhodesia[90] and Nyasaland.[91] It covered a total area of 485,000 square miles and had a population of almost eight million. When the population was broken down, the majority were African, a mere 300,000 European, and 35,000 Asian and mixed race. In the same way as it had been during our time in South Africa, we were to see, almost exclusively, the European or 'white' side of life throughout the latter part of our visit also.

Nyasaland was the most densely populated of the three regions, while Northern Rhodesia was the most thinly populated. The Federation was inaugurated eight years previously, in 1953, and the Queen was represented by the Governor-General, assisted by a cabinet of eight members drawn from the Federal Assembly of 59 members. The main functions of the Federal Government at the time related to external affairs, defence, immigration, finance and economic affairs, inter-territorial roads, railways, airways, European agriculture, posts and telegraphs and education (other than primary and secondary education for Africans). Mining was the basis of the Federation's economy, particularly copper mining in Northern Rhodesia which had a very rich copper belt north of its capital city, Lusaka.

Agriculturally, the Federation was self-supporting in most basic foodstuffs. In the field of secondary industry, there had been a very marked increase in the number and variety of factories (especially in Southern Rhodesia), which had been established since World War Two. Notable examples were the iron, steel and engineering industries, cotton spinning and weaving, the manufacture of textiles and food processing. The principal exports were copper, tobacco, asbestos, gold, chrome, ore, tea, zinc, lead, textiles and cotton goods.

Further long journeys beckoned for the Shamrocks and despite sore and tired muscles, we packed our suitcases for onward travel. We had heard talk of proposed visits to the Kariba Dam, Bulawayo and other places of interest, but all

88 Geographical Map (Federal Information Department. Salisbury, 1955.)
89 Now Zimbabwe.
90 Now Zambia.
91 Now Malawi.

tour members agreed that one excursion not to be missed, apart from the match itself, would be the outing to Victoria Falls, Central Africa's premier tourist attraction.

I made the most of the last days of my wonderful African expedition and enjoyed all that was offered. On the social side, we were very well received yet again when we arrived in the heart of the Rhodesian veld and I enjoyed all the outings and the inevitable craic which accompanied them.

The hotels were very modern and comfortable,[92] with beautifully appointed bedrooms, excellent cuisine and spaciously luxurious public rooms. Most of them had a laundry service which was invariably one of my first services to use on arrival. What a facility. They had our clothes returned to us in twelve hours. A far cry from having to write to my mother asking her to send some on! I developed a liking for refreshments such as a bottle of cold Caste lager, served straight from the fridge, in the residents' private air-conditioned cocktail bar. It was advertised as being "full of flavour, the friendliest, most satisfying beer" but to me, it just didn't come close to my favourite tipple, Guinness.

* * *

The journey from Salisbury to Bulawayo brought us through, or close to, some towns with interesting names and histories.[93] I heard about places such as Que Que (pronounced 'kwekwe',). In the early days, both Mziligazi and Lobengula tribes had cattle posts in this district; and as a result of diseases such as rinderpest and scab, which wiped out most of the beasts on occasions, the area became known as the country of the scab or mange ('ilizwe lweiskwekwe') which evolved into the abbreviated version on the tourists' map. As we progressed towards our destination, African sounding names such as Makwiro sat side by side with the English names such as Hartley, named after the man who discovered gold in this area. Our guide pointed out the signpost 20 miles from Gwelo, for the place called Hunters Road, and told us that it was the famous road used by the pre-pioneer hunters.

Bulawayo, the second largest city in the territories, was located in the area selected by Lobengula, the last of the Matabele kings, for his personal kraal. The Government House, designed by Sir Herbert Baker[94], stood on the site which was at the end of Lady Stanley Avenue (sometimes called Victoria Falls Road).

---

92 Gateway To Central Africa, *Union Of South Africa Travel Digest*, 1960. Wallachs P. & P. Co. Ltd., Pretoria and 'Bulawayo

93 'Sign Posts Of The Rhodesian Veld – The Origin Of Names- Gwelo To Salisbury Isibindi', *Africa Calls From Rhodesia And Nyasaland*, 1961. Rhodesia And Nyasaland Tourist Board, pp. 42 – 43.

94 Sir Herbert Baker (1862-1946) was an English architect who worked for many years in Africa. He was knighted in 1926 and was awarded the Royal Institute of British Architects' Royal Gold Medal for Architecture in 1927.

Bulawayo was generally interpreted as having derived from 'bulala', to kill, and referred to incidents in Matabele history and to a place in Zululand, with which the Matabele were originally associated. It had been conferred with the honour of the title 'city' as recently as 1943, 50 years after being occupied by the Pioneer Columns, following the Matabele War. It stood astride the three main lines of communication – road, rail and air – between the North and South African subcontinents, and was especially favoured for its geographical position as an industrial, commercial and tourist centre. It was the ideal place from which to plan our ongoing tours.

As we were driven through the streets of the city we observed the large untitled statue, of Rhodes[95] himself, at the north-facing intersection between Eighth Avenue and Main Street. We were shown the War Memorial on the west side of Main Street, between Selborne and Eighth Avenues. It was an interesting cloister, built in Pasipas sandstone with a rough monolith of Matopo granite as a central feature. The names of the fallen in the two World Wars were inscribed on the walls. There were many other monuments located nearby, such as the Rebellion Memorial, erected in memory of the civilians and soldiers killed in the Matabele Rebellion, the Lendy Memorial, an obelisk in memory of another war commander, and the Colenbrander Memorial, dedicated to what our guide described as "one of Southern Africa's foremost frontiersmen". We were told there was a memorial to a Matabele Chief also, but it was out on the old Gwanda Road, 14 miles away to the south of the city, on the site of his kraal at Mhlahladela, where he had died. But we weren't brought to see that.

I examined the Coat of Arms of the Federation on the front of the brochure which rested on my lap wondering what the motto "Magni Esse Mereamur"[96] meant. It was granted by Royal Warrant just seven years before my visit. A wreath of azure, black and white enclosed an angry looking red lion with blue fangs extended. Above the crest a large golden eagle, wings extended, was perched on a silver fish which it had clutched in its talons. On the right hand side stood a spotted leopard, while an equally upright sable antelope kept guard on the opposing side.

* * *

At the time of our visit, the great double curvature concrete arch Kariba Dam project,[97] with its six distinctive floodgates, had recently been completed at an estimated cost of £80 million, and the biggest man-made lake in the world was in

95 Cecil John Rhodes (1853-1902) A prospector and politician, he brought Northern and Southern Rhodesia (now Zambia and Zimbabwe) into the British Empire.

96 "Let us deserve to be great."

97 Kariba – Federation Of Rhodesia And Nyasaland, Federal Power Board, Brochure By Rhoprint – 26343.

the process of being formed. Part of the phased works had involved diversion of the great Zambezi River and exposure of the riverbed. Phase four of the project, which involved proceeding with the final construction of the dam, while keeping ahead of the rising waters, had been completed in June 1959 and already the lake was 175 miles long and up to 20 miles wide.

With the rising of the waters, thousands of the Batonka Tribe[98] who had lived along the northern banks of the Zambezi, and some of the Valley Tonga Tribe from the southern banks, had to be moved away from their traditional homes and re-settled on the plateau, some miles inland from the river valley. At a time of such progress in the white man's world, these tribal people still covered their offspring's' hair in a mixture of red ochre and goat fat, and lived mainly on subsistence farming. Despite an initial outcry at the move, the officials had convinced the tribes that they would be much better off than ever before, telling them they looked sleek, well-fed and healthy and would continue to enjoy this new worry free life, where the Rhodesian Government would occasionally distribute 'gifts' of items such as salt to them. The Irishmen were kept well away from the sight of the practically naked tribal women, smoking their pipes, and gazing nonchalantly out of wide, large eyes perched over high cheekbones.

As I sat on that tour bus, I realised I was approaching the end of my 'so near, but yet so far' experience in Africa and knew that this was it. Even though Andy Mulligan was more than likely approaching the end of his playing career at this level, I accepted that I would probably never play for my country. There was too much talent coming along behind me. I may have missed the boat. This was it.

I kept no mementos of the final match. Rhodesia was beaten 24-0. I didn't play.

98 'British Cabinet Minister Visits The Batonka' Cicely Williams, *Africa Calls From Rhodesia And Nyasaland*, 1961, Salisbury. pp. 8 – 12.

WHEELING

While I was there I heard it said that in every sense South Africa is picture country.[99] From the moment of my arrival on tour in that fabulous part of the world, I witnessed an ever-changing series of pictures. The images of that beautiful country which were impressed most deeply on my mind were the ones I took home with me in the treasure vault of my memory – and it was those which sustained me on many a dark night when I pulled them up from the depths, to remember and enjoy in the years afterwards. I was there.

It was also in South Africa that I experienced a very varied range of emotions. From the initial hope that I might gain a 'proper' cap, to the bitter disappointment and sense of powerlessness when I did not. From the thrill of playing in Mossel Bay to the 'couldn't be bothered with the detail' of the Salisbury encounter. From the quiet joy of swimming in the Indian Ocean to the exciting bustle and activity in the major cities.

The written words, maps, brochures and photographs, which I took home with me in my number seven suitcase, were the only tangible things I had to look at and examine in the more barren years of my life. You can't even begin to imagine the impact this trip had on me... and my life. Whether those words and pictures were captured on canvas, film, paper, or merely in my mind, they were my only reminder that the South African trip was an unforgettable experience for me in so many different ways. These items were more than just a record of me as a sportsman or tourist. I have often tried to explain what this tour actually meant to me. But I was usually so drunk when these feelings bubbled to the surface that nobody wanted to listen to my ramblings. What did it do to me? In many ways it destroyed me. Because all I brought home was a pennant, a silver tankard and some brochures. My decline began the day I landed back on Irish soil with nothing much to show for my trip of a lifetime, except a leather pouffe for my mother, a pair of ornamental wooden elephants and suitcase number seven.

---

99 *South Africa – A Portrait In Colour.* The Simonsberg, Cape, South African Tourist Corporation, Hamilton House, Pretoria, p. 3.

Above: Aerial View of Victoria Falls, Central Africa, November 1982
Below: Cataract View of Victoria Falls, Central Africa, November 1982
From author's own collection of photographs

African sunset
Photograph by Mary Collett (neé Deegan).

Compilation of souvenir images from Tom's suitcase.
Native drawing by Barbara Tyrrell.

KNOCKING-ON

South Africa and Rhodesia were an important part of my journey in life. It was a watershed. What an exciting opportunity for a young man in those days, over 40 years ago, to travel to what seemed like the end of the earth and stand overlooking the spot where the Atlantic and Indian oceans meet. I also stood on the spot where the first trade between white man and black man took place in 1497. I got to spend time in exclusive hotels, the likes of which I had never before experienced. Enormous, spacious places where my every need was easily catered for. I joined the group on tours of places as varied as ostrich farms and gold mines. I was treated to a variety of native dances. I went down underneath the earth into the renowned Cango caves. I swam in the beautiful Indian Ocean. I stood on the brink of the famous mile-wide Victoria Falls and watched as the flood waters of the Zambezi tumbled 350 feet into the gorge below at a rate of 75 million gallons a minute. And I had many laughs on that tour.

I saw huge cities in places where not many years before there had only been a wilderness. I absorbed the history of the place. I experienced first-hand the only crowds, in the world perhaps, to whom rugby was more important than in my beloved Limerick. I represented my country as a 'Shamrock' when the touring side played against one of the provincial teams. Yet, still I came home feeling drained and unfulfilled. I hadn't played in the only international match of the trip. I had no cap.

Although I enjoyed the trip immensely, it was also a time when I also had to finally accept that maybe, I'd never gain the ultimate distinction in Irish rugby. I felt empty. In the modern game, you could perhaps compare my bench experiences with those in the career of Shane Byrne, the current Leinster and Irish hooker:[100]

> ...His late emergence with Ireland is a gripping tale of what can be achieved through unwavering faith. He had many squad call-ups and got to tour far-flung places like Australia and South Africa, but the closest the man with the striking mullet ever got to action was bench duty.

---

100 'It's Crazy, I Was Worried That It Would Never Happen. Now It's Just A Case Of Taking Ireland Games As They Come' Liam Heagney, *Ireland on Sunday*, 6th February 2005, pp. 84-85.

Unlike me though, his luck eventually turned:

> With Wood on Lions duty in 2001, Byrne got back on the Irish bench for the first time in a while and, 66 minutes into what was a meaningless game on a June weekend that doubled up as his stag in Bucharest, the moment he had waited for finally arrived.

In Shane Byrne's own words:

> To put on that Irish jersey is still one of the most special things I can do. The experience is just absolutely awesome. It's crazy (that I've won this many caps); I was so delighted with my first cap as I was very worried that it wasn't going to happen at all. Now it's just a case of taking every game one at a time and to enjoy it to the absolute limit.
>
> But, even now, when you get into that changing room and you see that jersey in front of you, it's still like your first Irish cap. You still get that feeling of the joy of just being there. The standing out there for the national anthems. There's nothing like it. It's a very selfish moment and I find it very calming.

That's the experience I missed out on. I was so close to that thrill, that joy, that selfish, calming moment. Maybe it's ironic, in a strange way, that my ego never got that chance. One of my old Bohemian and Munster friends, Brendan O'Dowd, used to tell me that I was one of the most unselfish men he had ever met.

In Brendan's estimation, I was one of the few seasoned men who always looked out for the welfare of the younger players on the team in Bohemians. Brendan often spoke of the time I cried off an Irish trial due to 'flu. I wasn't sick at all but Bohs were to meet Old Wesley in Donnybrook on the same day as the trial was due to take place and I felt I couldn't let the club down for my own selfish interests. As it turned out I was instrumental in winning the match for Bohs. Just as I was leaving the pitch a reporter told me that if the selectors had seen me playing that day I would have been a cert for the Irish team.

"I wasn't playing today... when you're filing your report name someone else as scrum-half," I said.

And so I possibly lost out by putting the club before myself. That's one count where I have no regrets. I was a true Bohemian.

* * *

I fell in love with one of those beautiful Limerick girls and actually proposed to her. Her identity will remain my secret. That is the one thing I will not reveal. Oh, she's there in the suitcase somewhere. She refused me. Well actually, what she

asked of me in return for her hand in marriage was too tall an order for me – so we both went our separate ways. She said she would marry me if I gave up the booze. But I couldn't do that or she might get to know who I really was – so I broke her heart instead ... and my own into the bargain. I can recall only two occasions in later years when I spoke of this, both on nights I'd had a bellyful. I can't count the number of tear-soaked pillows I have had over the years, when I have cried myself to sleep for the want of her. Just one touch. It was a physical pain; a heartache which never left me. The most heartbreaking part of this particular romance, was that my beloved went on to marry my friend and I was best man at their wedding. Runner-up again. But I can't begin to describe my pain at this particular loss.

I was crushed, flattened, devastated. Even though these feelings came from a choice I made myself, I was affected deeply on emotional, physical and spiritual levels. The uncertainty of my future was compounded by this rejection. This was the time when the foundations of my life began to crumble and my entire world moved out of kilter. For some reason the aria called 'O Silver Moon' from Rusalka (Dvorak) is a very evocative one for me. Whenever I hear it, I am transported back to the days of the love of my life. The story goes that the water nymph, Rusalka, confides her innermost thoughts to the moon. She has fallen in love with a mortal prince and wishes to acquire human form in order to experience the joys of earthly love – even though, should her love prove false, they would both be damned forever. It is a very moving piece and one of the few things that could reduce me to tears in the latter part of my life.

I had many long years to ponder that I had let my self-esteem get so low that I thought the love of my life was only interested in me for my after-dinner speeches and pitch performances. At that stage I thought that if the booze went, these abilities would go too and I couldn't let that happen or she'd see right through me. Foolishly, I decided, she wouldn't like the shy Tom. I truly believed that what she used to call "my gentlemanly ways" and my ability to charm and entertain were dependent on the amount of alcohol I had on board. It had become such a crutch that I felt I could not live without it, even at this relatively early stage of my life.

On top of that, I must admit, the thought of the responsibilities of married life terrified me. I had never taken responsibility for myself, let alone for another person. The prospect of additional dependents, if children came along, paralysed me. I enjoyed visiting Helen or Michael and their families and I adored their children. I loved being an uncle but I didn't particularly want to be a father. Not yet anyway. It was great to be able to hand them back if they wanted anything (other than fun). Maybe it was all too much to think about. Maybe I wanted to remain the eternal child that unfortunately, I eventually became. Oh, how different my life might have been. But sadly, once my proposal was rejected my world began to fall apart.

Mullingar, early 1960s
Back row: Nuala Connolly (neighbour), Helen Kane (Tom's sister)
Front row: Gerard and Ursula Kane (Tom's nephew and niece)

By 1961, I had taken up a position with a third firm of accountants in Limerick, having taken a year out, in between, to work in the family business in Carrick. I had failed my accountancy exams. Aunt Bid's money was running out. My proposal of marriage had been refused and I was best man as she wed my friend. My parents were living on the hallowed ground of my childhood tennis court. My brother John was an ordained priest. Two of my siblings (Helen and Michael) had given me two nieces and two nephews and were getting on with their lives. My baby brother, Gerry, was studying dentistry and soon to be engaged.

But I went a different way. I had found something which changed my life more than any other single thing. For me, alcohol allowed me to hide my shy nature and gave me a voice that was listened to. It gave me the ability to talk. I realised that with a few jars on board, I was able to charm the girls and entertain the boys with a confident patter and gracious manner. They were not to know the low self-esteem that lurked beneath.

Even in latter years I was never sloppy with drink . . . chatty yes, but never sloppy. All my troubles vanished when I drank. With booze, in a hazy delight, I enjoyed short periods of inner peace in my efforts to escape from myself. But, as I discovered, time and time again, the happiness I was seeking wasn't in the bottle or glass. Sadly, it was to be many years before I found out that I already possessed what I sought all that time. Because, as I eventually found out, years later, happiness comes from within.

* * *

I don't have many mementos of my rugby days after the South African trip. At Bohemians, we suffered grievously through injury in the 1962 campaign and they had to replace players such as myself (in my 14th season on the First XV) and Paddy O'Callaghan for the Munster Cup Final against Old Crescent. Bill Mulcahy of Rathkeale was a towering figure in his one full senior season for the club and Seán MacHale*, later to play for Ireland with distinction, was in the front row. The team went on to win that match 8–3 and, as a member of the squad, I received my third Munster medal. Within months of that triumph, many of my mates left Limerick and Bohemians, or married, so the glory days of the boys in red went into decline. And so did I.

The truth was that I had no choice but to leave Limerick. I couldn't keep up the pretence any longer. It was too painful to watch the happy couple. The love of my life was married to my friend and I was left to struggle alone with personal issues such as lack of security, low self-esteem and borderline depression. It was my own fault, but I felt unable to talk about it, so the task of recovery overwhelmed me. Big boys don't cry. The unfortunate result was that my life after Limerick was never as full as it might have been. I was to spend it mostly tripping over shadows.

Tom (back row extreme left) – in the twilight of his career with Bohemians.
Standing; Tom Cleary, Jim O'Brien, Brendan O'Dowd, Johnny Ryan,
Kevin Prdendergast, Johnny Nagle, Bill Mulcahy.
Sitting: Gerry Sheehan, Ray Doyle, Billy Slattery, Marcus Mc Mahon,
Paddy O'Callaghan.
Ground: Séan MacHale, Pat Sheehan

PART SEVEN

Tom

REF NO. LVW/MAC

SHELBOURNE HOTEL
DUBLIN

TELEPHONE: 66471-7 (14 LINES)
TELEGRAMS:
"SHELOTEL DUBLIN"

11th February 1963.

T. J. Cleary, Esq.,
9, Lower Mallow Street,
LIMERICK

Dear Mr. Cleary,

As promised at our interview on Saturday last, we now write to offer you officially the post of Accountant within our group Trust Houses (Ireland) Limited. In the first instance Shelbourne Hotel, Limited, the senior company within the group, would employ you. In offering you this position, we would consider your first three months as a trial period at a salary of £700 per annum. Should you be confirmed in the position at the end of the trial period, your salary would then be £750 per annum.

Whilst we fully understand that your loyalties to your present employer would make you wish to give them the maximum period of notice, we would hope that this period need not exceed one month and that you would be in a position to take up your employment here about the middle of March or as soon thereafter as possible. It is most urgent for us that the position of Accountant is filled as soon as possible.

We should be grateful if you would confirm your acceptance of our offer and, at the same time, let us know when you will be in a position to start your duties here.

Yours faithfully,
For: TRUST HOUSES (IRELAND) LIMITED
L. V White Secretary

Tom, around the time he was appointed
Accountant at the Shelbourne Hotel in Dublin.

Kicking to touch

In February 1963 I was offered the post of Accountant at the Shelbourne Hotel in Dublin. I had burned my boats with the accountancy firms in Limerick. I moved "temporarily" into the flat my student brother Gerry was sharing with his friend Leslie Dowley. Palmerstown Road was to be my address for the next number of years. "Temporarily" wasn't in my vocabulary though. (As time went on everyone discovered that!) But, at this stage, it was more a state of mental paralysis than laziness, with me. Life was finally asking me to take responsibility for myself and I didn't like it. And it was going to be doubly difficult to manage such a resounding change in my life without the handy crutch of sport and sporting friends. I was on my own. It wasn't going to be easy. The brother's flat would be a handy way to ease myself into a new life. It was just for a while. Until I got out of the uncertainty and despondency.

* * *

After all my glorious years in Limerick, in the prime of youth and manhood, when the time came to leave I felt very lonely, uncertain and fearful of what lay ahead. I had finally admitted to myself that I'd never get that cap. Deeply disappointed and with only broken dreams for company, as I left the south west to head for Ireland's capital city, a sharp dose of reality struck and I became gradually swamped in a sense of depression. Had I allowed my talent to be stifled and degraded by over-indulgence in drink? Or was it just sheer bad luck? For years I asked myself those questions. And I discovered that the reason didn't really matter in the end.

Did my family ever realise that for almost 30 years my proudest possession was there on the sideboard, in full view? Did anyone ever know (or care) what it really meant to me? That beautifully decorative silver tray presented to me, as I left Limerick, in 1963, by my club, Bohemians. The one place in my entire life where I felt truly at home.

I often wondered afterwards whether I imagined that I was a better scrum-half than I actually was. I pondered on the many reasons why my rugby career didn't deliver the ultimate accolade. I asked myself, over and over, whether I was a bit naïve in my expectations. But there were no answers. None that satisfied me at any rate.

However, the prestigious Shelbourne Hotel, one of Dublin's finest, beckoned. My first impression was of lots of rooms with high ceilings and detailed plasterwork. The place was furnished with antiques and had numerous large Victorian fireplaces, all in constant use. A busy and bustling place, it was situated in the heart of the city overlooking St. Stephen's Green, just a stone's throw from the sights and sounds of Georgian Dublin. The hotel had a history of hosting both the royal and famous since opening its doors in 1824 and had also been immortalised in the writings of Joyce, Moore and Thackeray. But it also remained accessible to the ordinary man. I had done well to obtain a position here (although I must admit, there was some 'pull' involved). This was to be a new beginning for me.

The hotel was a well known gathering place for rugby aficionados, who used to congregate there from early morning on international match days. The ideal place to start a pub crawl en route to Lansdowne Road, many of my Limerick mates would meet up with me there for a mid morning start on these occasions. Later, large groups of us invariably made our way back to the Shelbourne in the evening, for match post mortems and further drinks, lasting well into the early hours of the following morning.

That first evening, when I arrived at the flat, Gerry and his friend Les were studying for their final exams. As Gerry himself used to say I "descended on the flat for a short stay" until I could arrange lodgings for myself. They lived on the top floor of the house in Palmerstown Road. I had been there before but that was just visiting or crashing out for the night of an international match. Now I took a serious look around. There was lots of space with two bedrooms (one of which was very large), a sitting room, kitchen, bathroom and toilet. I soon settled in and it wasn't too long before I started coming home later and later each evening until, eventually, it would be ten or eleven o'clock at night before they'd see me. I had been going straight from work to the pub and was inevitably in "good form" when I'd return to base.

By this time of night Les and Gerry were usually to be found studying in the kitchen, with all their books out on the table. They were both coming up to exams and were cramming until after midnight most nights. For the first night or two they were quite sociable and chatty with me and put their books away as soon as I came in. Slowly it began to dawn on them that an alternative plan of action was required or they'd never get anything done with these night-time interruptions. So they decided to study until ten o'clock and then take a break. Some nights they'd go over to Dawson's pub across the road from the flat, for a pint, but mostly they just had a cup of coffee or a bit of supper. This break was timed so that they'd be back at their books before I came in. Les would sit at one side of the table, Gerry at the other, and they "would – not – say – one – word"! If one threatened to break the silence, the other gave a warning kick under the table. One or other of them might get a bit restless listening to me "going on", talking away to myself, or cooking and eating supper, but once there was no con-

versation I, quite happily, would go off to bed. When Gerry eventually left that flat, I continued to share with Les for the rest of my time in the Shelbourne.

I didn't spend much of my time appreciating the medieval, Georgian and modern architecture of Dublin city during my sojourn there. I didn't have many interests, apart from rugby and a few jars. I hardly noticed the beautiful public buildings, such as Trinity College, Leinster House and the Bank of Ireland at College Green, as I travelled to work each day. The fact that literary greats such as Joyce, Beckett and Wilde were sons of that city went over my head. The luxury of having a ready-made 27 acre park on my doorstep in the heart of the city centre was wasted on me. St. Stephen's Green provided a pleasant lunchtime retreat for many people on sunny days, but I wasn't interested. And anyway I had nobody to share it with. I preferred the pub. Rugby international days were the highlight of my life. Almost everyone gathered in the Shelbourne and I had a blast with true Limerick friends beside me. That's what life was like for me then. I had few real pals in Dublin, apart from a couple of newly acquired drinking mates. I decided to bunk in with my baby brother and his friend, partly out of sheer laziness, and partly out of fear of being alone.

* * *

19th September 1964 – Gerry Cleary's wedding day
St. John's Church, Waterford
Leslie Dowley (friend of the groom), Tom (Best Man and brother of the groom),
Gerry (groom), Dick (father of the groom) and Michael (2) (brother of the groom)

If I had a penny for all the times I was best man at a wedding, I'd be a wealthy man. In the family (close and extended) there were so many such occasions, I can barely recall them. However, my cousin Jack Walsh's is a wedding day I remember particularly well, for some reason. I've lost count of all the times when I carried out this duty in Limerick. I inevitably, and readily, agreed to do the honours when asked. But, as time went on, there was one condition which I imposed.

"Please don't ask me to be godfather to your first baby. I have so many godchildren in Limerick, I can't keep up with them. I mightn't be a good godfather."

The most painful marriage for me (emotionally) was the day my darling married my good friend. Then there were times when weddings proved painful (physically) due to over-indulgence in alcohol the night before. Afterwards, however, when the happy couples were showing off their wedding albums, nobody would ever have guessed how I was feeling. I always took care with my appearance for these big days. And, to a certain extent, I wore a mask.

As for a wedding gift, I always purchased a set of silver candlesticks. As a child, I loved the candelabra on the dining room table in Bridge Street, so I thought it would be an appropriate and useful gift for the newly married couples. Of course I could never have known how times would change. I could never

have envisaged the day when families would not gather, three times a day, around the dining table for their meals. The advent of microwave meals and eating off a tray in front of the television were a long way off yet.

* * *

I have often wondered how I ended up living in Mullingar. It just sort of happened. At this stage the family were fairly fed up trying to solve my problems for me. I'm sure they could see obvious answers to my difficulties that I couldn't (or wouldn't). Deep down, I felt that my father and mother hadn't appreciated my independent nature when I was younger. Maybe, because I used to get more attention as a child when I became difficult, I subconsciously decided to continue that behaviour in adulthood. My talent at sport was a useful tool in manipulating people, my mother in particular. And although my parents obviously did their best, they never actually insisted that I live my own life. In ways I was grateful not to have to take responsibility for myself. In other ways I hated all the advice and what I saw as interference.

As time went by, I chose to become an uncooperative, permanent child, who was decidedly unhappy and, in many ways, resented other members of the family. I was an adult, who should have been responsible for my own life. But I wasn't. And so I ended up in Mullingar with Helen, my only sister. I often felt sorry for the angry mutterings at night, the unacceptable behaviour by day. I sometimes wondered how she felt about having her brother, adult child that he was, living in her home. I knew that she often had to call in favours from old friends because of me and she lived with a lot of disturbance on my behalf. Believe me, I appreciated that. But she never would have known. I never told her.

Where would I have been without the practical, emotional and financial support of Helen and my brothers? My cousin Delma and her husband Tom Morrissey from Carrickbeg also often "put me up" (or should I say "put up with me"?) for holiday breaks and numerous other long spells of time throughout the years.

I could so easily have become homeless.

* * *

PART EIGHT

Ursula

Forward pass

By the summer of 1966 your time in the Shelbourne is over, so you come on "holidays" for two weeks to our home in Mullingar, a large four-storey house in Dominick Street. The ground floor is mostly made up of the hardware and pub business, with a kitchen to the rear. The other three storeys are occupied by my mother, Helen[101], her three children (me being the middle child), Josie who helps out with the housework and various female tenants who live in bed-sits. One of the flats is empty, between tenants, so Mammy is able to put you on the top floor in the back room. It's a large room, with a small window and so is quite dark. But it was only for a fortnight, wasn't it? Sorry, I forgot, you don't do temporary. If I remember correctly, you ended up staying a year!

By July you've got a part-time job with J. J. Raleigh, Chartered Accountant, over the Central Hotel in Oliver Plunkett Street. Just a stone's throw from Jack Lynam's pub. Very handy for you, that. Your sister, Helen, agrees that you can stay on condition that you pay her rent. My first vivid memory of you is around the following December when you agree to escort Mammy to the New Year's Eve Champagne Ball. A dress affair, you both look wonderful, as you head out together. So glamorous.

She's been to the hairdressers that day and now sports a short, elegant, sophisticated hairstyle and has her nails painted. Mammy never has her nails painted! She lets me watch, as she gets ready for this rare night out. After her bath, I watch in admiration as she 'dresses up' in a gorgeous blue, glittery, taffeta gown the likes of which I've never seen close-up before. She puts on some light make-up and then uses a long, thin, pencil-like lipstick, around the contours of her lips. Afterwards she puts on her ordinary lipstick, purses her lips together on a piece of tissue to remove any surplus and gives me a beaming smile. "How do I look?" she asks, doing a little twirl for my benefit. I'm breathless. Speechless. For me, as a child, it's magical. Prince Charming with my Mammy.

One evening, about a month after the Ball, myself, Gerard and his pal, Pat, are sitting doing our homework in the downstairs kitchen at the back of the shop. Helen's gone up to the sitting room to get the fire going so that the room will be warm by the time we're finished and we can play there until bedtime. A

---

101 Helen Cleary-Kane (Tom's sister. Mother of the author.)

gas heater is going full blast in the middle of the kitchen floor and the windows are all steamed up, but I don't mind. I'm tucked cosily into the corner, underneath the shelf, beside the yellow and green crockery press with its patterned glass doors and drop-down leaf. The pale pink, formica table is turned around so that the big raised bubble, where I burned it the previous week with the iron, is down the boys' end.

We don't hear you coming until the kitchen door creaks and then opens slowly.

"Sshh..." you say, your forefinger up to your mouth "... where's your mother?"

We all turn towards the door.

"Upstairs" I say.

The boys say nothing – they just look at you.

"Sshh..." you continue even though we're saying nothing. Closing the door quietly behind you, you go over to the sink and pour some water into the kettle, then fiddling with the gas cooker, you strike a match, light the burner and proceed to put the water on to boil. Next, you open the door of the enormous fridge in the corner and take out some leftover bacon that Mammy is saving for the next day's dinner. You start to make a sandwich with some of that day's lovely fresh bread from Mullally's bakery (up the street). I watch as you cut and then butter the doorstep slices, plaster the pink and white, fatty meat on the bottom one, spread yellow mustard all over it and clap the lid on top. Much more interesting than homework but the boys work on, oblivious to it. You cut your sandwich into four bulky triangles, take out a clean handkerchief from your pocket, to use as a napkin, then you turn and wink at me, as, standing beside the cooker, you bend your head slightly forward and take your first bite.

I try to wink back but it's more of a blinking grimace because you start to laugh and then you wink again, more slowly this time. The kettle is singing, so you wet yourself a pot of tea and there you remain, enjoying it all, standing and eating because we're using the table. I wonder why you didn't have your tea earlier with the rest of us. All consumed, you wipe your mouth, and start shuffling in a mini dance step over to the sink with the dishes. Pat looks over at you.

"Seniority," you say. Pat looks at me, quizzically.

"...that's what it's all about...seniority," you continue to no one in particular. Pat glances at Gerard, who continues to work, head down. Gerard wants to get upstairs to the real heat of the coal fire and nothing is going to distract him. Or so he thinks.

You rinse the plate and saucer, cup and cutlery and leave them to dry on the draining board. That'll drive Mammy mad, I think to myself but I say nothing. Next you start looking over the boys' shoulders, to see what they're doing.

"Need any help with the sums, boys?" you ask, at the same time putting your hand in your pocket and rattling a few coins. I get that smell off you that you sometimes have when you come home late, but I don't realise that it's a curious mixture of smoke and alcohol. Gerard lifts his head slowly, weighing up the possibilities. He knows you have been drinking. If he says "yes", he risks giving you an opening to start talking nonsense, which would delay the homework for up to 15 minutes. On the other hand, he might be lucky enough to get a couple of pennies for sweets, in Jane's shop next door, or in Kate Ryan's in Mary Street, on his way to school the next morning.

However Pat is the first to respond. "No thanks, Mr. Cleary," he says "we're fine."

"MISTER Cleary" you announce, appreciatively. "What manners...you know what seniority means, young man." At that, you pull your clenched fist out of the pocket of your trousers and open it out to display an array of silver and copper.

"Sshh ...," you say, gesturing and grinning.

You select three two shilling pieces and give us one each and, putting the rest of the change back in your pocket, you pirouette on one heel, open the door and leave the room. We three look at the fortune now in our possession, speechless.

The door opens, and you stick your head back in. My heart sinks. You're only teasing us. No way are you giving us this much money ...each.

"Not a word to your mother," you warn and are gone again.

Pat eventually breaks the shocked silence.

"He must be very rich, your uncle."

"Not really," I reply, not really knowing.

Then Gerard finally speaks, "Well, he is a famous rugby player."

* * *

The Kane children, (Paula, Ursula and Gerard)
Christmas 1965, not long before Tom came to Mullingar "on holidays for a fortnight!"

Another of my memories from childhood is how you often used to ferry a car-load of us kids over to the heated swimming pool in Longford on a Sunday afternoon. These were the days when the Mullingar pool was still on the drawing board. Paula was considered too young, so she would stay at home with Mammy. But you always brought Gerard and me with, sometimes, our Buckley cousins, Des and Gerry, or our friend Nuala Connolly. On other days Anne, Stella or Peter Lynch would get their turn, or Gerard's pal Pat Broder, or maybe some of the other neighbours. The waiting list was endless. We all loved swimming at the 'diving club' at Lough Owel in the summer months, but swimming in a pool was a new and exciting departure for us. To be able to swim in wintertime was such a treat.

All week we'd be hoping that you'd be well enough to drive us, the 26 miles each way, the following Sunday. Sometimes you just weren't able to oblige and you'd stay in your bed all day. We mightn't miss out on our swim as a result, because Mammy or some of the other parents would do the needful, but the days you drove were different because you always waited for us in the pub across the road. After our swim, when we'd meet you there, your special treat for us was a lovely hot and beefy Bovril drink, with lots and lots of bread and butter. I still think of you every time I see a jar of Bovril. And to this day I love butter on my bread. What a fond memory.

* * *

Of course, in those early days we, even as children, sometimes didn't respect you. You were never a father figure in our house. Handy for a few bob when you had drink in you, someone to tease and belittle, maybe, but that was about it. Basically we watched you coming and going at a distance. Just like the other tenants.

"Hurry up, he'll be here soon."

"How d'ya know?"

"Just do."

I've my hands in the washhandbasin, while my friend Nuala tries to fold the large sheets of brown wrapping paper into a more manageable size. She plunges a few sheets into the warm water.

"Don't splash," I shout.

"Stop telling me what to do."

"One sheet at a time," I instruct.

She peels one off the bundle and I slowly soak it in the soapy basin. When it's well soaked, I squeeze it, but not too tightly, then roll it into a lump. The bathroom floor is all wet.

"How d'ya think that looks?" I ask.

"Not bad, but a bit too wet."

I squeeze more water out of the gloopy mass.

"That's more like it," she says.

"How many'll I do?"

"Oh, five or six."

I know Mammy will kill us if she finds us at this. I once heard her telling the man who works in the shop how expensive the brown paper is, and not to waste it. She tries to save it for wrapping the parcels of wallpaper and paints. We're not even allowed to cover our schoolbooks with it; we have to use old samples out of the wallpaper pattern books for that.

I look over at the low, white bathroom chair, where Nuala has put her first sloppy lump. Doesn't look very realistic from here I think.

"Keep going," she urges, as she pushes another sheet into the water.

When we have six pieces, of varying shapes and consistency lined up on the chair, we decide to put the plan into action. We move out into the narrow corridor outside the bathroom door. She turns right, I turn left. We have three pieces each.

"Put one of yours into the toilet, and two on the floor" I'm told. Making sure they're spaced out, but not too evenly, I look back at Nuala's display. They look more real from a distance I decide.

And so we leave our fake pieces of pooh for Uncle Tom to stumble on when he comes in from 'work'! We haven't bargained on the fact that the toilet will need to be used in the meantime, or that brown paper slop doesn't flush very well.

We are lucky our heads aren't used as plungers when our workmanship is discovered. And, after all that, Uncle Tom never even sees it.

He might have heard about it, though!

* * *

Ursula on her Confirmation Day, 1968
Photograph taken outside the shop in Dominick Street

After a year or so in Mullingar you return to Dublin once more and take up employment in Kennedy Crowley & Co., Chartered Accountants. By now it's well recognised, within the family at least, that you have a 'drink problem', though it is not spoken about openly. Meanwhile, your father is getting very old and feeble, and has been admitted to hospital in Waterford. Most Saturday nights, after shutting up shop, Helen, Paula and I[102] make the trip to Carrick, so that we can visit him on the Sunday. The arrangement is that you'll take the train from Dublin to Portlaoise and we'll collect you there so that you can visit Granddad[103] too.

* * *

Hurry... uuupppp.... I almost say it aloud.

"I'm not sure," the customer says "whether to go for the green or the pink."

"The green is nice," I venture, getting a pain in my outstretched arm as I dutifully hold up the roll of wallpaper for her to view. Perched halfway up the ladder, I know that if she'd only make up her mind one way or the other I'll have her out of here before she knows what's hit her.

"Let me see the pink again," she orders.

"'Tell you what," says I, "I'll let you see the two of them side by side and see what you think." Despite my rushing I know Mammy'll be delighted if I sell eleven rolls of the embossed paper and the paste to go with it, at this hour on a Saturday evening.

"It must be a very big room," I had commented when the woman said she thought she'd need eleven rolls.

" 'Tis," was her only response as she pondered her possible purchase.

I jump down from the third step of the ladder, directly onto the cement floor, spread out some old wallpaper at her feet and bend down with a roll of the leafy pattern in each hand. Placing the rolls on the paper on the ground and catching their edges in one fell swoop, I pull up to my tippy-toes and stick the ends into the prepared nails on the bottom of the wallpaper shelves just above my head.

"Oh, that's better," she remarks, standing back towards the counter to make the most of the view.

"What do you think," she asks.

"Well, I like the green," I offer once more. I couldn't care less really, so long as you decide, I think to myself.

"The pink is nice too.... Oh it's so hard to choose," she continues.

I sigh. I can see I'm losing her. After spending almost an hour up and down that ladder, and with rolls of paper sticking out from all angles on the shelves, in

102 Gerard Kane (Ref. 2) is at boarding school in Castleknock at this stage.
103 Dick Cleary.

what had been a tidy display, I have two choices. Pander to her a bit more, or busy myself tidying up so that she'll get the hint it's closing time.

I'm thinking of the planned journey to Carrick that night and feel that at this rate we'll never get going. Then I hear my mother's footsteps on the wooden floorboards behind the counter.

"Everything alright here?" she asks.

"Oh, hello Mrs. Kane. I'm trying to decide between the pink and the green."

"Well, hello Mary, let me see now. I've sold a lot of the pink, so maybe the green would be a bit different. You won't see it in the neighbours' houses," my mother continues, always the professional, moving out from behind the counter to stand closer to the customer.

She leans against the ladder as she speaks, putting one foot back behind her onto the bottom step. "The only person who has the green, as far as I know, lives out in Coralstown and the pink all went out towards the Lynn Road, so you'll be the only one with it up your way, Mary, if you opt for that pattern. It *is* lovely isn't it?" she goes in for the kill as she touches the side of the roll. "I'd use it myself, only we did the sitting room up last year."

That swings it. No one out her way has it; Mrs. Kane'd love to have it herself, and anyway it is lovely. All swirling leaves with a raised pattern and an embossed finish, bright but not exactly loud. I can almost see Mary's mind working, as she imagines it on the walls on her house and no one else up there having anything like it. *This was one of the benefits of shopping with Mrs. Kane,* she was most likely thinking (as I watched her). *Mrs. Kane knows her customers and she wouldn't knowingly sell it to her if she had sold it to a neighbour. The girl is alright, and she's done a fair job in showing the selections, but the mother knows her business.*

The deal is done.

Mary is delighted.

Mammy smiles, tiredly, at me.

"Go on up and get ready" she jerks her head towards the wooden panelled ceiling. "I'll finish up here."

Thank you God, I whisper. *We'll surely make Portlaoise on time now.* I skip up the stairs two at a time, go to the loo, throw my bag over my shoulder calling for Paula as I come back down towards the hall door.

"Going soon," I shout.

In no time at all we're in the car, a Ford Escort station wagon, which doubles-up as the shop delivery van. The back seat is collapsible and the Horan brothers,[104] who help in the shop after school, can load nine cylinders of gas in the rear. We have two custom cut pieces of chipboard, which make a false floor to hold the cylinders evenly and ensure that they don't rattle too much. Tonight

104 Danny, Séamus, Paddy and Bobby Horan all worked in the shop at various stages over the years.

however, it's the family car and we're off to see Granny and Granddad. I'm in the front passenger seat, and Paula is in the back, stretched out with her dolly, thumb in her mouth, as we bounce along, through Kilbeggan and Tullamore.

"Will the Christmas tree be up in Mountmellick yet?" I wonder out loud.

"Too soon," my mother replies. "Sure it's only November."

"I can't wait to see it," I say eagerly.

"A lot could happen before you see that tree."

With no prospect of seeing the tree, my thoughts turn to Portlaoise.

"Will we make the station?" I ask.

"Maybe."

"Hope so."

"Maybe not!" she adds.

I say nothing. I don't want her to know how much I hate going into the pubs in the square looking for you. The best days are when we reach the station before the train. You would join us, having travelled from Dublin and make the rest of your journey home with us in the car. Sometimes you'd take over the driving from Mammy, but if we were late she always stayed at the wheel and you might sit in the back, very quiet.

Suddenly, I hear her say "Road works ahead."

"Oh no!"

That does it. The delay isn't long but it makes the difference between the station and the square for me. So out I have to get in Portlaoise, and go to the pubs looking for you while Mammy keeps a watchful eye on me and where I'm going.

I have my routine down to a fine art at this stage, having done it on numerous occasions. Into the pub on the left at the corner. Only one door in and one door out as far as I know in this one. No sign of you. Across the road then to the next. Two doors here, so I can walk straight through and not have to retrace my steps. The smell, Ugh! No Tom. A few doors down to the next. Small and smoky, I particularly hate this one and always leave it until last. Still no Tom. Have I missed you? Back to the car.

"Can't find him."

"You'd better try that one over there," Mammy points to one I haven't had to look in before.

"He never goes in there. Maybe he missed the train."

"Try it anyway," she urges.

"Okay so," I sigh "It's freezing out here, you know..." I don't know which is worse. Looking in the pubs myself, or Mammy looking, and me staying in the car minding Paula. I always opt for the former, preferring the action role rather than having to sit there worrying that maybe Mammy mightn't come back, for some reason.

You are about to start a fresh pint. "Is that your second or third?" I creep up behind you.

"Now, now, Madam," you remonstrate, turning round to face me, with a Guinness moustache and a smirk.

"I wish it wasn't such a treasure hunt to find you," I moan, but I can't help smiling at my dear Uncle Tom. It's so hard to be cross with you. "Why can't you always be in the one place?"

"And be so predictable?" he laughs.

"You'd better hurry up and finish that one. Mammy's getting fairly fed up waiting out there and it's COLD."

"I'll be out in a minute."

"You have to come out WITH ME, you know that," I almost shout at him.

"I know the rules at this stage," he half-jokes.

"Well, I didn't make them."

"Have a Club Orange."

"No'oooh," I can barely suppress my annoyance.

"No thank you," he reminds me.

"No thank you," I repeat automatically.

"A Coke then," he offers.

"TOM..... if – you – don't – hurry – up...." staccato-like.

"OKAY Just a mo..." he lifts the enormous glass of black and cream to his lips and takes a satisfyingly large swallow. "Just one sec..." and the remainder of the pint disappears down his gullet.

And so we travel in smelly silence the remaining two hours to Carrick in the dark, Mammy driving, Paula sleeping, you muttering and me wondering.

You are not to last long at independent living. By the early 1970s you have once more returned to your sister, Helen, and the midlands. It is to remain your home for the remainder of your life.

* * *

Gerry and Ann moved back to Ireland from London in the early 1970s with their young daughter, Geraldine. Soon you have two more nieces, when Jenny and then Aisling are born over the next few years. But still to this day when I think back to the 1970s I mainly recall it as a time of many family funerals. Dick died in 1968 and it seemed to me as if he opened a floodgate when he got to heaven. As the following decade progressed we seemed to be gazing into freshly dug graves on a regular basis. We said goodbye to Brendan, his sister Pearlie, and Maureen[105] in that decade. All of them were only in their 40s. Your favourite uncle, Paddy Feehan, died in 1975 and your mother, Kitty, in 1977. And people continued to trust you, as you were named executor of some of their wills.

---

105 Maureen Cleary neé O'Callaghan – see list of family relations in Post Mortem section of the book for further details.

Your employment record during your years in Mullingar doesn't make for great reading. It was quite sporadic. In the early days you worked for Jimmy Raleigh. When you return in the 1970s, you work again once more with Jimmy who by now was a partner in Oliver Freaney & Co. Not too long afterwards you move to work at Dencon Ltd. and later at Stenson's. You never really hold a job down for long.

When I knew I was about to start this book, I had a chat with our local G.P., Dr. Trevor Winckworth (since deceased) about your rugby influence locally. He told me that at the time you arrived in town, Mullingar rugby was played in the racecourse grounds. He recalled that once, in the early days of your involvement with the club, you travelled on a tour to Holyhead.

Your role was that of general advisor and supporter extraordinaire. You don't play but you wave the Mullingar jersey with gusto and a great time is had by all. You go on to serve on the committee for a number of years and are an avid attendee at matches and meetings ....to begin with. But eventually you become unreliable. Story of your life, eh, Tom? You referee a bit and you coach the youth teams when they come on stream in the 1970s. The kids have all heard of your prowess at rugby and some are in awe of you. You continue to follow the game very closely.

When the Mullingar racecourse was sold to the Industrial Development Association in the late 1960s, the rugby club transferred to St. Loman's Hospital grounds and played a few matches there. Then a local farmer and club member, Michael Rooney of Irishtown, offered the club the use of a field as a "pitch". It's slightly sloped, going down at one side and has "quite a dip in it", yet the club goes on to play there for two seasons. The players have to come back a couple of miles to town and into Broder's Hotel for their showers after the game. Following an extraordinary meeting of the club in the early 1970s, negotiations begin for the purchase of a field and eventually the club buys a few acres at Cullion from the Land Commission. There follows a huge amount of drainage on what Trevor describes as "an awful field with a little pond in the middle of it". Unhealthy looking, bad land, it is generally felt, but the club drains it and puts sand in. You are very helpful at this stage and advise as best you can, from your experience of rugby pitches in your heyday. The club goes on to put grass on top with huge layers of sand underneath.

You are one of the proud members present at the 1977 official opening, when the club is blessed by Fr. Regan and Canon MacDougall and a Wolfhounds XV play against a Mullingar XV. Soon after this you donate to the club your green triangular pennant, which you had been presented with on your Irish tour to South Africa. It's still there, on display in the inner lounge, the room dedicated to the local character and rugby aficionado, Roche T.[106] Trevor laughs as he tells me of many conversations which took place, down through the years, between

106 Tommy Roche was a well-known character in Mullingar and was known (and referred to) far and wide as Roche T.

yourself (with drink on board) and Roche T (who had a speech impediment). *I can imagine!*

* * *

During my research, in one of my chats with Bill Mulcahy, we talked of his friend Don Mosey, who had accompanied the Irish/Shamrocks team on the short tour to South Africa in 1961. (He was a reporter for the *Daily Mail* at that time and went on to become the well-known BBC cricket commentator.) There was a letter from Don in your suitcase. I have calculated that he wrote it in 1975.

After the Mart at Dominick Street Square, Mullingar.
Tom, Joe Caulfield and Roche T.
Bridget Daly and Rita Caulfield in background.

You were living in Mullingar by that time and you have recorded that you received the letter two days after he wrote it. (Not a bad postal system as he more than likely addressed it to Mullingar rugby club.) I cannot find out whether you succeeded in meeting up or not, but he obviously thought highly of you and was looking forward to catching up on your progress since you had last met. I guess, knowing what your life was like by then, ...you didn't go. You owed Jack Foy's Menswear £56.05, some of which was outstanding for over three years. You left the invoice for us to find.

(Received by Tom on 10th December, no year on letter)

Morecambe,
England.

8th December.

My dear Tom,
In the hope that this eventually reaches you, may I say that I have never failed to ask after you on my visits to the Republic, whether professional or on pleasure.

This week I had a note from my good friend Wigs Mulcahy in which he mentioned that you now lived in Mullingar & were active in the Club there so I very much hope that this finds you in due course.

I shall be over for the England match on February 5th & I do hope we shall be able to get together for a jar (or two, or three......)

Normally, on such occasions, I have Jo with me & we stay with Bill, but once a year I have a rugby weekend with a group of my BBC colleagues. These are becoming progressively more popular &, in parallel, more riotous & while we shall be six in number, I have a waiting list of 16, all hoping that one of the chosen breaks a leg before February.

We shall probably be staying at the Burlington (awaiting confirmation) on the Friday & Saturday nights &, as I say, I do hope we can get together.

I won't write at greater length in case this gets lost, but in the hope that it doesn't I shall look forward to hearing from you & then, perhaps, we can bring each other up to date with 14 years or so.

Yours ever,
Don Mosey.

Mauling

I have an entire file of documents relating to your dealings with the Department of Social Welfare. The bottom line is that by the early 1980s you end up on the dole and eventually get a disability allowance. As far as we knew, at the time, it was all down to your "nerves being at you", although that was never really said aloud. Some family members reckoned (rather harshly I thought) that you must have got a kick on the head playing rugby and it was only coming against you now.

Sometimes the disability was disallowed when your medical check-up declared you were "not incapable of work". Then it was back to the dole. All through the 1980s and 1990s I can see the record of your appeals regarding your ongoing eligibility for this allowance. At one stage your local T.D. made representations on your behalf to the office of the director of social welfare services. If Helen hadn't prompted you, supported you and personally walked you down to their offices on more than one occasion, you would have been so much worse off. Did you realise that? Maybe you did, maybe you didn't. Did you appreciate her?

You were not easy to live with at this stage. Maybe we, children, were getting older and were noticing things more, but your constant drinking by day and talking to yourself by night were hard to bear. As a result we just ignored it. When the money ran out, you were a model tenant. Quiet, meticulous, affable, obliging, gentle and a good cook to boot.

I can see you now, getting the car ready to drive us somewhere. Dominick Street was quieter in those days. The bonnet of the car is raised for a thorough once-over and left in that position while you wander back upstairs to the new kitchen to get water for the wipers. Another trip upstairs has to be made for a cloth to use as you check the oil levels. Each tyre in turn is kicked to test them but just to be sure you drive across the street to Paddy O'Callaghan's garage and pump the wheels. But Helen would have to buy the petrol before take-off or en route. Because when you were in this diligent state it meant you had no money.

I recall the many times you cooked for us in the kitchen. You would never serve pork without the apple sauce, or beef without horseradish. At Christmas-time, you would often cater for the extended family and friends, but never, ever dine with the guests. You would eat alone. You loved your food. I picture you now, tasting something that's just a wee bit too hot for you and rolling it about in your mouth and when you eventually swallow it, you take out your hankie to wipe your lips.

You almost always left the kitchen in an awful mess. Every dish and pot, pan and grill pan, slotted spoon, wooden spoon, fish-slice and potato masher in the place would have been used and left God only knows where. It used to drive Helen up the walls. She might leave a tidy kitchen and go out for a while only to return to a place that resembled the scene after a tornado. No matter how much she threatened or how much we pleaded with you, it was always the same. We were invariably greeted by a sink full of pots and dishes waiting to be washed. Or else a draining board full of half-washed pots and dishes waiting to be washed properly. Sticky potato remnants on wet pots are a vivid memory for me. Strange the things we miss.

I see a recipe for minestrone soup in with your mementos. Did you ever get to try it out? The last meal you cooked for me was just a few days before you died. Helen was in America. I was at work. You were staying with us in Irishtown "for a few days" while she was away. The reality of it all was that she knew, when she was leaving Mullingar, that she would never see you alive again. But she had to go because you wouldn't give in and admit what we all knew. You were dying. But you preferred to look on yourself as still living. You were a mere shadow of your former self, unable to swallow solids, death warmed up, but you cooked a lunch of smoked haddock in white sauce for me that day. When I arrived home you pointed out where you had left what, and disappeared to your bedroom with a dessert bowl of almost liquidised fish, spud and sauce. But you couldn't eat it. You never ate anything again.

* * *

In autumn 1983 Helen sold the Dominick Street shop and house and we all moved to our new home at 'Willsboro' in Ballinderry on the outskirts of Mullingar. A reasonably new house, it was spacious, modern and has beautiful gardens, front and back. With five bedrooms, one en suite, it is more than ample for our needs. In addition to the main sitting room it has a small and cosy "family room" beside, but separate from, the kitchen. Helen allows you to take up position in this room and make it your own and it is soon to become known as "Tom's room". In this way you are afforded a luxury that very few men in your position would have, a bedroom and a sitting room to yourself. From these two rooms you are aware of all the comings and goings in the house, without ever really being a part of them.

'Willsboro' is good for you. You are that bit further removed from the temptations of the pub and bookies. Somehow it takes more effort to get yourself up the town and into your haunts than when you had been living smack bang in the middle of things. As the seasons change you begin to take an interest in the garden and mowing the lawn becomes your responsibility. You spend a lot of time pottering around outside and taking pride in your work, neither of which you've had for a long time up until now.

As time goes by, you begin to cycle to town (on my old bike!) and you slide back into the old familiar ways, coming in at all hours, chatting away to yourself. It is at times like these that the appeal of our modern home pales for the rest of us and we often wish we still had the four storey house, with your room right at the top instead of living in such close proximity to your meanderings.

In summer 1985, Helen and I decide to go on a pilgrimage to Lourdes. Neither of us has ever been there before. There's great excitement in the preparation, the trip to the airport, the flight and when we get there, we love every minute of it. The candlelit procession leaves a lasting impression on us both. The baths are worth the long wait (and all the Ave Marias in various languages!) just to come into contact with such a large volume of Lourdes water on our skin. And it is true. We don't need to dry off afterwards. It's a strange sensation.

Tom just strolling along
St. Brendan's Parish Church Grounds, Coolock, Dublin.

But you are having your own "strange sensations" while we're away. One day after a few jars in the pub, you decide to use Helen's car to drop a mate home. You're over the limit and you're caught. Drunken driving. I feel humiliated on your behalf as I read the leaflet "Information for Persons in custody" which starts off with a section entitled "Reason for arrest". How did it come to this? Where was the champion now? Had to be at rock bottom, surely. Or was there worse to come?

We're both disgusted and disappointed when we get home. No wonder Helen feels you can't be trusted; can't be left on your own. For once I see her point of view, where you are concerned. I'm furious with you.

* * *

If the 1970s was the decade of death, then the 1980s was a time of celebration. Your widowed brother, Michael married Bernadette Moran. Her two sons, Ken and Derry, joined the family and Zoë, your youngest niece, was born in 1983. You kept many of the invitations and Mass booklets from the celebrations of that time. I found the invitations to Stephanie Cleary's 21st birthday party, later her marriage with Eddie Keating, a 21st for Michael Cleary Junior[107], your brother John's silver jubilee celebrations, and some of the Kane cousins' weddings. Most of my friends, it seems, invited you to either their actual weddings or to the 'afters'. I came across a lovely photo of you taken with Anne Halpin-Deegan (or Annie as you used to call her) on her wedding day. You look quite impish in it. It is so "you". I love it.

My brother, Gerard's studies for the priesthood are progressing all through the 1980s and we celebrate his religious profession, diaconate, ordination and First Mass. Paula and I both get engaged in 1987 and married in 1988. You give us both away. You're chuffed and proud to do it. We might have been more relaxed about the speeches if we had known what a seasoned speaker you had been in your prime. Imagine we didn't fully realise that! You had responded to speeches and toasts aplenty in your days as captain of Bohemians and Munster teams (on several occasions). And you did us proud on our big days. We needn't have worried about you rambling on with a few jars inside you, à la comedian Brendan Grace's 'father of the bride' sketch.

I made a little speech myself on my wedding day, saying that you were probably delighted to 'give me away'! At least you'd be able to have a bit of a rest with me gone out of the house, I joked. You were always so good to me. I thanked you for being my personal manservant, secretary, chef, assistant and gardener for the previous number of years. I could always ask you to do almost anything for me.

I remember one day, while we were still living in Dominick Street, a workmate

---

107 Michael (Ref. 3), Tom's nephew. See list of family relations in Post Mortem section of book for reference and further details.

and I had planned to go browsing around the shops for the afternoon. But she rang around lunchtime to tell me she had been delayed and to go on ahead without her. You took the call and the message you passed on to me went something like this:

"Mary rang to say she got the lead," (you pronounced it "led").

"What's that supposed to mean?"

"How should I know what she means, but that's what she said – she got the lead."

"What lead?" I asked, picturing a large solid lump of metal.

"I don't know, do I? She said you'd understand and to go on ahead without her."

"I don't understand!" I said, intrigued.

"Well, if you don't understand, how do you expect me to?" you asked and went away muttering something about never understanding the workings of the female mind.

It was some time before it dawned on me that her enunciation and diction meant that she pronounced 'delayed' as 'de-led' and you interpreted it as 'the lead'. I still laugh when I recall your bewilderment that day.

On the other hand, I was fairly bewildered myself once when you told me you were thinking of preparing chicken Thai for lunch the following day.

"Mmm," I thought, "that should be nice. He must have been leafing through the recipe books for this one."

In all the years you had lived with us, I had never known you to serve this dish before. I was already looking forward to my lunch as I cycled off to work that day. All morning, as I cared for the patients on Ward Four, I had visions of succulent chicken fillet served with a lovely mild curry sauce on a bed of white rice. Maybe you might serve some trimmings, such as banana or coconut flakes on the side. I could hardly wait.

Chicken Thai?.... it was not! I think I hid my disappointment fairly well. Expectations aside, even your chicken thigh was nice to come home to.

Tom with Ursula's friend Annie (Anne Halpin-Deegan)
on her wedding day in December 1987
Photograph by Yvonne Martyn

After Gerard Kane's First Mass – June 1987
Standing: Fr. John, Tom, Michael and Gerry Cleary
Sitting: Helen (Cleary-Kane) and Fr. Gerard Kane

Walking up the aisle with Paula, August 1988. St. Paul's Church, Mullingar

Walking up the aisle with Ursula, October 1988. Franciscan Friary, Multyfarnham

Tom making his speech at Paula's and Jim's wedding, 24th August 1988
Fr. Gerard Kane (brother of the bride), Fr. Gerard Kane (uncle of the bride), Tom, Marie Kelly (mother of the groom), Barry Kelly (Best Man - brother of the groom)

Michael Cleary and Anne Wallace's Wedding day, March 1989
Gainstown Church, Mullingar
Tom, Stephanie (Cleary) Keating, Gerard Cleary (3), Hugh Cafferty,
Ann (Tilson) Cleary and Gerry Cleary (1)

PLAYING

Your good friend Seán Elliffe wrote some lovely letters to you while you were ill in hospital. They didn't make much sense to me when I found them in the suitcase, so I invited Seán out to the house to tell me the stories behind the letters. He misses you dreadfully. Some of the stories he told were hilarious, others were you to a tee, more were sad and lonely, but I began to get a picture of what you might be "up-to" on one of your many days up the town. For instance:

"The top of the morning to you, Tom." Seán stops for a chat one day as you stroll past Mullingar Dog Track wheeling your bike one-handed towards the railway bridge.

"Ditto Sir," you respond, smiling. You adjust your bicycle clips, open your jacket and rub your hands down the suede panels on the front of that old brown cardigan of yours.

"And how is your health, might I enquire," this is said half jokingly.

"Excellent, my good man," you attempt a grand accent.

"As it would be impolite for me to pass such a gentleman on this delightful day, I simply had to pause and make my enquiry," the jocular vein continues.

"Glad to see you still recognise class when you see it!" eyes twinkling.

"What's your prediction for the match, Sir?" Seán asks.

And oblivious to the speeding, mid-week traffic and resultant noise, there ensues a mutually satisfying, long conversation, between you two friends, about the pros and cons of both teams, the state of the pitch, the latest training methods, the sad lack of passing the ball, the intricacies of the scrum and more besides.

"Must go," Seán says eventually. "See you in 'Number 44' later."

"Maybe," you reply. You aren't going to be tied down to one pub in particular.

* * *

"Good morning, ladies[108]," you push the door of the bookie's office open wide, oblivious to the sweet wrappers and dust swirling in from the street.

"'Morning, Tom. You're early today."

---

108 Ladies such as Mary Barry, Delma Connell, Joan Daly, Maureen Gowran and Louise Milner were always very accommodating when it came to overnight bicycle storage.

"Sshh," you place your forefinger to your pursed lips. "Don't tell my sister I was here," you warn her friends and wheel the bike in behind the door, for safe keeping for the day.

"I'll collect it later," you wave to the two women behind the counter as you leave, having placed a small 20 pence bet on a sure cert for the twelve o'clock, with the few coins you have left in your pocket. "Just off to do my rounds," you joke.

Your next stop is the Post Office to collect your pension, and you take your place in the long queue of women wearing headscarves, carrying old fashioned shopping baskets looped across their arms and chit-chatting about the major issues of the day, such as the price of butter and where Mrs. so-and-so is today.

"Must be sick," says one.

"What makes you say that?"

"Well she's always here at this time, every week." Head nodding.

"Not always," says another who's wearing a plain red scarf. "I remember when her grandchild was making her First Communion she didn't come for two weeks so that she'd have a few bob saved to help with the dress."

"That was years ago. Her grandchild must be 20 by now," says the nodder.

"Sure she's married," says the red headscarf.

"Mrs. Smith GOT MARRIED?" shouts the first speaker, just as she's called to the desk, and that was the only piece of the conversation that the people in the entire line heard. And so another rumour starts in Mullingar!

You watch quietly as you wait for your turn. Ah! These are different days, you think. In the era of Maura Brennan in the old Post Office you'd have been summoned to the front for preferential treatment by now. Just as well you have no pressing engagements, you reflect, as the frazzled girl in the glass box that passes for a desk calls "NEXT". The thought enters your mind that the word "please" wouldn't go astray and you stroll towards her with all the time in the world at your disposal.

Out in the unseasonal weather, money in your pocket, as you take time to adjust your eyes to the bright sunshine, the biggest decision you have to make is whether to turn right or left. Right means Murray's (which you still referred to as Tommy Lynch's although it has changed hands several times since Tommy had been proprietor). Left means a selection of pubs and sporting friends in greater abundance for you to choose from. You decide to head for Murray's for a quiet pint or two, while you watch your race, with the intention of rambling further afield as the day progresses and eventually reaching 'Number 44' (your pet name for Jimmy Wallace's pub in Mount Street) on the run home for a self-appointed teatime. You've consumed your usual grilled feed before you left the house that morning, lining your stomach well for the day's activities ahead, just in case.

As the day progresses you meander down the town from Murray's, stopping off once more at the bookie's office to put on a few more small bets and a yankee. You're feeling very prosperous and relaxed, with a few pounds in your pocket and a few pints in your system. Ducking past Paddy Gallagher's pub (you remember that you had overstayed your welcome there recently – better to let sleeping dogs lie) you stay on the sunny side of the street and carry on past Days Bazaar and Dr. Winckworth's. Glancing at the window display in one of the boutiques that has sprung up lately, you notice that the blonde wig on one of the scantily clad wooden dummies has fallen askew, and you imagine it gives her a rakish look which could have been directed solely at yourself! You cross at the traffic lights towards the Arcade corner and turn down Mount Street.

As usual, you go in the lower door of the affectionately named 'Number 44'. You prefer the older end of the pub to the new extension. It's more seasoned somehow. Leave the brighter, higher end to the yuppies, is your motto. Your favourite publican is behind the bar in his shirtsleeves, immaculate as ever.

"Not too many in yet," you comment.

His face turns to thunder as soon as he sees you. With a jerk of his head he motions you towards the upper end and points to a seat in the corner away from the bar, behind the railings. You feel like a prisoner, but what is your crime, you wonder? Have you blotted your copybook here, too? However, you follow the directions and do as instructed by the all-powerful. After all, he's the boss!

"What's this about?" you enquire politely.

"It's a neutral corner for you today, Tom!" he says, as looks down the bar.

"Before I even wet me whistle?" It's only then that you twig your friend the painter, working furiously at varnishing the benches at the lower end. The boss knows that if the "artist" and this particular customer get together that will be the end of varnishing for the day. So a wee bit of manoeuvring is required.

"No point in letting rain stop play, Tom. Too early in the day." he half jokes.

Your pal winks up at you, paintbrush dripping.

Later in the day, when Seán arrives, you are still in your little cell, sent to Coventry by the proprietor. But, boy, do you get mileage out of it. You regale to all who will listen, the tale of such an act.

"If you saw the look that he gave me. He cut me in two and I didn't even say mine's a pint and what's your pleasure?"

"Mum's the word," says Seán, laughing and putting his forefinger to his lips, mimicking one of your own familiar gestures.

"Like a schoolboy, he took his place in that corner and didn't budge," says the boss when he comes over to collect empties.

"And 'yer man' can't understand what he did to me that I didn't speak," you chuckle.

And the end of the story is that the job is completed in record time, thanks to the owner's timely intervention.

That evening, as you're making slow progress home, chatting to yourself after a bellyful of pints and craic with the lads, you come across the extraordinary sight of your bicycle mangled beyond recognition. A little worse for wear and trying hard to focus, you sit upon a low wall to study the scene before you.

The jumbled confusion of metal is a sorry sight to see, but what you can't figure out is how it got to be there in the first place. Maybe some little brat saw that bike behind the door in the bookie's office and stole it; you swear to yourself. Muttering, you look across the road to where it lies, its handlebars twisted back to front and the wheels buckled. What are you to do? You continue to sit and ponder, having a full blown conversation with yourself and that's where Seán comes across you some time later, not far from the spot you had met him that morning. Seán gasps when he notices the wreckage.

"I can't imagine Tom was riding this bike," Seán mulls. "Are you waiting for a lift home, Tom?" he asks.

You look up slowly into the eyes of your friend but the lights of a car blind you as it comes around the bend and you turn away. Seán recognises the driver and flags him down. The taxi driver slows to a halt and gets out of his car. He looks at Seán and then he looks at you.

"Has he come off the bike?" he asks.

"No, I don't think it's Tom's bike," Seán answers "but he needs a lift home."

The two men examine the scene before them. "He's fairly tanked up," Seán remarks more to himself than to Mick.

And so, Mick O'Neill, another good friend came to your rescue at Seán's behest and kindly drove you safely home to Ballinderry. They never found out who owned the wrecked bike, because yours was located safe and sound where you had left it behind the door, in Power's bookmakers in Dominick Place the next time you went up town.

There are many people who looked out for you in similar ways to Seán and Mick and all your good pals. We only heard many of the stories after your death. The Dominick Street friends, such as Jim and Irene Connolly, who always treated you as one of their own. Denis and Celine Johnston, who encouraged you to continue with your tennis and Jane Brennan, who gave you credit when you'd run out of fags (despite having been told not to do so by Helen!). Joe Caulfield, one of numerous publicans, who listened patiently to your stories, no matter how often you repeated them. People like Trish Devine (or Molloy as you used to call her) who often gave you a lift home from the Rugby Club in her little Mini. But only on condition that you didn't talk 'rubbish' on the way and you had to get out of the car immediately when she stopped outside the Post Office! Others include the Mulderry family and Jack and Eva Foy – to mention just a few.

In more recent times, Brian and Marie Willoughby often picked you up on your way down the (appropriately named) Gaol Hill at night and delivered you safely home to 'Willsboro'. Mick Burke was a good listener and admirer of yours. The Corbett, Egan and Cosgrave families were great friends and neighbours, as was Mrs. Kiernan, from across the road, who, with great patience used to repair your trousers for you, even when they were at a stage where they should have been thrown out. I hear Joe Tynan often lent you a few bob when you ran short, in latter years. You had many, many more true friends and people who were genuinely kind to you (too numerous to mention, as they say in all the best obituary acknowledgements!). And they all still remember you as 'such a gentleman' whenever your name is mentioned.

* * *

I see you kept a brochure of De Paul House, the seminary in Celbridge, where you used to spend your holidays in the 1980s. Your brother, John, who had been chaplain to the deaf for 13 years, was appointed Superior there around that time. To give both yourself and Helen a break from each other, he used to ask you to "care-take" there during the summer when many of the residents were away on holiday. I wonder if you found that a bit patronising?

The decline in vocations to the priesthood in the 1970s resulted in the two Vincentian seminaries in Blackrock and Glenart being closed down. Opened in 1977, De Paul House was a modern bungalow type complex, far from what most people imagined seminaries to be. The house is still there, beautifully situated along the road between Leixlip and Celbridge, in lovely surroundings, with the River Liffey just at the end of the back garden. It would have suited you there, Tom. Lots of space and quiet. You made some good friends during your time there too. Members of staff and clergy alike loved you... most of the time.

At least they did until the summer of 1988 when you were found to be 'over the limit' following an accident in a De Paul House car. It resulted, eventually, in your driving licence being endorsed:

> Disqualified from Driving for 3 years 3.1.89 under Section 49 of Road Traffic Act 1961/68

This was the second time you lost your licence, Tom. Can you imagine how disappointed everyone was with you? Not half as disappointed and mad with you as you were with yourself, I suppose. Yet you still get the mandate form witnessed by your publican!

And people still stand by you. Your brother, John, goes to great rounds to make certain that the insurers covered you for the accident, because originally they queried your eligibility to drive under the Vincentian block policy. And you also kept all that detail in the suitcase. It's almost as if you were making sure that we were left with the full picture after your death – not just the good bits.

Something else you left for us was a lovely card received from one of your De Paul contacts. He was one of the priests who wrote to you, years later, after Michael's death and not long before your own, even though he was having difficult times himself and a future which, at the time he wrote, looked "bleak". He obviously thought highly of you because, despite his own circumstances, he took the time to write a beautiful letter to you.

* * *

I'm not sure exactly when you were accepted as an annuitant of RUKBA (Royal United Kingdom Benefit Association[109]). It was thanks, once again, to Helen's perseverance that you were even considered by this group. You kept a little orange booklet, issued in 1996 as a centenary edition of their magazine, entitled "The Golden Link". It tells me that the association was founded in 1863 with one of its objectives being "awarding annuities to persons of professional or similar background, resident in the British Isles, who are aged or in need, or who are over 40 years of age but unable for reasons of infirmity to earn their own livelihood."

You fitted into the latter category and received assistance on occasions towards the purchase of new clothes or other essential items that dole money alone would not have allowed you to buy. By this stage most of your clothing came compliments of Christmas presents from the family, or the St. Vincent de Paul Society's shop.

I can only imagine how you felt at accepting such "charity". You were really on the slagheap at this stage. A far cry from the big man, the sporting genius who had flashed Aunt Bid's legacy in Limerick not so many years before. To be

---

109 Now known as independent*age* – supporting older people at home – www.independentage.org.uk

'hail fellow well met' wasn't so easy now, I'd safely say. And yet, you had your Mullingar pals, men who truly liked you. They genuinely enjoyed your company and all your tales of sporting endeavours from the past. They kept you going. They were interested.

Over the years you had developed a keen interest in placing small bets on horse racing. A number of tattered, old, yellow dockets were in the suitcase, detailing yankees, doubles and accumulators which had obviously failed to come through for you. No doubt you watched those races in the pub as you tried to fill the long, boring days. And then on the days when the money had run out, you might see some of these same horses being victorious. Luck of the draw!

* * *

When we have all 'left home' and settled down, Helen decides to start bed and breakfast at 'Willsboro'. Her main worry about this is the risk of you arriving home drunk and annoying the guests. We advise her to pretend, if she receives any complaints, that you're one of them. Just another guest staying for the night, but one who's had a few too many. After all, you mostly came in talking (albeit loudly) to yourself. Oh.... and cursing! She decides to give it a try.

It works out fairly well early on and you even help her out, in that you are often there to take bookings by phone or receive guests in the afternoons, when Helen is out. She begins to build up a nice little trade and, before long, has guests, choosing to stay a second and third time and some become regulars. One morning she notices one of these regular guests studying the silverware on the sideboard.

"Is he 'casing the joint'?" she wonders. He seems to be a nice man, well dressed and quite polite, but "you never know these days", she thinks. However, when he leaves she forgets all about it.

Not long afterwards, this man books in again. And once more, the following morning, when Helen goes in to serve him his breakfast, there he is at the sideboard. She gives him her speciality 'dirty look'. He seems to be trying to read the inscriptions on the cups and large silver tray and when Helen is pouring his tea he volunteers that he is interested in knowing who has won all the trophies. He tells her that his son plays rugby and he has an interest in the game. So she gives him the bones of your story. The cups belong to her brother, an all-round sportsman who captained the Munster rugby team in the late 1950s and early 1960s, had almost been capped for Ireland, remained a bachelor, and now lives with her. And when he goes home he tells his son about you.

I'm not sure if you ever actually met this man, but he was intrigued by your story and never failed to ask about you any time he stayed after that. It turned out that his son, Jeremy Davidson[*], was playing for Ulster, Ireland and the Lions at that time. After your death, Jeremy donated a rugby ball in your honour. It had been used in the second test in Durban, South Africa in June 1997 and is signed by all the members of that Lions tour. The family gave it out on loan to Mullingar R.F.C. to put on view for a short time and then we donated it to the 'boys in red' at Bohemians in Limerick. It is on display there, in a dedicated glass cabinet. After all, Mullingar has your pennant. We decided to share you around a bit!

As time goes on, at the B & B, the incidents of late night chatting and bad language begin to take their toll on Helen and it becomes very difficult for her to run a business with that worry hanging over her all the time. Eventually, after a family 'powwow', we decide to move you out to the little, self-contained, granny flat beside the house, which has just become vacant. For the plan to succeed, though, she has to be guaranteed the rent every week. In the house, she can (and often has to) endure you not always helping out with the finances, but the flat is a different kettle of fish. She needs that money.

I have often thought since that this must have been soul destroying for you, Tom. Although Paula and I 'sold' you the idea of independent living, basically it must have seemed to you that you were being thrown out of your home.

The flat is nice, but very small and for someone who likes space, it is confining to say the least. We apply for free electricity and rent allowance for you, move out your own familiar bed (with great difficulty I might add – Paula and I nearly broke our backs as you directed proceedings) and a few other items, and try as best we can to help you settle in. Soon, however, as suspected, you begin to fall back on the rent. Helen has had enough. And that is when you have no choice but to agree to giving me your pension book. The final indignity?

On Thursdays, from there on in, I meet you at the Post Office during my lunch break, give you your book to collect the money; wait outside until you give me the rent for Helen and return the book to me, until the next week. What you did with the remainder of the cash was your own business. While this method of rent collection worked for us, I realised it must have been very hard for you. It left you with very little pride. But you gave us no choice. You could be so difficult at times.

Converting

As I reach this stage in the suitcase I am reminded of a quote, attributed to Cardinal Basil Hume, which you frequently used in the latter years of your life. Often when you were up staying with your brother John in Iona Road in Dublin you might wander over to visit your friends Noel and Olive Oates. Some days you'd vary your route, so you could call in to Our Lady of Dolours Church in Glasnevin for some prayer and contemplation beforehand. Inscribed in the nave there, is a quotation which seemed to have particular resonance for you:

> Every saint has a past, every sinner has a future.[110]

I suspect, somehow, that you identified with the sinner rather than the saint, Tom. Did you still keep faith in an unknown future? Despite the apparent hopelessness of your situation?

* * *

I don't think I have ever seen you as elated about anything as you were when you were reading Tony O'Reilly's autobiography. It was summer 1996. I can still picture you in your blue, short-sleeved tee shirt, book clutched under your arm, in the garden in 'Willsboro', making a point about some detail or other in the book. Anyone who would listen to you was treated to a diatribe of sorts. The marked difference was that you were doing this when you were stone cold sober. The book excited you; it brought you back to times long gone and told tales and stories of a life that you had been part of. We watched in amazement when your face was transformed (and dare I say joyful) as you spoke about the book.

This book had such an impact on you that you actually put pen to paper and wrote to the man for his 60th birthday. The carefully opened envelope containing his reply was kept safely in your suitcase. He thanked you for your good wishes, spoke about being "touched on the shoulder by one's own mortality" on reaching 60 and went on to invite you to the Heinz '57 races the following August. You were THRILLED! I remember it well. Because it was around the same time I was worrying about your weight loss and lack of appetite. And you

110 Cardinal Basil Hume, (1923-1999) Ninth Archbishop of Westminster.

A Sunday visit to Irishtown
Tom and Hugh

had always had a great appetite. Drunk or sober, hung-over or well, you were always able to enjoy a good feed.

Most Sundays since I had married in 1988, you used to come out to Hugh[III] and me for dinner after 12.30 Mass. Some days you would leave your bicycle at the cathedral and wander down to our usual parking spot for a lift out; other days you would cycle the short journey, trouser legs tucked into your socks, plastic bag of titbits for the dogs dangling from the handlebars. In the spring and early summer of 1996, while you still came out to the house, you didn't dine with us. You began to say you weren't hungry or that you'd had a late breakfast and I would duly wrap the plated dinner in cling film or tin foil and you would take it home to heat up in the microwave later. You would walk the dogs while we ate.

Indeed it is one such Sunday, around this time, that you make a detour via Lynch's pub on your way home. After a couple of pints of the creamy stuff, yourself and Johnny Eivers (one of the last drovers in Westmeath) get chatting. Now for some reason, Johnny thinks you were a teacher, and so it is by that title that he refers to you as he recounts this story to Hugh not long afterwards. Seemingly, the conversation between the two of you is getting interesting as the shadows begin to lengthen, and you both realise that it's coming on for tea-time and you haven't even had dinner yet.

"Just one sec," you say. "Haven't I a bit of grub in the bag here!"

You call the barman and order two sets of cutlery and a plate.

III Hugh Cafferty (1943-1999) husband of the author.

Now to those readers who don't know this pub, it wouldn't have been known at the time for serving meals. Sandwiches and soup maybe, but never a main course. So sets of cutlery might have been scarce and hard to come by and this request would have offered a fair challenge to the barman. However he came up trumps with some knives, spoons and a soup plate, and Sunday lunch was divided equally between the "teacher" and the drover, and both went home content.

In mid June the invitation arrives from Tony O'Reilly. The Phoenix Stakes will be held in Leopardstown racecourse on 11th August, the day after your 66th birthday. It's addressed to Mr. & Mrs. Tom Cleary and GUESS who opens the envelope in error. Helen! Thank God I wasn't there for that little episode. I suppose it was all picture and no sound for a few days? You must have been fuming.

You proudly pull the invite out of your inside pocket after Mass the following Sunday and display it to Hugh and me.

"Who'll you bring with you?" I venture ... "I could pose as your wife!"

No comment, just a withering look is all I get in response. The next day, you ring the given RSVP number and explain that you are a bachelor and will be bringing a guest with you, not a wife. Mick O'Neill (your friend the taxi-driver) is the lucky man.

Tom bumped into a family friend on his day out at Leopardstown.
Maureen Gowran and Tom Cleary.

An Roinn Leasa Shóisialaigh
Department of Social Welfare

Ainm:
(Name) THOMAS CLEARY

Seoladh:
(Address) WILLSBORO
MULLINGAR

Cliant-Uimhir
Client No.
676655

Stádas:
(Status) 1

Signature/Síniú

As June passes into July, you begin to complain of a lump in your throat and say you've been to the doctor. A medical card holder, you are put on a waiting list to be sent into the hospital for tests. Soon you begin to complain of difficulty swallowing and the flesh starts to melt off your bones. You're a sorry looking sight by the time 11th August comes around.

* * *

Soon after your great day out at the races, you are called to the hospital at Mullingar to see a stomach specialist. You're to fast from midnight and attend the Day Ward for blood tests and a procedure. In my heart I knew your complaint was serious and had probably progressed quite far before you sought help. The family had been pleading with you for some time to get yourself seen to, all to no avail. However, on the day, ever hopeful, I prayed that, at least whatever they found, it would be operable.

You look so vulnerable on the trolley as you wait to go in for the examination. The usual backless theatre gown is flimsy and I glimpse how thin you actually are – and with your false teeth removed, your face is gaunt and you speak with a lisp. I am quite shocked. Afterwards when I speak with the consultant, the awful truth cannot be ignored any longer. (He told me more than he told you, Tom.) I feel very emotional but have to gather myself together before facing you. Did you wonder at my off-hand attitude when I called to take you home that day? As it happened, I had a huge lump in my own throat which stopped me from saying much. You're glad it's over and you tell me you have to wait for news from your G.P. But I know that you are shortly for the knife in a Dublin hospital. Not long afterwards you are given a date. You will be admitted in early October for prior tests and surgery will take place on 4th.

* * *

I'm on tenterhooks for the entire day of your operation. Up and down like a hen on an egg. It's difficult for me to concentrate on my work. I know that you are due to go to the operating theatre early in the morning so I reckon that, all going well, you should be back in intensive care before I go to lunch at one. It is all I can do to resist ringing earlier to see if there's any news. Eventually I ring St. James' Hospital to enquire. They have little information for me that I don't already know from my experience as a nurse.

"Mr. Cleary was sent to the operating theatre early this morning and will be transferred to intensive care soon after his procedure."

You're not expected back on their ward and that's all they'll say. I ring again immediately after lunch. The nurse who answers knows nothing.

"Sorry," she says "I've just come on duty at two."

"Could you put me through to the intensive care unit please and I'll enquire there?" I ask.

"Hold on."

The nurse in I.C.U. says you're still in theatre and to ring back in an hour. The prescribed hour later I try again. Still no joy.

"He's probably in recovery for a while following his procedure," I'm told. I am advised to give it another hour.

I'm very unsettled and cannot understand the delay. Why is your surgery taking so long? Why is there little or no information forthcoming? Would they not transfer you directly to I.C.U. rather than sidelining you into a recovery bay? In my mind, you seem to have disappeared into the ether somewhere between specialities in St. James' Hospital. I ring Paula who, after all, is listed as your next of kin. Maybe they'll give her some concrete information if she explains who she is. No such luck. "Ring back later," she's told.

By about five o'clock, fed up getting the run around, I ring for the umpteenth time. This time I ask for the sister in charge of the intensive care unit, one part of me not wanting to annoy her as I realise how busy she's likely to be.

"Sorry to bother you," I begin.

"No problem; how can I help?" She sounds nice.

"I'm enquiring about Tom Cleary, who was operated on today by Professor ... (I pause, forgetting the name!) He should be well back with you by now but nobody seems to know where he is. He's not on the ward; he doesn't seem to be in the recovery room; he's not with you; he couldn't possibly be still in theatre, so I am wondering what's happening?"

"And you are ...?"

"His niece. I'm a nurse myself," I add, voice wobbling, not sure as to how she will interpret that piece of information, knowing that sometimes nurses don't like being questioned by 'their own'.

"I'm very worried," I continue, in an effort to soften the tone.

"We are expecting a Mr. Cleary, but he hasn't arrived here yet," she offers. At least that's something for me to clutch at. "Perhaps you could ring back in an hour and I'll have further information for you."

I almost explode. "Do you realise how many time I've been told to ring back in an hour today? Something is wrong, isn't there?" I probe.

"Not at all," she responds confidently. "He's probably being kept in recovery for a while to be close to the team that carried out the surgery."

"I suppose that makes sense," I say doubtfully, but every instinct I have tells me all is not right. Hanging up the phone, I think of all the 'reassurance' I had given you before your surgery. All that pit-pat stuff about the waiting being the worst part and as soon as it was over you'd be concentrating so hard on your own recovery that you wouldn't have time to worry, or feel much pain, blah, blah, blah!! What does any of it mean now that you seem to have disappeared into a black hole somewhere in a Dublin hospital? My lack of control over the situation bothers me. If you were in Mullingar, this wouldn't have happened. At least in the hospital where I'm so well known, I'd have no problem getting information. Here I am, after one whole day, none the wiser than I had been first thing that morning. But then, I also know that if you were in Mullingar, you wouldn't be able to have this specialist surgery. Nothing to do but wait I suppose. Dejected, I tidy up at work and get ready for home.

Hugh can't believe it when I get home and tell him the news. "Surely, they're able to tell you something?" he asks.

"You try," I plead. "Tell them you're his nephew."

He has no better luck than me.

"If he has died they'd have to tell us wouldn't they?" I ask.

"Tom's not going to die. He's made of strong stuff," Hugh slaps the table with the palm of his hand, making me jump. Later, while we are playing with the food on our dinner plates the hall doorbell rings. It's my friend Annie, who is also a nurse, to enquire after the man she considers to be her own 'Uncle Tom'.

Incredulous, she tries to offer some consolation but I know she fears the worst, just like me. Next comes Rosie from next door. "Any news on Uncle Tom?" she calls from the hallway. When she comes as far as the kitchen, Hugh just shakes his head sadly. "Oh" is all she says, disappointed.

We're making small talk when the phone rings. Hugh answers it. "Hold on a minute and I'll let you talk to her," he passes the receiver to me. "Paula" he mouths.

She's upset. "A doctor from James' rang me and I don't know what he was saying. I'm on my own here and I couldn't understand what he was saying...."

"OH MY GOD"

"....he's going to ring you now, I gave him your number, so I'll hang up." She's gone.

"What is it?" Annie asks "... bad news?"

Breaking out in a cold sweat, I take off my jumper, saying nothing.

The phone interrupts the silence and I lunge for it.

"Mrs. Cafferty?"

"Yes, speaking..."

It's the doctor from St. James'. He tells me some scanty but shocking details of your appalling day. I can't take it all in. I tell him I've been ringing all day long and getting nowhere. The bottom line is that you are now in intensive care on a ventilator, with little chance of survival, and probably have suffered brain damage, following your total collapse in the operating theatre.

Following that phone call, I feel immense heat and take off another layer of clothing, all the time fanning my face and breathing in puffs. The shock is immense. I am unable to talk. My hands are sweating and my armpits are stinging. So much is running through my mind. The phone rings again. Paula. "I can't get any reply from home," she says. The sound of her voice brings me to my senses a bit and 'sensible me' takes over, outlining what I think we should do. We contact Gerard who says he'll join Paula and they'll head for the hospital together. Hugh rings work and takes the night off; Rosie and Annie pack our bags, as I put my jumper back on, and begin to contact the remainder of the family. Poor Paula, getting that phone call on her own, and she over six months pregnant. I'm kicking myself for the bright idea of Paula being named as next of kin, simply because she lives closest to the hospital. I berate myself. How could I have been so stupid?

Helen was at a funeral that day and now we can't manage to get in touch with her. She's not at home; she's not in her friend's house. In the end we arrange for someone to drive her to Dublin later on, and Hugh and I carry on without her. I pick up my mobile phone on the way out the door, although it's sort of pointless because very few even know I have one, let alone my number. We stop in

Kinnegad and I buy a call card for the public phone and some minty sweets. Something tells me it's going to be a long night.

The journey to Dublin passes mostly in silence, as thoughts race through my mind. By the time we arrive at the hospital, park the car, ask for directions at Reception, and find our way along interminable corridors (being passed at one stage by a porter on a bicycle!), Paula and Gerard are already there. We hug and cry. Maybe we hadn't realised how much you meant to us until we thought we mightn't have you back. And if we did get you back it now looked like it wouldn't be the same Tom who would be returning. Time enough for that, I scolded myself, silently. Put those thoughts out of your head. They have not yet been in to see you but they have spoken to the nurse on duty and are waiting for the doctor.

We sit on the narrow bench outside the unit. It's very quiet. Occasionally someone rushes past us, not even glancing in our direction, in case we might make eye contact. *(Probably afraid we'll stop them and ask them something, I decide.)* Time passes in small talk and minty sweets. It's a cold unwelcoming space we find ourselves in.

"Why can't we go in to see him?"

"We've to wait for the doctor."

"I'm sick waiting all day, I want to see him."

"Sshh" Hugh consoles us "As the Lord said...can you not wait one hour with me," he quotes..." or something like that anyway, Father!" he nudges Gerard and winks at us.

Hugh's biblical quote lightens the moment for us all. We're smiling when the doctor arrives.

"Relatives of Mr. Cleary?" he enquires. He looks exhausted. Pale skin, five o'clock shadow, dark yellow rings under his eyes and cracked, dried lips.

"Yes, that's us," I say, even though there's no one else in the vicinity.

"Are you his children?" he asks politely.

"No, he's a bachelor," Gerard this time. "He's lived with us for about 30 years or so."

"Oh, so he's like a father figure to you." It's a statement. We look at each other, with sad smiles.

"Well, not exactly..." it's Paula who speaks, "more like an older brother really. A much older brother."

"I see," he says, doubtfully.

But he couldn't have seen. The truth is you have lived on the periphery of our lives for all the years you've been in our home, dipping in only when you feel like it, but always there, ready to help, without ever being intrusive. You never take much of an active role in what's going on.

"Well, as you know he is back in intensive care, on a ventilator as his surgery was not all plain sailing," he states the obvious, looking down at the patient chart in his hand.

"He's a very fit man," he says next.

I doubt it, but don't want to get into that with the doctor. *(He smokes and he drinks, he devours butter and he's your proverbial couch potato, but if you want to think he's a fit man, off you go.)*

"Not really," someone says.

"I would say he is," the doctor insists.

"Well he cycles a bike and goes for occasional walks..." I offer "...and he was a very active sportsman in his youth..." I trail off. It doesn't seem relevant.

"I have never seen any patient who put up such a fight as this man, ...ehm, Mr. Cleary," he says tiredly checking the notes once more.

"Tom, call him Tom."

"Tom fought a very hard battle today, one I was privileged to witness and be part of. In all my years, I've never seen a patient with such a will to live ... I only hope it is worth it for him," he says, finishing sadly.

And then he goes on to tell us the details of what has happened.

* * *

You had spent the entire day in the operating theatre. The tumour was at the end of your gullet, as feared, but it had tentacles, which snaked along onto the wall of your stomach and across your gastric artery. The team of surgeons and nursing staff did their best. The tumour was carefully removed while, at the same time, they discussed their options on the best solution for dealing with the feeler branch of its extension. In the end, once they were able to get a closer look, the only option open to them was to scrape it off the stomach wall and artery as best they could, in an effort to contain it.

This they did, as the anaesthetist observed your vital signs closely for any deterioration in your condition. It was slow, tedious and dangerous work. They closed you up eventually, and after a number of energy-sapping hours working on you, they stepped back from the table, pulling off their bloodied latex gloves and throwing them into the kick-bucket at their feet. There were sighs of relief all around. Your condition was described as stable at this stage. And from that doctor's description, I have often imagined the scene.

As some members of the team prepare to move out of the theatre, fresh nurses and porters begin to take over your care. Swab counts are being double-checked in the background as you're lifted onto the trolley, which is to take you out to the intensive care unit. It's then that all hell breaks loose. Your gastric artery bursts. All your vital signs drop rapidly and your abdomen begins to fill up with gushing arterial blood.

"HE'S COLLAPSED" someone shouts.

The team goes into action immediately. You're hoisted unceremoniously back onto that table in the blink of an eye. One nurse tears at your gown, as the surgeon literally rips you open once more. This is the emergency of emergencies. No time for careful scalpel technique here; there's barely time for sterile gloves. (I know what he did, Tom, you showed me the scars...remember?) They're losing you. Rapidly. Blood pressure plummeting, bright red blood spraying, heart stopping, resuscitation commencing, infusion under pressure, chaos reigning. I see it all. I almost panic even thinking about it.

All available hands from other theatres are called to assist. Six units of blood, which had been cross-matched for you, are available immediately and transfusion begins. But the blood is going nowhere. (It was described to us afterwards as being like "trying to fill a bucket that had an enormous hole in the bottom.") Urgent requests are sent to the laboratory for six more pints of blood.

"Make that ten," someone shouts.

Your abdomen is a swamp, as the surgeon tries to find the rupture. One vacuum unit is barely enough to suck the spurting blood away from the site of the tear. A porter is sent running for a large portable model to augment what's already there.

"Pull on those retractors," the surgeon calls desperately to his assistant, "it's a quagmire in here. I can't see anything."

"We're losing him," the anaesthetist warns.

High drama follows. Quicker than they pour the blood in through your veins, it bursts out of your arteries.

"He'll exsanguinate[112] soon if you don't find the source," someone states the obvious.

"We're losing him," the anaesthetist warns again.

"We heard you the first time."

"More blood needed."

"How many this time?"

"Better make it ten again."

About then, they find the gash in the artery. It is huge.

"Not much hope of closing this," but they continue to fight, because you are not letting go, Tom. You amaze them with your tenacity and will to live.

"He's a fit bugger, I'll give him that. What age is he?"

"All the sixes, 66," one of the nurses says, in a pun on bingo calling. It lightens the atmosphere for the team. They are used to working together. They understand each other and the parts they all play in the overall outcome for peoples' lives, every day of the week.

The porter returns with a message from the laboratory that they need to know well in advance if they are likely to require more blood than the 26 units

112 Bleed to death.

they have already ordered. It will have to come by special delivery from Blood Transfusion Headquarters, as the hospital's reserves of your type are quickly running out. It's looking as if they'll need more, was the reply.

"And a lot more, at that."

All day, until seven o'clock that evening, they fight for you, Tom, and all day you stay there with them. A battle of huge proportions. They think it's a losing battle, but they can't just give up on you. They have to keep trying. It's what they do. As for you, your spirit is not going to let you be runner-up in this one. This is an encounter unlike any of your sporting career, but this time you intend to come out the winner. In the end they transfuse you with over 40 units of blood, repair the rupture, close you up and hand you over for intensive care.

I had never heard the likes of it in all my days of nursing. I couldn't imagine how your body had survived. But I knew you were going to be a vegetable.

* * *

Helen and Freda[113] arrive, panting, before the doctor has finished giving us the details. More hugs and more tears. We all concentrate on the doctor's words, as he continues. Eventually he says he'll ask the nurse to come out to take some of us in to see you.

Paula and I are the first to go in to the abnormally bright warehouse that is the intensive care unit. Despite the warnings from the nurse, and despite my training, I get an enormous shock.

"Oh, Tom....." I gasp, putting my entire fist into my mouth to block the sound of my distress when I first see you. It's like something out of a film. You seem suspended in mid air, stripped to the waist, twice your usual size, bloated with fluids and other treatments, sedated into unconsciousness. Unrecognisable.

"He's like the Michelin Man," I say, tears blinding my eyes. You look like you're wired to the moon, surrounded by monitoring equipment, E.C.G. leads, drip counters, transfusions of blood and fluids, a catheter, a huge ventilator breathing for you, you don't look like my Uncle Tom. I can't take my eyes off your bare torso, with its massive padded dressing hiding the mutilated flesh beneath.

"You can touch him," the nurse speaks. I put my right palm on your forehead and stroke the back of your left hand lightly. "You're back in bed, it's all over," the nurse in me says. "Paula's here," I step aside. Paula tenderly touches your cheek, afraid to do any more because of the sophisticated equipment surrounding us and attached to your body. "Hi, Tom," she squeaks.

The nurse pulls up two little stools. "Sit there beside him for a while," she

113 A family friend.

suggests. We do as we're told, me closest to your head. It's then I see the familiar little suitcase with the number seven on the side of it, perched poignantly in behind the head of the bed; and a colossal rush of emotion overwhelms me. I can just picture you packing for the journey in your little flat before you left for Dublin. How worried you must have been, yet unable to voice it. You had no one really special to share those feelings with. All enquiries from interested family were brushed aside in your usual "I'm alright Jack" tone of voice.

"Look," I point the luggage out to Paula. We weep silently. It's not supposed to be like this. This isn't routine. This is the type of thing that happens to other people. Nightmare stuff. We feel so helpless. I begin to look for positive signs. Your colour is good; your monitor readings look alright to me, and you have some urine output in your catheter bag. But I am aware that I could actually be looking at a corpse which is being 'maintained'. I give you a little pinch. No response to painful stimuli, but then you're well sedated. What else, let me think. I say a little prayer. I wish I could look in the suitcase for your rosary beads and put them into your hand. Maybe they'd be in the way. I decide against it. The wee prayer will have to do. I know you have been anointed prior to surgery. I smile as I think about the time you had told me that piece of news. I said, "that's not Extreme Unction anymore, Tom; it's called the Sacrament of the Sick." You responded by telling me the world was definitely gone mad when even the Catholic Church was getting politically correct!

After a few moments I become aware of the noise of the equipment, beeping monitors, the hissing and clicking of the ventilator. I look around at the other patients nearby. Similar sounds surround them.

"That noise'll drive Tom mad," I say to Paula. Your sensitive hearing is a family joke, but I know in my heart of hearts that hearing is the last of the senses to go in a dying patient. I decide that after such a great fight you aren't 'gone' anywhere, you can hear all that noise and it is bugging you no end. The least we can do for you is reduce it a little bit. The nurse comes over. "Everything alright?" she asks pleasantly. We tell her that there are more people outside to see you and that we'll leave now and come back in the morning. I ask her to put some cotton wool in your ears to ease the noise for you. She looks at me doubtfully. She isn't too sure about that strange request. "Please," I ask, "he hates noise of any sort and this place will drive him wild. He wears cotton wool in his ears all the time at home." She says she will. Outside, four eager faces wait for news. We prepare them as best we can and they take their turns going in to see you. Gerard mentions the cotton wool once more before we leave for the night.

The following day we all gather mid-morning in Paula's house, joined by your brothers and their wives. It is a sombre gathering. Nobody had expected this outcome and the worry is apparent on all our faces. The reports from the hospital, however, are reasonably encouraging considering all you have been through. You've had a good night and the nurse on duty is happy with your condition.

"Critical but stable," she had said that morning. We fill John, Michael and Gerry in as best we can as to the present position and speak about your eventual prognosis, if you are to survive this. The possibility that moderate to severe brain damage is an almost foregone conclusion is uppermost in my mind. What's to become of you? How will we care for you? Nothing could have prepared me for this.

Paula caters for us all with tea, coffee and snack refreshments. We're discussing who should go in to the hospital first, knowing that we all can't arrive en masse and expect to see you. Michael is due to be admitted to St. Vincent's Hospital later that day for further tests following surgery which had taken place some time previously. He and Bernadette have their own worries but the rest of us are unaware of them at this moment in time. As we are sorting out how best to approach things, Paula's almost five-year-old daughter, Lisa, comes into the room, takes one look around at all the serious faces and announces "My Mammy has a baby in her tummy and she's wearing all Auntie Ursula's BIG BRAS!"

Injury time

The day after your surgery, family members are allowed in to see you in dribs and drabs, two at a time. You are still so heavily sedated that there is no way of knowing what way you are. Really are I mean. Like what way are you inside in your head? I'm raging that, despite being asked twice, and the reason having been explained twice, no one had thought to put cotton wool in your ears. In fact I am livid. That truly maddens me but also serves to emphasise how useless I feel. I ask once more. Someone who looks fairly senior this time.

"Will you attend to Mr. Cleary's daughter," she passes me, like a parcel, on to a young nurse.

"Niece," I say,

"Pardon?"

"He's a bachelor" *(...and if you were in any way bothered about your patients you might know that little bit of detail about him. I feel like screaming.)*

"Oh!" is all she says.

By the second morning after your operation, your sedation has been slightly reduced and we begin to get some response when we pinch you. Things look more hopeful as some of us head off for lunch. Ward rounds are due to take place and we need a breather anyway. We're advised to leave it until evening time to come back. The sister tells us that we'll, more than likely, be in it for the long haul and no point in everybody getting exhausted at this early stage. I know she's warning us about that vegetable we're going to have to bring home with us, eventually. My mind is working overtime as to how we will all deal with this.

Following an afternoon off, we return to the hospital to visit. I had bought some cotton wool to put into your ears myself because despite many oft repeated requests the staff had not attended to this little detail of your care. You're much more awake and seem to be communicating with your eyes. Better still, your hand responds when we squeeze. You are still surrounded by paraphernalia but somehow we don't notice that as much as we had before. They say you will be weaned off the ventilator by degrees and things will look even brighter then.

"Those eyes are too bright for someone with brain damage," I say hopefully to Helen as we leave the hospital that day.

"He pressed my hand," she says simply.

On the morning of day three, you are moved to a different position in the unit.

Helen almost panics. She thinks you are dead.

"Step down," I think immediately, "that has to be good news."

You are off the ventilator, propped up slightly, eyes closed, but peaceful.

"Tom?" we venture.

You slowly open your eyes, but just as soon close them again. We just sit beside you, quietly hoping for a miracle. I take a look around the unit. It's such a busy place, with people in all sorts of uniforms coming and going, doing their bit for patients or writing notes onto charts. Coming up to lunchtime, once again, we leave the unit and go for refreshments.

By the time we return, the doctors have done their rounds. The sister stops us before we go in to see you and fills us in on the happenings in our absence. She tells us you are much more alert, that, frankly, the entire team is stunned at your progress and it appears, to them at least, that you have all your faculties intact. She says that the family might notice some difference in your personality or mood but that there are no apparent ill effects at this stage from a medical perspective. In fact, she says, you've attempted to continue a conversation with the anaesthetist that started the night before your surgery.

"Something about an old school tie?" she ends in a questioning high tone.

Your eyes are open when we go back in, but your face is filled with pain. You speak. Wow! We're thrilled, but can't let you see that. We try to behave normally, as if everything is routine. As far as you're concerned, it's the day after your surgery and some time is to elapse before you realise the ordeal you have been through. For now it is enough for us that you're awake and, apparently, functioning. Helen goes out to make some phone calls with the good news, and I watch as a nurse comes to check your vital signs.

* * *

As the days pass you continue to astound medics and family alike. Despite your major struggle, the loss of blood, deprivation of oxygen and critical condition, it seems that fears for your potential status as a 'vegetable' are diminishing. To add to that good news, we realise that the anaesthetist has been true to his word and has passed on your message to an old rugby pal. Soon, news of your illness spreads and the lads from your Limerick days begin to rally. Some visit you, others write letters or send get-well cards. Your Mullingar mates meet with Limerick and Irish Greats in the waiting room of the hospital and the craic is mighty. In no time at all you are transferred to the high dependency ward (or as you used to refer to it 'the high deficiency ward'!).

Word travels, and many of your erstwhile friends are saddened and upset to hear of your generally 'reduced circumstances'. Most of them have assumed through the years that, after your Limerick days, you settled down, married and have a family. They have difficulty correlating the man of the past with that of the present. But their faith in your ability to overcome the hurdle of this illness remains constant and I'm sure their belief in you helps to boost your immune system no end.

Your condition continues to improve and not long afterwards there is talk of your discharge from hospital. You still don't realise how near to death you have been. We decide, and you agree, that you should recuperate with Hugh and me in Irishtown. And so you come to live with us for a while. In no time at all you settle in. You have space and time alone while we're out at work, but I'm no distance away if you feel you need help. Helen calls to see you daily with the newspapers. Your friends set up a telephone account in the bookies for you. We're thrilled to have you staying with us and to see your strength improving. You still have quite a few visitors and lots of phone calls. Soon I begin to recognise the voices on the telephone. The most regular callers from your sporting days are 'Mo' Moran, 'Gooser' Geary and 'Wigs' Mulcahy, but there are many more. And finally I think you understand the essence of what rugby is all about. Caps don't matter!

* * *

Do you remember the day, in late October, when you were recuperating at our house and you started to read some of the letters you received from your friend Seán Elliffe while you were in hospital? I could see in your eyes that his friendship meant a lot to you. He was a great support to you, in good times and bad. I suspect he was one of the few people, in latter years, that you 'let in' to see the real Tom.

You had other pals such as George Lord (ex tobacco factory), Tommy 'Tosser' Houlihan (the great hurler), Matt 'Rasher' Ryan and Harry Bauer (both former butchers), Eamon 'Killer' Byrne (the great boxer), 'Fast Brush' (painter and decorator), the Naughton brothers, Johnny Eivers (the cattle drover), Ollie Hynes (first man to arrive at the funeral home the night of your removal), Maurice Sinnott (a genuine teacher), Johnny Byrne ('the man from Borrisoleigh'), Tommy Farrell (kindness itself) and many more. Over the years, your 'meetings' in the local with these men kept your spirits up, gave you a purpose of sorts and the joke amongst you was about committee membership in this club of sorts. But Seán was special. Between the two of you, you had a language all of your own, as the following letter will testify. When you read it aloud to me I hadn't a clue what you were on about for most of it, but it was obviously special to you. At the time I dared not ask for too many explanations or I might have run the risk of you closing up and refusing to share it with me.

> "A Chara Tomás," you began to read:
> Before we go to press the Senior Committee and the inner circle has directed me to convey our best wishes for a speedy recovery – the vote was unanimous, including the back benchers.

You chuckled at this and went on:

> The Friday delegation led by Billy Boy and our Belfast representative were delighted to see you making progress and fighting the good fight and no holes [sic] barred. The scrum is never far away and you always come to mind in any given sport.

I remember your eyes were bright and there was an expression of pure joy on your face as you read this letter aloud to me:

> Who said "a man of few words?" (would it be the man from Borrisoleigh?) Must be the understatement of the year!

"That's referring to my friend Johnny Byrne," you explained to me:

> Several comments were made, nothing signed, observations were made and you were sorely missed at Church Parade on Sundays.

"That'd be a gathering in Coughlan's pub after Mass on Sunday," you tried to enlighten me.

"Coughlan's?" I queried.

"Now Jimmy Wallace's pub," you looked over your glasses at me:

> I suppose, Tom, you could do with what's happening in the street and the boys on the hill (Ballinderry – Lodge 13).

"What's that?" I interrupted.

"Oh some of the boys heard that when the Orange Lodge was marching, that Ballinderry Lodge 13 was the oldest Lodge in the North and so that's what we call the Naughton brothers' house in Ballinderry .... for the craic," you giggled:

> On Sunday, Maurice joined us at the Sacred Heart 9.30 Mass with the Naughton clan. (Colm was excused – late night manoeuvres) Bill was duty chef and the pan was on at high. Maurice said "Grace" (addressed his own synod!) – Ballinderry is saved!

"I don't get that," I ventured not too sure of your reaction.

"Maurice Sinnott addressed his own synod," you said, not one bit exasperated at my lack of understanding at the pun.

"Oh."

You went on:

> We reported to the clinic one o'clock assembly."

I laughed out loud. "I know where that was," I said, thinking of Jimmy Wallace's pub!

You beamed, continuing:

> Ollie was in the chair. Some strange client being interrogated. The barman 'mein host' keeping a beady eye and no sign of Crowley.

"No sign of Paddy Crowley," you explained before I had to ask:

> Tosser marked absent (all night séance). Rasher was out in sympathy. A mixed agenda – condolences were passed. "Fast Brush" gone to eternal reward (interred in his native Letterkenny). The meeting broke up, scattered by three o'clock for the match in Cusack Park (Eire Óg versus Kinnegad, 1-10 to 0-10). Meanwhile I had a near miss with my Iron Horse at the Ballinderry Roundabout. New pothole development, Frank McIntyre be warned.

"Is that the Councillor?" I asked.

"'Tis," you said chortling. "We are always joking that we are his representatives around the town on our 'iron horse bicycles'."

> That's it Tom – it's time for school.

"Seán's on a Fás[114] scheme at the boys' school" you clarified.

> Meanwhile, Tosser is game for anything – rabbit rare – hare or wild duck. Keep your head down – nothin' is sacred in the country!!
>
> Slán, God Bless, Seán.
>
> P.S. Ollie wants to know has Tony O'Reilly been in touch?"

* * *

114 Ireland's Employment and Training Authority.

I often recall one day in particular when you were in tip-top form after a visit from Seán and you and Hugh were having a chat about the happenings in the town.

You regale Hugh with up-to-date tales of the lads. Seán and Colm Naughton have attended a tree planting ceremony in honour of Blessed Edmund Rice at the Christian Brothers' School in College Street, across from the Garda Station where Hugh is based. Ruth Illingworth, local historian, speaks while the boys and the remainder of the gathering listen. You describe Seán's version of the antics of the local acoustics expert, Johnny Mullen, as he struggles with feedback near the famine tree. The lads retire to 'H.Q.' afterwards where there is lots of banter.

"I miss it," you confide.

"You'll be back soon," Hugh consoles you.

"I wonder if I'll ever be able to swallow a pint again."

"Of course you will," Hugh resists the urge to give you a slap of reassurance on the back – you are too delicate. He realises that even a small tap risks knocking you into the middle of next week. You are so frail. As it is he is afraid even to touch you.

"Seán told me that my 'Party Political Broadcasts' are sorely missed."

"Of course they are." What else can Hugh say?

"Not to mention Ollie's 'cross examination' during tea break," you continue.

There's a lull in conversation and a far-away look in your eyes.

"And Sinnott has the 'flu." you recall more of the chat with Seán. "Off the cocktails for a while like myself" At this, you throw a butt into the grate and make an effort to rise out of the armchair by the fire. Hugh supports your elbow and passes you the walking stick.

"I'm going to lie down for a bit," you say sadly.

Mullingar
Monday Morning 25th November 1996

Hello Tom,

I'm listening to the recording of Micheál Ó Hehir's[115] "Voice of Irish Sport" whose sad passing yesterday will affect us all. Born in Glasnevin 2nd June 1920 – Remember he did his first broadcast in our own Cusack Park – 1938.

On my way to 12.30 Mass yesterday (Feast of Christ the King) I was intercepted by Tosser in Mary Street. There's two ducks ready for the

115 Micheál Ó Hehir (1920-1996). Legendary Irish radio and television sports commentator. Noted for his Gaelic (football & hurling) and racing commentaries. Micheál did his first Gaelic Athletic Association commentary on 14th August 1938 when Galway defeated Monaghan in the All-Ireland Senior Football Semi-Final at Cusack Park in Mullingar.

Hill. Can I collect? No doubt he was looking forward to collecting "the bounty". I reported to the Clinic on "Q" – Ollie and Colm opened the meeting and Jimmy called "last orders – three o'clock adjournment." Topic of conversation Albert's damages[116] – Rasher's weight – and a possible comeback by the Tosser's shootin' ability. (Camán if not the gun!) Old photos were produced – notably Paddy Coughlan[117]- action shot behind the Bar. We also had time to "fill in" a few potholes!

Not a word about the "Three Irish Tenors" performance in the Cathedral the night previous. Ollie interrupted! It would cost you another tenner to get in!! – No argument. I mentioned the Rugby at Lansdowne[118] – better ask Tom Cleary was the response, so can I have a written report for next meeting?!

Well Tom, it's time I asked, "How are you?" Whatever you thought about the performance at Lansdowne – a marked improvement since losing to Samoa[119]. McIvor* had a very good game, but the Aussies proved their class, especially in the closing stages when superior fitness told. I bet you were glued to the set. What did you think?

The match in Cusack Park versus Antrim was postponed yesterday due to weather after early inspection to facilitate supporters. That didn't worry Tosser (he had a late appointment in Murray's followed by "All our yesterdays" in 'Number 44').

The weather must be curtailing your "training programme" and daily exercises. Snow showers Saturday night made Ballinderry a "no go area" early Sunday. I went to 12.30 Mass in the Cathedral. I made it to the Hill later. Smoke was coming from the chimney pots including Messrs. Dolans' and the cats were on alert, on duty outside the Naughton demesne!

Colm told me Bill is due back from London this week and was asking for you before he left – hopes to see you soon.

Well Tom, I "sign on" this morning. I finished at school last

---

116 Albert Reynolds, former Irish Taoiseach. This refers to his 1996 libel battle with the *Sunday Times* newspaper. The paper libelled Mr. Reynolds when it said that he had lied to the Dáil in relation to the delay in extraditing Father Brendan Smyth (one of Ireland's most notorious paedophiles, who was eventually sentenced to 12 years in prison for 74 sexual assaults). The knock-on effect eventually brought down the Fianna Fail-Labour coalition in 1994. Mr. Reynolds won the six-week action but was awarded only one penny in damages.

117 Former owner of Jimmy Wallace's pub, Mount Street, Mullingar.

118 Ireland v Australia, Lansdowne Road, 23rd November 1996. Final score was Ireland 12, Australia 22.

119 Ireland v Samoa, Lansdowne Road, 12th November 1996. Final score was Ireland 25, Samoa 40.

Friday and hope for a recall early 1997 – so does the Rasher "finished with the nuns". Will try for the Brothers! Any vacancies in Irishtown? – foundations etc. etc.

In the meantime, take good care Tom. Keep "cosy" and those feet moving.

God Bless,
Seán .

Not long after your surgery, while you are staying with us in Irishtown, you tell me about a 'dream' you had in the operating theatre. You are up on a height looking down at a very large, bright house. The house has two doors, one at the front and one at the side. There's a long queue of people waiting to get in the side door, while only a few linger at the front door. You know you have to make your way down the slope and gain entry into this house, so you start out on your way, looking up occasionally to check the state of the queue. When you get to the bottom of the hill, you head for the side door, but before you get there you change your mind. That queue is too long. You change direction and proceed towards the front door. It'll be quicker this way, you decide. But for no apparent reason, you turn at the corner of the house and walk back up that hill without looking behind you.

"Wasn't that a strange dream?" you ask me.

"Tom, I don't think that was a dream," I say.

"What do you mean?"

"You know you nearly didn't make it out of the operating theatre?"

"Yea, but what do you mean?"

"People don't normally dream under anaesthetic, Tom," I say.

"What are you saying?"

"I think that was a near death experience," I answer.

This is the first time you realise how ill you have actually been. You ask me to fill you in on the details of those few missing days and are shocked to hear the truth.

* * *

One Sunday evening about a month after you get out of hospital, I drive you into town to 'Number 44' for a quiet drink. It'll be your first since the surgery. The pub is very quiet. We sit on the soft seats just inside the lower door. We don't know any of the customers. We don't even know the new barmaid who is on duty. (I was a bit disappointed actually. Here we were on a major outing and nobody realised it or passed any remarks. Pity the boss man wasn't about.) I order two glasses of Guinness. You ask me to buy ten cigarettes. You look at the drink for quite a while after it's served before you take your first sip and swallow. A few small sips later you light a cigarette and try to smoke. After two puffs you feel sick and stub it out. You've had enough and want to leave. You've consumed less than half a glass of the black stuff, and can't wait to get back to the chair beside the fire in Irishtown but you are delighted with yourself. You feel you've made some progress, however small.

And indeed you are making great progress. You begin to cook a little bit, a sure sign you're feeling better. You're able to tolerate the smell of food and eat small portions. Cleaning up was never your strong point, so I usually face into that when I come in from work. Small price to pay. You battle valiantly and succeed eventually in getting back on the fags, despite making yourself physically sick on occasions. It's almost like a rite of passage. You approach that task with such willpower that we are all truly amazed. Maybe you feel more 'normal' if you have the familiar cigarette in your mouth.

As you begin to show some improvement, following your surgery, your younger brother, Michael, is slowly dying at home in Carrick. The Cleary family business has been sold; all his affairs have been settled and he retires to the bungalow to live out his final days and nights. In the care of his wife, Bernadette, his close family, the hospice nurses and other devoted carers, he begins to slip away. You travel to Carrick to visit him the weekend before his death, an arduous journey for a man in your condition. The two of you have a heart-to-heart and you come home exhausted, looking stooped and bent, old and frail. You return to the south a week later for his removal and funeral. People wonder who the old man is. They are shocked by your appearance and are in no doubt that you will soon be following Michael on a similar journey. The December weather is bitterly cold and the entire ordeal takes a lot out of you, but your spirits remain high and you actually enjoy meeting many old friends and acquaintances. You take up residence in the bedroom of your youngest niece (15 year old Zoë is evicted on the night her Dad is removed to the church) and there is a constant trail of visitors up and down the corridor to see you.

You decide to spend Christmas alone in Irishtown. Hugh and I are off to London for the festive season and you refuse to go to Helen, or anyone else for that matter. It isn't for want of invitations. You just want to be on your own so we respect your decision. What a lonely prospect, everyone thinks, but as it turns out you have a very pleasant day. One neighbour, Eileen, gives you a lift to Mass in the cathedral. Another neighbour, Rosie, gives you a small, tasty portion of Christmas dinner with all the trimmings. All the family and lots of friends ring you throughout the day and you enjoy the quiet comfort of your own company for the remainder of the afternoon and evening.

I always laugh when I think of my phone call to you that Christmas evening. Before Hugh and I headed off, I had given you the six-digit password for the telephone answering service, so that you could listen to any messages that might have come for you while you were out at Mass, or even in the event of a missed call while resting in bed. You sounded in good enough form when I rang, even though it was late enough in the evening. You gave me a run-down on how your day had gone and we chatted for a while.

When I asked you if you had received any messages on the phone you said, "he won't give them to me!"

"What do you mean," I asked.

"He just keeps telling me it's the wrong number," you said.

"What number are you using?" I was puzzled.

You were using the correct number alright. I couldn't understand it. I asked you to go through what you had been doing, step by step, to see where you could possibly be going wrong. I couldn't figure it out. I had written it all down for you.

"I pick up the phone, wait until I hear your voice telling me it's your phone, and then the man comes on and says 'please enter your password' – so I do. Then he says again 'please enter your password' so I do. And AGAIN he says the same thing – 'please enter your password' and I shout at him that I've already entered it and he hasn't listened to a thing I've said"

It turns out that you have been speaking the password instead of putting it in, using the keypad. You didn't realise it was a recording. You thought all along that you were actually talking to this man and had been giving out to him. How we laughed. Poor Tom. Modern technology was never your thing. You hated change. You'd never have coped with the mobile phone epidemic which has swept the country since your death.

Christmas comes and goes and the evenings begin to get a bit longer. Some days we drop you into town for an hour or so and you ring us when you want a lift home. Gradually, these outings become extended and before we know it, you're getting a taxi home. We worry about you, but have to let you have your independence. Next thing you start doing your own laundry again, washing your 'smalls' by hand. Thrilled we are. This is further progress. Thrilled that is, until the day I come in from work and see all your underpants and socks draped around the fireplace in the sitting room across the brass fire-irons.... and a visitor sitting there being entertained by you!

Hugh tells me to chill, that you are only trying to help out, but the truth is you are getting so much better that you're beginning to get on my nerves. Time to return to the little flat, I'm thinking. And in the end you actually broach the subject yourself. You want your independence back and our house is a bit far out from town for you. It's time to reacquaint yourself with the lads. So, with lots of support from friends and family, you go home and settle back into your tiny apartment.

In the early spring of 1997, you attend the christening of Paula's and Jim's second daughter, Aoife, in Dublin. Another very cold day, as you pose for the family photos in the church, I wonder to myself how much longer you have left to live. Afterwards, you merely nibble at the food on offer and you are tired out on the journey home. You look so feeble as you get out of the car and head towards the hall door. But, despite the physical deterioration, your state of mind appears to be good and you are more or less 'your old self'.

Around this time, Paddy Moran organises a "whip around" amongst old sporting contacts and sends the money to me to mind. These funds offer you a level of financial freedom which you haven't had for many years. I give you back your pension book and the lads' gift pays for the rent and essentials, leaving you with your own few bob and a bit of pride. What a get-well gift! I don't think any of them truly realised how much this gesture meant to you. As Dermot Geary wrote to me:

> It's nice to know that there are so many people still around who hold the name of Tom Cleary in high esteem.

At the time though, you didn't exactly warm to the notion that I controlled the money. I hope you understand and forgive me now. We were afraid of what it might do to you. The collection was carried out discreetly, via a network of old friends who were anxious to do something concrete, to let you know how they felt. They didn't want to cause you any embarrassment and I know that this also meant a lot to you. One day in particular stands out in my mind, sometime in the early summer of 1997 when Helen, you and I met some of those men in a local hotel for lunch. You paid for the meal with familiarity and pride, as if you had been in a position to do it that way all your life and I caught a tiny glimpse of the Limerick Tom. After lunch you headed off with the lads, bringing them on a comprehensive tour of Mullingar and surrounding areas.

Everyone who was part of your life at this time could see that, even though you had suffered so much from your illness and surgery, there was something to be learned by all of us from the way you were now dealing with the experience. You seemed to have a new love and respect for life. Your renewed acquaintances helped you to shift your attention from the more recent and mundane parts of your life and you were able to relive the quality times. You also seemed to develop a new awareness of the basic human need for other people in life. The awful emptiness and desolation of your latter years were actually banished and you truly began to live again. You appreciated your second chance.

And, all that time, you still maintained your sense of humour. While we were tiptoeing around you, especially in relation to the obvious fact that you were not long for this world, all the time you knew. You were preparing the suitcase of memories for us to find. As the revised version of the well-known old saying goes, 'he who laughs last...thinks slowest!' I don't think so.

Health-wise, at this time, you are giving nothing away and in a letter to Paddy Moran in July 1997, I wrote:

> It's difficult to know how he really is, as any queries are interpreted as 'fussing'. We try to be optimistic but we worry about even minor symptoms at times. He is still extremely thin, under ten stone I would think now. He is also very hoarse. Enquiries as to his appetite are greeted with scorn! However he is well able to drink his Guinness and gives his publican a hard time because he won't serve him a whacker of brandy ('to warm his stomach'). Only a half! Sometimes he walks up town and sometimes he gets a taxi.
>
> I have organised a course of massage for him for a troublesome pain in his shoulder blade which has been annoying him for some time. His first session is this evening so I hope it helps him and I also hope he sticks with it.

You spend your final birthday, 10th August 1997, care-taking the Vincentian house in Iona Road, Glasnevin. You stay there for about a fortnight, some days pottering around the city, meeting old school and rugby pals, others just being quiet. You pay a final visit to the church there and read the 'saints and sinners' quotation one last time.

By the time you return home in mid-August, you are visibly failing rapidly. You refuse to talk about your worsening health. By mid September, as you approach the first anniversary of your surgery, you are mere skin and bone, struggling to do even minor things, but adamant that you want to stay in your flat. Some days it takes enormous reserves of your depleted energy to drag yourself out of bed and shuffle the short few steps to the toilet. Afterwards you sit, exhausted, on the side of the bed before you can summon the energy to lift your legs up and crawl back underneath the covers. You are eating and drinking almost nothing. It is heart-rending to watch and feel so powerless.

One evening, Gerry and Ann travel over from Athy to see you. We tell you that they have come over to wish Helen well for a forthcoming holiday, but you are not fooled for a minute. Your comment on hearing the news of their visit?

"If you FART in Mullingar, they're over from Athy to see what's up!"

That evening we all plead with you to either move back into the house with Helen or come to us in Irishtown. You refuse. You continually say, "I'll be alright by the 4th". I grow to hate that flat. I look on it as your prison.

Of course we all know what you are waiting for. The end of the month. Helen is due to visit Paula, Jim and the children, who are now living in the States. It's a holiday she has been looking forward to for a long time but she knows that if she goes, you will be dead before she returns. You know that too, Tom. But you

THE LAST TWO PHOTOGRAPHS

Photographs taken in Jimmy Wallace's pub on 2nd September 1997, less than a month before Tom died.

Tommy Braiden, Harry Bauer and Tom Cleary.
(Note the cotton wool in Tom's ear. He always had sensitive hearing and hated noise of any kind.)

Harry Bauer, Paddy Crowley (just back after a trip to Canada, hence the celebration), Sean Elliffe, Tommy Braiden, Jimmy Wallace, Tom Cleary.

want her to go. So she goes. And the day she leaves, we finally convince you that you will be better off staying with Hugh and me for a while, 'until you pick up a bit'. You agree. All your objections dissipate that day, as you journey towards your final destination. Within days, you finally speak, for the first time, of your impending death.

* * *

It's a Sunday night. You have been with us for a few days, eating little or nothing, resting a lot but in reasonable form (considering how ill you are) and looking a little better than when you had been alone in that awful flat. Even your spirits seem to have picked up a bit. But then you have a massive bleed. It's like you have vomited your guts up. Large, lumpy, clotted blood everywhere. Bed, pyjamas, toilet, floor ... all bright red. Sweat pours out of you, and your breath comes in gasps out of your gaping bloody mouth. You're terrified. I say, "you know what this means, don't you, Tom?" You nod, another clot tumbling out of your mouth and onto your chest.

"It's the beginning of the end."

You nod again, too weak to do anything else.

"I'm dying," you say simply, when you've had a chance to catch your breath and clean your mouth.

I squeeze your hand. "Yes, Tom, it looks like this is the beginning of the end," I say again.

I go on to reassure you that we'll all be there for you. Once you have rested a bit, I ask you if you would prefer to stay at home with me or go into hospital. You opt to stay at home. So I settle you down as best I can and decide to contact the doctor and the hospice in the morning. You have a fairly restful night, all things considered. My brother, Gerard, comes down from Dublin the next morning and between us we try to organise the place a bit better for you. He goes in to town to buy navy sheets and a dark green basin so that if you vomit again, the blood against the dark colours won't look as shocking to you as it had the night before against the white sheets.

Your G.P. is away so a young locum arrives out to see you mid-morning. She isn't very pro-hospice and tries to convince me that you would be better off in hospital. Despite my misgivings, she goes on to convince you that you would be better off in there. I'm not so sure, but by then you have agreed to go. We don't want to upset or frighten you any more than you already are so, reluctantly, we agree. But I'm not happy. I would have preferred to look after you at home. I feel it would have been more dignified and less intrusive for you.

You have to be admitted through the casualty department. Lovely staff, but the conditions are awful. It's a cold and draughty pre-fab building and the room you are examined in seems to double as a store for supplies and equipment.

People are continually nipping in and out, looking for bits and pieces and I feel that, to many of them, you are just in the way. Even though I work in that hospital, it's as if I have never really looked at the place properly before. Soon afterwards, however, Rita, the hospice nurse comes down to see us. She is brilliant. She calls me aside and gives me lots of advice; the most important thing she tells me that day is to stop thinking like a nurse but to start thinking like a relative. And then she goes in to see you, Tom. Whatever she says works wonders. You are almost smiling when the porter comes to take you to the ward.

You settle in, as best you can, to a corner bed in a six-bedded ward. You lie on your side with the sheet pulled right up almost covering your face. You have no pain, but speak of extreme heat in your stomach. You say it's like a burning sensation, and it's causing extreme discomfort and pressure in your upper tummy; and you're quite agitated and restless. A nurse comes in with a bag of blood for your drip. The physician comes to see you and orders a barrage of tests and says he will consult with the surgeon to arrange passing a tube down your gullet to see what exactly is happening down there. There is also talk of referring you back to the professor in Dublin. I am getting exasperated. This is exactly why I wanted to keep you at home. The image of you bouncing up the road to Dublin, in the back of an ambulance, in your condition, is distressing to say the least. All this poking and intervention is totally unnecessary when we all know you are dying. We want you to die with your self-respect and dignity intact, so Gerard and I have a heart-to-heart chat with you about these 'options'. It's very emotional for all three of us. You decide you want none of these interventions. Gerard then asks if you want him to anoint you and you agree. It is a privilege to be present, but my heart is breaking, as you and I respond to the prayers.

Afterwards, we tell the physician that you don't want to go through any more intrusive procedures and a referral to Dublin is out of the question. When the surgeon comes, we ask for something to relieve that awful sensation of heat in your tummy. (You have described it to me as being "regulo five". Witty to the last, you are referring to the oven temperature on a gas cooker.) He orders an injection and for the first time since your large bleed the night before, you truly settle. We pull the bed-screen around you and I sit at your bedside as you sleep for a while. At one stage you open an eye and, seeing me there, give a withering look and banish me to the end of the bed to the opposite side where you won't see me! This is as close as we are allowed to sit (for any length of time) from that moment until your final bleed a couple of days later. Your brothers come to visit and we set up a rota as best we can, so that you won't be alone for any period of time. We keep in touch with Helen and Paula in the States and tell them to be prepared for a return trip home.

Friends of the family and our cousins are a great help. People like Eva Wallace, Ann Woodhouse[120], Nuala Daly[121], Phil Flynn[122] and Mabie Kane[123], in particular,

---

120 Neé Lynam. 121 Neé Connolly. 122 Neé Kane. 123 Neé McCormack.

come to mind but there are many more. If we have to leave the hospital for any reason, they stay in the vicinity of the ward but do not actually sit beside you. It means that, just in case something happens while we are out for a break, there is someone close by for you, but we all know that you wouldn't want them 'hatching' by the bedside. They are so generous with their time, visiting without actually seeing you. Occasionally we tell you who is outside and you just nod your head in appreciation.

The hospice nurse, Rita, is a great support throughout those final days of your life. To us and to you. She spends time beside you, speaking gently and understanding your need for quiet without ever being told. She puts things in plain words to us, as she elaborates on how insecure and uncertain you will be feeling. She describes the drugs and what they are doing. She also outlines the medication that is on standby in the event of another major bleed. Rita also explains to us what it will be like for you at the end. She says that, in the event of a large final bleed, as it progresses and worsens, you will have a horrifying sensation of falling. She puts it to us that you will actually be falling – out of life into death – but that will not make it any less frightening for you as you experience it.

Thus armed we continue our bed-end vigil. You ask for little and are content that someone is close by. (Once we're not too close.) You have minor episodes of bleeding and often ask questions such as, "Where is it all coming from?" and "Will it stop soon?" The noise on the ward is getting on your nerves. Certain nurses' voices grate on you, immensely. In they come, chattering about this and that, or being bright-eyed and bushy-tailed with some other patient and we can see it's driving you mad. I think back to all the times I've possibly done the same and wonder briefly who I might have annoyed in my day.

As your condition worsens, thanks to the suggestion of Maeve, the ward sister, you are moved to a quieter three-bedded ward. A corner bed once more, it offers you a greater degree of privacy and, therefore, dignity. Your masseur, Noreen, visits and offers you a treatment. You've kept up your sessions with her since the summer and have experienced great relief from your shoulder pain. (I've often thought how this continuing massage must have offered you such healing. To have someone touch your skin in such a caring way, after all your bachelor years, was special. And your friends' gift had made this possible. It's not that the family wouldn't have arranged and financed it for you – you would never have let us.).

That night, your brother, John, and I are on duty. Towards midnight, he goes home to try and get some sleep and I take up position on the chair at the foot of your bed. You have a reasonable night and sleep for long periods. I know both of the night nurses well, Val and Mary, and when the big bleed comes it's Mary who answers my call first. It's coming on for six in the morning when you suddenly awake, alert, eyes wide open, gesturing frantically and I barely make it to the top of the bed before you start vomiting. It's as if it is all happening in slow motion for me.

Mary calls the doctor and gets the drugs. The large stainless steel receiver is totally inadequate for the volume coming up your throat. I grab some towels from your locker.

"This is it, Tom," I say. "This is the one you've been waiting for. You'll be alright when this one's over."

You can't answer but your eyes tell me you understand. You are propped up on your left elbow and clutch my arm in your right hand as you struggle with the enormity of large clots in your mouth. You start roaring in distress. I don't know what to do, except hold you.

When the doctor arrives to give the injections, you slowly become less distressed and we try to make you as comfortable as possible, but the blood keeps coming. This goes on for some time. Your level of consciousness is low by the time John arrives. Mary has started saying some beautiful prayers, softly, as she kneels at your back with her hand supporting your head. John and I sit facing you, using towels as wadding under your mouth for extra soakage. We put your rosary beads into your hands and the three of us continue to pray:

> You have come to my heart, dearest Jesus,
> I am holding You close to my breast,
> I am telling You over and over,
> You are welcome, O little White Guest.
>
> I love You, I love You, my Jesus,
> O please do not think I am bold,
> Of course You must know that I love You,
> But I am sure that You like to be told.
>
> I will whisper, "I love You, my Jesus",
> And ask that we never may part,
> I love You, O kind, loving Jesus,
> And press You still nearer my heart.
>
> And when I shall meet You in Heaven,
> my soul then will lean on Your breast,
> and we will recall our fond meetings,
> when You were my Little White Guest.

At that, your eyes open once more; you hold out your right hand as if you're reaching for something or someone in the mid-distance and you gurgle what sounds like "Mi...chhh..ae..llll...". To me it is the name of your younger brother who has died just ten months previously. I know then that you sense you will be safe. You feel free to go.

It is the first time ever I have witnessed someone vomiting to death. It has taken almost two hours.

The Hug
Tom and Ursula
October 1988

TOASTING

Homily at Tom's funeral Mass. [123]
4th October 1997.

Well Tom, today is your anniversary. A year ago today you had your operation, the biggest test of your life. You always said you would be alright by the 4th October, and you are; though maybe not in the way you had hoped. It really has been a great year for you. Do you remember at Michael's funeral, you said to Stephanie: "It's really great to be alive. Thanks be to God. You make great friends in sport. But I didn't know it until I got sick." That's what the last year has been about, hasn't it, Tom. You got your second chance, and you took it.

The best thing about the last year was the growth in your own self-esteem. At long last, you began to realise that you were loved. Of course, you wouldn't use that word. You'd say friendship. OK that's the word we'll use. Friendship. Maybe real men don't talk about love. Especially bachelors. But we both know what we are saying.

People have been telling you all your life how loveable you were. In Carrick and Limerick, in your heyday, so many people admired the talents and gifts God had given you. You were humble enough about it. You probably couldn't understand the fuss. It was God's gift to you. Men admired you, and women adored you, but that wasn't what drove you.

The sideboard at home was always full of your trophies. Cups of various shapes and sizes. And you were proud of them. Especially the tray from Bohemians. But over the last year you collected even more precious trophies. We took one of them from your pocket the day you died. Probably the trophy that meant most to you in the end: a simple list of your family and friends. The ones who, finally, managed to break through that illness of the soul that affects so many; low self-esteem. The disease that keeps us from receiving love. And that is what changed this last year. The cups and medals were replaced with letters and get-well cards. And this time you believed what they said.

---

123 Reproduced here courtesy of Tom's nephew, Fr. Gerard Kane (Ref. 2).

As your body began to decay, your soul started to sing. You had a new zest for life. It really was great to be alive. Everything was fresh, everything important. The names of your nurses and fellow patients. Their personal stories. New pride in yourself and your family. You were discovering so much, perhaps for the first time. And you remembered. You wrote it down. That is why it was so hard for you to let go, and so hard for us to watch you. Because you had finally started to really live. You wanted to stay; to appreciate the new life and self-esteem you had. To remember all the people who had remembered you. There was a freshness in your stride, a stronger beat in your heart.

We heard the stories of your friends. Stories you never told us. You weren't one to boast. But your friends told us. The ones who rallied round. Men with nicknames that make them sound like inmates in a zoo! But we also heard the friendship behind the names, and the love they represented. Love has many names, Tom. Friendship is only one. But it was the one that made most sense to you. It was the way that God reached out to you. God, who always comes to us in a way we can accept.

You were frightened, of course. And a little anxious about the future. And you took refuge in ways and in places that offer no real peace. Old habits die hard. Like so many others, you had a particular weakness, a fault, a thorn in the flesh. Previously, it had helped to blur the edges of a sometimes-harsh reality. At least for a time. But it was a false escape and you knew it. And now there was a difference. Anxiety and an understandable fear drove you.

I won't do you the injustice, Tom, of pretending you were a saint. You wouldn't believe me anyway. As a priest I get fed up at times. We don't seem to bury sinners any more. Every funeral is that of a saint. Maybe it's because the country as a whole is losing faith. We don't trust the mercy of God anymore, so we need to canonise people here on earth. I won't do that to you. You need the mercy of God, just like the rest of us. At times you were exasperating, and irritable; unpredictable and cranky. At times you drove us cracked. You never fully accepted responsibility for your own life. You arrived here nearly 30 years ago, for a two-week holiday, and never managed to leave. Some holiday! Mullingar truly became your home.

And there may have been deeper wounds in you. But as you yourself used to quote, "Every saint has a past; every sinner has a future." And your future is bright. You were so lovable, and so loved. And all that is but a pale imitation of the way God loves you. We're delighted you finally began to hear that. You found the pearl of great price.

I doubt if we ever really knew you, Tom, or what made you tick. I doubt if you knew yourself. Only God knows that. But we entrust you to Him today with great confidence. We thank Him for giving us the chance to see you begin to realise your full potential.

We are going to enjoy ourselves today. I'd say you would love to be here. I imagine it would be another long night. But you have other work to do now. There are books to be balanced. Accounts to be kept. But we know this audit will be successful. You'll pass this exam. Because you had begun, over the last year, to understand. You knew and finally believed in the love God has for you. You started to allow yourself to be loved by others, and through them, by God. You died as you lived, Tom: everyone's friend. And you know, though you may choose to call it friendship, it was love. And love is of God.

If only

This book was about my Uncle Tom, a sportsman in his youth,
A gentleman and scholar and never 'ere uncouth.
His talent it was natural; at many kinds of sport,
Such as tennis, golf and basketball, he really showed his worth.

He was an all-round athlete, his trophies there are many,
He lived for sport, he loved it..... it had no equal, any.
As a boy he played lawn tennis, vast skill he did display,
He was winning competitions from his very youngest day.

But when he went to boarding school and touched a rugby ball,
He found the game quite powerful and gave that sport his all.
At scrum-half he did find his niche, his heart began to soar,
His movements were mercurial, and the crowds began to roar.

He felt he was invincible, heart thumping in his chest,
He represented Leinster; as inter-pro, he gave his best.
On leaving school he travelled, to that southwest city fair,
Where "ball-hopping" comes natural and they recognised his flair.

In Limerick, at Bohemians, he showed his great panache,
And soon he played for Munster, with his duck and dodge and dash.
He donned that famous jersey, thought his heart would burst with pride,
Nothing could surpass this chance, being on brave Munster's side.

The province took him to themselves, they raised his self-esteem,
They praised the man and cherished him, as a lynchpin in their team.
His partnership with Mickey was a legend in its time,
Still talked about down south today, each performance was sublime.

When he was named as captain, on that noted Munster side,
People clapped him on the back with joy, with pleasure and with pride.
The girls they flocked around him, with their round adoring eyes,
'Most every lass had judged him as the ultimate rugby prize.

We have photos of some beauties clutched quite closely in his arms,
Or with others on the sandy beach as they work their worldly charms.
Most men admired him also, as the chap who had it all –
He had skill and charm and talent, he was handsome, he was tall.

These lads had various nicknames such as Gooser, Wigs and Mo,
Tom was Weary, Beery, Cleary, whether hail or rain or snow.
One day he got a letter, calling him for Irish trial,
A crunch and crucial challenge he'd been expecting for a while.

The test it went quite well for him, he dared hope in his heart,
"Sub-to-attend" was his next call, (which was the next best thing to "start").
In 'fifty-nine and 'sixty he travelled with the team to France,
To Scotland, Cardiff, Twickenham, but to play he got no chance.

Those were the days when starting teams, must play until the whistle,
No substitution on the field 'gainst cockerel, rose or thistle.
So although he travelled with them, he never got to play,
The cap remained elusive......'til 'sixty-one, in May.

A short tour to South Africa included Uncle Tom,
Excitement burned deep in his chest, though he acted with aplomb.
Could this be consolation for all the times he sat,
And watched his peers performing; would he get an Irish "hat"?

As it turned out.... he didn't.... that made seventeen times in all,
He kicked 'round with the chosen, but he never booted ball.
(It drives me mad to see today, caps handed willy-nilly
To lads who run on for a mo, to me it's more than silly.)

After all that disappointment, Tom's life began to slip,
The girl he loved said "no" to him, the lads were leaving ship.
As all his mates they married and began to settle down,
Poor Tom became quite rudderless and left old Limerick town.

He drifted between siblings or his home in Tipperary,
At storytelling he was great, though sometimes quite contrary.
He never held a job for long, he enjoyed time in the pub,
But nothing could compare for him, with fond Bohemians Club.

A fortnight's trip to our house, for his annual vacation,
Became so oft extended; Ma said "SEEK ACCOMMODATION!!!"
He worked awhile, but stayed with us, true bachelor at heart,
And new pals heard of better days when rugby played a part.

As time went on, and things got worse, he had to claim the dole,
He became quite introverted, he never felt quite whole.
Thirty years he stayed in Mullingar, like our bigger, older brother,
Always there, but "missing", causing heartache for our mother.

Did we take him for granted?....Yes! That might be so,
But we got a rude awakening, when his health began to go.
Investigations followed, when food he couldn't swallow,
Thank God, we didn't realise, the torment that would follow.

Down for major operation, he was absent for a day,
When we rang to make enquiries not one person could say.....
We asked them to transfer us, they bounced us forth and back,
Astounded that a hospital would be so bloody slack.

He wasn't in recovery, no Tom in I.C.U.,
The ward he'd left that morning, said they'd tell us if they knew.
It turned out, he'd been in theatre, that whole long awful day,
His gastric artery ruptured, bright, red blood began to spray.

They attempted to transfuse him, though he was gone for sure,
They tried to do their best for him, but they knew they had no cure.
Like "blood going in a bucket with a huge, enormous hole",
Was how the doctor did describe the day that Tom clutched to his soul.

He fought his bravest battle with his team of health care staff,
And tiger-like he struggled, through each tormented half.
He received a huge transfusion, pints numbered forty-two,
A volume seldom heard of, but what else could they do?

They had witnessed something special on that ordinary day,
When Tom kept striving for the line, he would simply not give way.
At times they thought they'd lost him but the heart would not give up,
As his body tried to let him down, his soul beheld the cup.

They said "He'll be a vegetable,... that's if he does survive;
At present we are not quite sure how this man is alive.
The odds were stacked against him, we were sure that he would die,
he's not out of the woods yet"; then we began to cry.

"We've never seen a patient, of his age, so fair and fit,
it tells at times of stress like this, if they've exercised a bit."
We looked at one another, then we stated it, quite clear,
"Our Tom's a couch potato, have you got the right man here?"

They let us in to see him, pumps and wires all around,
His carcass seemed suspended in that warehouse full of sound.
Tubes in every orifice; a bloated body bare,
Brought feelings out in all of us, we never knew were there.

"Oh, Tom" we gasped in unison, "what's happening to you here?"
A nurse came up beside me, "feel free to touch him, dear."
His progress was quite speedy, we hoped he might survive the week;
Then first he woke up slightly and then next began to speak.

When the doctor came to visit, a question Tom did ask,
"Did you pass on that short message that I gave you as a task?"
The family was bewildered, what was this gobbledegook?
Was this the bland meandering to which a usual vegetable took?

It seems a chance discussion on the night before the op,
With this esteemed anaesthetist, in Tom's head didn't stop.
He'd recognised an old school tie and erstwhile pals got mention,
The doc passed on his greetings, with soon renewed attention.

Those deep-rooted relationships, had stood the test of measure,
As their letters, cards and greetings gave ill Tom endless pleasure.
The staff they were astounded, hopes did soar that once did plummet,
Tom's tale was celebrated at case-conference and summit.

His recovery was rapid, soon old friends began to call,
With Tom in high-dependency, we witnessed Ireland's call.
They rallied 'round in numbers, remembering days of old,
and most talk was of friendship, not of silver or of gold.

They talked of camaraderie, they parleyed fond alliance,
They spoke of will and motivation and sometimes of defiance.
They met in solidarity with mates from Mullingar,
They all felt great affection for Munster's former star.

In next to no time, Tom returned, to his midland habitat,
As his body was recovering, I thought about that "hat".
Would it have made a difference, to how it all worked out?
Would Tom's time of distinction have carried much more clout?

Would his spirit not have sunk so far, would his self-esteem have soared,
If he had met the dragon once and put points on the board?
If that girl had only answered "aye" how different life might be,
I might have Limerick cousins, playing Hein-e-ken rug-by!

But as most of us will learn in life, "if onlys" are a waste,
Whether decisions taken slowly or even done in haste.
What we all gleaned from Uncle Tom, was to allow ourselves be loved,
He grabbed his slender second chance and trusted God above.

We learned that real men can eat quiche and real men also care,
And when he died, they saw him down, 'most everyone was there.
We had a mighty party, guest of honour called away,
But at his final audit, pure pleasure held the sway.

This memoir's partly fiction, but based on all that fact,
Posthumously, it might substitute for the emerald cap he lacked.
His label as the best scrum-half who never wore the green,
Might receive due recognition, as it's newly heard and seen.

So this was Tom's life story, it's a tale of ups and downs,
A tale of joy and happiness, but also tears and frowns.
I am very determined, that this book will serve to tell,
That success, it is not everything.... and failure isn't hell.

So to use the words of Grantland Rice, a sportswriter of note,
(I found it in Tom's suitcase, this simply perfect quote)
"For when the one great scorer comes to write against your name,
He marks – not how you won or lost – but how you played the game."

THE END

POST MORTEM

Acknowledgements

I've never written a book before.[124] But ever since the night, soon after his funeral in 1997, when we found my Uncle Tom's suitcase full of treasured memories, this book has been in my head, just waiting to get out. I hope you enjoyed it. I certainly enjoyed researching and writing it. This story is not just about one man, nor about sport, nor even just about rugby. It's about natural talent in the extreme, allied to a competitive nature and leadership ability – all in a man with an intensely low self-esteem. Blow by blow, life chips away at the gifts to reveal the 'illness of the soul' mentioned at his funeral. What I have learned, in putting pen to paper, is how important it is for each one of us to let our souls sing while we can. Not everyone gets a second chance like the man in this book.

I wish to thank my family for their encouragement and support during the 'looooonnng' gestation period. I extend special thanks to my mother Helen (chief research assistant and fountain of knowledge on the family tree), brother Gerard and sister Paula (proof readers extraordinaire and lots more besides). Mere words are not enough to thank the three of you for your faith in me, your hope and love for me, and also for everything you have done for me down through the years, but especially in recent times. I also wish to thank Jim (care, concern, good food and special deliveries), Lisa (wit), Aoife (hugs) and Niall (pure fun), all of whom have helped me in ways they will never know. To Tom's brother Gerry, his wife Ann and family in Athy, and to his sister-in-law, Bernadette, and everyone in Carrick-on-Suir; thank you all for never losing faith in my ability to complete this project.

I remember Tom's brothers Michael and Fr. John (both now sadly deceased) – I hope they would have been pleased with the outcome of my work. To my 'favourite' cousin, sports journalist and author, Gerry Buckley,[125] (no mean man with a pen himself) I say SNAP! Thank you for your help with research at the National Library of Ireland and for all your wise advice. To Phil Nolan, your painstaking attention to detail is much appreciated. Thanks to Rene Lysaght (my former Irish teacher) for double checking the spelling and translations of words in Irish. Thanks to cousin Stephanie Keating for giving up her time to

---

124 I have tried to stay faithful to the items I found in the suitcase, so there may be some discrepancies in the book. For instance, team members names are taken, in most cases, from Tom's souvenir programmes and menus so changes made before kick-off will not be included. Any errors or omissions will be corrected in subsequent editions, if the matter is drawn to the author's attention.

125 Author of The Millennium Handbook Of Westmeath Gaelic Games, Leinster Leader, Naas (2000) and Fifty Years Of The Hogan Cup, Leinster Leader, Naas (2003).

help me in lots of ways, including trawling through the graveyard at the Friary in Carrick looking for Aunt Bid's grave. To Peter Wallace, I say, a heartfelt thanks for your spark of genius (amongst other things!). To Clair Wallace, your guidance on cover design is much appreciated. To my many friends, too numerous to mention individually, I say 'you know who you are!'

I extend my gratitude and appreciation to the Social & Cultural Committee of Mullingar Credit Union – whose funding helped me with some of the ongoing expenses incurred in the writing of the book.

To Tom's Limerick friends who rallied around for his final year, I say "much appreciated' to you all, but I especially wish to mention Dermot 'Gooser' Geary (for his endless letter writing and phone calls in his efforts to assist me), Bill 'Wigs' Mulcahy (for many anecdotes on days of yore) and the late Paddy 'Mo' Moran (who passed away since I started this book, but who showed huge interest in the project at its beginning). Thanks to all Tom's other friends from Limerick and elsewhere, who rallied when he was ill and contributed to that wonderful 'whip around' in 1997 – most, if not all, of your names are acknowledged in the Post Mortem section of the book.

To his Mullingar friends and acquaintances (some also now deceased), who kept Tom's spirits up when he was feeling low and life had very little to offer him; I say 'well done – it wasn't always easy'. You gave him lots of fun and offered him hope for the future. Best wishes also to other, unknown friends, including people who may have quietly helped him through the years.

Thanks to the nursing and medical staff of St. James's Hospital, Dublin who fought so hard to give Tom that brilliant final year of his life, and to the nursing and medical staff of the Midlands Regional Hospital, Mullingar for your care and attention in life and dignity and respect in dying.

I extend sincere gratitude to Maeve Binchy and the National College of Ireland, (IFSC, Mayor Street, Dublin 1) for organising "The Maeve Binchy's Writers' Club" in the winter of 2003–04. I cannot praise that course enough. Every Wednesday for 20 weeks I travelled, without fail, from Mullingar to the NCI for lectures and enjoyed every single minute of it immensely. (I still have the badge from our graduation night that says, "I went all the way with Maeve"!) To the girls in group six – Suzanne Barry, Olive Dunne and Marie O'Hanlon-Roche – thanks for the laughs and good luck with your own writing. To Stephen Glennon[126] from Roscommon, thanks for the offer of sharing the journey to the city with you – even though I never had to avail of it, it was very reassuring to have a contingency plan!

At the risk of inadvertently omitting some names I would also like to thank the following people, all of whom gave me assistance during my research for the book: Fr. Sam Clyne CM, President, and Ms. Rita Coyle, Union Secretary, Castleknock College for offering me unlimited access to the *Castleknock Chronicles* of 1945 to 1948; Mr. Sean Diffley, *Irish Independent*, for his prompt reply to my rugby queries; Mr. Willow Murray, Hon. Archivist, IRFU, for his patience

126 Author of *To Win Just Once* (2004).

and forbearance in trying to track down the 17 potential caps; Dr. Donal O'Shaughnessy, Hon. Medical Officer, I.R.F.U., for his advice on the aids at the disposal of the modern rugby player; Mr. Michael Coady, Carrick-man and author of *All Souls*; Mr. Noel Tracey of Castleview Tennis Club in Carrick for his wonderful 'action shot' of Tom at Fitzwilliam in 1948; Dr. Trevor Winckworth, Mullingar (since sadly deceased) for giving me a morning of his time, not long before his unexpected death, to recount Tom's input into Mullingar RFC in the early days at the present ground in Cullion; Mr. Hugh Woodhouse for seeking out old photographs from Mullingar RFC (for the book launch); Mr. Dom Dineen, Mr. Brendan O'Dowd and Mr Donal Holland for their help in putting names to faces in some of the photographs; Ms. Siobhan Lynam, Publisher of *A Country Boy* by Tom Lynam for her advice on printing and publishing; Ms. Connie Miller, U.S.A., who gave me permission to use the extract from the 1928 diary of her great-aunt; Mr. Paddy O'Byrne, a schoolmate of Tom's in Castleknock, now residing in Mullingar, for his descriptions of trips to Lansdowne Road in the 1940s and his meeting with Tom in South Africa in 1961; Mr. Mick English for replying to my letter; Mr. Kevin Whelan for the final proof-read; Mr. Charles Foster for help with printing and publishing.

Most of the newspaper cuttings in Tom's suitcase, relating to the matches in South Africa, were from the *Daily Mail* and were written by Staff Reporter, Donald Mosey (later to become well-known as the famed B.B.C. cricket commentator nicknamed 'The Alderman') who had travelled with the team. Peter McMullan, of *Rugby World*, was an Irish journalist who also travelled with the team and his articles gave me a good idea of the social side of things on the tour. The numerous match programmes which Tom kept were another great source of information.

The quotation used at the end of my verse "If Only", is by Grantland Rice (1880–1954), the celebrated American sportswriter.

And, finally I dedicate this book to the memory of my late, adored husband Hugh Cafferty, who died suddenly in 1999. We discussed this project many times together. He was intrigued with the collection of items in the suitcase and amazed that so much information could be contained in such a small space. Hugh was the only person who was aware of the original working title of the book ("Just Hoppin' the Ball"), a title which I had decided on long before one word was written (and before I realised it was a well known Limerick term and not merely one of Uncle Tom's sayings!). Hugh never doubted for a moment that I would write this book. How lonely it is that he is not here to share it with me now.

May the Lord bless you and keep you,
May the Lord make his face shine upon you, and be gracious unto you,
May the Lord lift up his countenance upon you and give you peace.

Numbers 6:24 – 26

List of family members' relationship to Tom

Christian Name	Surname	Comment	Relationship to Tom	Remarks
Aisling	Sheil	neé Cleary	Niece	Daughter of Gerard (1) (Gerry) & Ann
Alan	Carter		Nephew-in-law (in waiting)	Fiancé of Geraldine Cleary
Amy	Breashears	m. K Moran	Step Niece-in-law	Wife of Ken
Andrew (1)	Cleary		Great Grandfather	Father of Thomas
Andrew (2)	Cleary		Grandnephew	Son of Gerard (3) & Silvia
Anita	Morrissey		First cousin once removed	Daughter of Delma & Tom
Ann	Cleary	neé Tilson	Sister-in-law	Wife of Gerard (1) (Gerry)
Anne	Cleary	neé Wallace	Niece-in-law	Wife of Michael (3)
Aoife	Broxton	m. D. Moran	Step Niece-in-law	Wife of Derry
Aoife	Kelly		Grandniece	Daughter of Paula & Jim
Bernadette	Cleary	neé Butler (m. J. Moran)	Sister-in-law	Second Wife of Michael (2)
Brendan	Kane		Brother-in-law	Husband of Helen
Bridget	Cleary	neé Whitty	Grandmother	Mother of Dick
Colette	Keating		Grandniece	Daughter of Stephanie & Eddie
Delma	Morrissey	neé Feehan	First Cousin	Daughter of Paddy & Ita
Derry	Moran		Step-Nephew	Son of Bernadette & Jerry Moran and Step-son of Michael (2)
Dick (Richard)	Cleary		Father	Husband of Kitty
Eddie	Keating		Nephew-in-law	Husband of Stephanie Cleary
Elizabeth	Morrissey		First cousin once removed	Daughter of Delma & Tom
Ellen	Feehan	neé Barron	Grandmother	Mother of Kitty
Eoghan	Cleary		Grandnephew	Son of Michael (3) & Anne
Geraldine	Cleary		Niece	Daughter of Gerard (1) (Gerry) & Ann
Gerard (1) (Gerry)	Cleary		Brother	Son of Dick & Kitty
Gerard (2)	Kane	Priest	Nephew	Son of Helen & Brendan
Gerard (3)	Cleary		Nephew	Son of Michael (2) & Maureen (1)
Grace	Sheil		Grandniece	Daughter of Aisling & Greg
Greg	Sheil		Nephew-in-law	Husband of Aisling
Hannah	Moran		Step Grandniece	Daughter of Derry & Aoife
Helen	Kane	neé Cleary	Sister	Daughter of Dick & Kitty
Helena	Marsden	neé Feehan	First Cousin	Daughter of Paddy & Ita
Hugh	Cafferty		Nephew-in-law	Husband of Ursula (author)
Irene	Downie	neé Feehan	First Cousin	Daughter of Paddy & Ita
Ita	Feehan	neé Widger	Aunt-in-law	Wife of Paddy
Jennifer	Keating		Grandniece	Daughter of Stephanie & Eddie
Jennifer (Jenny)	Joyce	neé Cleary	Niece	Daughter of Gerard (1) (Gerry) & Ann
Jim	Kelly		Nephew-in-law	Husband of Paula
John	Feehan		First Cousin	Son of Paddy & Ita
John	Cleary	Vincentian Priest	Brother	Son of Dick & Kitty
John-Thomas	Feehan		Grandfather	Father of Kitty
Kate	Joyce		Grandniece	Daughter of Jenny & Peter
Ken	Moran		Step-Nephew	Son of Bernadette & Jerry Moran and Step-son of Michael (2)
Kitty	Cleary	neé Feehan	Mother	Wife of Dick
Lisa	Kelly		Grandniece	Daughter of Paula & Jim
Lucia	Cleary		Grandniece	Daughter of Gerard (3) & Silvia
Margaret-Jean	Morrissey		First cousin once removed	Daughter of Delma & Tom

Christian Name	Surname	Comment	Relationship to Tom	Remarks
Mary-Anne	Sheehan		Grandaunt	Aunt of Paddy
Maureen (1)	Cleary	neé O'Callaghan	Sister-in-law	First wife of Michael (2)
Maureen (2)	Cleary		Grandniece	Daughter of Michael (3) & Anne
Michael (1)	Cleary		Uncle	Brother of Dick
Michael (2)	Cleary		Brother	Son of Dick & Kitty
Michael (3)	Cleary		Nephew	Son of Michael (2) & Maureen (1)
Niall	Kelly		Grandnephew	Son of Paula & Jim
Nicola	Whelan		Grandniece	Daughter of Geraldine Cleary & Aidan Whelan
Paddy	Feehan		Uncle	Brother of Kitty
Patrick	Joyce		Grandnephew	Son of Jenny & Peter
Paul	Cleary		Grandnephew	Son of Gerard (3) & Silvia
Paul	Morrissey		First cousin once removed	Son of Delma & Tom
Paula	Kelly	neé Kane	Niece	Daughter of Helen & Brendan
Peter	Joyce		Nephew-in-law	Husband of Jennifer (Jenny) Cleary
Rebecca	Whelan		Grandniece	Daughter of Geraldine Cleary & Aidan Whelan
Silvia	Valderrama	m. G. Cleary	Niece-in-law	Wife of Gerard (3)
Stephanie	Keating	neé Cleary	Niece	Daughter of Michael (2) & Maureen (1)
Stephen	Cleary		Grandnephew	Son of Michael (3) & Anne
Stephie	Keating		Grandniece	Daughter of Stephanie & Eddie
Thomas	Cleary		Grandfather	Father of Dick
Tom	Morrissey		First Cousin-in-law	Husband of Delma
Ursula	Cafferty	neé Kane (author)	Niece	Daughter of Helen & Brendan
Zoë	Cleary		Niece	Daughter of Michael (2) & Bernadette

Tom's Family Tree

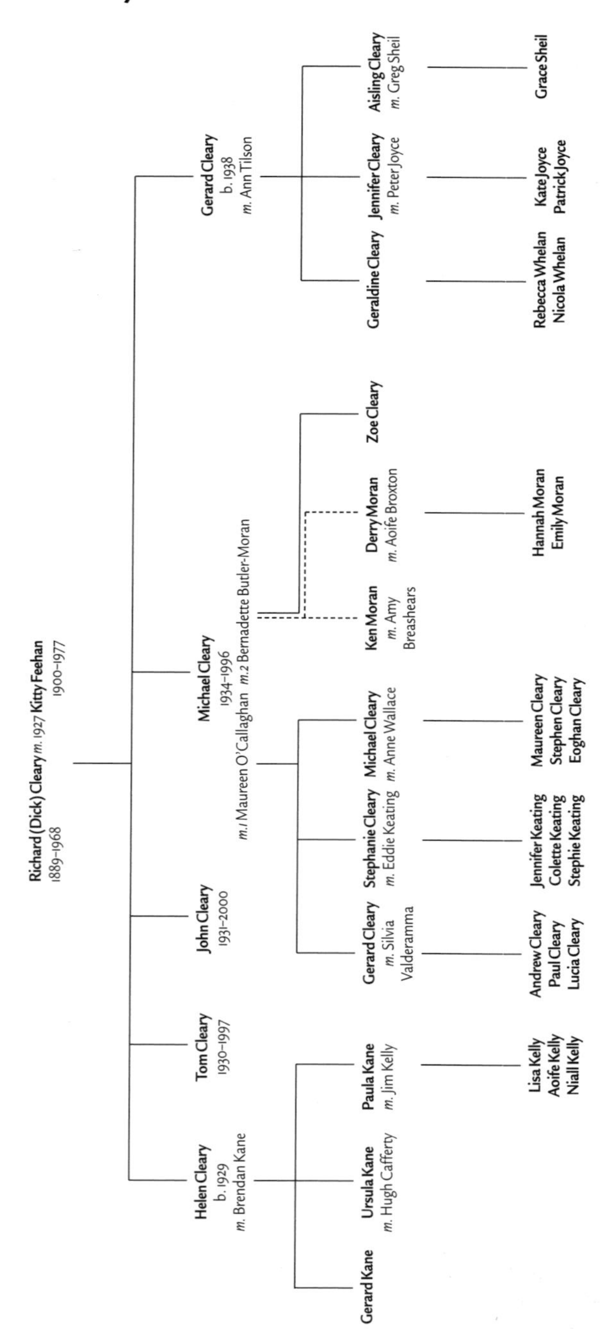
Richard (Dick) Cleary m. 1927 Kitty Feehan
1889–1968
1900–1977
Helen Cleary
b. 1929
m. Brendan Kane
Tom Cleary
1930–1997
John Cleary
1931–2000
Michael Cleary
1934–1996
m.1 Maureen O'Callaghan m.2 Bernadette Butler-Moran
Gerard Cleary
b. 1938
m. Ann Tilson
Gerard Kane
Ursula Kane
m. Hugh Cafferty
Paula Kane
m. Jim Kelly
Gerard Cleary
m. Silvia Valderamma
Stephanie Cleary
m. Eddie Keating
Michael Cleary
m. Anne Wallace
Ken Moran
m. Amy Breashears
Derry Moran
m. Aoife Broxton
Zoe Cleary
Geraldine Cleary
Jennifer Cleary
m. Peter Joyce
Aisling Cleary
m. Greg Sheil
Lisa Kelly
Aoife Kelly
Niall Kelly
Andrew Cleary
Paul Cleary
Lucia Cleary
Jennifer Keating
Colette Keating
Stephie Keating
Maureen Cleary
Stephen Cleary
Eoghan Cleary
Hannah Moran
Emily Moran
Rebecca Whelan
Nicola Whelan
Kate Joyce
Patrick Joyce
Grace Sheil

Tom's Paternal Relations

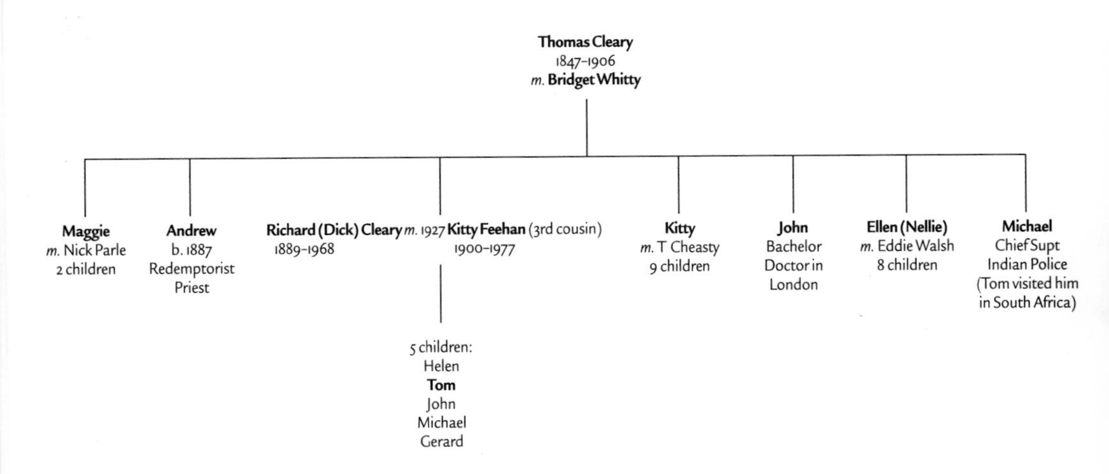

Tom's Maternal Relations

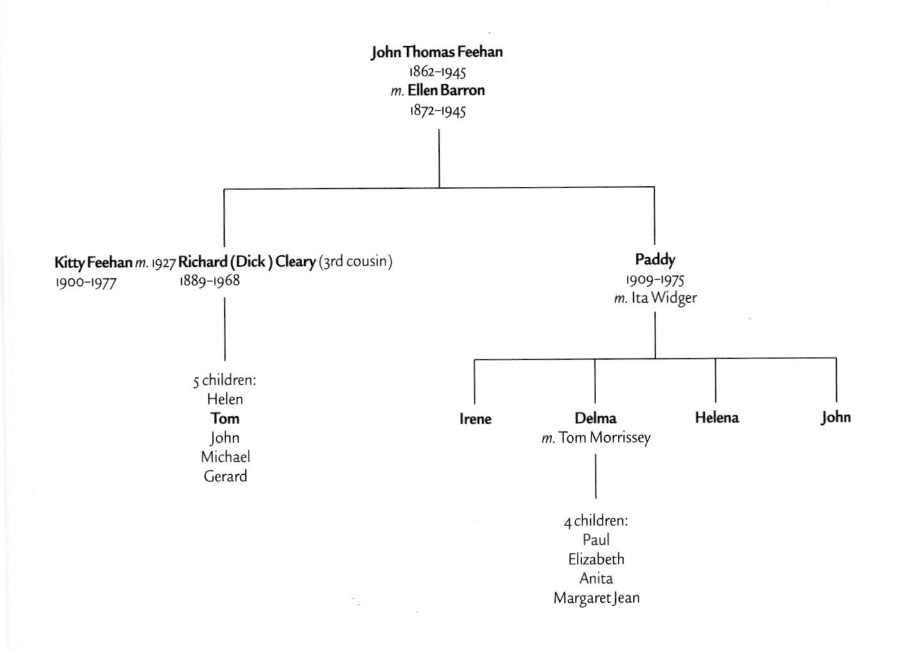

Carrickbeg Lady's Will
Bridget Mary Feehan-Hurley (1867-1946)

A newspaper cutting gives details of Tom's Grandaunt Bid's will:

"Mrs. Bridget Mary Hurley, of 1 Fairview, Priests Road, Tramore, widow of Frank Hurley, left personal estate in England and Eire valued at £46,912 (duty paid £10,153). Probate has been granted to Richard Cleary of Bridge Street, Carrick-on-Suir and James Fox, Tramore. She left £2,000 to the Catherine Walshe charity, £500 each to the Little Sisters of the Poor, Waterford and the Luke Wadding charity; £300 each to the Vincent de Paul Society at Tramore and Carrick-on-Suir; £200 to the Presentation Convent, Carrick-on-Suir, for the poor; £650 for Masses; £18,500 upon trust for Helen, Thomas, John, Michael and Gerard Cleary. Irene, Fidelma, Helena and John Feehan, Thomas and John* Hurley; £2000 to Mella Cunningham; an insurance policy to her grandniece Helena, and the residue to the Parish Priest of Carrick-beg for the poor."

* Print blurred on press cutting in suitcase. This could be John or Joan.

Rugby Positions Explained

Number	Position in the modern game	Line	Also referred to as
15	Full-Back	Back	
14	Right Wing	Three-Quarters	Winger
13	Outside Centre	Three-Quarters	
12	Inside Centre	Three-Quarters	Second five-eighth
11	Left Wing	Three-Quarters	Winger
10	Out-Half	Halves	Fly-Half Outside-half Stand-off First five-eighth
9	Scrum-Half	Halves	
1	Loose Head Prop	Front Row Forwards	Front Row Outside
2	Hooker	Front Row Forwards	Front Row Hooker
3	Tight Head Prop	Front Row Forwards	Front Row Inside Tight Head
4	Lock	Second Row Forwards	Second Row Lock
5	Lock	Second Row Forwards	Second Row Lock
6	Blindside Wing Forward	Forwards	Back Row Wing Flanker Flank Forward Breakaway Forward
8	No. 8	Forwards	Back Row Lock Loose Forward
7	Openside Wing Forward	Forwards	Back Row Wing Flanker Flank Forward Breakaway Forward

Munster Challenge Cup Campaign 1958

30th March, 1958 – Second Round Match

Bohemians – 9: Dolphin – 3

Referee – Mr. S. O'Sullivan
Bohemians – P. Downes, M. Mortell, B. Fitzgibbon, C. English, P. Moran, M. English, T. J. Cleary, J. Walsh, D. Geary, K. Doyle, K. Powell, C. Purcell, J. Ryan, W. Hurley, W. Slattery.
Dolphin – J. Kiernan, D. McCormick, N. McCormick, P. Crowley, R. Roche, V. Harrisson, N. Coleman, V. Giltinan, D. Barry, L. Dillon, J. Horgan, J. Sullivan, P. O'Callaghan, M. Sullivan, R. Dowley.

12th April, 1958 -Semi Final

Bohemians – 19: Old Crescent – 6

Referee – Mr. H. D. Cashell
Bohemians – P. Downes, P. Moran, C. English, B. Fitzgibbon, M. Mortell, M. English, T. J. Cleary, J. Walsh, D. Geary, F. Nagle, T. Watson, C. Powell, W. Slattery, W. Hurley, J. Ryan.
Old Crescent – J. Riordan, J. Clancy, S. McRedmond, V. Collins, M. Manning, J, Roche, W. Leahy, B. Downes, P. Lane, J. Reynolds, M. Spillane, L. Dundon, J. O'Keeffe, P. Molloy, C. Downes.

26th April, 1958 – Final

Bohemians – 9: Highfield – 0

Referee – Mr. J. A. Donovan
Bohemians – P. Downes, M. Mortell, B. Fitzgibbon, C. English, P. Moran (captain), M. English, T. J. Cleary, J. Nagle, D. Geary, W. Slattery, E. Watson, J. Mulcahy, J. Ryan, C. Powell, W. Hurley.
Highfield – P. Coughlan, J. Curtin, T. Finn, F. Buckley, D. Wixted, B. Russell, C. Odlum, L. Ormonde (captain), P. Dempsey, T. Stack, M. Leahy, N. Dillon, J. Dennehy, C. O'Driscoll, K. Clancy.

Munster Challenge Cup Campaign 1959

17th March, 1959 -First Round Match

Bohemians – 12: Sunday's Well – 3

Referee – Mr. P. Frawley
Bohemians – P. Downes, P. Moran, B. Fitzgibbon, C. English, M. Walsh, M. English, T. J. Cleary, P. O'Callaghan, D. Geary, W. Hurley, B. O'Dowd, J. Meaney, W. Slattery, C. Powell, J. Ryan.
Sunday's Well – D. Bradley, J. Daly, J. Lynch, D. Daly, M. Walley, T. Jackson, J. Healy, P. Attridge, P. Comerford, J. Harrington, B. Wilkinson, T. Wilkinson, N. Molloy, W. Egar, K. McCarthy.

4th April, 1959 -Semi Final

Bohemians – 3: Cork Constitution – 0

Referee – Comdt. T. Furlong
Bohemians – P. Downes, M. Walshe, B. Fitzgibbon, C. English, P. Moran, M. English, T. J. Cleary, P. O'Callaghan, D. Geary, W. Hurley, B. O'Dowd, J. Meany, J. Ryan, C. Powell, W. Slattery.
Cork Constitution – R. Hennessy, D. Scannell, T. Murphy, G. Horgan, F. O'Sullivan, G. Fleming, Ted Murphy, F. Murphy, K. Caniffe, J. Pyne, J. Crowley, D. Lynch, N. Murphy, D. O'Flynn, L. Coughlan.

25th April, 1959 – Drawn Final

Bohemians – 6: Shannon – 6

Referee – Mr. H. D. Cashell
Bohemians – P. Downes, W. Walsh, B. Fitzgibbon, C. English, P. Moran, J. McGovern, T. J. Cleary, W. Hurley, D. Geary (captain), P. O'Callaghan, B. O'Dowd, J. Meaney, W. Slattery, C. Powell, J. Ryan.
Shannon – M. Clancy, A. Sheehan, A. Sheppard, B. O'Brien, A. McInerney, E. Keane, S. O'Carroll, F. O'Flynn, D. Flannery, M. N. Ryan, J. O'Donovan, P' O'Flynn, F. Gallaghar, E. Clancy (captain), J. McNamara.

2nd May, 1959 – Final Replay

Bohemians – 12: Shannon – 3

Referee – Mr. S. D. Wilson
Bohemians – P. Downes, M. Walshe, B. Fitzgibbon, C. English, P. Moran, J. McGovern, T. J. Cleary, P. O'Callaghan, D. Geary (captain), W. Hurley, B. O'Dowd, J. Meaney, W. Slattery, C. Powell, J. Ryan.
Shannon – M. Clancy, G. O'Carroll, A. Sheppard, R. Keane, A. McInerney, E. Keane, S. O'Carroll, F. O'Flynn, D. Flannery, M. N. Ryan, J. O'Donovan, P. O'Flynn, F. Gallaghar, J. O'Shaughnessy, J. McNamara.

Munster Challenge Cup Campaign 1962

Munster Cup winning team 1962 (trained by Dom A. Dineen)

W. A. Mulcahy, K. Prendergast, M. McMahon, J. Ryan, D. Chambers, B. O'Dowd, D. Stack, J. Nagle, P. Sheehan, G. Sheehan, W. Slattery, T. O'Brien, C. English (captain), H. Wood, S. MacHale, P. O'Callaghan, M.A. English, T. J. Cleary, S. Kenny.

Munster Matches (Details from Tom's suitcase[127])

Munster v Leinster – November, 1958

Leinster – 32: Munster – 0

Leinster – N. Connolly (Blackrock), M. Fitzsimons (Lansdowne), K. Flynn (Wanderers), A. J. O'Reilly (Old Belvedere), N. Brophy (Blackrock), S. Kelly (Lansdowne), A. Twomey (Lansdowne), M. Cuddy (Bective), A. R. Dawson (captain) (Wanderers), J. Thomas (Blackrock), W. Mulcahy (U.C.D.), G. Culliton (Wanderers), T. Fahy (U.C.D.), R. Kavanagh (Wanderers), G. Kavanagh (Wanderers).

Munster – P. Berkery (London Irish), D. McCormack (Dolphin), J. Walsh (U.C.C.), J. Hill (Highfield), M. English (Bohemians), T. J. Cleary (Bohemians), G. Wood (Garryowen), D. Geary (Bohemians), J. O'Sullivan (Dolphin), M. Spillane (Old Crescent), T. Nesdale (Garryowen), N. Murphy (captain) (Cork Constitution), M. O'Connell (Young Munster), J. Ryan (Garryowen).

Munster v Connacht – 29th October, 1959

Munster – 6: Connacht – 0

Referee – Mr. K. D. Kelleher (Leinster)

Munster – R. Hennessy (Cork Constitution), D. Kennefick (Cork Constitution), B. Fitzgibbon (Bohemians), T. Kiernan (U.C.C.), F. Buckley (Highfield), M. English (Bohemians), T. J. Cleary (captain) (Bohemians), P. O'Callaghan (Bohemians), D. Geary (Bohemians), R. Dowley (Dolphin), M. Spillane (Old Crescent), T. Nesdale (Garryowen), L. Coughlan (Cork Constitution), T. McGrath (Garryowen), T. Coffey (Garryowen).

Connacht – S. Calleary (Galwegians), R. E. Roche (Galwegians), J. F. Dooley (Galwegians), G. W. Hackett (London Irish), J. Greally (U.C.G.), P. J. Kilcommins (Athlone), D. Armstrong (Corinthians), T. O'Neill (Corinthians), L. Butler (Blackrock College), R. McLoughlin (U.C.D. and Ballinasloe), B. N. Guerin (Galwegians), M. Leahy (Highfield), J. Armstrong (Corinthians), P. J. A. O'Sullivan (Galwegians), W. N. Carey (Athlone).

---

127 Tom saved the details from only four of his 14 senior appearances for Munster. He captained the province to inter provincial championship honours in 1959–1960. He also led the side in the four matches played by Munster during the 1960–1961 season. His Munster appearances were:
Season 1957/58 v Connacht, Ulster, Leinster & Lourdes.
Season 1958/59 v Connacht, Ulster & Leinster .
Season 1959/60 v Connacht, Ulster & Leinster.
Season 1960/61 v Connacht, Ulster, Leinster & South Africa.

Munster v Ulster – 14th November, 1959

Munster – 18: Ulster – 0

Referee – Mr. R. Mitchell (Leinster)
Munster – R. Hennessy (Cork Constitution), D. Kennefick (Cork Constitution), J. Walsh (U.C.C.), T. Kiernan (U.C.C.), F. Buckley (Highfield), M. English (Bohemians), T. J. Cleary (captain) (Bohemians), R. Dowley (Dolphin),[128] D. Geary (Terenure and Bohemians), P. O'Callaghan (Bohemians), T. Nesdale (Garryowen), M. Spillane (Old Crescent), L. Coughlan (Cork Constitution), T. McGrath (Garryowen), T. Coffey (Garryowen).
Ulster – N. J. Henderson (N.I.F.C.), J. W. Keepe,[129] A. Gurd (N.I.F.C.), D. C. Glass (Collegians), J. J. Kyle (Service), A. C. Pedlow (captain) (C.I.Y.M.S.), W Whiteside (Queens), E. D. Lindsey (Instonians), I. Butler (Dungannon), J. W. Foote N.I.F.C.), K. Mulligan (Malone), T. S. Martin (N.I.F.C.), E. L. Brown (Instonians), J. A. Donaldson (Collegians), J. M. Crabbe (Ballymena).

Munster v Leinster – 28th November, 1959

Munster – 18: Leinster – 14

Referee – Mr. M. E. Holland (Connacht)
Munster – R. Hennessy (Cork Constitution), D. Kennefick (Cork Constitution), J. Walsh (U.C.C.), T. Kiernan (U.C.C.), F. Buckley (Highfield), M. English (Bohemians), T. J. Cleary (captain) (Bohemians), G. Wood, (Lansdowne and Garryowen), D. Geary (Terenure and Bohemians), P. O'Callaghan (Bohemians), T. Nesdale (Garryowen), M. Spillane (Old Crescent), N. Murphy (Cork Constitution), T. McGrath (Garryowen), L. Coughlan (Cork Constitution).
Leinster – F. Keogh (Bective Rangers), W. Bornemann (Wanderers), K. Flynn (Wanderers), N. Nolan (Blackrock), J. Fortune (Clontarf), P. Goff (Blackrock), J. Kelly (St. Mary's), J. Thomas (Blackrock), B. Rigney (Bective Rangers), M. Cuddy (Bective Rangers), G. Culliton (Wanderers), P. Costelloe (Bective Rangers), G. Kavanagh (Wanderers), R. Kavanagh (captain) (Wanderers), F. O'Rourke (Bective Rangers).

128 M. Cunningham of Cork Constitution may have played in lieu of R. Dowley.
129 R. Nichol may have played in lieu of J. W. Keepe.

Other matches

An International XV v Ballymena: Ballymena Rugby Football Club
The Opening of New Pavilion on 29th April, 1960

Referee – Dr. J. Stewart (Queen's University)

International XV – N. J. Henderson (N.I.F.C. and Ireland), L. N. Brophy (U.C.D. and Ireland), A. C. Pedlow (C.I.Y.M.S. and Ireland), D. Hewitt (Queen's University and Ireland), A. J. F. O'Reilly (Old Belvedere, Leicester and Ireland), G. Sharpe (Stewart's College F. P. and Scotland), T. J. Cleary (Bohemians and Munster), B. G. M. Wood (Lansdowne and Ireland), A. R. Dawson (captain) (Wanderers and Ireland), T. R. Prosser (Pontypool and Wales), M. G. Culliton (Wanderers and Ireland), G. R. P. Ross (C.I.Y.M.S. and Ireland), N. A. A. Murphy (Cork Constitution and Ireland), P. J. A. O'Sullivan (Galwegians and Ireland), J. Donaldson (Collegians and Ireland).

Ballymena[130] – R. J. Gregg (Ireland), J. Rainey, W. R. McKane, R. W. Ewart, R. K. Murphy, J. E. B. McGarvey, J. W. Moffett (Ulster), J. S. Gardiner, B. Bolton, S. Millar (Ireland and Lions), J. E. Leslie (captain), W. J. McBride (Ulster), T. J. Finney, J. M. Crabbe (Ulster), I. Hamilton.

South African Springboks v Munster – 22nd December, 1960

South Africa – 9: Munster – 3

Referee – Mr. K. Kelleher, Limerick.

South African Springboks – L. G. Wilson, M. J. G. Antelme, J. L. Gainsford, F. Roux, J. P. Engelbrecht, D. A. Stewart, P. de W. Uys, S. P. Kuhn, G. F. Malan, J. L. Myburgh, F. C. Du Preez, H. S. Van Der Merwe, J. T. Claassen (captain), G. H. Van Zyl, A. P. Baard.

Munster – R. Hennessy (Cork Constitution), P. McGrath (U.C.C.), J. C. Walsh (U.C.C.), T. J. Kiernan (U.C.C.), F. Buckley (Highfield), M. English (Bohemians), T. J. Cleary (captain) (Bohemians), B. G. Wood, (Lansdowne), D. Geary (Terenure and Bohemians), M. O'Callaghan (Sundays Well), L. Murphy (Highfield), T. Nesdale (Garryowen), M. Spillane (Old Crescent), N. A. Murphy (Garryowen), T. McGrath (Garryowen), L. Coughlan (Cork Constitution).

Oxford and Cambridge XV v Wolfhounds
Lansdowne Road, Dublin on 13th September 1958.

Oxford and Cambridge XV – 14: Wolfhounds – 11

Referee: Mr. R. Mitchell

Oxford and Cambridge XV. – J. S. M. Scott (Oxford), M.S. Phillips (Oxford), L. D. Watts (Oxford), A. R. Smith (Cambridge), J. P. Horrocks-Taylor (Cambridge), A. A. Mulligan, (Cambridge), L. T. Lombard (Oxford), A. H. M. Hoare (Oxford), W. H. Downey (Cambridge), captain, J. D. Ourrie (Oxford), J. Loveday (Oxford), D. MacSweeney (Cambridge). R. H. Davies (Oxford), S. H. Wilcock (Oxford).

Wolfhounds XV – R. Tooth (North of Ireland), S. Quinlan (Blackrock), D. C. Glass (Collegians), R. T. Wells (Cardiff), P. H. Thompson (Headingley), M. English (Bohemians), T. J. Cleary (Bohemians), P. Dowley (Dolphin), A. R. Dawson (Wanderers), S. A. Millar (Ballymena), W. A. Mulcahy (U.C.D.), M. R. M. Evans (Harlequins), N. R. Murphy (Dolphin), J. T. Greenwood (Perthshire Academicals), R. Kavanagh (Wanderers), captain.

---

130 Ballymena had four international players in their ranks at this time, with 27 caps between them by this date. Robin Gregg (7 caps), Joe Gaston (9 caps), Sydney Millar (9 caps), Barton McCallan (2 caps). Willie John McBride, who played on the Ballymena team that day, had represented Ulster but had not yet gained a cap for Ireland. His first cap was to come almost two years later, against England at Twickenham in 1962.

Wolfhounds v Tom Clifford's XV – Thomond Park, Limerick on 14th September 1958.

Wolfhounds – 28: Tom Clifford's XV – 11

Referee: Mr. D. Meany
Wolfhounds – J. S. Scott (Oxford), P. R. Mills (Cambridge), M. S. Phillips (Oxford), L. D. Watts (Oxford), P. H. Thomas (Headingley), A. B. Thomas (Cambridge), S. Smith (Cambridge), D. Jesson (Oxford), N. A. H. Creese (Oxford), W. J. Downey (Cambridge), captain, H. R. Moore (Oxford), M. R. Evans (Harlequins), R. H. Davies (Oxford), H. S. O'Connor (Dublin University), J. McGowan (Bective Rangers).
Tom Clifford's XV – R. Hennessey (Constitution), F. Buckley (Highfield), C. Grealy (Galwegians), J. Roche (Old Crescent), D. McCormack (Dolphin), M. English (Bohemians), T. J. Cleary (Bohemians), F. O'Flynn (Shannon), D. Geary (Bohemians), W. Allen (Young Munster), captain. C. Powell (Bohemians), M. Spillane (Old Crescent), N. Murphy (Constitution), T. McGrath (Garryowen), M. O'Connell (Young Munster).

Wolfhounds v Waterpark Selected Kiloohan Park, Waterford on 10th September 1959.

Wolfhounds – 17: Waterpark Selected – 16

Referee: Mr. D. Kennealy
Wolfhounds XV – R. J. Macken (Old Wesley), A. R. Smith (Eddwvale and Scotland), J. Dooley (Galwegians and Ireland), C. A. H. Davis (Llanelly and Wales), A. Reid Smith (Dublin University), C. Littlewood (Oxford), P. Danos (Beziere and France), D. C. Main (London Welsh and Wales), L. Butler (Blackrock), D. Fitzpatrick (Dublin University), M. Celaya (Biarritz and France), M. Leahy (Highfield), D. Curry (Old Belvedere), A. O'Sullivan (Galwegians and Ireland), F. O'Rourke (Bective Rangers) captain.
Waterpark Selected XV – R. Hennessy (Constitution), W. Davis (Waterpark) captain, T. Kiernan (U.C.C.), J. McAleese (Old Belvedere), C. English (Bohemians), G. Hardy (Bective Rangers), T. J. Cleary (Bohemians), R. Dowley (Dolphin), D, Geary (Bohemians), M. Cuddy (Bective Rangers), E. Fitzgerald (Waterpark), P. Traynor (Clontarf), T. Coffey (Garryowen), T. McGrath (Garryowen), L. Coughlan (Constitution).

Skerries (Selected) XV v Wolfhounds XV – 13th September 1959.

Skerries – 10: Wolfhounds – 12

Referee: A. B. Robertson.
Skerries (Selected) XV: N. Connolly (Blackrock College), L. Tynan (Old Belvedere), E. McCarville (U.C.D.), N. McGrath (Old Belvedere), J. Fortune (Clontarf), F. McMullen (Clontarf), D. Armstrong (Corinthians), S. Cole (Skerries), J. McCurdy (Skerries) captain, J. Thomas (Blackrock College), G. Pullar (Dunbar), P. Traynor (Clontarf), P. Murray (U.C.D.), E. Pembrey (Blackrock College), D. Kissane (Blackrock College).
Wolfhounds XV: J. Meynard (Cognac), A. Reid-Smith (Dublin University), J. Dooley (Galwegians), J. McAleese (Old Belvedere), P. H. Thompson (Waterloo) captain, C. Ashton (Aberavon), T. J. Cleary (Bohemians), D. Main (London-Welsh), D. Geary (Bohemians), T. Gleeson (Lansdowne), M. Leahy (Highfield), C. Payne (Oxford University), D. Curry (Old Belvedere), A. J. O'Sullivan (Galwegians), T. McGrath (Garryowen).

Carrick v Cashel in the Garryowen Cup Clanwilliam Park, April 1960.

Carrick – 10: Cashel – 0

Referee: J. Sheridan.
Carrick XV: M. O'Keeffe, W. Galvin, L. Dowley, M. Cleary, T. Morrissey, T. J. Cleary, G. Cleary, M. O'Dwyer, T. Foley, P. Dowley (captain), J. Connolly, J. McGrath, . Phelan, R. Dowley, M. Mullins.
Cashel XV: T. Walsh, R. Allison, G. Ryan, T. Ryan, N. Dowling (captain), J. McGovern, P. O'Dwyer, D. Spearman, B. Boles, P. Caplice, E. O'Donovan, P. Caplice, J. Ryan, J.O'Connor, J. Maxwell.

Young Munster Selection v Wolfhounds XV – 18th September 1960.

Referee: J. A. O'Donovan.
Young Munster: C. Carey (Young Munster), D. Kennefick (Constitution), J. Walsh (U.C.C.), J. Dooley (Galwegians), W. Bornemann (Wanderers), M. English (Bohemians), T. J. Cleary (Bohemians), A. Quin (Young Munster) captain, D. Flannery (Shannon), P. O'Callaghan (Bohemians), T. Nesdale (Garryowen), M. Spillane (Old Crescent), N. Murphy (Garryowen), T. McGrath (Garryowen), L. Coughlan (Constitution).
Wolfhounds XV: J. Wilcox (Oxford), P. Dawkins (Oxford), J. McPartlin (Oxford), P. Barnett (Oxford), J. Glover (Oxford), B. Risman (Manchester University), A. Mulligan (Cambridge & London Irish) captain, C. Rigby (Oxford), L. Butler (Blackrock), J. Bagnall (St. Mary's), P. Costello (Bective Rangers), J. D. Currie (Harlequins), D. Mac Sweeney (Cambridge), J. Saux (Lourdes), R. Butler (Oxford).

Combined Universities v Rest of Ireland Donnybrook on 8th January 1961

Combined Universities – 6: Rest of Ireland – 0

Referee: Mr. R. Mitchell
Rest of Ireland – R. McMullen (Dublin University), R. J. McCarten (London Irish), M. Moore (Dublin University),[131] A. J. O'Reilly (Dolphin), W. Bornemann (Wanderers), M. English (Bohemians), T. J. Cleary (Bohemians) captain, J. Thomas (Blackrock College), B. Rigney (Bective Rangers), M. O'Callaghan (Sunday's Well), B. McBride (Ballymena), C. J. Dick (Ballymena), G. Kavanagh (Wanderers), K. E. Lappin (Collegians), D. Scott (Malone).
Combined Universities – T. Kiernan (U.C.C.) captain, F. Byrne (U.C.D.), J. Dillon (U.C.D.), J. C. Walsh (U.C.C.), J. Greally (U.C.G.), G. Tormey (U.C.D.), M. Mullins (U.C.C.), A. Gillen (Queens University), R. Meates (Dublin University), J. Dick (Queens University), W. A. Mulcahy (U.C.D.), B. O'Halloran (U.C.D.), E. Maguire (U.C.G.), C. Powell (Dublin University), H. Wall (U.C.D.).

131 Newspaper reports name Moore as having played. The programme from Tom's suitcase names J. F. Dooley (Ireland and Galwegians) at Right Centre.

Irish Rugby Football Union Touring Team 1961[132]

Brophy, N.

Niall Henry Brophy. Born on 19th November 1935. Wing. Gained a total of 20 caps for Ireland and two caps for the Lions, between 1957 and 1967.

Cleary, T. J.

Thomas Joseph Cleary. Born on 10th August 1930. First played for Munster in 1950 Went on to captain Bohemians (Limerick) and the Munster inter-provincial team (including the match v South Africa in December 1960). Was in a number of final trials, and named as substitute to attend for international matches versus England, Scotland, Wales and France on numerous occasions, but did not gain the ultimate distinction of a cap for Ireland.

Culliton, M. G.

Michael Gerard Culliton. Born on 15th June 1936. Lock. Gained a total of 19 caps for Ireland between 1959 and 1964.

Dawson, A. R. (captain)

Alfred Ronald Dawson. Born on 5th June 1932. Hooker. Gained a total of 27 caps (16 as captain) for Ireland and six caps for the Lions between 1958 and 1964. He captained the Lions in a record breaking six successive test games in 1959, was an Irish selector between 1969-1971, coach to international side in 1974, became a member of the International Board and was President of the IRFU in 1990. An architect by profession he is credited with much of the modern development of the Lansdowne Road ground in the '70s and '80s.

Dick, C. J.

Charles John Dick (known as Ian). Born on 26th January 1937. Number 8. Gained eight caps for Ireland between 1961 and 1963.

Dick, J. S.

James S. Dick. Born on 24th October 1939. Hooker. Gained one cap for Ireland (v England) on 10th February 1962.

Dooley, J. F.

John Francis Dooley. Born on 10th August 1934. Centre. Gained three caps for Ireland in 1959.

Glass, D. C.

Dion Caldwell Glass. Born on 15th May 1934. Gained a total of four caps for Ireland between 1958 and 1961. Best known as a full back.

Hewitt, W. J.

William John Hewitt. 1 on 6th June 1928. Gained four caps for Ireland between 1954 and 1961. Best known as a fly-half.

Houston, K.

Kenneth James Houston. Born on 20th July 1941. Wing. Gained a total of six caps for Ireland between 1961 and 1965.

---

132 Rugby statistics from www.scrum.com accessed on 19th April 2005. Please note that on the 1952 Irish tour of Argentina and Chile the international matches were not recognised as Irish caps. Hence they are not included in the total number of caps mentioned for each player.

Jeffares R. W. (Secretary)

Billy Jeffares, (Junior). International referee eight times in all. President of Lansdowne Club in 1945. Secretary and Treasurer of the IRFU at the time of this tour (a role he took over from his father, Rupert, in 1951). The *Cape Argus*, on April 19th 1961 states "one of the games he refereed was the Ireland-New Zealand match of 1935. This unique situation, of an Irishman refereeing his own country's match, happened through the non-arrival of the scheduled Scottish referee. New Zealand won 17-9."

Kavanagh, J. R.

James Ronald Kavanagh. Born on 21st January 1931. Flanker. Gained a total of 35 caps for Ireland between 1953 and 1962.

Kiernan, T. J.

Thomas Joseph Kiernan. Born on 7th January 1939. Gained a total of 54 caps for Ireland (24 as captain) and five for the Lions, between 1960 and 1973. Originally a centre, he played mostly at full back. Went on to become Ireland's national coach, President of the IRFU, a member of the International RFB and chairman of European Rugby Cup Ltd.

McGrath, T.

Timothy McGrath. Born on 3rd October 1933. Number 8. Gained a total of seven caps for Ireland between 1956 and 1961.

Millar, S.

John Sydney Millar. Born on 23rd May 1934. Prop. Went on to gain a total of 37 caps for Ireland and nine caps for the Lions, between 1958 and 1970. Chairman of the International Rugby Board at time of writing.

Mulcahy, W.A.

William Albert Mulcahy, (known as Bill and/or Wigs). Born on 7th January 1935. Lock. Gained a total of 35 caps for Ireland and six caps for the Lions between 1958 and 1965.

Mulligan, A. A.

Andrew Armstrong Mulligan. Born on 4th February 1936. Scrum-half. Gained a total of 22 caps for Ireland and one cap for the Lions, between 1956 and 1961.

Murphy, N. A. A.

Noel Arthur Augustine Murphy. Born on 22nd February 1937. Flanker. Gained 41 caps for Ireland and eight for the Lions between 1958 and 1969. Son of Noel Francis Murphy (tour manager)

Murphy, N. (Senior) (Hon. Manager)

Noel Francis Murphy, President of the Irish Rugby Football Union in 1961. Gained 11 caps as a wing forward for Ireland between 1930 and 1933. He was the father of Noel Arthur Augustine Murphy, also included in the touring team.

O'Reilly, A. J. F.

Anthony Joseph Francis (Kevin) O'Reilly. Born on 7th May 1936. Wing. Gained a total of 29 caps for Ireland and ten caps for the Lions, between 1955 and 1970.

O'Reilly, T. A. (Hon. Assistant Manager)

Thomas A. O'Reilly, played as scrum-half for Lansdowne between 1925 and 1935 when virtually all the three-quarters from that club represented Ireland. Gained many inter-provincial and Irish trial honours, but did not gain the ultimate distinction of a cap for Ireland. Was President of Lansdowne in 1953.

Scott, D.

Dennis Scott. Born on 19th November 1933. Flanker. Gained a total of three caps for Ireland between 1961 and 1962.

Thomas, J.

James Noel Thomas. Born on 15th December 1932. Prop. Represented Leinster on ten occasions prior to this South African tour. Played and captained in the final Irish trials, was named as sub to attend at international level, but did not gain the ultimate distinction of a cap for Ireland.

Tormey, W. G.

Gerry (Jerry) Tormey. Fly-half. Represented (U.C.D.) on Combined Universities v Rest of Ireland. Had been Leinster out-half to Tom's brother, Gerry, who played at scrum-half, in the schools inter-provincial matches in 1957. They were also the half-back partnership on the Dental Hospital rugby team for three years around the time of this South African tour. Jerry, like Tom, did not gain the ultimate distinction of a cap for Ireland.

Walsh, J. C.

Jeremiah Charles Walsh. Born on 3rd November 1938. Centre. Gained a total of 26 caps for Ireland, between 1960 and 1967.

Wood, B. G. M.

Benjamin Gordon Malison Wood. Born on 20th June 1931. Prop. Gained a total of 29 caps for Ireland and two caps for the Lions, between 1956 and 1961.

The Teams
Ireland v South Africa on 13th May 1961 at Newlands

S.A. 15
Lionel Geoffrey Wilson, (Western Province). Born on 25th May 1933. Full back. Went on to gain a total of 28 caps for South Africa, between 1960 and 1965.

S.A. 14
Barend Pieter Van Zyl, (Western Province). Born on 1st August 1935. Wing. This was his only cap for South Africa.

S.A. 13
Gideon Hugo Van Zyl, (Transvaal). Born on 20th August 1932. Flanker. Went on to gain a total of 17 caps for South Africa, between 1958 and 1962.

S.A. 12
Colin Marius Greenwood, (Western Province). Born on 25th January 1936. Centre. This was his only cap for South Africa.

S.A. 11
David Alfred Stewart, (Western Province). Born 14th July 1935. Centre. Went on to gain a total of 11 caps for South Africa, between 1960 and 1965.

S.A. 10
Charles Frederick Nimb, (Western Province). Born on 6th September 1938. Fly-half. This was his only cap for South Africa.

S.A. 9
Pieter de Waal Uys, (Northern Transvaal). Born on 10th December 1937. Scrum-half. Went on to gain a total of twelve caps for South Africa, between 1960 and 1969.

S.A. 1
Stefanus Petrus Kuhn, (Transvaal). Born on 12th June 1935. Prop. Went on to gain a total of 19 caps for South Africa, between 1960 and 1965.

S.A. 2
Ronald Andrew Hill, (Rhodesia). .Born on 20th December 1934. Hooker. Went on to gain a total of 7 caps for South Africa, between 1960 and 1963.

S.A. 3
Pieter Stephanus Du Toit, (Boland). Born on 9th October 1935. Prop. Went on to gain a total of 14 caps for South Africa, between 1958 and 1961.

S.A. 4
Johannes Theodorus Claassen, (Western Transvaal). Born on 23rd September 1929. Lock. Went on to gain a total of 28 caps for South Africa (9 as captain), between 1955 and 1962.

S.A. 5
Pieter Johannes Van Zyl, (Western Province). Born on 23rd July 1933. Lock. This was his only cap for South Africa.

S.A. 6
Gideon Hugo Van Zyl, (Western Province). Born on 20th August 1932. Flanker. Went on to gain a total of 17 caps for South Africa, between 1958 and 1962.

S.A. 7
Hendrik Jacobus Martin Pelser, (Transvaal). Born on 23rd March 1934. Flanker. Went on to gain a total of 11 caps for South Africa, between 1958 and 1961.

S.A. 8
Douglas John Hopwood, (Western Province). Born on 3rd June 1934. Number 8. Went on to gain 22 caps for South Africa, between 1960 and 1965.

* * *

Irl. 15
Thomas Joseph Kiernan, (University College Cork). Born on 7th January 1939, he went on to gain a total of 54 caps for Ireland (24 as captain) and five for the Lions, between 1960 and 1973. Originally a centre he played mostly at full back. Went on to become Ireland's national coach, President of the IRFU, a member of the International RFB and chairman of European Rugby Cup Ltd.

Irl. 14
Anthony Joseph Francis (Kevin) O'Reilly, (Dolphin). Born on 7th May 1936. Wing. Went on to gain a total of 29 caps for Ireland and ten caps for the Lions, between 1955 and 1970.

Irl. 13
William John Hewitt, (Instonians). Born on 6th June 1928. This was his final cap of four gained for Ireland between 1954 and 1961. Best known as a fly-half.

Irl. 12
Kenneth James Houston, (Queens). Born on 20th July 1941. Wing. Went on to gain a total of six caps for Ireland between 1961 and 1965.

Irl. 11
Jeremiah Charles Walsh, (University College Cork). Born on 3rd November 1938. Centre. Went on to gain a total of 26 caps for Ireland, between 1960 and 1967.

Irl. 10
Dion Caldwell Glass, (Collegians). Born on 15th May 1934. This was his final cap of four gained between 1958 and 1961. Best known as a full back.

Irl. 9
Andrew Armstrong Mulligan, (London Irish). Born on 4th February 1936. Scrum-half. Gained a total of 22 caps for Ireland and one cap for the Lions, between 1956 and 1961. This was his final cap.

Irl. 1
John Sydney Millar, (Ballymena). Born on 23rd May 1934. Prop. Went on to gain a total of 37 caps for Ireland and nine caps for the Lions, between 1958 and 1970. Current Chairman of the International Rugby Board.

Irl. 2
Alfred Ronald Dawson (Wanderers). Born on 5th June 1932. Hooker. Went on to gain a total of 27 caps (16 as captain) for Ireland and six caps for the Lions between 1958 and 1964.

Irl. 3
Benjamin Gordon Malison Wood, (Lansdowne). Born on 20th June 1931. Prop. Gained a total of 29 caps for Ireland and two caps for the Lions, between 1956 and 1961. This was his final cap.

Irl. 4
Charles John Dick (known as Ian), (Ballymena). Born on 26th January 1937. Number 8. Gained eight caps for Ireland between 1961 and 1963.

Irl. 5
William Albert Mulcahy, (known as Bill and/or Wigs), (University College Dublin). Born on 7th January 1935. Lock. Gained a total of 35 caps for Ireland and six caps for the Lions between 1958 and 1965.

Irl. 6
Dennis Scott, (Malone). Born on 19th November 1933. Flanker. Went on to gain a total of three caps for Ireland between 1961 and 1962.

Irl. 7
James Ronald Kavanagh, (Wanderers). Born on 21st January 1931. Flanker. Gained a total of 35 caps for Ireland between 1953 and 1962. (Had made a new record earlier in 1961 when he passed out the most capped Irish forward for over 50 years – George Hamlet.)

Irl. 8
Timothy McGrath, (Garryowen). Born on 3rd October 1933. Number 8. Gained a total of seven caps for Ireland between 1956 and 1961.

Touch Judge
Noel Francis Murphy, (Manager of the team) President of the Irish Rugby Football Union in 1961. Gained 11 caps as a wing forward for Ireland between 1930 and 1933. He was the father of Noel Arthur Augustine Murphy, also included in the touring team.

Referee
Pieter Melt Hertzog Calitz, Western Province, South Africa. He was a master at Jan Van Riebeck High School. This was the only international match he refereed.

Irish scrum-halves during Tom's era (1950–1962)

Raymond Carroll – Born in Dublin on 9th February 1926. Gained 3 caps as scrum-half for Ireland between 25th January 1947 and 11th March 1950.

John Hume Burges – Born in Tipperary on 26th October 1928. Gained 2 caps as scrum-half for Ireland on 28th January 1950 and 11th February 1950.

John Anthony O'Meara – Born in Cork on 26th June 1929. Gained 22 caps as scrum-half for Ireland, between 27th January 1951 and 15th March 1958.

Herbert Lowry McCracken – Born in Belfast on 8th July 1927. Gained 1 cap as scrum-half for Ireland on 13th March 1954.

Sean Joseph McDermott – Born in Kinsale on 28th March 1932. Gained 2 caps as scrum-half for Ireland on 26th February 1955 and 12th March 1955.

Andrew Armstrong Mulligan – Born in India on 4th February 1936. Gained 22 caps as scrum-half for Ireland between 28th January 1956 and 13th May 1961. 1 cap for Lions v New Zealand on 19th September 1959.

Jonathan Wallace Moffett – Born in Belfast on 30th April 1937. Gained 2 caps as scrum-half for Ireland on 11th February 1961 and 25th February 1961.

James Charles Kelly – Born in Dublin on 8th April 1940. Gained 11 caps as scrum-half for Ireland between 14th April 1962 and 11th April 1964.

Press Cuttings From Tom's Suitcase

May 9th

Injured Malan to miss Test against Ireland

From Donald Mosey (Johannesburg, Tuesday).

IRELAND'S Rugby tourists arrived at Jan Smuts Airport here this afternoon. Avril Malan, skipper of the 1960-61 Springboks in Britain, was in the reception committee and the first news he gave me was: "I am out of the test on Saturday. I took a heavy tackle on the right thigh in a Club game and it has not recovered enough for me to say I am fit."
Thousands of British spectators who saw Malan lead his team last winter unbeaten until that dramatic Barbarian's game know just how much his captaincy meant.
Johannes Claassen, Malan's lock forward partner, is tipped to take over as skipper and Piet Van Zyl to fill the vacancy. That would bring the Van Zyl representation in the team up to four – Hugo, Rennie, Piet and Ben-Piet.

All fit and well
The tourists had a three-hour stop at the airport to await a flight to Capetown, their headquarters for the first week of the tour. They landed in brilliant sunshine with the temperatures in the 70's after a tiring journey of nearly 20 hours, but all are fit and well.
A crowd of 1,000 waited at the airport to welcome them, along with officials of the Transvaal Rugby Union.
A photographer asked a group to pose in front of an Irish Republic flag. They all came from Northern Ireland. It was all cheerfully laughed off.

Cape Times, Wednesday May 10th 1961

Malan Out – Piet v. Zyl In S.A. XV

Claassen is captain

By Maxwell Price
Twenty-seven-year-old Piet van Zyl, 6 ft 4 in, and weighing 230 lb., is the selectors' choice as lock replacement for Avril Malan, the Springbok captain, who withdrew from the South African team to play Ireland at Newlands on Saturday.

Van Zyl, a cousin of the Springbok flanker, Hugo van Zyl, wins his first Test cap and is the eighth Western Province player in the team.

There are now four Van Zyls in the Springbok team, the other two being the wings Hennie van Zyl and Piet-Ben van Zyl.

Johan Claassen will captain South Africa. He led the Springboks against France in 1958. The withdrawal of Avril Malan came as no surprise.

As was stated in the "Cape Times" last week his Test position was uncertain following an injury received in the Transvaal-Western Province fame at Newlands on April 29.

After that fame he said that he was not satisfied with his performance. "I am not properly fit yet", said Malan, who later withdrew from the Springbok trials at Port Elizabeth. Malan has a troublesome thigh injury which has not yet responded to rest and treatment.

While congratulating Piet van Zyl, one cannot help consoling at the same time with Frik du Preez, the Springbok flanker, who played such good rugby in the lock position at Port Elizabeth on Saturday.

But Piet van Zyl also did well, and while Du Preez may have been more prominent at the line-out, Van Zyl also caught the eye there as well as being extremely active in the loose mauls.

He was up to join in a spectacular move once with Dave Stewart and Keith Oxlee.

Du Preez's additional asset, of course, is his goal-kicking. He displayed better form in this department at the trials than Charlie Nimb, who is the Springbok goal-kicker in Saturday's test match.

The Springbok team will assemble in Cape Town to-morrow. Like the Irish they will live at Sea Point but in a different hotel.

The Cape Argus, Thursday, May 11th 1961

'SPRINGBOKS WILL HAVE FULL PRACTICE TO-MORROW'
– Hennie Muller
–
By A. C. PARKER

"WE have been given very little time to prepare for Saturday's international against Ireland, and I intend arranging a full work-out for the Springbok team to-morrow morning," Mr. Hennie Muller (manager of the South African side) said to-day.

Pointing out that the Transvaal players, including the captain (Johan Claassen) are not due to arrive in Cape Town until late this afternoon by air, Mr. Muller said that in any event no preparatory work could be undertaken before to-morrow as to-day was a religious holiday.

'We will have a team talk after dinner tonight and I intend impressing on the Springboks that they will be up against a very fit and capable side.'

The former Springbok captain. who so successfully managed the South African test teams against the All Blacks last year, made it clear that he would not be a party to dour, 'safety-first' tactics against the Irish on Saturday.

'BALANCED RUGBY'
'We want to win, of course, but the Springboks should aim at playing balanced rugby. By this I mean that the three-quarters must be brought into the game and that the type of rugby played by South Africa should be attractive,' he said.

Muller added that 'short-tour' tests were not meant to be battles of attrition, and he was pleased that Ronnie Dawson, the Irish captain, had also promised attacking play by his team.

HILL ARRIVES
Ronnie Hill, the Rhodesian hooker, arrived in Cape Town by air last night and. was the first Springbok to check in at the team's Sea Point hotel. The eight Western Province players and Piet du Toit of Boland were due to book in this afternoon.

Hill, who will be playing in his third internationals complained this morning of a sore throat and was to see a doctor. He was unable to have a meal last night. 'Otherwise, I feel fit enough, physically, and expect the trouble to clear up,' Hill said today.

Rumours were circulating last night about the fitness of two Springboks – Doug Hopwood and Charlie Nimb – being in doubt. Both, however, reported 'one hundred per cent fit' to-day.

Nimb had a painful boil on the face lanced yesterday afternoon. The rumour about Hopwood apparently originated from a slight bump he received on the knee on Tuesday night when practising at Brookside.

Nimb practised on his own at St. Joseph's College this morning and has been giving special attention to his place-kicking.

The Irish players had a two hour training session at the Hamiltons ground yesterday afternoon, when the greater part of it was devoted to loosening-up and exercises under the direction of Ronnie Dawson.

SPLIT UP

In the last 45 minutes the tourists got down to serious practice, the forwards splitting up under the supervision of Dawson and the backs under Andy Mulligan.

Dawson had Saturday's test pack scrumming against the rest who were augmented by Peter McMullan, the 'Belfast Telegraph' correspondent. It was significant that the Irish captain called for a concentrated, powerful shove.

Mulligan, after a tactical talk, had the backs running. Tony O'Reilly, who has filled out a lot, still has plenty of pace.

This afternoon the Irishmen were to run at Newlands and they will have a final work-out tomorrow morning – after the two test teams have been photographed together.

Mr. Jaap Theron, the South African Rugby Board representative with the team, said to-day that the Irish party would fly to Oudtshoorn in two Dakotas on Tuesday morning. From Oudtshoorn they will travel by car to Mossel Bay for next Wednesday's match there against South Western Districts.

The tourists will board a Port Elizabeth-bound aircraft at George next Thursday morning and will fly from there to Johannesburg.

As they are keen to do some shopping in Johannesburg, the Irish will not leave for Potchefstroom – where they play Western Transvaal on May 20 – until the Friday night.

SPORT 1
NO BLACKBOARD OF TEST – SAYS HENNIE MULLER
By Maxwell Price

Springbok manager, homespun Hennie Muller, turned his nose up at the very mention of it. "Blackboard talks", he said, " Blackboard talks! No, this team will not have any of that". He explained that he had no wish to have the thinking of his team complicated by blueprints. "We just want to play good, attacking rugby against the Irish at Newlands on Saturday".

Blackboard talks have often in the past been part of the Springboks Test preparation.

The full Springbok team to play Ireland assembled before dinner at their Sea Point hotel last night, and Muller, having congratulated all the players on being chosen, outlined the plan of preparation for the big game at Newlands.

"We will take them as they come." He had explained earlier, "Look, I don't like blackboard talks. You can't plan a game to the last letter." Blackboard talks are too theoretical. Often things don't work out as you think they will."

Muller added that he felt that he had a good workman-like Springbok team. "we will play attacking rugby, on orthodox lines – on a solid foundation ... of course there will be tricks and variations; but you cannot publish them."

Three Team Chats

He said that there would be three team talks. The one last night served to get the players together "as a team – thinking rugby."

Then today before practice he would outline the essentials he wished to rehearse at practice. On the eve of the Test tonight, "I hope to have the chaps set as a team, and the fundamentals of our tactics having been drilled into them, I will drive home the importance of the match itself, the honour of their being the select of South African rugby. What it means to play for the Springboks, more especially in a Test match."

He added, "I know I will get the best out of these boys. I hope they play well and they win' but should we lose, which can easily happen, we will be the first to congratulate our Irish visitors. You know how things go in rugby, you can never be too sure of winning!"

Wants Newlands
Hennie Muller was adamant about one thing last night. "I want the Springboks to have their turn on Newlands before the game. The chaps should benefit having a training spin there on the day before the game. They will get the feel of the turf and the Newlands atmosphere."

Last night it seemed likely that the Springbok team would have their Test rehearsal at Newlands about 11 a.m. today.

The Irish, under the shrewd Ronnie Dawson, trained at Newlands yesterday. Team manager, Mr. Noel Murphy, said, "This is a beautiful surface, a wonderful rugby atmosphere."

The practice was not over-severe. It consisted mainly of loosening up and running, with Irish wing, Tony O'Reilly, one not relishing the grind of practice, ever hugging the inside rail.

IRISHMEN HAVE CHANCE TO MAKE HISTORY: BUT ODDS FAVOUR S.A.

By A. C. PARKER

THOUSANDS OF MILES from O'Connell Street and Donegal Square, the 'dharlin bhoys' of Ireland will try, at Newlands tomorrow, to achieve a first rugby victory over South Africa – something they have found beyond their powers over the past 53 years in five matches at Balmoral, Ravenhill and Lansdowne Road.

Ireland, among the home countries, have always been regarded as 'unpredictable'. The aptness of this label was demonstrated as recently as five months ago in Dublin when Ronnie Dawson's men were written down by their own Press as having no chance of beating Avril Malan's Springboks.

In the event their traditional luck deserted the Irish only in injury time, and after as brave a fight as one has seen they went down by a rare 'pushover' try. No South African present at Lansdowne-Road, least of all the nine players in to-morrow's clash who were in the Springbok side that day, will be disposed to under-estimate Ireland's prospects of making history.

France have lost only one of their last 18 internationals – to Ireland. It's true that, after beating England, Dawson's men went down to Scotland, Wales and France in last season's internationals. But injuries played some part in the reverses against Wales and France.

LOSS OF FORM

Normally the Springboks, following their very successful tour of Britain, would start hot favourites to win to-morrow. One feels that the odds must still be slightly on South Africa, but the form of a number of established internationals so far this season has been disappointing enough to raise doubts about the outcome.

It's no secret that the preponderance of Western Province men in the Springbok team – five backs and three forwards – has been sharply criticized in other parts of the country. Some of them, indeed, have been a shade fortunate on current form to be preferred to their rivals. But the national selectors may have the last laugh.

SHREWD IRISH CAPTAIN
Dawson, who led the Barbarians to their 6-0 win over the Fifth Springboks, is perhaps the shrewdest captain in the Rugby Union game to-day. He knows full well that the Irish team to-morrow is a long way from being the strongest that could be fielded were all their best players available. There are potential weak spots in key inside back positions.

No one knows better than Dawson, too, that for his team to stand an even chance of success to-morrow the Springbok forwards must be matched and contained at every phase. The Irish pack came close to parity on December 17.

A major contribution to the Barbarians' victory in Cardiff was the way their forwards, by a tremendous effort in the tight, forced the Springboks to play more often to their backs than they might otherwise have done.

BACKS ISOLATED
The Barbarians succeeded in isolating the Springbok backs from their customary forward support and through Gainsford, in particular, often brought off a primary break though nothing came of it.

Dawson, one feels, will rely heavily on his forwards and trust to opportunism by his backs. Tony O'Reilly must always be reckoned with in this respect to turn the odd scoring chance to account.

The Irish pack (average weight 207lb.) unquestionably is one to be respected, particularly solid in the tight positions. Psychologically, it would have been a sound move to have seven of the pack that did so well in Dublin by including the experienced Gerry Culliton and Noel Murphy.

Ian Dick, however, is reported to have played well in the second row against France and Denis Scott and Tim McGrath are believed to have been chosen for their mobility.

Gordon Wood and Syd Millar are two excellent heavy props who will fully test Piet du Toit and Franie Kuhn, and the hooking duel between Dawson and Ronnie Hill should be keen.

Bill Mulcahy (who plays in a white strip to protect his ears) and Ron Kavanagh are two other grand forwards, and Johan Claassen and Piet van Zyl will not have things their own way at the line-outs – the Irish exploit the French 'peeling-off' tactics.

However, one saw these Springboks so often produce great forward play overseas that they are capable of getting on top of even this good Irish pack.

Claassen, playing in his 22nd test, was freely criticized when he last led South Africa at Newlands against France in 1958 and Avril Malan's ability to inspire his forwards may be missed.

But Claassen is surely experienced enough by now to sum up the situation.

Doug Hopwood was unable to play against Ireland in Dublin, and Hugo van Zyl and Martin Pelser are always more effective working in co-operation with him.

HALF-BACKS THE KEY

The game is likely to turn on the use the Springbok inside backs make of what is bound to be a liberal share of possession, and it may well be won or lost at half-back.

Charlie Nimb has his big chance to justify the confidence placed in him by the selectors and he and Piet Uys could prove superior as a pair to Dion Glass and Andy Mulligan, who apparently will be playing together for the first time.

Mulligan, of course, is a wily, experienced scrum-half who can open up a defence with his wide break, and he will no doubt be closely watched around the scrum.

The role of the centres will be vital, especially in creating scope for the wings, and here Dave Stewart and Colin Greenwood may have the edge on Jerry Walsh and the 19-year-old new cap, Ken Houston. Walsh was one of the best defensive centres the Springbok struck in Britain.

Tom Kiernan had an impressive game at full-back a few months ago and Lionel Wilson, a man for the big occasion, will have to improve on recent form to match him.

Kiernan is also a reliable goal-kicker who can be assisted in this direction by Glass. Nimb, though off target with his place-kicking of late, has had his on days in the past.

It looks like a South African win, but Newlands will give the likeable Irishmen a great reception if they pull it off.

TEAMS

IRELAND: T. J. Kiernan; A. J, F. O'Reilly, J. C. Walsh, K. J. Houston, W. J. Hewitt; D. C. Glass, A. A. Mulligan; S. Millar, A.R. Dawson (captain), B.G.M. Wood, D. Scott, W. A. Mulcahy, C..J. Dick, J. R. Kavanagh, T. McGrath.

SOUTH AFRICA: L. G. Wilson; Hennie Van Zyl, D. A. Stewart, C. Greenwood, Ben-Piet Van Zyl; C. Nimb, P. de W. Uys; S.P. Kuhn, R. A. Hill, P. S. du Toit, Hugo Van Zyl, J. T. Claassen (captain); Piet Van Zyl, H. J. M. Pelser, D. J. Hopwood.

Referee: Mr. P. M. Calitz. Kick-off, 4 p.m.

IRELAND GIVE KEN HOUSTON HIS FIRST CAP
CAPETOWN, Wednesday.

KEN Houston, 19-year-old science student from Queen's University, Belfast, gets his first Irish Rugby cap as centre to John Hewitt in the team to meet South Africa at Newlands, Capetown, on Saturday.

Houston is scarcely known south of the border and has not even played for Ulster, but he gets his chance first because injury and studies kept three of Ireland's top backs at home and secondly, because of his startling and consistent club form in the latter part of last season.

One other selection and one omission caused a few raised eyebrows in Capetown today. Dion Glass was named as stand-off half after winning his three caps at either wing or centre, and Gerry Culliton, Wanderers wing forward and 13 times capped, was omitted.

But the Irish themselves have one or two pointed views on the strength of the opposition.

They have a poor view of Dave Stewart's defensive qualities and his selection at centre has been particularly noted, especially in view of Houston's love of the dashing break.

Key Factor

Avril Malan's injury, which deprives the Springboks of their finest leader for years, is taken as by far the strongest factor in any chance of a shock win by the tourists.

Coming on top of John Gainsford's absence – he is another thigh-injury victim – it has started a great deal of speculation on that interesting possibility.

Gainsford, who called to welcome the party this morning, told me he will be out of Rugby for another two weeks.

With eight Western Province men in the Springbok side, an Irish win would be welcomed almost as much in the Transvaal as in Ireland.

There was a tremendous howl up north when the team were announced shortly after Transvaal visited Capetown and beat Western Province.

The controversy will at least make certain of a crowd of 40,000-plus.

Mr. Noel Murphy, the Irish R.U. President and senior tour manager, has laid down his policy as "to play the type of Rugby which will be attractive to your spectators."

And when he was faced with the catch-question, "How then, can you beat a Springbok pack?", he twinkled back smartly: "... Good forward play can be very attractive you know."

South Africa go into the Test without a recognised goal kicker since they have brought in Piet Van Zyl as forecast, rather than Frik Du Preez who kicked so well in Britain and especially in Ireland.

Criticism

But the point worrying South Africans most is that Johan Claassen takes over from Malan as skipper and that, they say, is likely to be Ireland's greatest asset.

Claassen was the Springbok captain three years ago when the French shattered South African Rugby pride by winning one and drawing the other game, and this is not merely a matter of looking at history for a precedent.

Claassen's captaincy on the field was, and still is, the subject of detailed criticism.

Ireland have seven men from the Six Counties in their team for the first time since anyone in this party can remember.

Daily Mail, Saturday, May 13th 1961

First Test Forecasts are puzzling the Tourists

IRISH BACK THEIR PACK

AND TIPSTERS SAY THEY'LL BEAT THIS SPRINGBOK SIDE

Capetown, Friday From Donald Mosey
Daily Mail staff reporter, who is travelling with the Irish team.
(His test Match report will appear on Monday.)

THE last official photograph has been taken, the last official party has finished, and the stage is set for Ireland's first ever Test match in South Africa.

They came out here not even giving themselves a chance, apart from the natural fighting response of the Irish to a challenge. Today they find themselves being widely tipped to beat the Springboks.

It is forecasting they cannot understand, because it is based entirely on a negative approach to tomorrow's game.

The tipsters are not looking at the potentialities of the tourists at all, but at the many faults they find with the South African selectors and with a handful of the men they have picked.

Their Plan
The advice most freely given to the Irish is "give the ball to your backs and let them run, and the Springbok pack will never get into the game."

But the fact is that the tourists are not too happy about the strength of their backs and are working understandably on the idea that their main force is in the forwards.

If David Hewitt, Niall Brophy, and Mike English had been here their approach might have been different, but the strength of the backs as a combined force, with so many enforced changes and positional switches, is problematical.

The poker-faced Tom Kiernan is safe enough at full-back and the rampaging Springbok forwards will not ruffle him.

Tony O'Reilly is just as likely to fade out of the picture in an overseas Test as he is to justify his tremendous popularity.

Versatile John Hewitt is just about incapable of playing a bad game in any position and Andy Mulligan and Jerry Walsh have plenty of experience to add to their ability.

Ordeal

For Ken Houston the game will be something of an ordeal. To take a man who has not played provincial Rugby in Ireland and put him against the Springboks at Newlands for his first big game is rather like taking a talented Fourth Division footballer in England and dropping him into the F.A. Cup Final at Wembley.

Dion Glass has not played for Ireland at stand-off half but has three caps in the three-quarter line, and it is generally accepted that his best work is done in the half-backs.

As for the forwards, the front row came off far better against the Springboks on their tour of Britain than any three have done for a long time, and that includes the All-Blacks, while Ronnie Dawson is a far greater captain than Claasens.

In the second row, the two doctors, Bill Mulcahy and Ian Dick, look capable of diagnosing any trouble from the opposition and treating it in the approved manner.

Tireless

The back three prove something of a contrast from Ronnie Kavanagh, the most capped Irishman, through the roving and tireless Tim McGrath to Dennis Scott, who played nearly all his first international against France a couple of months ago as an emergency full-back when the team were crippled by injuries.

The South African critics who feel the Irish have more than an even money chance say the Springboks are weary after their own six months' season – a visit from the All-Blacks, an exhausting tour of Britain and now their own new season starting with last week's trials in Port Elizabeth.

They have had no time for team training for this game.

The Springboks met yesterday, five days after being selected, and had no change to work-out because Ascension Day is observed very strictly here, with banks shops, pubs, and cinemas closed, and no sport taking place at all.

So they were left to make all their preparation on the day before the Test.

Pep Talks
They will have a loosener at Newlands and three pep talks from manager Hennie Muller, who scorns theoretical rugby and the use of a blackboard. Whatever the result the game promises to be a classic example of a fight between the Irish, averaging 14st 7lb, and the Springboks, 15st. 6lb.

If Ronnie Dawson's men can hold these heavyweights, South Africa might regret going into the game without a recognized goal-kicker, but I doubt whether it will become merely a matter of penalties.

The Irish can expect a good deal of support. Apart from the traditional backing of the coloured fans, they will be urged on by many rugby followers here who would be delighted to see the lordly Springboks humbled at their own headquarters.

If I doubt whether this can be done it is in no way a criticism of the Irish but born of a wholesome respect for the supreme efficiency of South African Rugby.

CAPE TIMES, SATURDAY MAY 13th. 1961

FIGHTING IRISH WILL BE HARD TO BEAT
Bright Test Match is Expected at Newlands To-day
By MAXWELL PRICE.

The Springboks, on home ground, start as favourites today against Ireland, a country which has yet to master South Africa at rugby. They have come near to doing it on Irish soil, but the honour has eluded them. Perhaps today at Newlands, playing for the traditional green, Ronnie Dawson's Irish XV will be inspired to such great endeavour as to make the occasion historic for Ireland.

But on record and against the background of the recent Springbok tour and that team's performance in Ireland the odds are against them; a fact which far from dismaying our rugby visitors will bring forth that tremendous Irish fighting spirit and a will to win.

The Springboks will not find it easy quelling the force and fire of this internationally-experienced pack of forwards; and it is fortunate that on this occasion they can pit against them in scrums and line-outs eight forwards equally experienced and perhaps just a little stronger.

This is the pack which on tour, except for the Barbarians game, when Claassen and Du Toit were absentees, cut down the forward opposition before them with some ease.

At the line-out and loose phases things did not go too well against Ireland at Lansdowne Road; but a persistent deep throw-in by the Springboks played into the Irish hands that day, and the absence of Doug Hopwood robbed the Springboks of great technique and intelligent play behind the scrum.

Nevertheless it was the Springbok pack which in the end brought victory, in "injury time", with a push-over try after the backs, having been given a generous supply of the ball, had repeatedly dissipated chances.

A LEADING ROLE

It was a day when Dick Lockyear (scrum-half) played one of his worst games of the tour, and inside-back play suffered accordingly.

Hopwood's absence from the Springbok team was perhaps a more important factor that day. Hopwood, on tour, played a leading role in three international successes against Wales, England and Scotland.

There is no doubt that his presence is a boon to the backs in the sphere of backing up and covering.

It is an advantage that Piet Uys, scrum-half, has an understanding of the Hopwood game.

Good rugby could be seen from the Springboks; for there is plenty of talent and speed behind the scrum. Charlie Nimb, fly-half, has the chance today to prove the selectors wise in their choice.

His centres, Dave Stewart and Colin Greenwood, are full of rugby, as the saying goes; and there is drive and speed on the wing as presented by Ben-Piet can Zyl, the Stellenbosch speed merchant, and "Houtperd" (Rocking Horse) Hennie van Zyl.

Lionel Wilson has only to be his usual consistent self to give the Springboks all the assurance a team needs from its full-back, and Johan Claassen, a Test captain, recalled to duty by injury to Avril Malan, has the chance to prove his fine rugby qualities. He has a sound pack of forwards, good in all departments and a proved and tested international unit.

The newcomer, Piet van Zyl is an excellent lock forward, a line-out leaper among the best, and has surprising speed for a man his size. His form this season has been outstanding.

While I can see the Springboks superior at line-out and possibly in the loose the Irish have the advantage of having one of the best hookers in world rugby in Ronnie Dawson, their captain, whose props, Gordon Wood and Syd Millar, are proved campaigners. Springbok hooker Ronnie Hill will not have it easy.

The Irish loose forwards are quick on the ball, with Ron Kavanagh a hard, fit exponent of the linking game. In the Dublin Test he fastened on to the deep ball at line-outs to link profitably with his backs.

EXPERIMENTAL TOUCH

Andy Mulligan. as scrum-half, is competent, and while there is the touch of the experimental about the inside backs with 19 year-old Ken Houston making his international debut at centre, experienced men like Mulligan, Jerry Walsh (Centre) and the wings, O'Reilly and Hewitt, provide the balance which gives the Irish line the look of efficiency.

Tom Kiernan, at full-back, gives strength to this Irish team. He is also a useful goal kicker. Nimb, Claassen and Wilson practised goal-kicking yesterday, Nimb being particularly accurate.

The Springboks rehearsed various back movements at their Newlands runabout yesterday, and it is clear that they will play to their backs. This is the idea uppermost in the minds of the Irish as well, so with fair weather promised there is every hope of seeing sprightly rugby at Newlands today.

The Teams:

IRELAND	S.A.
T. J. Kiernan	L.G. Wilson
A, J. F. O'Reilly	B. J. van Zyl
J. C. Walsh	D. A. Stewart
K. M. Huston	C. Greenwood
W. J. Hewitt	B.-P. van Zyl
D. C. Glass	C. F. Nimb
A. A. Mulligan	P. de W. Uys
B. G. M. Wood	S. P. Kuhn
A, R. Dawson (captain)	R. A. Hill
S. Millar	P. S. du Toit
J. R. Kavanagh	G. H. van Zyl
W. A. Mulcahy	J. T. Claassen (captain)
C. J. Dick	P. J. van Zyl
D. Scott	H. J. M. Pelser
T. J, McGrath	D. J. Hopwood

Referee: P. M. Calitz.

SPRINGBOKS DELIGHT CROWD OF 35,000 AT RUGBY TEST
By A. C. Parker

The Cape Argus, Saturday, May 13th 1961

Playing the running game before a delighted crowd of 35,000 at Newlands this afternoon, South Africa outclassed Ireland by 24 points (three goals, two tries, and a penalty goal) to eight (a goal and a try). The Springboks led 13-0 at half time.

There was no question about South Africa's superiority at every phase and the 16-point margin by no means flattered them. Ireland, to their credit, always tried to bring their backs into play.

Colin Greenwood and Ben-Piet van Zyl, two backs playing in their first international, each crossed the Irish line twice. The other Springbok try was scored by the number eight, Doug Hopwood, with Charlie Nimb kicking three excellent conversions from the touchline and goaling a prodigious 55-yard penalty.

Tom Kiernan, the Ireland fullback, scored all the points for his team late in the second half – a try, a conversion and an easy penalty.

This much-criticized Springbok side 'clicked' from the start and the Irish defence simply could not cope with the passing movements in which the forwards played their full part.

Johan Claassen had a tremendous game, controlling the short line-outs and excelling in the tight – loose Hopwood, Pelser and Hugo van Zyl were a rampant trio of breakaways and Piet van Zyl also playing in his first test excelled in the fluid exchanges.

SUPERB PACK

Uys had a fine game behind a superb, winning pack – Hill out-hooked Dawson 3-1 in heels against the head – and Nimb, at fly-half effectively answered his detractors with his well-balanced, pivotal display.

Stewart was a big success at centre, but had to move to fullback for most of the second half because of a shoulder injury to Wilson. Greenwood showed a lot of thrust in the first half, and Ben Piet van Zyl ran beautifully. It was not Ireland's day.

McGrath and Mulcahy worked hard in the pack and Mulligan, at scrum-half, had ideas. But Glass did not look the part at fly-half and the Irish defence was well below the standard expected, though with the way the Springboks played to-day the gaps kept coming It was all in all a most attractive game and the South African selectors have cause to be happy men.

A crowd officially estimated at 35,000 in perfect weather saw the match open on a bright note with both teams prepared to use their backs.

Stewart, receiving on the blind side, put the Springboks on the attack, finding touch in the Irish 25.

In the sixth minute Mulligan was penalized for putting the ball in unfairly. The kick was just outside the Irish 25 but only five yards in from touch and Nimb was narrow.

South Africa looked dangerous when Hopwood broke away down the left and cross-kicked for Hugo van Zyl to gather, but he could not get his pass away before being smothered.

OPENED SCORE

In the 13th minute, however, South Africa opened the score with a clever try. From a scrum 10 yards outside the 25, Uys fed Nimb who dummy-scissored with Stewart and put Ben-Piet van Zyl clear.

The right-wing was checked by Hewitt but passed inside to Greenwood who dived over in the right-hand corner – a great start for Greenwood in this his first international match.

Nimb's kick from the corner looked like going just wide but curved inside the far upright for South Africa to lead 5-0.

The Irish came back strongly only for the fly-half, Glass, whose handling had been shaky, to drop his pass.

In the 17th minute Hopwood had to receive attention to his shoulder.

IRISH CHANCE

After 19 minutes Ireland had a chance when Hill was penalized for foot up. Kiernan, however, had bad luck with his kick from 35 yards, hitting the upright, and Stewart cleared from the rebound.

Two minutes later Hugo van Zyl was caught offside and Kiernan, incurring mild disapproval, was just short from fully 50 yards.

When Nimb knocked on an awkward pass from Uys inside his 25, Ireland heeled and O'Reilly, the blind side wing, kicked high across. Walsh was penalized for offside as Wilson caught the ball.

The Springbok wings were using the short throw-in to Claassen. who was getting the ball back repeatedly.

South Africa, after a defensive spell, struck again in the 28th minute to go into a substantial 10-0 lead. Greenwood made the initial penetration by picking up a loose ball and bursting into the open. His inside pass found Piet van Zyl who gave inside to Hopwood, and the no. 8 shaking off three tackles, crossed far out. Nimb added the conversion with a beautiful kick.

CONFIDENT MOOD

These scores put the Springboks in confident mood and only a forward pass from Kuhn after Pelser and Hugo van Zyl had broken away and inter-passed saved Ireland.

The Springboks, however, added a third score in the 33rd minute – through a breakdown in the Irish line.

Houston, their outside centre, was tackled in possession by Stewart, and Pelser, picking up, gave to Hopwood, who, with O'Reilly drawn inside, sent Greenwood across for his second try far out. This time Nimb could not convert.

The Springboks were outplaying their opponents at this stage and Greenwood, side-stepping Walsh, made a clean break and Stewart and Uys handled for the hooker, Hill, to drop his pass with the crowd standing up to hail another try. Greenwood was proving a big success.

Close on half-time he was heavily tackled and the ambulance men came on to the field but he waved them away.

There had been a rhythm in the South African back-play that one has not seen for some time. Greenwood and Stewart especially were combining well. In the first half Hill led Dawson by the only two heels recorded against the head.

Half Time: South Africa 13, Ireland 0.

Three minutes after the resumption Hopwood lost a gift try when he kicked high and Kiernan knocked on in front of his line. The Springbok No. 8 fumbled with the line at his mercy.

In the 17th minute Nimb hit the upright high up with a fine attempt to goal a penalty from just inside the Irish 10-yard line.

This was not Ireland's day and a minute later their defence was caught badly out of position when the Springbok forwards forced quick possession from a loose scrum after Mulligan had fallen on the ball.

Pelser flung out a long pass to the unmarked Ben-Piet van Zyl who crossed in the right-hand corner. Nimb's kick was true all the way and South Africa led 18-0.

Then an interception by Hugo van Zyl saw the flanker put in a 40-yard run which. was ended by Kiernan forcing him into touch.

In the 13th minute South Africa had to re-arrange their team through a shoulder injury to Wilson. Wilson was hurt in making a tackle. Hopwood was taken out of the pack to play right-wing, Stewart moving to full-back and Ben-Piet van Zyl switching to centre.

A promising attack by Ireland with O'Reilly cutting infield and passing to the No 8 was checked in front of the South African posts by Piet van Zyl, who intercepted and saved well. Then Piet du Toit was on the spot to touch down just ahead of Glass.

Ireland, with seven forwards against them, were more m the picture now but, when Stewart brilliantly initiated a counterattack, only a forward pass from Hennie van Zyl to Ben-Piet van Zyl prevented another Springbok score.

TREMENDOUS KICK

Wilson returned to the field in the 23rd minute and Nimb went close with a long-range penalty. Stewart, however, stayed in the full-back position with Wilson, whose right hand was limp, just behind him.

Though a well-beaten side, Ireland were throwing the ball about enterprisingly.

The next South African score, after 31 minutes, took the form of a tremendous 55-yard penalty kick by Nimb from just inside the halfway which cleared the bar by a good margin.

With time running out, Ireland raised a big cheer with two scores in quick succession. First, Kiernan goaled an easy penalty when Uys was penalised in front of his posts, and then a good movement down the left saw Houston kick infield. Hennie van Zyl failed to gather and Kiernan collected to score between the posts, the full-back adding the conversion.

This roused the Springboks, and Uys broke strongly round the blind-side to send Ben-Piet van Zyl over for his second try. Nimb's kick failed and South Africa led 24-8.

DAILY MAIL WEDNESDAY, MAY 17th 1961

Brophy plays on tourists' left wing.
from DONALD MOSEY

Oudtshoorn, Cape Province,
Tuesday.

A 75-MINUTE flight from Capetown this morning brought the Shamrocks touring party to this lovely little town 56 miles inland from Mossel Bay, where tomorrow's game against South-Western Districts will be played.

From the airport the whole party was whisked away in cars to visit the famous Cango Caves in a valley more beautiful than anything even the blue hills of Kerry can offer.

As Oudtshoorn is the biggest Ostrich farming centre in the world, a visit to one of the farms was in the programme as well, before the 56-mile drive over the mountains to Mossel Bay.

No walk-over
This fixture should give the Shamrocks a chance to find their feet for S W. Districts are reputedly the weakest provincial side in the country. But, as this judgment is by current South African standards it will still be far from a walkover.

Personality of the side is Bruce Lynn, a No 8, who made the Junior Springbok trials for the Aussies tour two years ago. For tomorrow's game Districts include a scrum-half, Geldenhuys, who has never played in senior Rugby of any kind, and Koos Du Toit, the former Boland centre.

Strong pack
Niall Brophy will be Shamrocks' left winger, just two days after arriving from Ireland, with Tony O'Reilly on the other side to round off the open game. The Tourists hope to stage an exhibition style match. With Gerry Culliton, Syd Millar and Noel Brophy in the pack, they are expected to beat the Districts forward and give the backs all the chances they want.

HEWITT FORCED TO CRY OFF
IRISH PRESS Special
The Irish rugby team should register the first victory of their South African tour at Mossel Bay, Cape Province, today, when they meet South-Western Districts.

They are not looking on it as an easy game, however. The Districts put up a good Show against the All-Blacks, losing 6-19, after trailing 0-13 at half time.

The Districts finished bottom in the last Currie Cup Tournament, but many touring teams in the past have found that it was wrong to underestimate the weaker South African provincial teams.

All the players who were not included in the Irish team beaten by South Africa in the international at Cape Town on Saturday will be in action today, plus Niall Brophy, wing-three-quarter of the 1959 'Lions', who joined the party on Sunday.

The South Western Districts have a mobile pack, although it is light by South African standards, the average weight being just over 14 st. 4 lb.

The Irish team will have a weight advantage in the scrum, but Jimmy Dick, who is playing his first game of the tour, will be up against a fine hooker in Piet van Zyl.

The Districts have two fast wings in Horne and Sefrontein, but it would be too much to expect them to outpace Tony O'Reilly and Brophy, while John Dooley and Jerry Walsh should give Ireland the advantage at centre.

G. Tormey, brought into the party when Mick English was forced to withdraw with an injured calf muscle, is at out-half and scrum-half Tom Cleary, who captained Munster against Avril Malan's Springboks, should provide him with a good service.

Ireland plan to play another fast open game and intend to throw the ball about as much as possible. Their forwards should get on top early in the game, with weight advantage of about 7 lb. a man.

John Hewitt, who was to have captained the Irish team withdrew after testing his injured knee late yesterday. Hewitt received the injury in Saturday's match against South Africa. He had been having treatment for fluid on the knee.

Tom Kiernan, who excelled in the international, will play at full back – in which position Hewitt was to have played – and front row forward Syd Millar will captain the Irish side.
Ireland: T. Kiernan, A. O'Reilly, J. Dooley,. J. Walsh. N, Brophy; G. Tormey. T. Cleary; J. Thomas. J. Dick, S, Millar; I. Dick; G. Culliton, D Scott, T. McGrath. N. Murphy

IRELAND FIGHT HARD FOR 11-6 VICTORY AFTER GREAT S.W.D. RALLY
From Maxwell Price

Mossel Bay. Greater enterprise and speed behind the scrum helped Ireland to an 11 – 6 win over South Western Districts here yesterday. Ireland led 8 – 0 at half-time, but when the home side narrowed the gap with two penalties in the second half, the crowd of 5,000 urged them to greater endeavour.

Forwards and backs tried desperately to snatch a win to make the occasion an historic one (it was the first international rugby visit to Mossel Bay for 51 years) but Ireland fought back.

Three minutes from time, Tom Kiernan, who played another great full-back game, stole up to the fly-half post to drop a goal and make the issue safe for Ireland, who won the match with a goal, a dropped goal and a penalty to two penalties.

The Irish back line, with Tormey operating at fly-half, looked more businesslike than it did against South Africa in the Test on Saturday. Tom Cleary, scrum-half, substituted ably for Mulligan. Had the centre play of Walsh and Dooley been more consistent, the Irish wings O'Reilly and Brophy would probably have been in for tries.

Valuable Ground

Towards the end on a sound forward platform, Tormey kicked the ball into the open space for the wings. This manoeuvre gained valuable ground.

South Westerns gave stouter opposition than expected. Their forwards, led by a competent hooker in Flip van Zyl, gained more than a fair share of the ball at the scrums, but Ireland, with Jim Thomas prop, Culliton and Noel Murphy often in the picture, were on top at the line-out and in the loose.

There was more speed generally about the Irish play, backs and forwards.

The close nature of the second-half scoring kept interest at fever pitch. Kiernan, the Irish full-back, not only dropped the all-important goal, but goaled a penalty and converted splendidly from touch in the first half – eight points out of 11 which made his tally 16 out of 19 points in the first two games of the short tour.

Good Pace

As with the Test on Saturday, the game was played at a rattling good pace with the Irish willing to attack from their own half. Their loose forwards, Murphy, McGrath and Scott were a boon to the half-backs as they sped to the loose ball, or were up for support.

Noel Murphy, who played against South Africa in the Dublin Test, was the best loose forward on the field. Jim Thomas, a tough, mauling forward with a useful knack of dispossessing at the line-out, was a busy prop how now and again also showed a fair turn of speed.

South Westerns were more or less out of the picture in the first half, but once Bruce Lynn goaled his penalty from half-way early in the second half they found new heart and Ireland was forced to fight hard for the victory.

Ireland Attack

A good dribbling rush put Ireland early on the attack. Offside at the line-out gave Tom Kiernan a chance, but he missed an easy 30-yard penalty. He made no mistake with an easier one for "foot up" a moment later, and within six minutes Ireland led 3-0.

Following a spell of midfield mauling and fruitless kicking, Noel Murphy, with a nice run from the loose, returned Ireland to the home half. Dooley did well in a line move to keep Ireland attacking, and after Cleary had picked up well from a wheeled scrum Murphy was there to take the pass and send hooker Jimmy Dick over for a splendid try. Kiernan converted from touch to put Ireland 8-0 up after 21 minutes.

Heartened by this score, the Irish attacked through their backs, Kiernan joining the line splendidly.

For most of the first half South-Westerns and made virtually no impression in spite of good leaping at the line-out by Strydom. Nortje, centre and Lynn, number eight, tackled well at times.

There was greater liveliness in the Irish play, both among the backs and forwards, but Wagner, the South-Westerns full-back, defended well under pressure.

The Irish seemed through for a certain try after a break by Jerry Walsh, but Millar tried to barge over with the line open and Dooley and Brophy unmarked at his side. Half-time: Ireland 8 South-Westerns 0.

There was a sensational start to the second half when Bruce Lynn goaled a great penalty from half-way within the first minute (8-3). Excitement reached high pitch when Geldenhuys, home scrum-half, caught his own short kick and sent wing Sefrontein on a run to the line, but Tormey, failing back, brought off a great tackle.

South Westerns seemed revitalised. Barnard kicked up and Kiernan was bowled over, but a bad pass robbed South Westerns of another chance of a score.

With 17 minutes to go, Ireland were penalized at the line-out amid boos from non-European spectators. Hanekom goaled from the "25" near touch (8-6).

Pass Intercepted

Ireland were desperate to maintain their narrow lead, and Tormey sent a high kick to the corner. Only weight of numbers brought O'Reilly to the ground as he tried to bulldoze his way over. Then Tormey broke, but Lynn intercepted his pass.

There were eight minutes left with play ranging mostly in midfield. Ireland, with Kiernan and Murphy prominent, played desperately to maintain the narrow lead.

Culliton booted through to force a scrum at the posts. Ireland heeled and Kiernan, who had come up to take the scrum-half's pass, dropped the goal which made Ireland breathe more easily (11-6).

GOOD DEFENCE KEEPS IRISH SCORE LOW

Tourists score only one try
The Friend's Special Representatives

Mossel Bay, Wednesday
After shaping like comfortable winners in the first half, the touring Irishmen had to play for all their worth to beat a spirited South-Western Districts side by 11 points to six before a crowd of about 4,000 here this afternoon.

The Shamrocks, who led 8-0 at half time, scored a goal, a penalty goal and a dropped goal to two penalty goals.

Kiernan, who played an outstanding game at full back – he came in for the injured John Hewitt – contributed eight points with an easy penalty, a touchline conversion of hooker Jimmy Dick's try and just before time, a drop from a five-yards scrum.

South Westerns penalties were goaled by the no. 8 Bruce Lynn (a prodigious kick from just inside the half way) and the front-ranker, Koos Hanekom.

There was much excitement when Hanekom kicked his penalty to make the score 8-6 in the 24th minute of the second half and the issue was in doubt up to the final whistle. But it was far from being an exceptional game because of numerous handling mistakes by the Irish.

The tourists, who were much the more enterprising side, fully deserved their win. It was only the excellent defensive work of the South-Western Districts men that kept them in the game with a chance, their tackling and covering being of tenacious quality throughout. In this respect, Nortje at centre and Lynn at No. 8 excelled.

Strong Kicking
The South-Western backs, who saw far less of the ball, hardly had a single line movement, but the value of fly-half Barnard's strong kicking with both feet in driving the tourists back, was a considerable factor in the home team's creditable performance.

Jimmy Dick, who scored the only try of the game when the scrum-half Tom Cleary and flank forward Noel Murphy combined in a clever move from a set scrum, out-hooked Philip van Zyl to gain a 6-1 lead on the tight head count. And at the line-outs Ian Dick and

Gerry Culliton gave Ireland the advantage, though Strydom worked hard in this department.

Jerry Tormey proved a better fly-half than Dion Glass had done in Saturday's Test, but the line still lacked punch, though once it was only a great cover-tackle by Lynn that stopped Walsh on the corner flag.

On this form it is doubtful whether the tourists will beat Western Transvaal or Rhodesia.

TRANSVAAL TREK IS A TOUGH ONE FOR THE SHAMROCKS

FROM Donald Mosey

Johannesburg, Friday.
Daily Mail, Saturday May 20, 1961

SOME of the snags of a short tour involving four games are beginning to show as the Irish Shamrocks go into their third game of the tour at Potchefstroom tomorrow.

They spent the whole of yesterday travelling, first by coach for 30 miles, then in two aircraft with a whole series of stops which prevented their getting any sort of rest.

It took just over nine hours to reach Johannesburg from Mossel Bay.

That left a minimum of time for the casualities to have treatment and put the tourists in the position of having to train today – the eve of a game against Western Transvaal which promises to be nearly as tough as the Test from the forwards' point of view.

Ron Kavanagh is having treatment for a bruised heel, Tim McGrath has a badly blistered foot, and it looks as though John Hewitt's game at Newlands was his first and last of the tour.

A heavy tackle early in the Test left Hewitt with a damaged knee and shin, on which the fluid is proving difficult to move.

Strong Team

Nevertheless, with Kavanagh fit as he expects to be, Shamrocks field a strong team against the Transvaalers, who are anxious to point our that, well as the Springboks played in the Test, the selectors were still wrong to include so many Western Province men at the expense of the North.

Western Transvaal are led by the immensely powerful Johan Claassen who insists he will retire at the end of the season although he is playing as well as anyone has ever seen him.

He is joined in the second row by "Tiny" Pretorius and the giant wing forwards Lofty Nel (two tests against New Zealand) and Koos Bezuidenhout (a junior Springbok).

It seems certain that Shamrocks are going to be outweighted even more than they were at Newlands.

If they can win this game they can win back some of the prestige they lost by their disappointing show at Mossel Bay, which had not even the saving grace of being attractive to watch.

Late Trip

To play at Potchefstroom the tourists have to make an 84-mile coach trip tonight, arriving very late, and then drive back the same distance tomorrow night after the game.

No one is looking forward to the journey very much, but it is part of the sacrifice which has to be made to take touring sides to centres where the population may not be very large but where enthusiasm is just as high as the big city.

The teams are:

Transvaal: Cilliers; Swemmer, Jordaan, Carlstein, Powell, Grundlingh, Moodle, Pienaar, Buitendach, Putter, Claassen, Pretorius, Bezuidenhout, Kotze, Nel.

Shamrocks: Kiernan; Brophy, Walsh, Houston, O'Reilly, Tormey, Mulligan, Wood, Dawson, Millar, Mulcahy, Dick, Murphy, Kavanagh, Culliton.

RONNIE DAWSON SETS THE STYLE IN AGONY
From DONALD MOSEY: Potchefstroom, Sunday May 22nd

WESTERN TRANSVAAL - 6 SHAMROCKS - 16

This was more like it. This morale and prestige boosting win was a triumph for the tactical brilliance of Ronnie Dawson and the result of a tremendous all-round improvement in the work of the Irish tourists.

Consider the disadvantages they had to contend with in meeting one of the mightiest packs in South Africa, led by Test skipper Johann Claassen in his greatest form.. They were playing at an altitude of 4,600 ft. where a burst of even 25 yards has you labouring to catch your breath.

The game started in a temperature of 75 deg. and a blaze of blinding sunshine, and continued in a clinging, clammy heat until the end.

Skipper Dawson played for three-quarters of the game in intense pain from badly torn ligaments in his right wrist.

Murphy hurt

Noel Murphy who was off for treatment for five minutes in the first half, limped through the remainder of the game with a nasty twist of the right ankle. Yet despite all this, the tourists brought off a notable, clean-cut win against a team which beat both the Lions and the Barbarians on their last visits.

South African critics blame the Western Transvaal backs for the defeat in rather comprehensive terms. Apparently, they have not stopped to consider how much their performance was governed by the way Dawson dictated the course of the game with consummate skill, and how magnificently his plans were carried out by his men.

Take the line-out as one example of how the Irish played above themselves.

Bill Mulcahy and Ian Dick were up against Claassen, at 6ft 4in, and 16st. 10lb, and "Tiny" Pretorius, biggest forward in South Africa at 6ft. 6 in. and 17st. 12 lb. Yet, through the supremely efficient working of a system they have practised diligently, and which involved the vital co-operation of Ron Kavanagh and Gerry Culliton, Shamrocks got the ball back 24 times to the Transvaal side's 23.

Scoring Kiernan
Mulcahy's marking of Claassen was terrific. So was much of Dick's individual effort – what a vastly improved player he is! And Kavanagh was going better than any man on the field at the end of those exhausting, energy-sapping 80 minutes.

The backs. too, must come in for a share of the credit. This was by far the best game Tony O'Reilly has played on tour. His try, three minutes from the end was a model of how to capitalise on the stand-off half kick to the wing. Gerry Tormey, who had a good game. placed his punt perfectly.

Andy Mulligan varied his game cleverly and worked a dropped goal for Tom Kiernan with a brilliant feint.

The magnificent Kiernan, whom everyone here expects to see next year with the Lions, had a personal haul of ten points, making a total of 20 out of the 25 the tourists have scored in three games.

Again, Shamrocks had a little referee trouble. A South African official completely missed a mark by Mulcahy which cost the Irish the one try they conceded and he completely mystified the team by disallowing what looked like a perfectly good dropped goal by Ken Houston. Fortunately, it didn't matter this time.

This was not always an attractive game to watch, but a win for the Irish was important both for their own spirit and the success of the final game at Salisbury, Rhodesia, on Wednesday.

Dawson, who has no time for pious phrases like "the game is the thing and the result unimportant" was determined to win it, and laid his plans accordingly.

He deserves immense credit for doing so, and for his personal example in playing while plainly suffering agonies from his damaged wrist.

Friendship Roll

R. Hurley
W. A. & E. R. Barry
T. J. & Roisin Nesdale
Michael English
W.G. Hurley, Providers
Owen and Mary Ryan
M. J. Hoctor
James F. Walsh
Dynan Fitzpatrick
P. F. & A. Walsh
Tom Kirby, Electrical
W. M. Peacocke
S. MacHale
M. McMahon
Donal Chambers
Michael Kirby
Mathew McNamara
John G. Ryan
James Baggott
D. M. Hanrahan
Dominic Dineen
F. J. & Patricia Horne
Oliver Walker
James and Anastasia Mc Govern
Caleb and Gillian Powell
Paddy Moran
D. M. Murphy
C. English
B. J. Nesbitt
A. Condell
J. Finnucane
Anthony G. O'Sullivan
Edmond J. Kelleher
D. R. Lawlor
Patrick Keogh
G. E. Russell
Patrick A. Lyons
W. J Slattery
Dermot Fitzgerald
W. Trevor McMorrow
P. T. Moran
J. H. Wood

The above list contains the names of friends[133] who rallied around when Tom was recovering from his surgery in October 1996. At this late stage, it is obviously not an exhaustive list and there may be some names inadvertently omitted and, if so, I apologise. All of the above people made donations to a "whip around" for Tom, which gave him an element of financial freedom for the first time in 30 years. The collection was organised mainly by the late Paddy (Mo) Moran in conjunction with Dermot (Gooser) Geary, two Bohemians men from days of yore.

133 Found in Tom's suitcase.

LIFE GOES ON
ONGOING SNAPSHOTS FROM THE FAMILY ALBUM

Standing: Michael (3) Cleary, Anne Cleary, Gerard (2) Kane, Silvia Valderrama, Gerard (3) Cleary, Stephanie Keating, Paula Kelly, Eddie Keating, Irene Connolly (family friend)
Middle row: Jim Kelly, Ann Cleary, Helen Kane, Gerry Cleary, Nuala Daly (neé Connolly, family friend)
Front row: Aisling Sheil, Zoë Cleary, Geraldine Cleary, Jenny Joyce

The next generation
Back row: Maureen Cleary, Lisa Kelly, Rebecca Whelan, Colette Keating, Stephen Cleary
Front row: Andrew Cleary, Stephie Keating, Paul Cleary, Jennifer Keating, Nicola Whelan, Aoife Kelly.

Tom's extended family (Athy Branch)
Back: Ann Cleary, Aisling & Greg Sheil, Rebecca Whelan, Jenny Joyce, Alan Carter and Geraldine Cleary
Front: Gerry Cleary, Nicola Whelan, Peter Joyce, Baby Patrick Joyce, Kate Joyce (on Jenny's knee)

Tom's extended family (Carrick-on-Suir Branch)
Standing: Stephanie Keating, Gerard Cleary (3), Michael Cleary (3), Derry Moran, Ken Moran, Eddie Keating, Aoife Broxton
Sitting: Anne Cleary, Silvia Valderrama, Bernadette Cleary, Zoë Cleary, Amy Breashears

Tom's extended family (Mullingar Branch)
(Photograph of Tom playing tennis in background)
Back row: Gerard Kane, Niall Kelly, Paula Kelly, Aoife Kelly, Helen Kane, Jim Kelly
Front: Ursula Kane Cafferty with Lisa Kelly

January 2004

Standing; Rebecca Whelan holding Baby Kate Joyce,
Middle row, left to right; Jennifer Keating, Lisa Kelly, Maureen Cleary, Colette Keating
Front row, left to right; Stephie Keating holding Niall Kelly, Stephen Cleary, Aoife Kelly, Eoghan Cleary, Nicola Whelan

October 2004

Nicola Whelan, Niall Kelly, Lisa Kelly, Rebecca Whelan,
Aoife Kelly, Maureen Cleary, Eoghan Cleary

Bohemians men of yore.
Bloomfield March 2005
Brendan O'Dowd, Donal Holland and Dom Dineen

Bloomfield March 2005
Brendan O'Dowd (Former President Munster Branch I.R.F.U.), Ursula Kane Cafferty, Donal Holland, Helen Kane and Dom Dineen (President I.R.F.U. 1971-1972)

Endnotes: International careers of players mentioned in the narrative

Please note that on the 1952 Irish tour of Argentina and Chile the international matches were not recognised as Irish caps. Hence they are not included in the total number of caps mentioned for each player.

Albaladejo, Pierre. Born on 14th December 1933. Fly-half and full-back. Went on to gain a total of 30 caps for France between 1954 and 1964. (He kicked a total of 12 drop goals in his entire ten year career, of which three were against Ireland in 1960. See p. 105.)

Baard, Adriaan Pieter. Born on 17th May 1933. Number 8. This was his only cap for South Africa.

Berkery, Patrick Joseph. Born on 3rd February 1929. Full-back. Went on to gain 11 caps for Ireland between 1954 and 1958.

Boniface, Guy. Born on 6th March 1937. Centre. Went on to gain a total of 35 caps for France between 1960 and 1966.

Bornemann, Walter William. Born on 19th January 1936. Wing. Went on to gain four caps for Ireland in 1960.

Brophy, Niall Henry. Born on 19th November 1935. Wing. Went on to gain a total of 20 caps for Ireland and two caps for the Lions between 1957 and 1967.

Burges, John Hume. Born on 26th October 1928. Scrum-half. Went on to gain two caps for Ireland in 1950.

Celaya, Michel. Born on 4th July 1930. Back-row. Went on to gain 50 caps for France (12 as captain) between 1953 and 1961.

Claassen, Johannes Theodorus. Born on 23rd September 1929. Lock. Went on to gain a total of 28 caps for South Africa (nine as captain) between 1955 and 1962.

Clifford, Jeremiah Thomas. Born on 15th November 1923. Prop. Went on to gain 14 caps for Ireland and five caps for Lions between 1949 and 1952.

Crauste, Michel. Born on 6th July 1934. Back-row and flanker. Went on to gain a total of 63 caps for France (22 as captain) between 1957 and 1966.

Craven, Daniel Hartman. Born on 11th October 1910. Scrum-half. Went on to gain a total of 16 caps for South Africa between 1931 and 1938. Chairman of the South African Rugby Board at time of Tom's involvement.

Culliton, Michael Gerard. Born on 15th June 1936. Lock. Went on to gain a total of 19 caps for Ireland between 1959 and 1964.

Danos, Pierre. Born on 4th June 1929. Scrum-half. Went on to gain 17 caps for France between 1954 and 1960.

Davidson, Jeremy William. Born on 28th April 1974. Lock. Went on to gain 32 caps for Ireland and three for the Lions between 1995 and 2001.

Davies, Cyril Allan Harvard. Born on 21st November 1936. Centre. Went on to gain seven caps for Wales between 1957 and 1961.

Dawson, Alfred Ronald. Born on 5th June 1932. Hooker. Went on to gain a total of 27 caps (16 as captain) for Ireland and six caps for the Lions between 1958 and 1964. He captained the Lions in a record breaking six successive test games in 1959, was an Irish selector between 1969-1971, coach to international side in 1974, became a member of the International Rugby Board and was President of the IRFU in 1990. An architect by profession he is credited with much of the modern development of the Lansdowne Road ground in the 1970s and 1980s.

Dick, Charles John (known as Ian.) Born on 26th January 1937. Number 8. Went on to gain eight caps for Ireland between 1961 and 1963.

Dick, James S. Born on 24th October 1939. Hooker. Went on to gain one cap for Ireland (v England) on 10th February 1962.

Domenech, Ameédeé . (Unable to locate date of birth.) Went on to gain a total of 52 caps for France between 1954 and 1963.

Dooley, John Francis. Born on 10th August 1934. Centre. Went on to gain three caps for Ireland in 1959.

Du Preez, Frederick Christoffel Hendrik. Born on 28th November 1935. Lock. Went on to gain a total of 38 caps for South Africa between 1961 and 1971.

Du Toit, Pieter Stephanus. Born on 9th October 1935. Prop. Went on to gain a total of 14 caps for South Africa between 1958 and 1961.

Dupuy, Jean-Vincent. Born on 25th May 1934. Wing and centre. Went on to gain a total of 40 caps for France between 1956 and 1964.

Edwards, Gareth Owen. Born on 12th July 1947. Scrum-half. Went on to gain 53 caps for Wales and ten for the Lions between 1967 and 1978. Also gained one cap on a World XV team and made five appearances for Wales in non-capped matches.

English, Michael Anthony Francis. Born on 2nd June 1933. Out-half. Went on to gain a total of 16 caps for Ireland between 1958 and 1963. Was selected for the Lions tour of Australia and New Zealand in 1959 but was not capped as he didn't play in a test match. He broke his leg on that tour and returned to Ireland by boat in the company of Niall Brophy who was also injured (see endnote re Niall Brophy below). Also referred to as Mick and/or Mickey, he and Tom were recognised as easily the best club partnership in the country in the late 1950s and early 1960s.

Flynn, Michael Kevin. Born on 20th March 1939. Centre. Went on to gain a total of 22 caps for Ireland between 1959 and 1973.

Gainsford, John Leslie. Born on 4th August 1938. Centre. Went on to gain 33 caps for South Africa between 1960 and 1967.

Glass, Dion Caldwell. Born on 15th May 1934. Went on to gain a total of four caps for Ireland between 1958 and 1961. Best known as a full back.

Greenwood, Colin Marius. Born on 25th January 1936. Centre. This was his only cap for South Africa.

Guerin, Brendan Noel. Born on 2nd January 1930. Lock. Went on to gain one cap for Ireland on 25th February 1956.

Hardy, Gerald Gabriel. Born on 29th March 1937. Fly-half. Went on to gain one cap for Ireland on 24th February 1962.

Hewitt, David (Dave.) Born on 9th September 1939. Centre. Went on to gain 18 caps for Ireland and six for the Lions between 1958 and 1965.

Hewitt, William John. Born on 6th June 1928. Fly-half. Went on to gain four caps for Ireland between 1954 and 1961.

Hill, Ronald Andrew. Born on 20th December 1934. Hooker. Went on to gain a total of seven caps for South Africa between 1960 and 1963.

Hopwood, Douglas John. Born on 3rd June 1934. Number 8. Went on to gain 22 caps for South Africa between 1960 and 1965.

Horrocks-Taylor, John Philip. Born on 27th October 1934. Fly-half. Went on to gain nine caps for England and one for the Lions between 1958 and 1964.

Houston, Kenneth James. Born on 20th July 1941. Wing. Went on to gain a total of six caps for Ireland between 1961 and 1965.

Kavanagh, James Ronald. Born on 21st January 1931. Flanker. Went on to gain a total of 35 caps for Ireland between 1953 and 1962.

Kiernan, Thomas Joseph. Born on 7th January 1939. Centre and full back. Went on to gain 54 caps for Ireland (24 as captain) and five for the Lions between 1960 and 1973. Went on to become Ireland's national coach, President of the IRFU, a member of the international RFB and chairman of European Rugby Cup Ltd.

Kuhn, Stefanus Petrus. Born on 12th June 1935. Went on to gain a total of 19 caps as prop for South Africa between 1960 and 1965.

Kyle, John Wilson. Born on 10th January 1926. Fly-half. Went on to gain a total of 46 caps for Ireland and six for the Lions between 1947 and 1958.

Lane, Michael Francis. Born on 3rd April 1926. Wing. Went on to gain 17 caps for Ireland between 1947 and 1953 and two caps for the Lions in 1950.

Lockyear, Richard John. Born on 26th June 1931. Scrum-half. Went on to gain a total of six caps for South Africa between 1960 and 1961.

MacHale, Seán. Born on 6th April 1936. Prop. Went on to gain 12 caps for Ireland between 1965 and 1967.

Main, Derrick Roy. Born on 29th November 1931. Prop. Went on to gain four caps for Wales in 1959.

Malan, Avril Stéfan. Born on 9th April 1937. Went on to gain a total of 16 caps as a lock for South Africa, (ten as captain) between 1960 and 1965.

McCarthy, James Stephen. Born on 30th January 1926. Flanker. Went on to gain 28 caps for Ireland between 1948 and 1955.

McGrath, Timothy. Born on 3rd October 1933. Number 8. Went on to gain a total of seven caps for Ireland between 1956 and 1961. This was his final cap.

McIvor, Stephen Charles. Born on 5th February 1969. Scrum-half. Went on to gain three caps for Ireland between 1996 and 1997. He was also an unused substitute on the bench on a number of occasions in 1997 and 1998.

McMorrow, Angus. Born on 6th November 1927. Went on to gain one cap as full-back for Ireland on 10th March 1951.

Meredith, Brinley Victor. Born on 21st November 1930. Hooker. Went on to gain a total of 34 caps for Wales and eight for the Lions between 1954 and 1962.

Millar, John Sydney. Born on 23rd May 1934. Prop. Went on to gain a total of 37 caps for Ireland and nine caps for the Lions between 1958 and 1970. Chairman of the International Rugby Board at time of writing.

Moffett, Jonathan Wallace. Born on 30th April 1937. Scrum-half. Went on to gain two caps for Ireland in 1961.

Moncla, Francois. Born on 1st April 1932. Flanker and Lock. Went on to gain a total of 31 caps for France (18 as captain) between 1956 and 1961.

Morgan, William George Derek. Born on 30th November 1935. Number 8. Went on to gain 9 caps for England between 1960 and 1961.

Morgan, Haydn John. Born on 30th July 1936. Flanker. Went on to gain 27 caps for Wales and four for the Lions between 1958 and 1966.

Mulcahy, William Albert (known as Bill and/or Wigs). Born on 7th January 1935. Lock. Went on to gain a total of 35 caps for Ireland and six caps for the Lions between 1958 and 1965.

Mullen, Karl Daniel. Born on 26th November 1926. Hooker. Went on to gain 25 caps for Ireland (18 as captain) and three for the Lions between 1947 and 1952.

Muller, Hendrik Scholtz Vosloo. Born on 26th March 1922. Number 8. Went on to gain 13 caps (nine as captain) for South Africa, between 1949 and 1953.

Mulligan, Andrew Armstrong. Born on 4th February 1936. Scrum-half. Went on to gain a total of 22 caps for Ireland and one cap for the Lions between 1956 and 1961. This was his final cap. Andy was the scrum-half who played in the international matches every time Tom was named as 'sub-to-attend'. See Post Mortem section of the book for further detail.

Murphy, Noel Arthur Augustine (son of Noel Francis Murphy). Born on 22nd February 1937. Flanker. Went on to gain 41 caps for Ireland and eight for the Lions between 1958 and 1969.

Murphy, Noel Francis (Manager). President of the Irish Rugby Football Union in 1961. Wing forward. Gained 11 caps for Ireland between 1930 and 1933. He was the father of Noel Arthur Augustine Murphy, also included in Ireland's 1961 touring team .

Nesdale, Thomas Jude. Born on 18th August 1933. Flanker. Went on to gain one cap for Ireland in 1961.

Nimb, Charles Frederick. Born on 6th September 1938. Fly-half. This was his only cap for South Africa.

O'Neill, William Arthur. Born on 15th November 1928. Prop. Went on to gain six caps for Ireland between 1952 and 1954.

O'Meara, John Anthony. Born on 26th June 1929. Scrum-half. Went on to gain 22 caps for Ireland between 1951 and 1958.

O'Reilly, Anthony Joseph Francis Kevin. Born on 7th May 1936. Wing. Went on to gain 29 caps for Ireland and ten caps for the Lions, between 1955 and 1970.

O'Sullivan, Patrick Joseph Anthony. Born on 2nd June 1933. Number 8. Went on to gain 15 caps for Ireland between 1957 and 1963.

Pelser, Hendrik Jacobus Martin. Born on 23rd March 1934. Flanker. Went on to gain a total of 11 caps for South Africa, between 1958 and 1961.

Richards, Kenneth Henry Llewellyn. Born on 29th January 1934. Fly-half. Went on to gain five caps for Wales between 1960 and 1961.

Risman, Augustus Beverley Walter. Born on 23rd November 1937. Fly-half. Went on to gain a total of 8 caps for England and 4 for the Lions between 1959 and 1961. To the regret of his many admirers, he turned professional and moved to Rugby League early in 1961 when he was dropped by the England selectors.

Roques, Alfred. Born on 17th February 1925. Prop. Went on to gain a total of 30 caps for France between 1958 and 1963.

Scotland, Kenneth James Forbes. Born on 29th August 1936. Full-back. Went on to gain a total of 27 caps for Scotland (four as captain) and five for the Lions between 1957 and 1965.

Scott, Dennis. Born on 19th November 1933. Flanker. Went on to gain a total of three caps for Ireland between 1961 and 1962.

Stewart, David Alfred. Born 14th July 1935. Centre. Went on to gain a total of 11 caps for South Africa between 1960 and 1965.

Stringer, Peter Alexander. Born on 13th December 1977. Scrum-half. Went on to gain 56 caps for Ireland between 2000 and date of research (June 2005). He was also an unused substitute on the bench three times in that period.

Thomson, Ronald Hew. Born on 12th October 1936. Wing. Went on to gain a total of 15 caps for Scotland between 1960 and 1964.

Uys, Pieter De Waal. Born on 10th December 1937. Scrum-half. Went on to gain a total of 12 caps as for South Africa, between 1960 and 1969.

Van Zyl, Barend Pieter. Born on 1st August 1935. Wing. This was his only cap for South Africa.

Van Zyl, Gideon Hugo. Born on 20th August 1932. Flanker. Went on to gain a total of 17 caps for South Africa, between 1958 and 1962.

Van Zyl, Hendrik Jacobus. Born on 31st January 1936. Wing. Went on to gain a total of ten caps for South Africa between 1960 and 1961.

Van Zyl, Pieter Johannes. Born on 23rd July 1933. Lock. This was his only cap for South Africa.

Vannier, Michel. Born on 21st July 1931. Full-back. Went on to gain a total of 43 caps for France between 1955 and 1961.

Walsh, Jeremiah Charles. Born on 3rd November 1938. Centre. Went on to gain a total of 26 caps for Ireland, between 1960 and 1967.

Wilson, Lionel Geoffrey. Born on 25th May 1933. Full back. Went on to gain a total of 28 caps for South Africa between 1960 and 1965.

Wood, Benjamin Gordon Malison. Born on 20th June 1931. Prop. Went on to gain a total of 29 caps for Ireland and two caps for the Lions between 1956 and 1961. His final cap was gained on the tour to South Africa in 1961.